"Don't try to find out who you are Courtney. You may uncover horrors you're better off not knowing. Let the door stay closed."

But Courtney Marsh would not let the door stay closed. Against all warnings she pursued the elusive and dangerous discovery of who she really was. . . .

"FASCINATING. . . . Will haunt you until you finish—and maybe for a while after that."

—*Lincoln Journal and Star*

The
Golden Unicorn

A NOVEL BY

Phyllis A. Whitney

A FAWCETT CREST BOOK

Fawcett Publications, Inc., Greenwich, Connecticut

THE GOLDEN UNICORN

THIS BOOK CONTAINS THE COMPLETE TEXT OF
THE ORIGINAL HARDCOVER EDITION.

A Fawcett Crest Book reprinted by arrangement with
Doubleday and Company, Inc.

Copyright © 1976 by Phyllis A. Whitney

ISBN 0-449-23104-6

Selection of the Literary Guild, August 1976

Printed in the United States of America

10 9 8 7 6 5 4 3 2 1

Acknowledgments

My special thanks to Miss Dorothy King of the East Hampton Free Library for her assistance when I was doing my research for this book. I am also grateful to Mrs. Amy Bassford and Mrs. Condie Lamb, who helped me immensely.

The background is as I saw it and responded to it in that charming village. However, I "built" my own house on the dunes, and the family that lives at The Shingles is peopled entirely from my imagination. That, too, is the source of all the story happenings.

The
Golden Unicorn

1

Except for the mumbling of the television set, the living room of my New York apartment seemed utterly still and empty—without life. My presence hardly appeared to matter, and I wondered if it ever had. I had dressed for bed in my georgette gown with its matching blue robe—but there was no one to see, and I had a strange, glowing feeling that nothing about me or the room had any reality. I felt as static as the room itself, emotionally drained—as empty as the apartment. The loss I had suffered two months ago in July, as well as what had happened to me that afternoon, was having a delayed effect. But I couldn't seem to fight this reaction, or counteract my depression.

If I was honest, what had happened today wasn't even terribly important, but just another setback in a long list of setbacks. I wasn't completely bereft of hope. Tomorrow I would be on my way to East Hampton and my searching would go on. But for now, for this moment, I was numb with discouragement.

On the television screen the talk-show host was putting on his best now-I-am-about-to-present expression and I tried to focus my attention. It was necessary to watch, to listen to his words.

"I want you to meet a young woman who has enjoyed an amazing success," he was saying. "She has become known to us all in the last few years because of her outstanding articles in *National Weekly*. I'm sure you've read her interviews with American women of accomplishment, and you know what lively and penetrating pieces she writes. I want you to welcome Miss Courtney Marsh."

The audience applauded with flattering enthusiasm, and the girl came out from the back of the set while I watched with the blank feeling of never having seen her before.

Don't swing your arms when you walk, I thought, but I had no other real criticism. She was slim, blond, smartly dressed in a dark red sheath which hinted at a good figure and revealed a well-shaped pair of legs. She moved with poise and assurance, shook hands with the host and the other guests with accustomed grace, and sat down in her chair, smiling without self-consciousness—well used to being in the public eye. Her fair hair fell to her shoulders with a brushed shine, swinging when she moved her head. She began to answer questions intelligently in a clear voice and with an attractive effect of modesty, speaking of the surprising success she had made for herself in the last few years. She was a complete stranger to me.

"You're still in your twenties, aren't you?" Hal Winser said. "How did you become such a whiz so soon? How come people tell you so much in your interviews?"

"I've always been interested in other people," she told him smoothly. "I like to find out what makes them tick."

"But now you specialize in women only—and not even particularly famous women. Why?"

"I suppose I've become aware of a great many women around the country today who're doing outstanding work in the arts and the professions. Most of them are working quietly without a great deal of recognition. I've wanted to learn about them myself and I try to give them a little of the credit they deserve—and haven't sought."

"Did you always like to write, Courtney?" he asked with the easy familiarity of his breed, though he'd never seen the girl he called by her first name until this moment. "Did your parents encourage you when you were young?"

I left my chair and turned off the set with a sharp click. I ought to watch critically for whatever I could learn, but that girl on the screen had nothing to do with me, and I didn't want to hear any glib talk about her parents.

Courtney Marsh.

I was Courtney Marsh—whoever that was. Yet right now I could hardly recall the taping of that show weeks before. It had lost all reality for me. Indeed, I sometimes wondered what reality there had ever been for me in my whole life.

Without warning, memory whipped back over the years to a very young Courtney in fifth grade. I had been adopted when I was two months old, and my loving adoptive parents had never kept this fact from me. No one had ever made anything of it until that day in school. I could still hear the voice of the poisonous little boy who had sat next to me.

"My mom says you don't have any mother and father. My mom says you aren't real."

I had run away from school before classes were dismissed that day. I had run all the way home to Gwen Marsh's arms, and she had held me gently, pouring out comfort, consoling me for what could not be helped.

"Of course you're real, darling. You're the realest thing in our lives. Leon and I have had you since you were a baby. We *are* your mother and father, even though you weren't born to us."

I switched off the memory as sharply as I'd turned off the set. Because I wasn't real. What that boy had said was true and I had only been thrusting back the knowledge all these years while I explored other people's lives and made up fantasies about myself. I had always done that, wondering as a child if I could be the youngest daughter of a queen—kidnaped and lost until Gwen and Leon found me. Or—in a darker mood—perhaps I was the daughter of that horrible ax murderer who had terrified the country. What sort of blood ran in my veins? How could I know?

The only thing I knew for sure was that I was not the natural child of Gwen and Leon Marsh. They had been good and kind, but they had never understood my wild imaginings, my flights of fancy, or, later, my driving will to *be* somebody. They'd have been happy if I could have married a boy next door and grown up in suburban Connecticut without any thought of a career. My success had bewildered them. I was the cuckoo in the robins' nest, but they'd done the very best for me they could, and I had loved them both dearly.

Now they were lost to me too in that dreadful train accident near Rome during the summer, and I had felt devastated ever since. They hadn't been old enough to die and they should have had the comfortable old age I could have given them. Yet their loss had brought everything to a climax in my life, so that I was driven by a new urgency.

I felt terribly alone, and what that boy had said so long ago began to seem true—I wasn't real. The girl I had just seen on television wasn't real. How could she be when there was so much she didn't know—such as how to be a person in her own right, how to love a man and be a woman a man could love. There was a dark void out there that I was never free of, and because of it I couldn't be fully alive.

It wasn't as though I'd not had a happy life with Gwen and Leon. But I could only bring that back in memory. Across the room, the telephone was silent. Once I would have called them in Connecticut, told them I was feeling low, and their love would have poured out to me, even if they didn't fully understand my mood. Of course I had friends I could phone. I had Jim, who had brought me home this afternoon—if I wanted to call him. But apathy persisted.

I had never thought of myself as a self-pitying type, and I took real satisfaction in my job and the work I loved to do well. It mattered to me to be important in my field. Perhaps that was a part of who I really was—the long fight to prove my equality with all those who already knew everything about themselves. But self-pity or not, I was entitled for this one night to long for something others had that I had never known.

In recent years I had met other adoptees and I'd learned that our yearnings to *know* were the same, that I wasn't an oddball exception. We called what we were doing "The Search," and society had made it as difficult for us as possible to bring such a search to an end.

The phone rang as I stared at it, and I went reluctantly to pick up the receiver. Easy cheerfulness wasn't what I needed now and my "hello" wasn't exactly welcoming.

"Courtney, hon, you were terrific on Hal Winser's interview! You showed *him* how." That was Jim's voice. "All that glamour you project! And you couldn't have looked more elegant and sure of yourself. You did Courtney Marsh proud. I liked the way you turned some of those snide questions about professional women back on him without being in the least rude—really great!"

"I couldn't watch," I said.

There was a small silence at the other end of the line. Then Jim came on again. "Darling, don't let what happened this afternoon get you down. It doesn't matter. Why should it? You've got things all mixed up in that pretty head of yours."

"I'm not real," I said. "Good night, Jim."

I put the phone aside and looked about the room as though I were seeing it for the first time. Thinly worn antique Persian rugs, their colors muted against the austere black and white room. A few Thonet pieces, complemented by some Art Deco. A Castiglioni lamp and elaborate stereo, with original oils and name lithos on the walls. Who did this room belong to? What was it trying to prove? Good breeding and a sophisticated taste—good blood? All acquired and superficial—perhaps not even mine.

I turned my back on it and went into the bedroom, where I swallowed a sleeping pill, threw off my robe, switched out the lights, and got into bed. I wasn't Jim Healy's darling. Courtney Marsh wasn't anybody's darling. How could she be with a great part of her vital identity missing? That girl on television was only a stranger talking to other strangers. She had no self of her own to talk about. She was nothing but a façade—and no one around her knew it.

"Go to sleep and stop being a fool," I told myself. "You've got a career that most girls would give an arm and a leg for. You've compensated beautifully. Your name is well known, you're at the top of your profession, and you're only twenty-five. What on earth do you want? Every life has something wrong in it, goodness knows. What do you expect?"

I answered my own critical self. "Not all that much. Just to know who I am. Everyone else knows—so why shouldn't I?"

I was done with waiting and brooding and imagining. The time had come for action—even though it was so desperately difficult to find a course of action that would take me anywhere. This afternoon I had tried—and once more failed. I went through the scene again in my mind. Quite intensely I had begun to hate the not unkind man I had talked with. Even as I had taken the chair offered me near his desk, I had known that Alton Pierce and I were antagonistic.

The lawyer was already on guard when I walked into his office. In order to make this late afternoon appointment, I'd had to give my identity, and he must have looked up my name in his files so that he was prepared to tell me nothing of what I wanted so terribly to know.

I was startled to find him younger than I expected, since I had been prepared to see the man with whom Gwen and Leon had dealt. He met me with a stiff, rather watchful manner that did not reassure me, and I began too abruptly, not trying to lead into my questions gracefully as I would have done if the interview had been on a subject other than myself.

"I believe it was your firm that handled the details when I was adopted nearly twenty-five years ago, Mr. Pierce."

The guarded look moved to a folder that lay on the desk before him, and he barely nodded. "My father handled the case, Miss Marsh. He has since died. Has the adoption worked out well for you?"

Well? How could I answer that when the ramifications were so many, when mixed into my love for Gwen and Leon and their love for me were all the inner questions and longings that I couldn't begin to make anyone understand?

"It has gone very well," I said. "But that doesn't mean I haven't a right to know who I am."

He was shaking his head before I'd finished the sentence. "I'm sorry, but you have no right, Miss Marsh. No legal right at all. You must know that. These matters are sealed—and very sensibly so, in order to protect all the parties concerned."

I couldn't help the bitterness that crept into my voice. "Yes, I've been to the agencies where such records are kept. They wouldn't give me anything."

"You didn't expect them to, did you?"

"I suppose not. I had to try. But I was told some years ago that Pierce and Benton had handled the case, and I knew you weren't bound by the same restrictive rules."

His look was not entirely without sympathy, but I could see that he didn't mean to give an inch. "Perhaps not. But we are governed by the ethics and the responsibility to those concerned. This is not anything I can possibly divulge, Miss Marsh."

He put a hand on the manila folder on his desk in a manner that told me the interview had already ended and there was nowhere else for me to go. In those papers before him, well within reach of my hand, were hidden all the answers to what I wanted to know—my mother's name, and perhaps my father's. Whether I was legitimate, perhaps even the reason why my mother hadn't wanted to keep me, had given me away. Yet the folder might just as well have been locked in a safe, for all the good it would do me.

"In this case," I said, "I think there is something more important than these rules of silence. I wonder if even the ethics you speak of matter any more? All this began more than twenty-five years ago. I can understand that adoptive parents must be protected from a young mother who might change her mind and cause trouble about a baby. Even the mother needs protection from exposure, if that's what she wants. But years have changed all this, and you must know, Mr. Pierce, that I have no intention of causing anyone trouble or embarrassment. I only want to know who I am."

"You are the daughter of Gwen and Leon Marsh, who so generously adopted you and gave you a good home," he said sternly. "Nothing else really matters. Haven't you considered the pain you may be bringing them by asking such questions now?"

I swallowed hard and tried to keep my voice steady. "They both died just two months ago in a train crash in Italy."

He looked a little shocked. "I'm very sorry. I can understand that this loss has left you with an emptiness you want to fill. But believe me, Miss Marsh, it would not be wise for you to pursue this search any further."

"Why not?" I snatched at his words. "What do you mean—'not wise'?"

"You have to remember that your mother gave you away. To speak bluntly, she's not likely to want you back in her life now."

"But I've told you I don't want to make any trouble for her. I probably wouldn't even let her know who I am. It's only my identity I'm seeking. Surely you can understand that?"

He shuffled the papers on his desk impatiently as his good nature began to run out.

"You think now that you'd be silent. But if you found your mother, or your family, you'd discover that sooner or later you would be driven to identify yourself. And that could be disastrous. It could hurt you all. Such things are better forgotten."

"If I live to be a hundred, I won't forget," I said.

"Then I am very sorry for you. Because there isn't any way for you to go on. It would be wiser to accept the end of the road in this office and stop fighting something that happened long ago and can't be changed now. All the decisions were in other hands than yours. You can't affect them and you have to learn to accept them."

"I won't accept them!" I cried. "Other people had no right to make decisions I could never agree to. And it's not the end of the road. There is one other thing."

His look was suddenly alert. "Yes?"

"I know where my mother lived. Her home was out on Long Island. In East Hampton."

"What makes you think that?"

"When I was going through his things after the crash, I found a latter addressed to Leon. It had been written many years ago by an elderly aunt of his who has since died. It asked how the little girl from East Hampton was doing."

The man behind the desk was silent, his expression still guarded, giving nothing away.

"Of course it referred to me, though they'd never told me where I came from. Gwen used to say that I had to be protected from the past when I began to ask too many questions."

"Very wise of her."

"Then you won't even confirm this small detail?"

He shook his head. I hadn't hoped for anything else.

"It doesn't matter," I said and stood up. "I'm going to East Hampton tomorrow."

"Without a single lead to follow? That's pretty foolish, isn't it?" He rose from his desk and came around to stand beside me. Now that I gave evidence of leaving, his manner softened a little. "I'm sorry I can't help you, Miss Marsh."

We had reached a complete impasse and I knew it was final. In the outer office Jim would be waiting for me, and there was nothing to do but rejoin him and let him take me back to my apartment.

Mr. Pierce came with me to the door and when he opened it for me I thanked him stiffly and went out. The receptionist glanced at her watch as though eager to be off, and Jim Healy tossed aside a copy of *National Weekly* and stood up. Jim and I worked together on the magazine, where he was an assistant editor.

"I've been rereading your story about Dr. Ruth Brooks," he said. "I'd never heard of her, but you did a good job of making her come through as a skilled doctor and a compassionate woman."

I couldn't have cared less. "I'd like a cup of coffee, please."

"Right away, lady," Jim said cheerfully and we walked

down the hall to the elevator. "You notice I'm not asking questions," he said when we were alone in the descending car, just ahead of the five o'clock crowds.

"I don't expect you need to."

"Right. Your face is a mile long. Let's go over to Bruno's."

I couldn't bear to talk while we walked the two blocks, and I let him rattle on, trying to amuse and cheer me. Jim found us a booth at the back and ordered coffee for me and a whiskey sour for himself.

"I warned you that a lawyer would tell you nothing," Jim said when the waitress went away. "Courtney, why don't you give this up? There aren't any open doors and you'll just keep banging yourself against stone walls. I don't like to see you hurt."

I found myself studying his rather broad, good-natured face in the dim light of the booth. I was fond of him. I respected his intelligence and his integrity, and he had taught me a lot about my job. But I wasn't in love with him. I hadn't ever been really in love with anyone, and sometimes I wondered if I ever would be.

"Listen," I said. "I'm an adult. I *do* have a right to know. None of the arrangements that were made had my consent. I have a right to know who I am."

He reached across the table and took my hand. "I know who you are. And what you are right now is enough. Just take me—I've got family galore, and you can have most of them as far as I'm concerned. Aunt Helga trying to run my life because she thinks I look like Uncle Hubert. Mother fussing if I stay out all night. Dad thinking I'm crazy to work on a magazine instead of getting a real job. Who needs relatives?"

I withdrew my hand gently and sipped hot coffee. Jim didn't understand, any more than anyone else ever had. How could there be understanding when I didn't truly understand myself? I only knew that I'd built up a façade to hide behind, and that somewhere there was a woman who needed to come out into the open and prove herself as flesh and blood—someone who was more than clever words on paper.

"What have you got to go on?" Jim demanded, setting

his glass down with a thump of protest. "You haven't any leads. And without a lead you can't even get started."

Around my neck, hidden beneath the collar of my blouse, I wore a pendant on a fine gold chain, and now I reached back and opened the clasp.

"I have this," I said, and held up the chain, so that the golden unicorn dangled from it—a tiny, perfect thing, its front legs prancing, the slender golden horn protruding from the forehead, the etched eyes somehow wise and knowing.

Jim had seen it before and he did not take it from me. "What can you possibly tell from that?"

"It came with me. It was around my neck when Gwen and Leon brought me home. It was a—a memento from someone. Someone who must have cared a little to leave such a precious thing with me."

"But it gives you no information of any kind."

"Perhaps it does. There's something you haven't seen." I opened my handbag and took out a yellowed clipping, spreading it open on the table between us. "When I went through their bank deposit box after Gwen and Leon died, I found this."

Jim bent over it, studying the newsprint with its hazy reproduction of a painting, trying to press out the folds with his forefinger. I didn't need to look. I had almost worn out the clipping since I'd found it. It reproduced—badly—a painting by an artist named Judith Rhodes: a beach scene with a desolate stretch of sand fading into the distance. It was a night scene with a full moon sailing an otherwise empty sky above the dark ocean.

Jim looked up at me, puzzled. "So what?"

"Read the penciled words on the margin," I said.

He turned the clipping sideways and read the words aloud. " 'Is this the unicorn in our Courtney's life?' " He shook his head at me. "Who wrote this? And what unicorn?"

"It's Gwen's handwriting. Look at the shadow on the moon."

It was there when he searched—the outline of cloud in the strange but unmistakable shape of a unicorn.

"It's not much to go on," Jim said. "Who is Judith Rhodes, anyhow? I've never heard of her."

"Neither had I. But when I found the clipping I took it to an art gallery on Fifty-seventh Street. The owner knew her work well and was enthusiastic, though she's apparently recognized and admired only by a small coterie of the knowledgeable because she won't exhibit often, and doesn't want to sell many of her paintings. He told me that the Rhodes are an old, wealthy family in East Hampton. That might—well it just might—tie in with the letter I showed you asking about the little girl from there. Evidently Judith Rhodes is something of a recluse. Her husband's in banking—plenty of money—and when she does have a show he brings in the paintings and sees to everything. She never comes in herself."

Jim shook his head. "So—what's the connection?"

"The man at the gallery told me she makes rather a thing of including unicorns in her pictures. You know, like Whistler's butterfly signature. She seems to use them often. There must have been some connection in Gwen's mind because she wrote those words in the margin of the clipping. Anyway, I'm going to East Hampton, Jim."

"Blindly, without any more of a lead than this?"

"What sort of reporter do you think I am? Judith Rhodes is an artist of unusual talent, yet she's one of those unknowns I like to interview. I wrote to her, and her husband answered. He's keen on the idea, and he's sold it to her, which is unusual. So I'm to go out there and stay for a visit—as long as it takes to get the material for my piece. And Jim—I'm not coming back to the office."

He looked at me, startled, waiting. I folded the clipping carefully and put it back in my bag.

"Today I turned in my resignation," I told him. "They can't do anything else at the office but accept it. I'll still free-lance a bit if they want me to, but after this piece I'm on my own."

"Why, Courtney—why?"

I didn't want to explain, and I wasn't even sure that I could explain, but I had to try. I owed him that.

"I've got to get away. I want to do a book—a collection of the articles I've been writing about my talented women.

I'll add to it, of course, and flesh the whole thing out. I even have a publisher who's interested."

"They'd give you time off from the magazine if you asked. They won't want to lose you."

"I don't want time off. I want to burn my bridges. Oh Jim—don't you see? I've got to burn them! I've got to find out how to be *me*. Going to Mr. Pierce's office was a start, and I'm grateful to you for coming with me. I'll admit I felt like a cub reporter going to see him under the circumstances. If you'll put me in a cab, I'll go home now. I need to pack so I can leave tomorrow."

He didn't like any of it, but there was nothing he could say or do to change my mind, and he knew it.

"I'll miss you around the office." He paid the check and we went out to the street.

I couldn't honestly tell him that I would miss him, nice as he was, though sometimes I wished I could. At the curb he halted, with a hand on my arm.

"Are you pinning some wild hope on having this Judith Rhodes turn out to be your mother?"

"No! No, really I'm not. There's not enough evidence to lead to that. I only want to find out why Gwen wrote those words on that newspaper clipping, and why there's a unicorn in my life."

He hailed a cab, kissed me, and let me go, and all the way home I sat numbly, letting New York slip by the cab windows without being conscious of it, smelling the smoke of bridges burning and feeling a little frightened.

Back in my apartment I had gone around turning on lights, trying to cheer up the living room. All that black and white! Why had I ever wanted it? I went out to my small kitchen and started a warm-up supper. My meeting with Alton Pierce had taken away my appetite, but when the food was hot I carried a tray into the living room, set it on the coffee table, and tried to eat. But I couldn't stop my churning thoughts, my memories.

I hadn't always been a rewarding daughter to Gwen and Leon. They had never stopped making me feel that I was cherished, valued, loved. Yet again and again while I was growing up I'd pestered them for information—information they didn't have to give me. In the ordinary conflict that must arise in any family between parental discipline and the waywardness of children, I had a special weapon that I learned to use shamefully: "How could you know? You're not my real mother. You're not my real father."

The cruelty of the young!

Uncomfortably, I remembered Mr. Pierce's words. He had said that I could only bring disaster if I walked into my mother's life today, and that I would very likely be unwelcome. I wondered if he had said that out of some knowledge of her now, or if he was just stating a general pattern.

I had been eating automatically, and somehow my plate was empty before me on the tray, and I poured myself another cup of coffee. But it cooled while vivid pictures surged through my mind.

I could see myself going into some public place, perhaps a store in East Hampton. The golden unicorn might rest outside my blouse and I could imagine the sudden attention upon that distinctive pendant, the abrupt pouncing, the question "Where did you get that?" My imaginings gave me a sudden fright. That was not the way I wanted it to happen. I wanted to view and appraise and know, before anyone knew me—almost the way I did before one of my interviews. I wanted to find out from a safe emotional distance, with no one guessing my identity. Just as the adoptive parents never knew who the real parents were, the real mother never knew where her baby had been given for adoption—so the name of Marsh would mean nothing out in East Hampton. Probably for the first weeks of my life I had gone by another name—a name I didn't even know. I had been given for adoption a little before I was two months old, but not immediately at birth, as was usually the custom. That much Gwen had been able to tell me because she knew my age and date of birth when I came to her, and I'd often wondered why I had been kept for that short space of time.

My own imaginings disturbed me. I would wear the pendant because it was a talisman, and it could identify me, if ever I wanted to be identified. But I would be sure to keep it hidden from view.

As the evening wore on, I had turned to Hal Winser's talk show on television, but I hadn't been able to watch for long, and my churning thoughts had never quieted. Now, as I lay in bed and waited for the sleeping pill I'd taken to work, I realized that my memories of this evening had come full circle.

The Search! We were all alike, we adopted children, in our wish, however secret we might keep it, to know where we had come from. It mattered more in the pattern of where we were going than outsiders ever understood.

I realized that such a search, if successful, might end unhappily—with parents I didn't want to accept, who wouldn't want to accept me. Even then, I wanted to know. Yet it didn't *have* to be that way. If she could only know, I might very well sympathize with a girl who had been alone and frightened and without money or help, and who had been forced to give away a baby she couldn't keep. I was sentimentalizing now.

If the Rhodes' name led anywhere, it might mean that disgrace, not poverty, had caused my being given away. I could sympathize there too. Even twenty-five years ago a baby born out of wedlock in a well-to-do family might have brought fear and grief to the mother. It comforted me to make allowances, and I fell asleep foolishly pitying that lost young girl who had been my mother, and whom I knew absolutely nothing about.

2

The next morning I made the long drive out toward the eastern tip of Long Island in my Volvo, and when Montauk Highway turned into Woods Lane, and then into Main Street, I was in the village of East Hampton. I liked its air of rural tranquility, its old houses and unique windmills. Drowsing in the center where the road divided lay the Town Pond and the Old South Burying Ground. On either side were houses of historical vintage, their shingles a silvered brown. As a reporter I had done my homework, and had been reading about East Hampton, so I already knew some of its landmarks.

When I had found a place to leave my car at the curb, I got out to walk. The Rhodes wouldn't expect me until early afternoon, so there was time to reconnoiter a bit, perhaps ask a few careful questions, and have lunch before I drove to the house.

Main Street was generously wide, laid out in an earlier century by those who were accustomed to wide spaces and uncramped living. Trees overhung the sidewalk, but I was to learn later that the hurricane of '38 had destroyed most of the great elms that had once arched above the street, and many of these were replacements.

As I walked along, I found myself wondering if I could have been born here. Was there a house in this town where I had slept in my crib until I was nearly two months old? Something in me quickened at the thought of coming at last to my own source. How would I accept the final ending to that search, I wondered—and what would it do to me? In spite of all those childish fantasies, I wasn't sure how I might react in the face of final reality, and that was a somewhat frightening thought.

In any case, I liked the casual, small-town flavor of the village, the informally dressed people who moved in the warm sunshine of early September without the urgency of New York. Yet it was a small town with a special distinction because it had long been a haven, not only for wealthy summer visitors, but for the arts as well, and the shops had a smart look about them that suggested a traveled clientele with cosmopolitan tastes. Writers lived here, and artists, and from John Drew to Laurette Taylor and on, the area had been a haven for those connected with the theater.

At a dress shop I stopped in to look around and speak to the woman behind the counter, mentioning that I was here to do an interview with Judith Rhodes. She was past middle age, and her response seemed oddly startled.

"Oh? Then you'll be going out to The Shingles?"

I knew the name of the house from the stationery on which Herndon Rhodes had written me.

"Yes. Is it one of those houses on the ocean?"

She nodded. "It's on the dunes, but it's not like the summer houses. Old Ethan Rhodes built for the year-round, and the family has always lived there."

Sensing both curiosity and hesitation, I let her catch her breath while I asked to see a yellow and brown scarf displayed in a glass case. When I'd bought it to go with the beige pants suit I was wearing, I went on, testing again.

"I'm looking forward to my visit. The Shingles sounds like an interesting place, and Judith Rhodes is a fine painter."

"Mm." The sound was noncommittal, yet I suspected that she was torn between a desire to talk and a natural reticence toward a stranger. I waited encouragingly until she continued. "Once when I was a little girl the Rhodes opened the house to visitors for an afternoon. We have a regular tour every summer, you know. It's a spooky old place. But they haven't been a part of our tour for a great many years now."

"Why is that?" I asked directly.

"Perhaps it was those deaths, coming so close together as they did. Even all that long ago. Anyway, they don't entertain much any more."

I knotted the scarf about my throat, further hiding the golden pendant, thanked her, and went outside again. It wasn't wise to ask too many questions of one person, but it might be to my advantage to collect what tidbits I could here and there.

A restaurant displayed its attractive interior through long windows, and I went in and took a table near the front. Bay scallops were in season on Long Island, and I ordered them with an accompanying salad. The young waitress was friendly.

"The Shingles? Oh, wow! Hardly anybody gets inside that house. Though I have a girl friend who works out there as a maid sometimes. She says there's a woman they shut up in the attic who paints pictures all the time. Though my friend never saw her when she worked there."

This was fantasy, and I ate my lunch without encouraging further revelations from this particular source. It was interesting, though, that mentioning The Shingles could bring so curious a response.

When I'd finished my meal I walked toward Hook Mill, turned down a cross street, and found a well-stocked book-store where I could buy a map and ask directions. The woman in charge had seen me on television the night before, and she was friendly and helpful—and much less lugubrious. Apparently members of the Rhodes family often dropped in for books, and she spoke of having borrowed paintings of Judith Rhodes occasionally to hang in the store.

"Herndon Rhodes comes in for books for his wife frequently. You'll like him, I think. And it should be a privilege to meet Judith."

"How many are there in the family?" I asked casually.

"Let me see . . . there's Stacia to begin with. She's the daughter of Herndon and Judith, and she lives at the house with her husband, Evan Faulkner. And of course there's John, Herndon's older brother. He does a lot of traveling, though he's at home right now. I saw him in here just yesterday." There was approval in her slight smile, as though John Rhodes was someone she liked.

"Is there a Nan Kemble too?" I asked. "Herndon Rhodes mentioned her in his letter. I'm supposed to stop at her gatehouse shop when I arrive."

"Yes, of course. You'll like Nan—unless you get off on the wrong foot with her. But she's not really a Rhodes. Her sister Alice was married to John, but Alice has been dead a long time now."

I shook my head in bewilderment and spread my map on the counter. "You've given me more names than I can handle, I'm afraid. Will you show me how to find The Shingles?"

"That's Ethan Lane, right there," she said, pointing a pencil on the map. "Ethan Rhodes built the house, you know, back in the mid-1800s. The lane is a dead end and it runs right into Rhodes property. There are several ways to find it. These crossroads along this section mostly run to the water. But you might go this way. . . ." She marked a few arrows on the map and I thanked her and went back to my car.

One of the roads that led south to the water lost me quickly in a maze of wide lanes dreaming green-gold in sunlight. It was going to be a late fall, and only a few trees had begun to turn. I drove slowly past well-trimmed privet hedges, past post and rail fences twined with rambling roses in late summer bloom. Now and then, through the hedges, or over the fences, I could glimpse enormous lawns leading to white mansions, most of them built in a much earlier day. Blue hydrangeas still bloomed along driveways, and there were signs to preserve privacy. Yet in the midst of all this luxury there would appear an unexpected potato field stretching between green lawns. Potatoes and summer people—these were the main business of this South Fork of Long Island.

I paid no attention to directions now, content to wander in my car and catch the flavor of a place that was like no other in which I had ever been. The lanes curved and ran off in every direction, and their names enchanted me—Maidstone, Dunemere, Asparagus, Pudding Hill, Georgica Road, and Lily Pond Lane. The latter would take me in the direction I wanted to go, and I followed it slowly, idly.

There were no other cars, no one on foot, no sidewalks. Just the quiet, empty lanes stretching between their high privet hedges. Here and there a certain wildness had taken over where hedges had gone untrimmed and grown fifteen feet or more in height. Some of the houses I glimpsed were already shuttered, as summer residents closed up for the season and left their homes to ocean winds and cold weather. There seemed a certain sadness about the shutting down, with all the outdoor summer activity over, and winter quiet already setting in. For a little while nature would hold its breath through the golden days of September and October, with leaves turning bright and falling to carpet the lawns in russet. Then it would be winter, with the summer visitors long gone, and the green world would vanish as everything battened down to meet the darker months.

I marveled a little at my own thoughts. I had never been here before as far as my memory went, yet there seemed a strange sense of familiarity. Perhaps I came of people who had braved whatever storms the ocean drove in upon these unprotected shores.

The sign came up without warning: Ethan Lane. Named perhaps after some distant relative of mine? But I mustn't think along those lines. I must not become emotionally involved or leap to eager conclusions that might well prove absurd. It was necessary to remember that I knew nothing at all, and it must remain that way until I had some reason to be sure, some reason to speak a name with the knowledge of true relationship. After all, I was a woman, a seasoned professional, and I must not behave like a teenager in my fantasies.

Green hedges shut me in again as the lane curved away out of sight. I followed it slowly, trying to ignore the sudden thumping of my heart. Remaining calm and reasonable was one thing—controlling my own pulse beat might be something else.

There were three or four houses along the beginning of the lane and then the way narrowed, as a wild tangle of scrub oak, beach plum, and stunted pines took over. Ahead rose two crumbling stone gateposts where the road came abruptly to an end. There was no sign, no nameplate, but I knew this was the place. Beyond the gate I could see the dark shingles of the old gatehouse, and I drove through and parked my car in a small clearing beyond.

Now taller oaks and maples, which must once have given the area a parklike aspect, replaced the tangle of wild growth, shutting out the sun, so that the air felt a little dank and chill. I could smell the sea now, though it was not in sight. The gravel drive wound away from where I stood and disappeared among the trees, and there was no main house in view. The gatehouse was brown-shingled, with a slanting roof that overhung the front door, and here there was a sign which said simply THE DITTY BOX. I wondered how customers ever found their way to a spot so remote and secluded.

No one seemed to be about and, since this was a shop, I opened the narrow door to step inside, but what I saw startled me and I paused in the doorway.

At first glance the shop was no more than a clutter of unidentified articles. It was the two women near a flight of stairs at the rear who arrested my attention. One was a blond girl of about my own age, while the other woman who stood facing her in some moment of crisis was probably in her mid-forties. The girl had clearly been crying, and one cheek was puffy and bruised. But her eyes sparked fury.

"He struck me, Nan, and I don't have to take anything like that! Evan's an absolute brute and you've got to talk to him. He won't listen to anyone else."

As I pushed the door fully open a bell jangled over my head, and both women turned surprised looks in my direction. The girl put a hand to her swollen cheek and ran upstairs out of sight, leaving the other woman to come toward me through the shop.

Casual brown slacks and yellow sweater suited her small, lean frame. Thick, iron-gray hair was worn in a straight and uncompromising bob, with long bangs down her forehead, and beneath them gray eyes appraised me as she crossed the shop. Her eyes, I thought, were her best feature—large and candid, truly beautiful.

I smiled at her. "Miss Kemble? I'm Courtney Marsh. Mr. Rhodes wrote that I was to stop in and let you know when I arrived."

She came briskly toward me, holding out her hand. Her clasp was strong, firm, slightly assertive, as though she might be trying to counteract any adverse impression I could have gained from the angry girl.

"Of course," she said. "I recognized you. I saw you on television last night. Did you have any trouble finding us?"

"No trouble at all. I stopped in the village for lunch and a map, and then I drove around for a while."

We were indulging in a polite circling of words, but I had the feeling that her real attention was not upon me, but upon that tearful girl with the bruised cheek who had run upstairs so hastily at my appearance. I looked about the shop for the first time and began to register an impression.

"The Ditty Box!" I said. "Now I understand."

She smiled at me, her rather plain—except for those arresting eyes—intelligent features warming to enthusiasm. "Yes—ditty boxes were what sailors kept their small possessions in on a voyage. And this place is strictly nautical. I specialize in nautical antiques, you know. Though what we sell isn't always small enough for a ditty box."

I could see that. On a nearby shelf stood a graceful model of a clipper ship made of wood and bone, and beyond it against the wall soared a pilothouse eagle, the paint still bright on its wings. Nearby stood a ship's wheel, and there was an octant, several compasses, and occupying a corner a battered figurehead of Davy Crockett, his hair long under his coonskin cap. Displayed in a glass case was a fascinating assortment of scrimshaw.

"What a marvelous idea!" I said. "But how does anyone find you back here in the woods?"

She moved among her treasures, her light touch owning them with pride, and I sensed her controlled vitality, the inner energy that drove her. Nan Kemble, I thought, would work hard at making her shop a success—indeed work hard at anything she attempted. My imagination was already leaping ahead to consider her as a possible subject for one of my articles.

"I advertise in the right places," she told me. "People have known about my shop for years, and those who are interested find me. But now I'd better phone the house and have someone come down to take you up."

"Can't I find my own way?"

"Probably you could. But I've had my instructions. I'll phone Herndon too, as he wants to come home from the bank. We all watched you on that program last night." She moved toward the telephone on her desk.

"What did you think of the interview?" I asked, wanting to keep her talking.

"Squirmy," she said without hesitation. "I can't stand Hal Winser. I wouldn't have been watching if Herndon hadn't insisted, and if I hadn't read your articles. I wanted to see what you were like. I'm glad you didn't let him get away with putting you down."

I was pleased that she hadn't indulged in empty flattery. " 'Squirmy' is the right word. I couldn't watch when the show came on last night."

She smiled again and picked up the phone. When she had called Herndon Rhodes to let him know that I had arrived, she phoned the house. Someone she called "Asher" answered, and apparently said he would convey her message.

"Evan will come for you. Evan Faulkner—Stacia's husband. You saw her just now at the back of the shop. She's a bit upset or she would have come down to greet you. Why don't you sit over here for a moment? I'd like to talk to you anyway. Will you have a cup of coffee?"

Her desk was set in an alcove with a counter at the back, on which a plugged-in percolator burbled. I accepted mine black, as she took her own, and sat down to look around the shop again. Apparently this big pine-paneled room had once been the living room of the gate lodge.

At the back, stairs led up to a narrow gallery off which opened two or three rooms.

"I think you'd better be somewhat prepared," Nan Kemble said, frowning into her cup. "I can't go into details, because it's a family matter—and you're a reporter. But something unsettling has just happened up at the house and everyone is in a tizzy. So don't judge by surface tension. We're not always like this. I don't know what's behind this—unpleasantness—but it needn't affect your story about Judith in any way."

"Thank you for warning me," I said. "Is there anything you want to tell me about Judith Rhodes ahead of time that will help me talk with her? I like to put people at ease from the start."

Nan Kemble nodded toward an opposite wall. "Have you seen Judith's paintings? That's one over there."

I studied the picture with its cool grays and blue-greens, its drifting mists that somehow lent a mystical and ghostly quality to a scene that might otherwise be totally real. Once more she had painted a beach, with white surf curling in upon white sand marked by a broken snow fence and a clump of beach grass bending in the wind. The mood was one of sadness, so that the scene seemed of a place bereft. Though the misty light appeared to be that of daylight, a strange globe sailed a sky of pale Persian blue. Something that was neither moon nor sun.

The painting drew me and I left my chair and walked to the wall where I could examine it more closely. The mysterious globe was a small, floating face, its cheeks pink and plump, its eyes staring and fixed, like blue glass. Not a child's face—it lacked any living quality—but more likely the face of a doll. It made the one touch of the surreal in the picture, and for some reason it chilled me.

"Why the floating face?" I asked, coming back to my chair.

Nan Kemble's shrug was expressive. "You don't ask Judith why, or what she means. I'm not sure she knows, or if it's necessary to know. She paints what she sees, and imagines. I suppose genius has its own reasons. You'll understand better, perhaps, when you visit her attic studio."

I smiled, remembering. "There was a young waitress in the restaurant where I had lunch who tried to startle me with a story about a woman who was shut away in an attic, painting pictures."

"People build legends about what they don't understand," Nan said, "and I expect Judith Rhodes makes fair game. She attracts slings and arrows."

"You do regard her as having genius, however?"

"That's a large word, of course. But yes—I think I do."

"That's why I'm here—because an expert in New York used that word. But I'm also interested in her as a woman behind the painter."

"I know. And that's what you do best. You get humanity into your writing. And I like your giving women a break. What an interesting cross-section of subjects you've tackled—lawyer, architect, poet, author, actress, doctor—I don't remember them all, but I like what you're doing. The rest of us need to read about these quiet successes women are making of their lives, as well as about the more spectacular achievements of the headline grabbers. But I'll warn you—Judith won't be easy to do."

I've sometimes been told that my antennae are sensitive when it comes to human emotion, and I felt a prickling now. Nan Kemble was enthusiastic about Judith as a painter, less enthusiastic about her as a woman.

"I've met other women who were difficult to interview," I told her. "Do you say that because she's something of a recluse?"

Nan shrugged again and I sensed caution settling in. "Judith goes her own way. She doesn't trouble about the world very much. Perhaps she lives in that fantasy country of sand and ocean and sky that she likes to paint. With mainly the gulls for company."

"What is she shutting out?" I asked, surprised by my own candor.

"I expect that's for you to discover for yourself. If there really is anything she needs to shut out."

"You said Stacia is her daughter. Are they close?"

A faintly troubled look touched Nan Kemble's face. "I suppose there's always friction along the way between mother and daughter. But growing up usually cures that."

She paused. "I guess it will take a while in Stacia's case."

I hesitated and then blurted out the question at the back of my mind. "Is Stacia an only child?"

"Yes. Judith isn't exactly the mothering type."

I decided to press a bit more, since Nan seemed willing to talk. "What does her husband think of Judith's painting?"

"He'd like to see her recognized, acclaimed." There was a hint of regret in Nan's tone that I did not understand. "But Judith doesn't want that. Sometimes I think she's afraid of it."

Which brought us back to what Judith Rhodes might be concealing, or refusing to face.

"Why afraid?" I asked.

Gray eyes appraised me, knowingly observant, and I knew her frankness had come to an end.

"I'm not the one you should interview," she said. "I recognize that you need to talk not only to Judith Rhodes but to those around her. However, I'm not the right person."

"But you must have known her for a long time. I believe your sister Alice was John Rhodes' wife?"

Nan picked up her cup and stirred sugarless coffee vigorously. "You might as well know that I sided with Judith against your coming here. I argued with Herndon against it. I think I was right. I'm not sure you're going to be good for any of us."

"I'm sorry," I said. "All I'm after is to be able to write an in-depth piece about a very gifted woman."

"And in doing that you may stir up old pain that needs to be forgotten."

Remembering who I was, and what my own place might be in this picture, I suddenly wanted to reassure her—perhaps to reassure myself.

"I'll be careful," I promised. "I assure you that I don't want to hurt anyone."

"That's not good enough. You won't know quicksand when you see it. The wisest, kindest thing you can do would be to go straight out that door and back to New York."

"I'm sorry," I said. "I can't do that."

She sipped coffee, apparently resigned to my response, accepting the fact that I was not to be discouraged from my course.

Wondering what "quicksand" she meant, I was silent too for a time. Had that word anything to do with giving away a baby nearly twenty-five years ago?

"Have you seen other work of Judith's around New York?" Nan asked more conversationally.

"Unfortunately, no. But I've talked to the owner of a gallery who is enthusiastic about her paintings, and who told me a lot about them. The only thing I've seen until now is a reproduction in a newspaper of a strange moonlight painting of another beach scene—with the shadow of a unicorn on the moon."

Nan nodded. "That's one of her best. You'll see it hanging in the living room at The Shingles."

"But why a unicorn?"

"She often uses it. There's some sort of Rhodes' legend. Get one of them to tell you about it. . . . I wonder what can be keeping Evan? He should be here by now."

"If I'm holding you from your work—" I began, but she had turned her head and was looking toward the rear of the shop behind me. I turned too and saw Stacia Faulkner coming down the stairs.

She looked slim and attractive in lime green slacks and a hemp-colored shirt, and she had apparently bathed the bruise on her cheek, washed away her tears, recovered herself, so that she held her head proudly high, daring anyone to notice the purpling skin below her left eye. Her fluff of blond hair was as fair as my own, though she wore it shorter, and her eyes were as deeply blue. We were of nearly the same build, average in height and fairly small-boned, but her lips seemed thinner, and perhaps a little petulant. At any rate, I hoped my own didn't carry an expression like that. Her nose had a completely different shape from mine. That I was seeking resemblance between myself and this girl who was nearly my own age, I knew very well. What might she be—a cousin, a sister? Silently I told myself to stop this sort of measuring at once. As far as I was concerned this girl was merely Judith Rhodes' daughter and might be useful to me for an article about her mother. I should not have to keep reminding myself to remain impersonal.

Nan introduced us and Stacia gave me a cool, firm clasp and released my hand immediately. Clearly, she didn't want me here either.

"Your timing couldn't be worse," she told me frankly. "My mother's in a terribly upset state."

Nan broke in. "Miss Marsh knows there's been an upheaval at the house. I've mentioned it."

Stacia turned her attention to Nan, waving an airy hand, on which I caught a shine of sapphire. "And a good thing, don't you think? Isn't it high time someone kicked up a fuss? Three people died, and no one ever looked into it. Not seriously."

"That's all ancient history, and there was nothing to look into," Nan said calmly. "Two were accidents and one was a natural death. But I don't think your father will want Miss Marsh troubled with all this past unhappiness."

Stacia made a face at the rebuke and then winced in pain from moving her cheek. "Sorry! I forgot what a loyal member of the clan you are, Nan, even if only through your sister's marriage. We can't have all the family skeletons paraded for publication, I suppose. Though it might be interesting, at that."

I was beginning to dislike Stacia Faulkner and take sides with Nan, even though family skeletons were exactly what I wanted to know more about.

"We'll talk again," Stacia said, turning to me. "In the meantime, can I take you up to the house?"

"Evan will be here any minute," Nan told her. "I've already phoned for him to come and fetch Miss Marsh."

"Courtney," I corrected, "—please."

"If Evan's coming, I'll get out of the way—fast!" Stacia caught up a jacket from a chair, waved a hand at both of us, and started for the door with a lithe, swift movement that reminded me of some jungle cat. But she was already too late.

The door opened just before she reached it, jangling the bell, and Evan Faulkner walked into the room. I found myself staring at this man whom I was prepared to dislike, since he was the author of the bruise on Stacia's cheek.

He was probably around thirty-five—a tall, strongly built man, though rather on the lean side, with tanned skin and dark hair, and eyes the color of gray ice as he looked at his wife. With a hand clapped to her cheek, as if to conceal the bruise, she ducked past him and out the door without a word.

"What's the matter with her?" he asked directly of Nan.

"That isn't hard to figure, is it?" Clearly, Nan had a temper that could surface easily. "I don't think you needed to play that rough." She turned apologetically to me. "The skeletons seem to be falling out of all our closets today, Courtney. I'm sorry, Evan. It's none of my business."

A dark flush had swept up lean cheeks to stain his forehead, but the stain was one of anger, not embarrassment, and I saw that those cold eyes could spark hotly. But he kept whatever he was thinking and feeling well under control and came across the shop to me, holding out his hand.

"Miss Marsh?" he said formally. "I'm Evan Faulkner. Would you like to go up to the house now? I expect you've had a long drive, so you'll probably like to rest."

Formal words, ordinary words, with a wild rage seething beneath them and held in check by that iron grip he kept upon himself. He was a man I would not want to make angry.

I stood up, feeling thoroughly uncomfortable and not in the least relishing this plunge into the middle of a family quarrel.

"Thank you," I said stiffly. "My car is outside."

"We'll go up in mine," he told me. "Asher can come for your car and bags later. Thanks, Nan, for taking care of Miss Marsh until I could get here."

Nan put out her hand to me. "Come and see me again. I owe you some quieter hospitality."

"I'd like to come," I said. "I'd love to see your shop when there's more time."

Evan Faulkner held the door and I went out to his battered gray station wagon and got into the passenger's seat. When the engine purred, belying the rough exterior, we started along the driveway, winding between thick undergrowth on either side, crowding the trees of what must once have been a lovely park. The present-day Rhodeses apparently liked wilderness and seclusion.

My sense of being thoroughly uncomfortable continued, and my dark-browed companion offered no small talk, driving in silence. At least the flush of rage faded, leaving his skin normally tan, though when I stole a look at him, I saw streaks of white about his tightened mouth. I tried to think of something to say that might ease the tension, ease my own discomfort, but my mind was a blank.

As we came around a curve in the gravel drive, he broke the silence for the first time, braking the car and startling me.

"This is the best spot from which to catch your first glimpse of The Shingles," he said.

His words prepared me to be impressed—so that I expected beauty, soaring architecture—some vista of loveliness. The house that lifted three stories into the air atop its high dune was anything but beautiful. Impressive, yes, with a great and brooding dignity as it raised shingled walls and tall brick chimneys against the blue sky, but its color was a dark umber, shading into ebony in the shadows, somehow heavy and oppressive. It had stood there since the last century, braving the storms that had burst over its head, riding like a ship into the very teeth of the gales and high seas that must have hurled themselves upon it. "The Shingles" seemed a modest name for so overpowering a structure.

There was a faint prickling at the back of my neck. Had I been born in that house? Had I belonged to it in those early months before I was adopted?

As I stared at that massive structure, I became aware that at my side Evan Faulkner was studying me as I studied the house. I turned my head to meet his look and felt an odd sense of disquiet go through me. Until now he had been too thoroughly lost in his own anger to see me as a person, but now he was aware of me, weighing and measuring me—so that I sensed dismissal as clearly as though he had spoken, and I thought I knew why. My smile was forced and slightly wry.

"I suppose you saw that dreadful television program last night?"

"Dreadful? I thought you were in control every minute," he said coolly.

I wanted to say, "That girl may have been, but she isn't me," though I could hardly say anything so absurd to this stranger, and when I spoke I knew my helpless resentment was showing.

"You sound as though you don't approve of women being in control."

He didn't rise to the foolish bait, but touched the gas pedal so that the car speeded up, climbing the slope of overgrown dune that led to the house. I felt as disgruntled as a child and resentful of him as a man. This was what men had been doing to women for centuries, only I wasn't used to being put down—if that was what had happened.

I tried to give my attention to the road the car followed, and I could understand now why everyone spoke of going "up" to the house. We were climbing the line of dunes that ridged the southern shore along the ocean. In the vicinity of The Shingles some order had been brought out of the wild tangle of beach vegetation, and the gravel drive rose to end at a brick parking area before a long garage.

Again Evan Faulkner braked the car. "Let's go up," he said shortly, discouraging any further conversation between us.

A herringbone brick walk mounted toward the foot of steps that rose steeply, ending in a sheltered alcove into which was set the massive front door. Just as we reached its double panels and huge brass knocker, one side opened and an old man stood peering out at us in the dim light of the recess.

"This is William Asher, who has looked after the Rhodes for many years," Evan Faulkner said. "Asher, will you take Miss Marsh to her room and then see that her bags and car are brought up from the gatehouse?"

The old man bowed and mumbled some greeting for me, regarding me with a look that seemed to measure and automatically find me wanting. My earlier annoyance evaporated and I suppressed an inclination to laugh at myself. New York had spoiled me. There I was accustomed to being treated not only as an equal but as someone rather special by the men I knew. Now two men who knew nothing about me seemed to have weighed my worth and found me wanting—and I had reacted with the same childish resentment and wish to stamp my feet that I'd thought nonsense in other women.

"Thank you," I said, being very gracious to Evan Faulkner, giving him my best smile. He nodded and went off down a long hallway. He wasn't going to bother about me further, now that he could pass the burden along.

The thin, bony figure of William Asher mounted the stairs ahead of me, leading the way, and when we reached the second floor I could discern the layout of the house. A long, rather narrow hall ran its width, with all the bedrooms facing the ocean, and a series of closets and storage rooms on the land side. Asher paused before the third door and opened it for me.

"In here, Miss Marsh. I'll be back soon with your bags. You can tell Mrs. Asher if there's anything you want. My wife takes charge of this part of the house, and there's a bell by the door that will call her."

I thanked him and he went off, leaving me to step into a room that shimmered with sea light. Two white-curtained windows looked out upon a tremendous view, and I went to stand at one of them. Below me the barrier dune humped itself down in a steep pitch from house to beach, and I saw that wooden steps descended over it. White sand stretched in either direction as far as I could see and the lacy surf of Judith's painting scalloped its edge, flowing up the sand, and then receding with that breathless sound of the ocean breathing. There was apparently little wind at the moment and the sea made a flat, endless plain clear to the horizon. Far out on the water the white wings of a sailboat hung limp, and I heard the throb of motor power in the distance.

Both windows were open on the sunny day and I breathed deeply of salt air, feeling an unexpected joy move through me—as though I had come to a place where I belonged and where I could find happiness and contentment. I smiled at the illusion, at my own imaginings. The dark, massive house still lay behind me, and I already knew there was something far from reassuring about it that I must eventually reckon with. But at least I could escape it and walk the beach whenever I pleased—as someone else was already doing.

The man on the sand was not young, in his fifties perhaps, as I judged by his silver-gray hair, but, dressed in white shorts and a gray pullover sweater, he was jogging along the hard sand at the water's edge with the vigor of a man much younger. As he came even with the house, he turned toward the steps and ran lightly up to the top of the dune. Beneath my window he came to a halt and stood looking up at me.

"Hello, Courtney Marsh," he said. "I'm John Rhodes. Sorry I wasn't inside to greet you. We've been looking forward to your arrival."

As I smiled and returned his greeting, I did calculations in my mind. John was Herndon's older brother, and he had been the husband of Nan Kemble's sister Alice—the one who had died.

"I was envying you your run on the sand," I said. "There have never been enough beaches in my life."

"At this time of the year it's all yours to enjoy." He gave a generous wave of his hand, and disappeared below me inside the house. So far, I decided, I liked him best of any of the family I'd met.

A knock on the door signaled Asher with my bags and a message.

"Mr. Herndon has phoned," he said as he set down my cases and coat. "He would like to see you downstairs in half an hour, if that is convenient, Miss Marsh." The words were properly courteous, the underlying disapproval was not.

"I'll be there," I assured him, and when he'd gone I unpacked a few things and hung them in the good-sized closet. Now I had time to admire my room.

It was simply furnished and quite charming. A walnut lowboy with brass pulls served as a dressing table, with a gilt-framed mirror above it. In a corner stood a gold-upholstered chair, and the spool bed wore a handsome quilt in a warm yellow fan design. The rug was a great braided oval of mottled green and yellow, and there were watercolor seascapes on the walls, none of them as arresting as the real view framed by the windows.

Charming though the room might be, however, I had no desire to sit down and wait out my half hour. John Rhodes had invited me to enjoy the beach—so why not? I would find my way down to it and follow that enticing rush of surf for a little way before my appointment with Herndon Rhodes in the living room.

At the dressing-table mirror I brushed out my shoulder-length hair that was as blond as Stacia's, touched up my lipstick, and studied my face for a moment in the glass. Was there any resemblance? No!—I must not follow that path again, lest my own yearning betray me. Just to think was to quicken my pulses, and along that road could lie sure disappointment and disillusionment. I was here as a reporter, an observer—interested, perhaps, in unicorns.

All the doors were closed along the corridor as I walked toward the stairs, passing framed abstracts that occupied the spaces in between. I couldn't make out the initials with which they were signed, but I didn't think they belonged to Judith Rhodes' brush. As I neared the stairs, a woman came down from the floor above, pausing to smile nervously when she saw me.

"I'm Mrs. Asher," she said. "If there is anything you want, Miss Marsh—?" She was years younger than her husband and might have been faintly pretty if she had released the severity of her hair, pulled back in a brown knob. Obviously she was far less sure of herself and her own position than her husband. Asher had an air of owning the house.

"There's nothing, thank you, I'm very comfortable," I said pleasantly and went on down the stairs that ended in a short hallway separating living room from dining room. Another, longer hall opened off it, running the width of the house at the back and paralleling the upstairs corridor. I could see an outside door at the far end, and I started toward it.

On the way, passing an open door, I glanced in upon a dark-paneled library with old books lining the shelves, and a long refectory table in the middle, heaped with boxes and papers, as though some sort of work was in progress. A library collection could be a good source of family information, I thought, and noted the room as a place to visit another time. But now I walked to the far door and went down steps to a grassy terrace that disappeared around the ocean side of the house. Idly, I walked along the terrace to a flagged section above the ocean, where beach furniture had been invitingly set, sheltered by a green-striped awning.

I decided to look around a little before I went down to the beach. The terrace followed the house, and as I moved into the open, I found that the wind was rising, bringing with it the soft roar of the surf just below me. Out on the water white sails plumped and power was shut off. A sense of the agelessness of sand and ocean possessed me and I knew that even these elderly houses which stretched along the dunes were young beside this vast sky and sea. But out here I felt none of the oppression that I had experienced inside the house.

As I reached the far end of the terrace, I came upon a sheltered alcove built into the lower floor—a square inner room, open to the ocean on one side, and boasting a fireplace, where one could sit protected from wind and sun, yet be almost outdoors.

But the house still crouched above me with its dark, weathered brown shingles—a preserver of secrets—and I was forced to look up at that broad façade that raised its three frowning stories into the sky. At a window high above, a curtain moved, and I knew that someone looked down at me—not openly as I had looked down at John Rhodes—but with an air of one who was curious, who wanted to watch without being seen. A hand touched the curtain and I caught the flash of a sapphire ring, remembering that I had seen such a ring on Stacia's finger. No matter. What did I care if she chose to peer at me from behind a curtain?

They were all rather strange in this family—even Nan Kemble, who was not blood-related, but whose life had been tied in with the Rhodes, as Evan Faulkner's life was tied in. Reluctantly, I found myself wondering about Evan. What was his work? And what strains had he been under which drove him into striking his wife so brutally?

Behind me something snuffled ominously. I whirled about, startled—and froze where I stood. The largest Great Dane I had ever seen watched me from a few feet away, his cropped, pointed ears held high and alert. He was black-masked, and his coat was a mottled white and blue-black, his skull and chest massive, his neck muscular with power. The dark eyes stared at me suspiciously and there was no wagging of his thin tail, which had the curve of a saber.

"Hello, boy," I said cautiously, not moving a finger.

His answer was a growl deep in his throat. Great Danes were bred as work dogs, watchdogs, I knew, and I didn't want to tangle with this fellow. Neither did I want to take fright and alarm him. Carefully, I took a step back toward the half-enclosed room off the terrace. There must be a door leading into the house—if I could reach it.

But as I stepped back, the dog drew closer, and I knew that he wasn't going to let me enter the house. I also sensed that he might be getting ready to spring. His sudden bark shook me with fright and I had to call out.

"Help me, someone! Please call the dog!"

There were open windows and someone heard. A door to the terrace room was flung open and a woman came running across the flagstones.

"Tudor!" she called. "Stay, boy. It's all right—stay!"

The dog halted his relentless approach and the long tail began to wag at the appearance of his mistress. She flew past me to reach him and knelt to put her arms about his great neck, and soothe him with quiet, loving words.

It was in this way, with a total lack of formality and without introduction, at a time when I could hardly have been more distraught, or she more in control of the situation—it was in this way that I met Judith Rhodes.

3

I stood well back from the Great Dane as she knelt beside him, and I found that I was trembling to my fingertips— partly because of the fright the dog had given me, partly because this was the woman I had come to confront, and I had no idea what she might mean to me, or what place she might have in my life. I could only stand there shivering, staring at her, waiting for her to turn and speak to me.

She wore a cotton peasant dress, flowing to the ground in bright patchwork squares, belted at her waist with a leather thong, and with a square neck that revealed a tanned space of skin meeting the tan of throat and face. Her hair was black and straight and very long as it fell about her, covering her back where she knelt crooning over the dog, slipping down in long silky strands that touched the terrace stones. I couldn't see her face until, having quieted the dog, she looked up at me, and I met the brilliant green of her eyes. Her nose was delicately formed, and the mouth that was like pink velvet was un- touched by lipstick. She must be as old as Nan Kemble, since she had a daughter nearly my age, yet there was an agelessness about her that allowed no naming of her years. More than anything else, however, she wore a serenity that somehow took me by surprise. If there had been some eccentricity evident, the shyness of a recluse, even a touch of derangement, I would not have been surprised, but when she rose to her sandaled feet, one hand resting on the dog's brass-studded collar, there was only a lovely calm worn as gracefully as she wore her patchwork gown.

"I'm sorry," she said, one hand smoothing long strands of hair back from her face. "I didn't know you were out here, or I'd never have let Tudor come onto the terrace."

I realized that introductions weren't necessary, and that she would not bother with them. She knew who I was, and I knew she was Judith Rhodes, and no naming of names seemed to matter. Yet introductions were ordinarily a method of crossing the bridge between strangers, and I found myself oddly shy and self-conscious, not knowing what to say—and I was still trembling.

Her voice had a low resonance as she began to talk, trying to reassure me.

"You needn't be afraid of him. He's a handsome fellow, isn't he? A Harlequin Dane they call his breed because of the mottling. A few years ago John Rhodes, my brother-in-law, brought him home from Germany for Stacia, but somehow he attached himself to me. We couldn't give him a German name—something royal, like Tudor, seemed right."

I found nothing to say, and her calm green gaze studied me thoughtfully, seeming to come to some conclusion.

"You aren't like the girl I saw on television last night," she stated. "You're not like her in the least. I think you'll be all right—so tomorrow morning we'll begin."

And that was all. With her hand still resting on the dog's collar, guiding him, she moved along the terrace, a straight, tall figure. I had no need to seek for resemblance here. There was no fairness of coloring about Judith Rhodes, no slightness of bone structure. Though tall, she was not a big woman, and her bones were good, but far more prominent than mine or Stacia's. Which meant nothing, of course. I had spoken not a single word, and she was already gone, out of sight around the far end of the house, leaving me gaping after her, and far more shaken than I could have believed. No wonder she had said I wasn't like the Courtney Marsh she had seen on television —I was a shaking lump of terrified, distraught flesh, without poise, without a voice.

In rueful response I began to laugh a little. Thank God for the grace of being able to laugh at oneself—if only in nervous reaction. It was something I'd forgotten lately in New York. But my mirth did me no good with Asher, who came rather peevishly out of the house, apparently having noted my encounter with the dog and with Judith Rhodes from a window.

"We didn't know you were coming out here, Miss Marsh," he chided me, clearly disapproving of laughter he could not understand. "I would have warned you about the dog. He doesn't like strangers wandering around."

"Then I was lucky," I said, sobering to accept my chastisement.

"Mr. Herndon is waiting for you in the living room," he went on with reproachful dignity. "If you will come in, please."

"Of course," I said. Laughing at myself had helped me to recovery, and my knees were no longer quaking as I walked through the door Asher held open for me and into the living room.

It was strange, but though I had played at times with the thought of Judith Rhodes being my mother, I'd had no fantasies about her husband. With a baby that had been given away, anyone could be the father. He was standing near a fire he had just lighted in the grate of a big brick fireplace when I came in, and he set the poker aside and came toward me, hand outstretched.

Herndon Rhodes' hair was completely gray and the face beneath seemed worn and faintly sad. He was a big man, though not as tall as Evan Faulkner, and he looked older than the older brother I'd seen jogging on the beach.

"I'm glad you've come, Courtney Marsh," he said as I gave him my hand.

"I'm happy that you were willing to let me come," I said. "I've just met your wife on the terrace—and I think I've been accepted."

He looked a little surprised and I hastened to add that Mrs. Rhodes had suggested that we could begin tomorrow morning.

"That was quick," he said. "I really haven't been sure what would happen when you arrived. Judith is doing this to please me, you know, and it's not something she really wants. Last night when she saw you on the program, she decided she wasn't going to like you. I think I'd better be frank and tell you that."

I smiled at him. "I don't blame her. I saw some of the program myself, and I didn't like that girl either. Perhaps I redeemed myself with Mrs. Rhodes just now by being practically eaten by her dog. I was so scared I couldn't even open my mouth, and that may have reassured her."

He smiled with a certain restraint. "I'm sorry about Tudor, but delighted if you got past Judith's guard."

He had seated me near the fire as he spoke, and as he moved about I had a further opportunity to study him. For a seemingly quiet, self-controlled man, there were surprising touches to his dress. A vest of red plaid and a tie only a shade less bright, gave him a certain flamboyance that hardly matched his rather subdued manner. In this man they seemed almost like costume touches.

But the place interested me even more than the man, and I took the opportunity to look about the big, high-ceilinged room. It was windowed along the water side, letting in a rippling sea light from the ocean, as well as brightness from the sky. The original dark woodwork had been replaced with creamy-pale paint, and unlike the exterior of the house, which seemed gloomy with age, this room shone with a bright aura of wealth, luxury, elegance. It was not a room through which one would run with wet bathing suits and sandy feet, and it was large enough to dwarf the grand piano that stood beside rear windows. Two great Chinese rugs covered the floor, their oblong beige centers bordered in blue and decorated with tiny pink flowers at each corner. On the mantel handsome porcelain, also Chinese, gleamed in blue and white. The sofas were Empire, and the rest a mixture of antique and richly comfortable modern pieces.

But the most arresting feature of the room was the large

oil painting I had seen before in its newspaper reproduction. A golden moon with its unicorn shadow shed an ambience over the beach scene that made the picture glow with an unearthly light. In the foreground an ancient figurehead—perhaps from a clipper ship—sat atilt in the sand, turning the sad, weathered face of a woman to the room.

The picture drew me and I left my chair to stand before it. Its mood was sadly haunting, as had been that of the other beach scene hanging in Nan's shop, the glow of moonlight lending a chill to the scene that seemed colder than the lapping waves of a gray ocean. Judith's work had indeed a quality of make-believe about it, a dreaming emptiness which the imagination could easily people with wraiths.

"I do believe that Judith Rhodes must be one of the fine painters in this country," I said. "That scene is real, and yet it's surreal at the same time, and it conveys a mood I won't easily shake off."

"Perhaps that's exactly the mood of this house," Herndon said softly, coming to stand behind me. "The Rhodeses are a haunted lot, I'm afraid. You'll sense this if you're here awhile, so I might as well warn you of it. Perhaps that is the very thing that has complemented something rare in Judith's talent. I'd like her to be recognized to a far greater extent than she is, you see. I have an ambition for her that she lacks for herself. Especially since—" He paused, then went on. "Especially since we may not have The Shingles in our possession too much longer—and then I don't know what will happen to Judith's painting. She has put down roots here."

His words startled me. "But the house has always belonged to your family, hasn't it?"

"Even so." He shrugged unhappily, and I knew that whatever might be bringing about a change, he was not instigating it. I wanted to question him directly, but I knew he would not tell me now.

"I'd like to know a little more about the family," I said.

"I'll see if I can telescope to some extent. I won't go back into ancient history, but we can start with Ethan Rhodes, who built this house. He was a whaler—more than a whaler, since he had a fleet of ships, though he captained only one. He lived originally in Sag Harbor, which was a great whaling center in the old days. When he retired he came here and built this house on the dunes, before any of the summer places went up. He built of wood because that's what could be had at the time. There was no stone around in this sandy soil, except what came in as ballast in ships."

"How are you related to Ethan Rhodes?"

"He was my great-grandfather. He had sons who scattered round the country. Only the eldest, Brian, stayed in this house. He was a sailor too. His son Lawrence was my father, but he turned to the law for his career."

"What about the women in the family?"

"Ethan's wife Hesther was of pretty stalwart stock. All the women stood by their husbands when they went off on long voyages. If you like, I'll write a few names down for you, so that you can keep relationships straight. If you're interested."

"Yes, please. For my own guidance. All this won't go into what I write, since your wife is only related by marriage. Are Lawrence and his wife dead—your father and mother?"

"Yes. Sara died at least thirty years ago. My father about five years later."

"You and John Rhodes are their only sons?"

"That's right. I married Judith, of course, and John married Alice Kemble. She died shortly before our father did."

I remembered the woman I'd talked to in the dress shop—"all those deaths, so close together . . ." she had said. But "all" would not pertain to only two. So who else had died? Stacia had said later that there were three deaths. And "all" had come about close to the time of my birth.

"Have there been other children in the family besides Stacia?" I asked tentatively.

"No—none."

Had he replied too quickly? So far everyone I'd met seemed quick to conceal, to turn away from certain questions. If the house had its secrets, so did the people who lived here and were the source. I threw out another tentative hook.

"Miss Kemble mentioned that I had come at a bad time—that something disturbing had happened recently which had upset all of you. I'm sorry if that makes having me here a burden."

"Let's sit down," he said. "The afternoon is getting on —would you like something to drink?"

"No, thank you," I said, and waited.

He went on, choosing his words carefully, and I had a feeling that here was a man who would have liked to be comfortably open, yet who had been forced by circumstances to play a different, more evasive role. Again I wondered about that bright vest.

"Miss Kemble shouldn't have worried you with this. What happened was nothing more than a malicious trick played by some irresponsible person. We shall simply ignore it."

"I understand," I said. "It's just that everything around Judith Rhodes interests me and I can't tell what may help me to know and understand her better."

A slight smile touched his mouth. "I doubt if you will ever know and understand her. I've been married to her for a good many years, and I've never achieved that felicitous state. Perhaps that's why she remains forever fascinating."

His words were slightly pedantic, yet there was a note of affection in his voice that seemed genuine, and seemed as well to hint at some sorrow. Perhaps Herndon Rhodes, the prosaic banker, had a greater complexity to his character than easily met the eye.

We were sitting once more and I gave my attention again to the painting over the mantel. "Can you tell me about the unicorn on the moon?"

He seemed glad to turn to history. "Ethan's wife, my great-grandmother Hesther, had a superstition about unicorns. She was given a little gold one by a visiting potentate and that started it off. Unicorns are supposed to bring good luck, but Hesther had a whimsical streak and she devised her own legend when she claimed to have seen a shadow like a unicorn drift across the moon. That was the night Ethan's father died, and after that she always said that a unicorn on the moon could mean either disaster or great good fortune for a Rhodes. It's all written down in her diary, and has been passed along in the family. Hesther's gold unicorn became a sort of talisman against any possible threat."

"And have other Rhodes seen the ghost unicorn? On the moon?"

He moved restlessly in his chair, as though my questions had begun to weary him. "I'm afraid I don't believe in that sort of thing, Miss Marsh."

I ventured a more pertinent approach. "What happened to Hesther Rhodes' golden unicorn?" I asked, and held my breath.

"Unfortunately, I don't know. Trinkets have a way of disappearing over the years. I asked Judith to look for it once, because I thought it should be given to Stacia, but she couldn't find it."

Involuntarily, my hand sought the throat of my blouse, but before I could find anything to say, Evan Faulkner appeared in the doorway.

"Have you seen Stacia?" he asked of Herndon.

The other man shook his head. "No, I haven't. I looked for her myself when I came in. Come join us, Evan—I'm about to order drinks."

"I want to find Stacia," Evan said.

He went off without a glance at me, and I sensed that he too was a troubled and preoccupied man. As would certainly be likely with that bruised cheek he had given Stacia.

Herndon looked after him thoughtfully. "Evan has been a great help to us. Lately he's been cataloguing the Rhodes' collection of books and papers and whaling captains' logs. Nearly everything has been preserved since Ethan's time, but it has never been properly inventoried and classified. Perhaps now, when Evan pulls it all together, it will be given to some museum, where it will prove of real value. He's taken time off from his work out at the Ocean Science Laboratory in Montauk, where he's a marine biologist, to take care of this. We're all grateful to him. It may be necessary to move fast."

"Why is that?"

He shook his head. "Nothing that need concern you." He looked suddenly weary, as though he carried some inner burden that was almost too great to bear.

"Perhaps I'll go upstairs and change for dinner," I said, wanting to let him escape the evident strain of talking to me. "Thank you for telling me something about the family."

He stood up as I rose and he nodded almost absently, as though his thoughts had already turned elsewhere. His mouth wore a grim look that was disturbing to see in the face of a man I had thought of as kindly and considerate.

As I hurried upstairs and down the hall to my room, I found myself troubled by a rising sense of disquiet. First the house itself had seemed to oppress me, and now the people who lived here were doing the same thing. Nan Kemble, with her secrets and concealments; Stacia, tearful and hurt, and trying to put on a brave front; Evan, driven by some dark anger that had led to a violence whose source I could not guess. And now Herndon, grimly withdrawing from my questions, although it was he who had invited me here to ask such questions. In my one glimpse of him, John Rhodes had seemed to carry about him a certain lighter charm, but he too might seem less open when I knew him better. That left me only Judith, with her calm, her serenity, her great creative force—yet perhaps she would prove to be the greatest enigma of all.

Which of these might be related to me? Any—or all? I remembered very well how sure I had been that if only I could trace my way back to my own roots, so that I could know something of the family that had bred me, I would be satisfied. But after so short a time in this house, I was already sensing complexities. There would be no easy answers, and there might exist in me a need to ask for more and more, until everything had been made clear—however disastrous full knowledge might be. Had that wretched lawyer been right, after all?

In my room I went to stand once more at the window, gazing out toward those ceaseless waves rolling in on the beach. There were waves like that in our lives—ebbing and flowing, urging us along, pulling us back, now threatening, now calming.

Since my encounter with the dog, I had steadied to some extent, yet there was still a surging of uncertainty in me, like those waves on the beach, and it brought with it a restlessness. My own tides were swollen with unanswered questions—with temptations to believe, when there was no proof and I must not believe. Yet there *was* the unicorn. Now I knew it belonged here. It belonged to the Rhodes' past and it had been placed about my neck. So did that make me a Rhodes? And if so, to what branch of the family might I belong? There was a hint of likeness between myself and Stacia, none at all to Judith. Nor did I find anything recognizable in Herndon or John. Both brothers had blue eyes, where Judith's were green, and before their hair had started to gray they had probably been blond. How little I had to go on. Especially since there seemed to be no missing child on the family tree. Though of course, if there were, that might be something to hide from a stranger like me. The important thing was not to become emotionally impatient. I must move slowly and carefully, remembering what Mr. Pierce had said about the certainty of my being unwelcome as a long-lost daughter at this late date.

In the bathroom I ran a hot tub and sprinkled in the fragrant mauve salts I found in a cabinet. When I felt rested and refreshed and some of those throbbing questions had been quieted, I dressed for dinner. I had no idea what was customary in this house, but my St. Laurent print chemise should be suitable, with its red roses scattered to the long hemline, and a decorous ribbon tie at the throat. But I could not wear my unicorn. The chain would show above the neck of the dress and this was not yet the time to flaunt my identity—even if I knew what that identity was.

I folded chain and pendant into tissue and tucked them into the drawer of the lowboy dressing table among my cosmetics. The ruby earrings I clipped on had been a gift one Christmas from Gwen and Leon, and they brought again the sharp pang of my loss. It was a loss I could never replace, didn't want to replace. Yet I must search on and try to find answers, even if they proved unhappy and disquieting. At least I liked the whaling background of the Rhodes. Old Ethan had made himself a part of history, and it might be satisfying to place myself somewhere within that heritage. When the opportunity arose perhaps I could seek out Evan Faulkner in the library and learn more about this family that might prove to be mine.

Nevertheless, I braced myself before I went downstairs, as though some sort of battle lay ahead of me. If this had been an ordinary visit, I would have enjoyed it, no matter what the atmosphere. I could have remained curious, but uninvolved. As things were, purpose must lie behind every move I made. I was here to find out, not only about Judith Rhodes, but about myself, and there was no time to be wasted. Even in this coming dinner encounter, I must watch and listen, and try to find the right questions to ask without ever betraying the true reason for my asking.

When I reached the living room, I found the three men standing before the fire, glasses in hand, clearly engaged in a conversation that could not have been cheerful. Herndon looked grimmer than ever, Evan angry, and even John had lost his cheerful air. They all turned and looked at me, pausing in their talk, and I knew that I was anything but welcome at that moment.

It was John who smiled first and came toward me. He was a tall man, with a handsome, rather saturnine look and flyaway eyebrows that could be cocked mockingly, and were less silver-blond than the hair above. Yet there was an ease about him which the other two lacked.

"We'll be glad for your company at the table tonight, Courtney Marsh," he said. "Stacia and Judith have decided to have their meals upstairs. Judith often does so, and Stacia isn't feeling well. So we need you badly."

His light touch was exactly right, helping me to relax, and in response the other two attempted to throw off the gloom which seemed to weigh them down. I accepted the glass of Dubonnet that John brought me, accepted his compliment about my dress, and recognized that he was not ignorant on the subject of fashion. John Rhodes was more of a cosmopolitan than anyone else in this house.

Yet of the three, it was Herndon who managed the most interesting sartorial touches, even though, in him, they were unexpected. Tonight, he wore under his jacket a smart, saffron-colored silk jersey turtleneck, modified for evening, that contrasted with the less imaginative clothes of the other two. Once more, I found myself wondering what this meant in Herndon. Vanity? He didn't seem a vain man. An effort to keep up with his dramatic and colorful wife? Perhaps. I couldn't decide.

When we went into the dining room John seated me in the place at the table's foot, opposite Herndon at the other end—undoubtedly the place which would belong to Judith when she came downstairs to dine. Candles had been lighted in crystal holders down the table, and old linen damask shone in a patina of pale light.

In those days when servants had abounded, Asher would have had others under him, doing his bidding. Now he served us himself, very correct, a little stiff in his joints, and decidedly dour of expression. I gathered that only Asher and his wife lived in the house. The cook and the housemaids came in from the village to take care of their duties, and went home at night.

Unlike the living room, the dark woodwork of the dining room had been left in its original state—perhaps because this was a truly rich and handsome room, with the dignity of another century that no one had wanted to tamper with. Again the ceiling was enormously high, and the windows on the ocean side correspondingly tall, with yards of burgundy draperies pulled across against the night. Above low mahogany paneling, raspberry wallpaper rose to the plate rail, where examples of Spode and Sèvres and Meissen were on display. The sideboard too was mahogany and huge, with a well-polished Georgian silver service set upon its top. In one corner stood an impressive glass cabinet filled with china and crystal.

All these things, I suspected, must have belonged for generations to the Rhodes family, and I wondered what would happen to them now, if the place, as Herndon had intimated, was to be sold. So few families had roots in the past these days that I already found myself regretting that this should happen. Perhaps this feeling was due to my own eagerness to belong to a real family, and if it was to be this one, I didn't want to see it dispersed so soon after I'd found it.

John was the only one who made much of an effort at conversation, drawing me out about my work on the magazine. We found that we had mutual friends in New York and it was easy to slip into small talk with him. Herndon appeared lost in a world of his own—concerned with matters I had no knowledge of, while Evan Faulkner was probably still harboring an anger that had nothing to do with me, and yet which caused me to feel the flick of it when he spoke. I wondered if Herndon knew that Evan had struck his daughter.

Once Herndon roused himself to somewhat stiff conversational effort, nodding toward the portrait of a woman that hung over the sideboard. "You were asking about members of the Rhodes family, Miss Marsh. That is a portrait of Alice Rhodes. When was it done, John?"

John did not look at the picture. "It was painted just after we were married. I never thought it a very good likeness."

I glanced up at the portrait, and the brown eyes of the girl who had posed for it seemed to meet mine quizzically. She wore a pale blue dress, with a touch of pink at the throat, and there was a pink rose in her brown hair. One cheek barely dimpled in a smile, and the portrait seemed to suggest that she might burst into gay laughter at any moment.

"I can remember her like that when she was very young," Herndon said. "But it's true that she was never a 'sweet Alice.' She was much more of a person than that."

"She was still young when she died," John said bleakly.

I wanted to ask how she had died, but this wasn't the time. Apparently John Rhodes had never married again.

Strangely enough, however, through soup and roast and salad, to the custards we were served for dessert, it was not Herndon and John who held my most interested attention —but Evan Faulkner, who was not a Rhodes at all. Once or twice I tried to draw him into talk about his work out at the lab in Montauk, but his resentment of me, somehow begun when he had seen me on television last night, seemed to have deepened, and his answers were in monosyllables, so that I gave up. I hadn't liked him in the beginning, and there was no reason to like him now, yet some perverse impulse in me kept trying to reach him. Why?—to stir up the sleeping tiger? I didn't like brutal, insensitive men. But as a reporter, a writer, I was seeking an answer to the antagonism that burned between this husband and wife.

Only once did he take me by surprise. I had given up trying to talk to him, and was lost in my own thoughts when I realized that Evan had asked me a question, and I hadn't been listening. I blinked into the waiting silence, forced to apologize.

"I'm sorry. I didn't hear what you asked."

His dark eyes regarded me steadily. "I was merely wondering aloud whether you would put anything about the Rhodes family and its history into the article you are going to write."

"That would be irrelevant," Herndon said quickly. "Judith is a Rhodes only by marriage."

I wondered at this quick attempt to discourage me. After all, he had told me something of the family.

"I haven't decided about that," I said quietly. "It depends on how things fit in. I don't like to discard anything until I'm sure it doesn't belong."

"The Rhodes have an interesting history," Evan said, as if he had at last decided to acknowledge my presence. "I suppose it's having my roots here in the Hamptons area that makes me want to see it preserved. That's what I'm trying to do now. If you've any interest, Miss Marsh, stop in the library sometime and I'll show you some of the materials on whaling. John can add a lot to this background as well."

I wondered why Evan was urging this upon me, but when I glanced at John he smiled at me easily. "Anything you want to know, of course. Sometimes I think Evan is more interested in all this whaling history than we are."

I wasn't sure what I wanted to know, but at least Evan Faulkner had made a civilized offer and I thanked him for it. If I went to the library to learn more about the

Rhodes and the past, it would be for reasons he could not suspect.

We had nearly finished the meal, and I was looking forward to escaping upstairs, when Asher came into the room, clearly agitated. He carried a salver on which lay a plain envelope, to place it before Herndon.

"It's another one, sir," Asher said. "I just found it."

Herndon regarded the envelope as he might have regarded a snake that could raise its head to strike at him.

"You'd better open it," John said quietly.

Herndon made no move to slit the envelope. "It might be wiser to burn it unread."

"Open it," Evan said. "It may give us some clue about the sender."

Herndon ripped open the envelope and unfolded the single sheet of cheap, lined paper inside. Then he looked up at Asher.

"Where did you find it?"

"Someone pushed it under the front door, sir," Asher said. "I was going through the hall and I saw it. I don't know how long it was there. No one was about when I looked outside."

"If there are any more, bring them to me at once," Herndon told him. "Not to anyone else. And take care that they don't reach Mrs. Rhodes."

"Of course, sir." Asher bowed his gray head and went off, though I suspected he would have liked to stay to see what would happen next.

"Well, what's in it?" John demanded. "What does it say this time?"

Herndon tapped the sheet before him. "There's just one word. Letters cut out of a newspaper again and pasted on ruled paper. They spell 'Anabel?' with a question mark added. That's all."

Evan said, "That could refer to the boat, of course."

"Not coming on the heels of the last note. I don't think so."

"Let's see it." John held out his hand.

Herndon gave the sheet to him and glanced in my direction. "I'm sorry, Miss Marsh. You might as well know that someone has started a series of anonymous notes which arrive at our door, without anyone seeing who brings them. Probably it's no more than malicious mischief."

"Mischief from someone who knows a remarkable lot about the family," Evan said. "You should show them to the police, as I've said before."

"No!" Coming from the quiet banker, the word was unexpectedly explosive. "I won't have Judith troubled with this sort of thing. She had to know about the first one because she was present when it came, but I would prefer it if you don't mention that there's been a second. Not any of you."

His manner was still formal and a little stiff, but there was no missing the underlying force. As I listened, I grew increasingly puzzled about the relationship between Herndon and John. Curiously, even though John was the older, Herndon seemed to be in charge, and the problem in hand was being deferred to him.

Evan was watching me, and when I caught his look it seemed to challenge me. "You understand, Miss Marsh, that this affair is off the record as far as you are concerned." He spoke coldly.

"Of course," I agreed.

John's smile was reassuring. "I don't think we need worry about Courtney. And let's dispense with this 'Miss Marsh' formality. The young lady is going to be part of the family for the time being—undoubtedly treated to our innermost secrets. So let's relax with her a little. I know her writing and she doesn't do hatchet jobs."

"Thank you, John," I said.

"In any case," he went on, "we all know that Judith did everything she could at the time these events occurred. What happened wasn't her fault."

"She still remembers," Herndon said. "It's vicious to open old wounds like this."

"You might consider that the wounds are mine too," John said.

Herndon sighed. "Yes, I know. I'm sorry."

Evan reached across the table to take the note from John and examined it carefully. He seemed to exert a certain authority in this family, and he was listened to.

"Since you don't want to go to the police with these, the only thing you can do is ignore them. Either the purpose behind the mischief will become evident, or whoever is playing tricks will tire of it and it will stop."

"I don't know." Herndon was staring up at the portrait of his dead sister-in-law.

"Is there anything—well—in doubt about that time when she died?" Evan went on. "Anything someone who disliked the Rhodes could make something of? The first note referred to Alice."

"There has always been gossip, of course," Herndon said. "But it had no base. What happened was a double tragedy, but simple enough in each case."

"Then you've nothing to worry about," Evan assured him. "There's no real harm being done, as John says, and from now on we'll tip the help off to be on the watch, and both Asher and his wife can keep an eye out. Miss Marsh—"

"Please make it Courtney," I said, backing John up.

Evan gave me a thin smile. "Of course, Courtney. I was about to suggest that you say nothing to Judith about this —as the others won't either."

He had not really softened toward me. His dark look challenged any opposition I might offer, and I felt the force of a will that would brook no contradiction. It was a look that gave me no trust, in spite of his use of my first name, and I resented it strongly.

"I've already said I won't use any of this, and of course I won't talk about it with Judith, if that's what you wish."

Herndon pushed back his chair, closing the subject without further comment, and we left the table.

I excused myself on the score of being tired, and started toward the stairs. I had had enough of uncomfortable undercurrents for one day, and I wanted to spend the rest of the evening alone. In my room there were books to read, but mainly I wanted to do a little sorting out when I was by myself. For reasons that I could not yet understand, I seemed to have stepped into a household stricken by more than anonymous messages. Some crisis seemed to be approaching, but its tide lay beneath the surface, its causes and meanings well hidden from my outsider's view.

Whether this was anything that concerned me as a possible member of the family, I couldn't tell. I had no interest in using such private matters in my piece about Judith—but I had a great deal of interest in them in the event that I was involved.

In any case, I climbed the stairs feeling increasingly depressed and discouraged. I, who had never known a family of my own blood, had built over the years an imaginary picture of what such a family should be like. None of that felicitous fancy appeared to exist in this household.

When I reached the upper landing, I was brought sharply out of my puzzling to find the dog, Tudor, stretched with his great mottled body across my path, looking down at me with antipathy in every muscle.

His tail did not thump when I tried to speak to him, and his black lip drew back unpleasantly from his teeth. A now familiar growl warned me, so that I turned away hastily, to discover John Rhodes at the foot of the stairs.

"It's all right," he assured me. "Tudor's not used to you yet. Come down, boy—come down at once."

At least the dog obeyed commands. He arose with swift grace and pushed past me down the stairs, so that I was thrust against the banister and felt the warmth of his great body as he rushed by. John gave him a pat on the flank and Tudor headed for the back of the house.

"I'm sorry," John said, his smile reassuring. "We'll see to it that Tudor is tied up after this, when he's not with Judith. Have a good sleep, and forget about the Rhodes or they'll give you nightmares."

I tried to return his smile, but my lips felt stiff, and I ran up the stairs quickly and hurried down the hall to my room. There I met with new disquiet. My door was ajar, though I knew I had left it closed. I pushed it open cautiously and looked into the room. Stacia Faulkner lay stretched upon the patchwork quilt on the bed, her arms behind her head, and her bruised cheek clearly in view as she turned her head to look at me.

"Hello," she said. "I hope you don't mind my waiting for you here."

4

I was not altogether pleased to find myself with a visitor —and particularly not with Stacia. I had looked forward to being alone, yet on the other hand she might be the one to tell me more about this curious household.

"I don't mind," I said, and went to drop into the gold-upholstered wing chair, waiting to hear what she wanted.

Stacia raised herself on an elbow, regarding me with large, rather luminous blue eyes. "That's a beautiful dress." Her tone was almost wistful, and I wondered why. Beautiful gowns would hardly be a rarity to this girl, who didn't need to work for her clothes as I did. "But it's lost in a place like this," she went on. "Wasted." She did not add "on a man like Evan," but I sensed that she was thinking of her husband.

"You didn't seek me out to talk about dresses," I said.

"No—you're right. What do you think of us so far, Courtney Marsh?"

"I don't know enough about you to think much of anything," I told her.

"I'll bet that's not true!" she challenged. "I think you're already liking and disliking, taking sides. And perhaps wrongly."

"I'm open to suggestions." Stacia was nearly my age, yet sometimes she seemed younger, more vulnerable than I would have expected.

"I can tell you one thing," she said. "Uncle John is the only real human being in this house."

"Are you discounting your father and mother?"

"Judith doesn't care about anything but her painting, and my father doesn't care about anything except her. Perhaps you need to know this before you start talking to her."

Behind her words lay old, angry resentment, and perhaps pain as well—perhaps the remembered pain of a child who had been neglected. Unexpected pity for her stirred in me.

"I'm glad you've had a friend in your uncle," I said. "I like him too. By the way, I don't really know what he does. His work, I mean."

She flashed me a smile that hinted at amusement rather than malice. "Perhaps he's mainly a parasite—like me. In his own way, I suppose he has a touch of genius—but he doesn't work at it hard enough. Of course I was born too late to know, but I understand that Grandfather Lawrence was enormously proud of that boat Uncle John designed— the *Anabel*. It's still in the marina over in Sag Harbor and I've gone sailing in it a few times. Grandfather was even ready to build a small shipyard, to try to revive ship-building here on Long Island—and let Uncle John design and build boats. But most of those plans are unfinished. Though he still promises to build a boat that he'll name for me."

"Who was Anabel?" I asked.

Stacia sat up on the bed and crossed her long legs in their green slacks. "It's a Kemble family name. I gather that the boat was already built, and Aunt Alice had named it before little Anabel was born. The poor little thing wasn't around very long anyway. Have you heard about the baby who died?"

I sat very still, hardly daring to breathe, all too aware of the sudden thumping of my heart. "No," I said, "I haven't heard. Whose baby was it?"

Restlessly, she left her perch on the bed and went to a

window to part draperies that had been drawn against sky and ocean. When she spoke it was over her shoulder.

"I'm talking out of turn. I keep forgetting you're a reporter. Ask Judith. Ask Judith to tell you—she knows everything about this family. And she was the one who found Aunt Alice when she died. But this isn't for me to talk about. Ask her."

I didn't believe that Stacia was given to reticence when it served her purpose. Some other motive moved her now.

"You sound like someone who is trying to stir up trouble," I said frankly.

"Perhaps I am!" She whirled to face me and I saw again the purplish bruise on her cheek and sensed the anger that drove her. There was nothing childlike about her now. She was a woman and furious. "They've got it coming to them! All except Uncle John. He's outside of it. He and I are safe."

"Safe?"

Her smile dazzled and mocked at the same time. "From you, perhaps? You're not going to write about *us*, are you? Only about Judith. And if you want to do an honest piece about my mother, perhaps you'd better learn some of the right questions to ask. Everything's going to be pulled down about their heads before long anyway, so a little more upheaval won't matter. We'll be leaving this house soon, and that will destroy Judith. I don't think she can work anywhere else."

"Why must she leave the house?"

"Because it will be sold. Whether they like it or not, it will be sold!"

"Who will sell it? I shouldn't think your father—?"

"That's another question you can ask her." Stacia left her place at the window and moved about the room, once more as lithe in her movements as a young leopard, and perhaps almost as dangerous. My feeling toward her was still mixed. It was possible that she had a right to her anger. Perhaps injury had been done to her long ago that she'd had no defense against—yet I was beginning to suspect that she asked for punishment, willfully pushing out at everyone in order to antagonize.

Finished with her prowling about the room, she threw herself on the bed and pressed an arm across her eyes. When she spoke she had lapsed back into her pose of youthfulness. "If it wasn't for Nan and John, I might have run away years ago. Nan listens to me. She's never tried to order me around, and she never scolds me."

I wondered if that was a mistake on Nan's part, but I didn't say so.

"I liked Nan Kemble when I met her this afternoon," I said. But it wasn't Nan I wanted to talk about. "I don't suppose you remember your grandfather—Lawrence Rhodes?"

"No. He died before I was born. Yet sometimes I think he's closer to me than those of my family who are living. Maybe I'm like him. I'd have made a good lady pirate."

"I thought Lawrence's field was the law."

"It was. Dry stuff—trusts and wills and estates. Not much room for pirating there. But he was a pirate, just the same. Captain Yellowbeard, whose word was law. He ruled them all with absolute power, and he would cut down anyone who disobeyed him."

"Aren't you making up some of this?"

"Maybe. I've built him up in my own mind, I know, and even though we may be a little alike, I'm afraid he would never approve of me. Family—that's what mattered to him. The Rhodes name and what he thought it stood for. That was make-believe too—but he fooled himself first of all. I don't think old Ethan was like that. All the family pride began with Brian, who was Lawrence's father. It got so the good name of the family and its importance in the community mattered more than anything else. Everyone had to be measured by what Lawrence considered infallible Rhodes' standards. And when a Rhodes turned up who didn't meet the measure, he was banished—or destroyed. I think old Lawrence destroyed my mother and father for all those false principles. Maybe he even destroyed himself. I'm not going to let him get at me, even though in some ways I admire him."

"When did Lawrence die? What happened?"

"He died only two or three months after Alice and the baby. But prosaically enough. A heart attack. Judith was with him. Isn't that a strange thing about my mother? She was always there when someone died—Alice, the baby, Lawrence. Oh, not that she had anything to do with causing anyone to die. The Rhodes name wouldn't stand for that. Close the ranks, protect, shut out the press, save the family! And I guess it was done very cleverly. So now Judith paints melancholy pictures of sea and sand, and floats severed heads across her scenes."

"I don't think I like what you're telling me, and I don't think I believe it," I said quietly.

"Why not? What do *you* care about the Rhodes?"

The question came so suddenly, so pointedly, that I froze for a moment, and then realized that she couldn't possibly know the main reason why I was here.

"I suppose I feel doubtful about accusations that seem to be made out of anger and resentment."

Abruptly, disconcertingly, Stacia dissolved into tears. She turned on her stomach and wept long, heaving sobs like a child, so that her cheeks turned pink and the bruise grew even puffier. Alarmed, I went to sit on the edge of the bed beside her, and put a quieting hand on her shoulder.

"I'm sorry," I said. "I have no right to harsh judgments concerning things I know nothing about. But even if you dislike your mother, you mustn't try to prejudice me against her."

"I don't dislike her!" she wailed. "I love her. I've always wished I could be beautiful and talented and have people love me so much they would give up their lives for me."

The outburst seemed utterly childish and forlorn, yet even as I tried to soothe her I wondered if there was a woman's calculation behind it. What did she want of me—and why?

I went into the bathroom and dampened a washcloth with cool water, brought it back to her. "Let me wipe your face. You mustn't cry like that." As I touched her a curious feeling came over me. An emotion I had never experienced before—as though I touched someone dear to me who was of my own blood. A sister, perhaps? But the feeling was only fleeting. Stacia herself took care of that.

As she reached up to hold the cold cloth against her

puffy cheek, the heaving sobs stopped abruptly and her weeping ended.

"Go look in the top drawer of that dressing table," she said. "I left something there for you. I thought it might give you a shock to find it, but you've been more decent than I deserve, so you'd better look now, while I'm here. Perhaps you don't enjoy severed heads."

Uneasily, I went to the lowboy and opened the drawer. This was where I had placed my golden unicorn, and I looked for it first, still wrapped in its tissue. Only a few other things were visible—brush and comb and my cosmetics case, and I glanced toward the bed, questioning.

"Feel back in the drawer. Way back," Stacia directed.

My fingers slid into the shallow space, searching the far corner at the rear until they touched something small and cold and round—something faintly human. I drew out the bisque head of an old-fashioned doll and stared at it with repugnance. Round cheeks had been tinted rosy, and the eyes clicked open as I held it up, staring at me, roundly blue and soulless. The hair had been removed and the head was hollow at the top, so that one could look into it and see the glued-in eyes, the joint that thrust up at the neck to enable the head to move on the body. But there was no body—only this small "severed" head.

I didn't like the feel of it in my fingers, and I didn't like the impulse that had placed it here in my room. I set it down and turned back to the girl on the bed. She was watching me, her tears forgotten and that air of amusement about her again.

"I spooked you, didn't I? But it's a kindness, really. It will help prepare you when you walk into Mother's studio tomorrow."

"What do you mean?"

"You'll see." Stacia pushed herself up from the bed, and once more I had the impression of a body limber as a cat's—a characteristic which mixed strangely with the child who had cried, and the woman who could be malevolent. My feeling of blood relationship had vanished, taking with it the momentary warmth I had felt toward her. Cousin? Sister? What might she be to me—if anything? And which of all these masquerades was she? Perhaps a mixture of all of them? For the first time I felt a twinge of sympathy for Evan Faulkner. It was possible to imagine being taunted into a rage by Stacia—but I still didn't care for a man who would strike a woman. I didn't care for human beings of either sex who showed violence toward each other.

She paused beside me on the way to the door, taking her leave. "You look terribly confused. But I think I rather like you. And I don't want to see you do a bad piece about Judith—but only an honest one. Will you try to do that—write honestly?"

"I always do try," I said stiffly.

She gave me an elusive smile and slipped past me out the door. When it closed behind her, I turned back to see the staring eyes of the doll's head fixed blankly upon me. Hastily I thrust it into another drawer, away from the unicorn, wishing she had taken it with her. My feeling was one of odd disorientation. So much had been hurled at me, yet all of it had amounted to nothing more substantial than fog—all wisps and patches, implied hints, nothing concrete, nothing sure and certain. I felt as though I'd been doing battle with a mist maiden—a creature without substance or reality—something out of one of Judith's paintings.

From my encounter with Stacia Faulkner, only one truth had emerged. There *had* been a baby. A baby named Anabel. And that was the name, complete with question mark, which had been written on the note so recently delivered to Herndon Rhodes. What was going on? Why had this name been thrown into a quiet ant heap, causing consternation and a scurrying for cover? Was it really possible that I had been that baby who was supposed to have died? Had I been named Anabel by my true parents? And who were those parents? Judith and Herndon? Alice and John?

I didn't know. Except for that brief moment with Stacia, I had experienced no sense of relationship to anyone, and I dared not even try to guess. I wasn't sure whether I had been armed by Stacia with questions I could ask Judith tomorrow, or whether I would do better to erase from my mind every word she had spoken in this room. When I had time, I might visit Nan Kemble again. I wanted to know a great deal more about Stacia herself, to know what her malice—if that's what it was—added up to, and Nan seemed to have befriended her.

But for now I'd had enough of The Shingles and this rather terrifying family who lived here. Severed heads, indeed! What a pretty choice of words!

When I'd undressed and turned off the lights, I opened the draperies at the window and looked out at a trillion stars, seldom to be seen by city eyes. A few flecks of cloud drifted across the spangled sky, over a moon that was not yet full. There were no unicorns. Beneath that vast spangling the dark ocean rolled in endless disquiet, waves breaking upon the beach below my window with a muffled roar. What would it be like out there when there was a storm? Probably pretty frightening. Along this south shore there were few inlets or bays, and no good harbors. Farther west, toward the city, the barrier of Fire Island sheltered the land, but here the shore was fully exposed to the elements and to any storms that might come pounding up the coastline from the hurricane belt.

I drew the draperies across and switched on the bed lamp, got into bed with a mystery novel, and read until my eyes tired. Then I fell soundly asleep, and if I dreamed I couldn't remember what about when I opened my eyes the next morning—and that was always best.

At least my spirits had risen and I was looking forward to a day that could hardly be less than interesting in this house. The dark feeling of stepping toward the brink of some dangerous quicksand had lifted, and I no longer had a sense of becoming too closely involved. No one knew who I was, and I remained a free agent. I could reject this family any time I chose and go back to New York with nothing changed for Courtney Marsh. Even if some certain evidence were given me that I was a Rhodes, I could take it or leave it as I chose.

Thus, feeling light-hearted and reassured, I dressed in white slacks and a turquoise shirt, and brushed my hair till it shone. The morning was beautiful, and when I went downstairs to breakfast I found bright sunlight pouring in at the tall dining-room windows. Stacia, John, and

Herndon—this morning his vest was green—were already at the table, and someone said Evan had eaten early and gone to his work in the library.

Stacia wore jeans and a pink pullover this morning, and her cheek had lost some of its puffiness, but she appeared subdued, greeting me briefly and returning to her own thoughts that seemed to shut out conversation. John ate with a hearty appetite, and I suspected that he of them all was the one who most savored the creature comforts. I wondered what he would do when The Shingles was sold.

"Judith will be ready for you around ten," Herndon told me. "Her studio is on the top floor in the attic. And, Courtney—don't worry if she doesn't talk to you easily at first. She's rather shy with visitors and it may take a while to get her to relax."

"That's my job," I said. "Most people are apt to be self-conscious at the beginning of an interview. It's like having a camera poked at you. Which reminds me—will she mind having a few pictures taken? I've brought my camera along."

"You'll have to ask her," Herndon said. "She's very photogenic, but I'm not sure she recognizes the fact."

"She recognizes it," John said, and I sensed a moment of tension between the two men. Then John folded his napkin, gave me a smile and a nod, and left the table.

Herndon looked after him with an expression in his eyes that I could not read. Was it sadness, resentment? It was hardly fondness for his brother.

"I'm calling on several of our bank branches in the area this morning," he said to me, "but if you need to reach me, ring up the number in East Hampton. They'll know where I am. I don't expect there will be any need."

"I'm sure there won't be," I agreed.

From her corner of the table, Stacia looked up. "Did you hear the weather report on the radio this morning, Dad? There's a hurricane starting up the coast from the Caribbean. I hope it comes this way!"

I stared at her. "Why on earth do you hope that?"

"Because I love storms." She flashed me her look of challenge. "And in this house we don't have to worry about them. Think of all the storms The Shingles has weathered. Old Ethan built for high seas and wild winds."

She gave her father a sly smile, excused herself, and left the table to disappear in the direction of the living room. In a few moments stormy music from the piano broke out, filling the house. The Valkyries were apparently going all out at this early hour, though I didn't recognize the music.

"She's very good. What is that composition?"

"It's her own. And she is good. This is the thing she does best. She could have taken it up professionally if she had wanted to—both playing and composing. She chose to get married instead."

"Would her husband object if she wanted a career?"

"No, I don't think so. In fact, if she wanted to, no one would be able to stop her." He smiled wryly. "It's her choice not to. Discipline has never been something she has welcomed—not even from herself."

Herndon, as I had begun to realize, was a rather private person, in spite of those touches of dress that invited attention. He was a quiet man, capable in his business work, undoubtedly, but willing to sit back and let other people do as they chose. Thus it was surprising that he had opened up to me about his daughter. He was no easier to understand than anyone else in this house of complexities.

He waited at the table until I had finished my toast and coffee, and then went off to one of his banks. I thanked Asher for serving me and wandered down the long rear hall toward the far end of the house. The library door stood open, and I paused to look in.

Evan Faulkner sat at the refectory table, pencil in hand and a ledger before him in which he was making an entry. He did not look up as I stood in the doorway and I could study him for a moment. Something about that dark, bent head, something about his strongly carved profile aroused once more a curious ambivalence in me. I disliked him because of what he had done to Stacia, and because of our previous encounters as well. Yet he held my interest, made me want to fathom the mystery of a sort of man I had never known before.

As I stood there unseen, a telephone rang, and I noted the library extension. Evan lifted the receiver.

"Hello," he said and then listened for a moment, while I saw a scowl crease his forehead. When he spoke the chill note I had heard before was in his voice. "No, you may not speak with her. I've left word that any call from you is to be transferred to me. . . . If you keep on along your present course, Olive, you can only end up on the wrong side of the law. . . . Don't bother making threats —do what you like. . . . What did you say? . . . Hello? . . . Olive? . . ."

Apparently the speaker had hung up, and I realized tardily that I was in a position of eavesdropping. Before I could turn away, however, I saw that I was not alone. A little way down the hall William Asher had come within hearing and looked thoroughly upset. When he noted my attention he gave me a haughty glance and disappeared into the dining room. I followed him a short distance and then returned down the hall, making more noise than before. Yet when I reached the doorway for the second time, Evan still did not look around.

"May I come in?" I asked.

Only then did he turn his head to regard me without welcome, rising reluctantly from his place at the table. He was as tall as I remembered, and as dark-haired and dark-browed. His eyes seemed to hold me off. I wondered whether it was because he disliked reporters in general, or me in particular, or whether it was because he had sensed and reacted to my own antagonism toward him. I had no time now to wonder about the speaker on the phone, or who "Olive" might be. At the moment I needed to tackle this bear of a man in his den.

"Last night you said you would be willing to tell me something about Ethan Rhodes and the great whaling days of Long Island," I reminded him.

"Then you've decided this is part of your story?"

"I haven't decided anything. I'd just like to know. The more material I have to draw from, the better. I can always discard. It's not having enough to write about that can do me in."

"Do you know anything about whaling?"

"Very little, I'm afraid. But I know very little about most subjects when I start on an interview assignment.

I'm a good learner. So I can begin anywhere. Whaling was a pretty brutal business, I've gathered."

"That's true enough. But necessity as well as greed was the contributing factor in the nineteenth century. There wasn't much else to produce lubrication and illumination, and almost every part of the whale was used—bones, teeth, millions of barrels of oil."

"I remember something Jacques Cousteau once said," I mused. "That there's more to life than hides and oil and meat and ivory."

"He was right and I agree. But at least in the old days the whale stood a chance against the man. A good many times the man lost. But the beasts don't stand a chance against modern equipment and there can be more whales taken in a year than are born. Most nations are trying to do something about that. Only the Soviet Union and Japan have been holding out."

I was still curious about him. "What fascinates you most about whaling?"

"The whales themselves. And of course the men who hunted them. It's a dramatic story that shouldn't be forgotten. Comparatively, the great whaling days lasted only a short time, but they were filled with drama and tragedy—both human and animal."

His eyes had brightened with an interest I had not seen before, and his voice came alive as he went on.

"I want to see these old books and papers preserved. There was a lot more to whaling than bringing home barrels of oil. The whalers were the country's early explorers and geographers and sociologists. Whaling ships might set out from Sag Harbor and other spots along the coast, but they sailed all the seas. They charted waterways we knew nothing about and they brought home word of distant places. They gave us knowledge we'd never had of faraway islands and the people who populated them."

I hadn't realized that this remote and rather cold man, whose only emotion seemed to be anger, could so warm to a subject. He cared about this task he had chosen to do, and listening to him, I began to sense its importance—an importance that would reach far beyond this room.

"What will happen to all these records?" I asked.

"I'm trying to pull them together, arrange some sort of chronological order, and make a full listing of everything that's here. Then the right place for all of it will be found—a museum, perhaps, as a Rhodes' gift, where it can be available for researchers, opened to the public as it has never been here. I need to finish before the house is sold."

"Who owns The Shingles? Who is selling it?"

"Do you mind if I get back to work?" he asked coolly as he pulled out his chair at the long table. "You can look around, if you like, and ask any questions about these things that occur to you."

"Thank you," I said, equally cool. "But it's the Rhodes I want most to know about. From Ethan on down. Why is everyone being mysterious about what is going to happen to this house?"

His smile was scarcely friendly. "You don't give up, do you?"

"I'm a reporter, and I'd like to know."

"It's hardly a secret—just uncomfortable to talk about. Perhaps the reason no one pins anything down for you is because no one is sure what will happen. At this moment, no one really owns the house."

"How can that be?"

"Herndon Rhodes, who isn't the oldest son, was the one in whose care Lawrence entrusted it. But it is only held in trust, in the sense that he has preserved and managed everything pertaining to it since his father died. His responsibility will come to an end in a few weeks, and then we'll all find out what's going to happen next. There's been talk of selling. Perhaps you might say a threat of selling."

I was still hopelessly in the dark. "But by whom?"

"By my wife, Stacia. On her twenty-fifth birthday."

For some reason that I did not understand a faint chill seemed to trace itself down my spine. What happened to the house meant nothing to me. I had no real kinship with any of these people, and yet I had been drawn to the very edge of a possible maelstrom. A few steps more, the answers to a few questions, and I could be plunged into the vortex—into an involvement I might not want. My task here was as a reporter and I must hold to that.

I dropped my questioning and began to move idly about the room. At the table Evan turned back to his work. I took books from a shelf, riffled through them absently, put them back. Next to the fireplace was a wall space where several pictures had been hung, and examining them, I saw that one was a yellowed photograph of a sailing vessel called the *Hesther*.

"Did this ship belong to Ethan Rhodes?" I asked.

The man at the table glanced toward the picture. "Yes. Hesther, of course, was the name of Ethan's wife. That was one of his last ships. It used to sail around the Horn."

"And this next picture?" It was of a graceful sloop, its sails filled with wind, and Evan answered with slightly more warmth in his voice.

"That one was built more recently. John designed and built her before his father died. She's a real beauty. The *Anabel*." A fondness for ships and sailing spoke in his words, but the name of the boat had distracted me.

The *Anabel*. That name which had also been given to a baby. A baby whose existence interested me.

"I wish I could sail in her," I said. "Perhaps John would take me out sometime."

"Aren't you a city girl? Do you belong in a sailboat?"

"You're thinking of the girl you saw on television. I'm someone else. New York City is on the water, and Long Island Sound is close-by. I've gone sailing. I can handle a tiller as well as a typewriter."

He studied me thoughtfully—as though I might be some curious marine specimen he'd just fished from the sea.

Then he said, "That next picture is of Brian Rhodes, Lawrence's father. He was a ship's captain too, but in a tamer day."

My great-grandfather? I wondered, never able to suppress the quick instinct to speculation. I moved closer to look at the photo. It was only an enlarged black and white snapshot of a man standing on the deck of a small boat. I couldn't make out his face very well and the picture meant nothing to me. Where was all that surging longing for a family with which I had started out from New York? Were the Rhodes themselves stamping it out, perhaps releasing me from an imaginary bondage that I'd suffered under all my life? No—I didn't believe that longing was entirely gone yet. It was somewhere inside me, surfacing unexpectedly at times— waiting. Waiting until I could be sure of something—as I was sure of nothing now.

I wandered back to the table and looked over Evan's shoulder, perhaps annoying him further. He had put his ledger aside and appeared to be checking a box of assorted oddments against a faded, handwritten list.

"Do you want to help?" he asked abruptly. "If you've nothing else to do."

For Evan Faulkner this was almost amiable—or perhaps he only wanted to stem my questions.

I pulled up a chair to sit down, and he pushed the box toward me. "I'll read the listing, and you can look for the matching item in the box."

Lying on the table beside the open box was the lid, and I bent to read the spidery writing across it in faded ink— a name, "Sara Rhodes," Lawrence's wife, who had died long before her husband.

"These were her things?" I said. "I wonder what they are doing in the library."

"A number of boxes of odds and ends have been carried into this room and stored wherever there was shelf space. I go through them as they turn up, in case there's something of importance."

This box seemed to contain little of real value. I plucked out a blackened bit of tubular silver. "I think this is a toothpick holder," I said. "Silver."

He checked it against the list he had found in the box, and read the next item. "Sugar tongs."

Again I found tarnished silver, and set the piece aside with the first.

We went through the box, checking off item after item. There was a lovely sunburst garnet pin that Evan laid aside for Judith, along with one or two other pieces of Victorian jewelry. There was a small ivory elephant with a cracked trunk, and a miniature carving of an ivory sailing vessel. I held up the latter in delight.

"Look—there's a name carved on the prow! It's the *Hesther*—Ethan's wife must have loved this."

As I held the tiny thing in my hand, Hesther Rhodes

began to seem more to me than a hazy figure out of history, and for the first time I had a sense of connecting to someone who had been flesh and blood—perhaps whose blood still flowed in my veins. For once I did not thrust the thought away from me.

The man beside me read the next item, and exclaimed, "Here's something the family has looked for for a long time! It lists a gold pendant in the shape of a unicorn."

My fingers poked idly through the remaining items in the box, but for a moment I couldn't breathe.

"Does the list give any description of the pendant?" I asked in a voice that was not entirely trustworthy.

He glanced at me and then studied the paper before him. "Yes—it says that the initial 'R' has been scratched onto one hoof. What does it matter, if the unicorn is there?"

"It isn't," I said. I didn't need to look. I knew very well that the golden pendant was upstairs in my room. I had never noticed an "R" scratched onto a hoof, but if there was such a marking, then any last doubt would be gone.

"Too bad," Evan said. "Herndon always wondered what became of Hesther's unicorn. He wanted it for Stacia."

I pushed my chair back from the table. "If you don't mind—I think I'm getting a headache. I'd better go and take an aspirin before ten o'clock when I'm to visit Mrs. Rhodes."

"Of course," he said carelessly. As though he hadn't expected me to be of much use. When I left the library he was working on the last articles in the box and I didn't look back. There was no need to take aspirin—my head was fine, but I couldn't wait a moment longer to take out my golden unicorn and examine its hoofs.

While I was out, my room had been made up and I went into it and closed the door. In a moment I had pulled open the drawer and had the fold of tissue in my hand. It felt light, with nothing lumpy in the center, and I knew before I spread the paper open. The unicorn was no longer there.

5

Minutes ticked by while I stood before the open drawer with the wad of tissue in my hand. Then I began a rather frantic search. The pendant was not in the drawer where I had left it. Nor was it in any of the other drawers I opened, although I came again upon the bisque head of the doll, its eyes closed now—which was the way I preferred them. I left it sleeping and searched on, even though I knew very well that my effort would be futile.

If someone had taken the pendant, it would surely be Stacia. She could have seen it last night when she put the doll's head in my drawer. Seen—and recognized it? Had she come back to take it away to show it to someone, or just appropriated it as something she felt I had no right to? And what was I to do about it now? I didn't want to ask her about this, or mention the missing pendant to anyone. It might be better to say nothing, merely to wait and see what developed. The unicorn was mine! Someone long ago had wanted me to have it, and I meant to get it back. But just for now I was forced to let the matter drift and wait for Stacia to make her next move.

In the meantime, I felt increasingly uneasy. Perhaps fear would be too strong a word, but it was there at the back of my mind, senseless, yet pervading my consciousness. Fear seemed to be the elusive quality that haunted this house. As though its members might fear one another—as I might fear them?

But surely this was nonsense. Even if someone discovered who I was, even if they all learned my identity eventually, what would it matter? They were nothing to me, any more than I was anything to them, and I would simply go away and never be heard from again in their lives. If the house was to come to Stacia on her twenty-fifty birthday, that had nothing to do with me, but must be part of a long-ago will of Lawrence Rhodes which left it to her. There was no reason for the smuggling away of the unicorn pendant—except that this seemed a house of secrets and animosities. There was a climate here that suited the growth of hidden motives, like mushrooms sprouting in a cellar. The anonymous notes that had so upset the household were more of the same, and so was that strange phone call from "Olive" that I'd overheard in the library. Even Asher's behavior had been strange and secretive.

I wanted none of this. Let me get my interview and go away as quickly as I could.

Something in me seemed to be building resistance against the knowledge I had so long sought, and it was as though I wanted to hold off any final revelation. I didn't really want Judith or Alice for my mother, or Herndon or John Rhodes for my father. At least I would have no trouble now in interviewing Judith. I was a reporter, a writer, and she was my subject—no more and no less.

When my watch hands reached ten, I picked up my small camera and notebook and walked into the hall to seek the stairs to the attic. They didn't rise from the top of the main staircase, and as I walked down the hall seeking them, Mrs. Asher came out of a bedroom, speaking over her shoulder to a maid. When she saw me she paused uncertainly, and I asked her about the stairs.

"They're right down there at the end of the hall, ma'am," she said, and would have scurried out of sight if I hadn't stopped her, seized by casual curiosity.

"Have you worked for the Rhodes a very long time?" I asked.

"No, ma'am. I've only been here for a few years—since I married William Asher." She waited for no more from me, but ducked back into the bedroom where I heard her talking again to the maid.

So this was a late marriage for William, I thought, and accounted for her being less at ease in the house than her husband.

I walked on toward the narrower flight of stairs, which reached upward at the end of the hall.

The stairs climbed steeply, as though they had never been intended for much use, and there was a square landing at the top, with a closed door straight ahead. I tapped on the panel and waited. For a moment I thought she must not have heard me, then Judith's voice called to me to come in. I opened the door and walked into the large attic expanse of Judith Rhodes' studio.

The woman at the easel sat on a high stool facing me, and I could not see her canvas as she worked in absorption with her brush. Having called to me to enter, it was as though she had already forgotten me, and I was content to stay where I was, gathering impressions of both woman and studio.

This morning she wore a rust-colored smock over light twill pants, and her long black hair was caught at the back of her neck with a rust-red velvet bow. She sat on her perch with a brush in one hand, palette in the other, a slight frown of concentration between dark brows. Her complete focus on what she was doing enabled me to study her openly, as I'd had no time to do yesterday. Her sun-tinted face was a long and beautiful oval, with those great green eyes and the lips so perfectly formed that she needed no brilliance of lipstick to enhance them. I was glad of color film in my camera.

"Do you mind if I take a picture?" I asked. "Just as you are now?"

The concentration was broken and her brush paused in midair as she looked toward me. Again there was surface serenity, but I wondered if it might perhaps be a controlled calm that she wore, something learned, something adopted. To conceal what?

"No pictures," she said quietly in the same low resonance I had heard yesterday.

"I'm disappointed," I said. "Our readers would like to see you at work. And you make such a perfect picture yourself, just as you are now."

"People *look* at photographs," she said enigmatically, and I sensed that being looked at might bring the outside world too close.

"People look at your paintings too. Your last show in New York must have brought pleasure to a great many."

"I didn't want that display. But at least they can't see *me* in the paintings."

I wasn't sure she was right about that. All artists betrayed something of themselves in their work—whether their medium was paint or the written word, clay or music—whatever. But I meant to seek no argument with Judith Rhodes until I knew her better, and I felt in her a slight resistance to me this morning.

"Do you mind if I look around?" I asked.

"As you please. I'll work a little while longer, and then we'll talk."

The heart and focus of the room was the woman, but now I looked about to find her frame. Overhead, the studio roof rose in the high, beamed peak of a cathedral ceiling, and it must have been well insulated to let her work up here the year-round. At the northern exposure a large glass window had been set into the slanting roof, throwing full daylight into the room—an artist's necessity, and evidence that this room had been remodeled in its every detail for the woman at the easel.

Because the roof swept down on each side from the central ridgepole to the floor, there was little space, and no standing room at the far edges. However, room dividers had been set about here and there, to bring the vast spaces in a bit closer, and on these, framed canvases had been hung, while other paintings were stacked in distant corners—the result of a good many years of continuous production. Now I would have the opportunity to taste my fill of Judith Rhodes' creative talent.

But as I started toward the nearest partition, there was movement beyond Judith's easel, and I saw Tudor ease himself to his feet and curl one black lip in an expression that was less than inviting. When he growled, Judith turned her head.

"Be quiet, Tudor. This is a friend."

The dog sat back on his great haunches, his look fixed upon me, but he was quiet now, accepting his mistress's command, even though he might not accept me.

Following the side of the room farthest from the dog, I stood before the first buff-colored partition and gazed at the four paintings mounted upon it. One looked out on a stormy sea, with waves crashing high over wet black rocks and a small round face floating on the stormy surface—as though cast adrift in that unlikely spot. Two were beach scenes, with gulls flying over misty water, only one of which carried that strange signature of a disembodied doll's face. The fourth was again a beach scene, on a calm day, and along the sand at the water's edge pranced a golden unicorn. All carried that unsettling air of fantasy imposed upon reality which seemed characteristic of Judith's painting.

"Your husband was telling me about the unicorn legend," I said. "It must appeal to you."

She slipped down from her stool with a smooth, quick movement, and began to clean her brushes. The odor of turpentine reached me as her answer came over her shoulder.

"I'm not sure that 'appeal' is the word. Perhaps a better word would be 'haunt.' "

"Do you think there's anything to the legend?"

"I don't know." The words seemed a little flat. "There have been Rhodes who claimed to have seen the unicorn moon before they died. Sara, Lawrence's wife, was one of them. And of course Hesther, who started it all."

"What about Lawrence Rhodes?" I asked. "Did he see it too?"

It was not a question I would have put to her as an interviewer—but one that came unbidden out of my own search for answers that lay in the past. I had not rid myself of that inner drive to know, after all.

She gave me a startled look as she put her brushes aside to come toward me.

"Yes, he saw it. There was a moon that night. As if I

could ever forget. It was shining full into the living room downstairs, and he told me he had seen the unicorn—that he was going to die."

I waited in silence, hoping she would go on, but that was all she meant to tell me. Her serenity was worn like a protective garment, so that she rested secure behind its covering.

"Let's sit down," she said, "where we can be comfortable."

At a short distance down the attic, East Indian prayer rugs made an island, with a sofa, chairs, and central coffee table arranged upon them. She led the way across the otherwise bare floor to this oasis, and now that I had moved past her easel I turned to look at the picture she was working on. Again there was a stormy sea, this time with a small boat, and vague figures in the mist, still unfinished. Once more a doll's face floated in the sky, the eyes closed this time, like those of the sleeping head in my dressing-table drawer downstairs.

She waited for me to take my place on the flowered couch, and then seated herself in a plain brown chair that set off her rust color to good effect. Settling back comfortably, she seemed completely poised and untroubled.

"There's fruit juice," she said, indicating a frosty pitcher on the table. "Please help yourself."

I poured juice into ruby glass and sipped the tangy mixture, taking time to formulate my next question. It must be an easy one for her to answer, something reassuring, in case she might be on guard against me. Instead, however, some inner prompting brought out a question I had not meant to ask so soon.

"Why do you paint dolls' heads into so many of your pictures, Mrs. Rhodes?"

"*I* can answer that!" The voice came from the door to the stairs that I had left open, and I looked toward it to see Stacia Faulkner walk into the studio. She still wore the jeans and pink pullover she'd had on at breakfast, and her fluff of fair hair was tousled, as though she might have come in from a run on the beach.

"Hello, Mother," she said, her hands set jauntily in

jeans pockets as she sauntered into the room. The words were a simple enough greeting, yet I sensed something more in the way she spoke them—some sort of defiance, some flouting she was directing at her mother.

"Good morning, Stacia." Judith Rhodes spoke quietly.

"What do you think of this?" Stacia asked, displaying her bruised cheek to the light. "What do you think, Mother dear, of a man who beats his wife?"

Her mother glanced at me. It was not a look of apology, but merely noted my presence as a captive audience to Stacia's scene. Stacia saw and threw a bright stare in my direction. I wondered if it indicated her knowledge of the unicorn, but I said nothing.

"We don't have to be proper with Courtney," Stacia went on. "She knows. Nan and everyone else knows by now that Evan struck me."

Though her daughter's words and behavior were outrageous, Judith still said nothing. Wide green eyes regarded her daughter without expression, and yet I caught a faint tightening of those full lips, and sensed that Judith was resisting a deliberate baiting by her daughter.

Their exchange of held glances lasted only a moment, and Stacia was the first to turn away, looking again at me, and so intently that I could almost feel the thought of my golden unicorn burning between us. I was suddenly sure that Stacia had it, and I wondered what it meant to her. Then she flicked a hand in the air as though she dismissed something she did not welcome and spoke to me.

"As I was saying, I can answer your question about the dolls' heads. Come and look."

She ran down the long room past display partitions to where a cabinet of drawers stood just under the slant of the roof. Not wanting to take sides, I followed her reluctantly. I would try to give Stacia the benefit of my doubts because she appeared to be the injured party when it came to Evan, and yet, more and more, I felt that I did not like this girl, and I hoped that she was neither my sister nor my cousin.

Kneeling before the cabinet, Stacia pulled out a bottom drawer and I stood behind her looking into it with a horrid fascination. Tumbled into the drawer helter-skelter lay what must have been two or three dozen dolls' heads. They were from every type of doll possible—bisque and wax, china and wood and plastic, some with hair, some without, some with ridged black hair painted on china skulls, some with cracks across pink cheeks, or a chipped nose, some innocently perfect, staring up at me with blue eyes and brown eyes, or in some cases no eyes at all in empty sockets.

Stacia jumped to her feet, leaving the drawer open, and waved a proud hand at the collection, as if at some accomplishment. "They're all mine. Or they used to be. When I decapitated them, Mother brought the heads up here. There's a doll graveyard out in the woods where all the bodies and arms and legs are buried."

I stared at her in disbelief. "You mean that as a child you broke every one of those dolls?"

"Right! There were more interesting things I could do with my life. Uncle John taught me to pitch a ball and sail a boat and climb trees. He rescued me from all that feminine nonsense girls are doomed to. The trouble was people kept on giving me dolls."

"Couldn't you have given them away to children who would have liked them?" I asked.

"It was more fun to smash them up. It upset people more. Even Uncle John didn't care for that."

With an inner revulsion I walked back to the sofa and sat down opposite Judith.

She had not moved. Her long hands, one of them showing a smear of chrome yellow on the back, lay quietly in her lap. Her head was slightly bent and her eyes seemed fixed upon her hands. I could not see their expression.

"At least you've put those broken dolls to good use," I said to her. "They seem to have become a sort of signature for your paintings, like the unicorns, and they lend a haunting quality that people remember."

Judith said nothing. She raised one hand absently and examined the yellow smear on its back. Stacia closed the drawer with a vigor that set the heads to rolling and clattering for a moment, and then they were all quiet again, shut away in the dark, staring at nothing.

"Go ahead with your interview," Stacia said sociably,

coming to drop down on the sofa beside me. "I'd like to listen."

She made my hackles rise. "I don't think that would be a good idea. This is something between your mother and me. I never like to work with an audience."

"Let her stay if she wants to," Judith said, raising neither her voice nor her eyes.

Stacia settled back with an air of triumphant expectancy and stared at me. There was nothing more I could do.

"Have you always liked to paint?" I asked Judith.

"Not always," she said and left it there.

"Not until all those people began to die," Stacia put in.

This time Judith looked at her daughter—a long, quiet look that carried an intensity which made the younger woman drop her own gaze.

"I was unhappy," Judith told me. "I was trying to escape from much that was tormenting me. So I began painting when I was in my early twenties. It helped me, satisfied me."

"And you could hide in it when other people needed you," Stacia put in. "Dad always said you mustn't be disturbed—to let you alone. So I did—I did! And I took to breaking up my dolls. Maybe because I couldn't get through to you. If it hadn't been for Uncle John—"

Judith's composure showed no crack. "I expect I was not always a good mother," she agreed. "But I don't think any of this can be interesting to Miss Marsh."

"I'd rather use what *you* tell me," I said, feeling increasingly outraged by Stacia and wishing she would go away. "Without any fanfare, working quietly on your own, you appear to have developed an enormous talent. Nan Kemble calls it genius. Did you know that?"

"Genius?" Judith repeated the word as though she sounded something in a foreign tongue. "Who knows what genius is?"

"Talent, at least. You can accept that. Exceptional talent. Did you work with a teacher in the beginning?"

"No, never. I only painted for my own amusement. But I wanted to do it well. I read books, and I used to go to museums."

"I remember," Stacia said. "You used to take me with

you. I can remember the times we had tea in the restaurant at the Metropolitan. But I hated those pictures you painted, and I don't need any psychiatrist to know why. They took you away from me."

"I'm sorry," Judith said softly. "I've always been sorry. But there wasn't anything else I could do. I had to paint."

"Real talent is probably compulsive," I said. "You have this in common with the other women I've talked with and written about. You all *had* to do what you had to do. And families aren't always happy with that."

Stacia yawned. "In me you see the sacrificial lamb. And what good does all that talent do—when she hides herself at The Shingles? She's always been one to hide her candle. I hope you'll bring her light out into the open, Courtney."

The words were not as kind as they seemed on the surface, but I ignored their cut.

"Such talent shouldn't continue to be hidden," I agreed. "And of course it won't be in the end. This sort of thing develops a life of its own. Even Emily Dickinson's poetry came out into the open eventually. But this should happen now. For the work itself. It should be seen. And it can even be an encouragement to other women. So many of us grow up thinking we can't achieve anything on our own—until we see someone else doing what we thought couldn't be done."

"I'm afraid I'm not a feminist, Miss Marsh," Judith said. "I've never suffered from being a woman."

"Because Dad was such an angel to you!" Stacia cried. "He protected you, gave you anything you wanted. Except the one thing you wanted most."

Judith did not move, her eyes downcast again, and I thought once more of her composure being worn like a cloak. But this time she reached out from behind her tranquility.

"What do you think I wanted most?" she asked her daughter.

Stacia sprang up from the sofa and circled the small island of furniture set apart in the huge attic, so that I was reminded again of a cat creature stalking.

"What you really wanted all the time was freedom from guilt—wasn't it, my darling Mother?"

I had heard enough, and I didn't mean to sit by and listen to Stacia trying to torment this quiet, reserved, gifted woman.

"I'll go downstairs now," I said, "and come back another time, when I can see you alone, Mrs. Rhodes."

"Please don't go." Judith's words surprised me, and I had an uncomfortable feeling that she did not want to be left alone with her daughter. Uncertainly, I hesitated, not sitting down.

"The trouble is," Stacia told me, "that you aren't asking my mother the right questions. Ask her what she's going to do when this house is sold and she has to leave."

"There's no need to ask that," Judith said calmly. "I shall never leave The Shingles." She looked up at her daughter. "Come here, Stacia. Come here to me."

But this time Stacia backed away, and I didn't know what would have happened next if there hadn't been a tap on the door.

Judith called, "Come in," and one of the maids from downstairs walked hesitantly into the room, clearly unsure of herself in these upper regions.

She carried an envelope, sans tray, as she came the length of the room to hand it to Judith, and I felt a quick flick of anxiety—since no more anonymous letters were supposed to come to her.

"I found this near the front door just now," the girl said. "Mr. Asher isn't about, so I brought it up to you. Your name is on it, Mrs. Rhodes."

"Another one!" Stacia cried.

"Thank you." Judith took the envelope and sat staring at it, while the girl went away.

Stacia said, "Do you want me to open it?"

Her mother shook her head and slit the envelope flap with a forefinger. From where I sat I could see the uneven pasting of cutout letters across the single, lined sheet. Judith read the words silently and leaned back in her chair, letting the envelope and page float to the floor. Stacia pounced upon the letter and held it up, reading the few words aloud.

" 'What did you do to Alice's baby?' "

I sat very still, watching Judith, my breath quickening with my heartbeat. She seemed so quiet, so frozen, that I wondered if she was going to faint, and I bent toward her.

"Are you all right, Mrs. Rhodes?"

For an instant she did not move, and then she raised her head to look at me blankly, as though she had forgotten who I was. When she spoke, she was not addressing either of us.

"Who is doing this to me? How can it be happening?"

There was anguish in her voice, yet I found myself regarding her sharply. Anguish was understandable enough when she was being tormented, but the thing that made me stare was my sudden suspicion of a false note. I didn't believe that her anguish was wholly real.

Stacia dropped the letter and moved quickly to the phone on the coffee table—apparently with a house connection, since I heard her speak to Asher.

"Please find Mr. Faulkner," she said. "Ask him to come upstairs to Mother's studio at once."

"You didn't need to do that," Judith said, as Stacia set down the phone.

"Yes, I did. You're looking positively ill. You shouldn't let some anonymous letter writer get to you like this. You haven't anything to hide. It really was an accident, wasn't it—when Alice's baby drowned?"

I wasn't sure whether Judith heard her words or not, but they were ringing through my mind. *Alice's baby.* Here were those words again. Did they mean John's baby as well? Had they anything to do with me?

"I don't think I'll stay around, Mother," Stacia said when Judith didn't speak. "I'll leave you to Courtney Marsh and Evan. After all, he has a vile temper and he might strike me again, mightn't he, dear?"

She flew down the room and I heard her clatter on the stairs. Judith raised her head, seeming to listen for a moment before she picked up the sheet that had fluttered to the floor and reached calmly for a packet of matches on the coffee table. While I watched, she lit a match, touched it to the corner of the paper, and held it while the small blaze flared up. When it burned close to her fingers she dropped it into a tray and watched it blacken into ash. Only then did she look at me.

"There was no letter," she said.

Her look held my own, and though I gave her no verbal promise, she must have read something in my eyes that reassured her. When she settled back in her chair, she seemed to have fully recovered her poise and her air of being a degree or two removed from everything that went on around her.

"You might as well know the truth," she said. "It wasn't Evan who struck my daughter. I did. She drove me too far, and I slapped her."

The hint of a melancholy smile touched her mouth, while it was my turn to sit frozen, staring at her.

She raised her right hand and regarded it as though she examined something objectively that belonged to someone else. "I'm really very strong, I slapped her quite hard. Does that shock you, Courtney Marsh? Will you write that into your article?"

It was she, now, who was baiting me, and I found myself wondering what might really lie seething under all this calm she turned toward the world.

"I can't say I blame you," I told her. "Stacia seems to ask for it."

"An eldritch child, born of a witch," Judith said lightly, and suddenly her laughter floated through the great echoing room beneath that high ceiling—a shocking outburst. I had never heard her laugh until now. It was a silvery sound quite different from the low resonance of her speaking voice, and somehow it sent a chill down my spine. All the sympathy I had been ready to bestow on Judith Rhodes was checked in its outpouring.

"Stacia thinks she has learned something that she is trying to use," Judith went on. "Something completely false, of course, but I think she's frightened. She's afraid she may not be able to turn me out of her house, after all, so she's bring other weapons to bear."

I stood up and started for the door. There was nothing I could say, and all I wanted at the moment was to escape this strange, beautiful, talented woman who seemed to occupy some plane of existence removed from the rest of us. But before I could escape her presence, I heard footsteps on the stairs and Evan Faulkner came into the room.

"What is it? What's happened?" he asked as he went directly to Judith.

She looked up at him, smiling, and held out her hands for him to take. "Another letter—that's all. Stacia was upset about it. Let's not tell Herndon and John. I've already burned it. I think we know who is writing them."

"I had another call this morning," he said. "I suppose we'll have to take some action."

She sighed. "It doesn't really matter. Nothing matters any more."

Evan let her hands go. "You know that isn't true."

"Sometimes I think you're my one friend in this house."

"That's not true either, as you know very well."

They had both ignored me during this exchange, as though they had nothing to conceal, but now Judith glanced in my direction.

"Please send this child from New York away for now," she pleaded. "She can be very persistent and I can't endure any more questioning."

Evan gave me a dark look of reproach. I started to speak indignantly, only to recognize that it would be no use. I kept my chin high as I walked the length of the studio, past Tudor, who raised his head watchfully, past the waiting easel with its scene of a boat in a storm, and went downstairs to the second floor. I felt thoroughly shaken, assaulted in all my senses and emotions, so that a quivering had begun inside me. If I had been unsure of my identity before I came to this house, I was totally torn and confused about it now.

What sort of "action" did Evan Faulkner intend, and why did Judith feel he was her only friend? More especially, who on earth was the Olive to whom he'd talked on the phone? Was she the source of these anonymous letters?

At the second-floor landing I hesitated, and then went quickly downstairs and into the dining room. There, over the great dark sideboard, hung the portrait of Alice Kemble Rhodes, and I leaned against that black walnut solidity and stared up at the mirthful face in the picture. A face that looked as though the young woman who had posed might burst into laughter at any moment. There had been disagreement as to whether it was a true portrait or not, but now I studied it with longing, trying to find a responsive emotion in myself. The large, beautiful eyes looked familiar and I realized they were like her sister Nan's eyes. Perhaps the two had resembled each other when they were young.

Was she my mother?

There had been no other child mentioned since I had come to this house—but only that reference to the baby who had died. Alice's baby—by drowning. If she had been my mother, what was Judith's involvement? What had happened to enable me to escape that death, and be given for adoption in New York?

I found myself standing on my toes, the better to study every detail of the painting. There seemed to be something Alice Rhodes had worn about her neck when she had posed in that summery blue dress. Yes!—there was a gold chain showing, and against the hollow of her throat lay a tiny pendant, painted vaguely in the shape of a unicorn. So now I knew. This girl had surely been my mother. Something terrible had happened—a drowning she could not have sought at that young age—and she had left a baby that others must have given away. My mother would have wanted me, since I had stayed with her for at least two months after my birth. But now, if I had found her, I had also lost her, for she had died a long time ago—leaving John as my father.

All my life I had been warned: "Don't try to find out who you are, Courtney. You may uncover horrors that you're better off not knowing. Be satisfied with the loving parents who raised you. Let the door stay closed."

But a door which has begun to open has a certain momentum of its own, and it does not swing itself shut of its own accord. I knew very well that I must walk through, that I wanted to walk through, no matter what it cost me, or how shocking the result might be.

So absorbed was I in my own thoughts that I didn't hear Asher come into the room until he stood at my elbow. Then I turned to see that he carried a tray of silver flatware which he apparently wanted to store in the sideboard. I stepped out of his way, wondering about this old man who ran the house for Judith and Herndon.

The question I asked him was the same one I'd asked his wife. "Have you been with the family for a long time?"

He answered me guardedly but proudly, not trusting me, yet wanting to admit to his own lineage with the family.

"I came here when I was a young man to work for Mr. and Mrs. Lawrence Rhodes," he said.

"That's a long time. The present family is fortunate to have you. I suppose you remember Alice Rhodes?" I looked up at the portrait again.

"Yes, of course, Miss Marsh. I was able to attend her wedding to Mr. John."

I asked my next question without warning. "How did she die?"

He started visibly and dropped his tray of silver on the sideboard so that the pieces rang against each other. But in a moment he had recovered and he answered me quietly.

"She died out near Montauk, where the Kemble family has a cottage. I believe she went swimming alone one morning and was drowned. Mrs. Judith found her where waves had rolled her upon the beach—but it was too late."

"And the baby—what happened to her after her mother died?"

"She was lost in an accident at sea only a few days later. It was very sad—especially for Mr. John, who had a double loss, and for Mr. Lawrence, who had been so pleased and happy over having an heir."

The old man began to sort the silver carefully into its flannel containers, and I thanked him and went away, only a little more informed than before.

An urge to escape this house, with all its secrets and its alarming deaths, had seized me. One death hadn't happened, if I had been that baby, Anabel. But the deception that had been perpetrated was disturbing in itself. Why—why? Why had someone gone to so much trouble to cover up?

When I'd run upstairs to fetch a jacket, I came down and let myself out the front door, with no word to anyone. Fog was beginning to blow in from the sea and I walked down into the mist gratefully, not wanting my car now, but only to walk into thick fog and let it close about me. Perhaps then I could be alone and free from that dark, shingled house that towered behind me and held so many ominous secrets.

6

My way lay downhill from the house, and mist cut off the tops of the old trees that had once made this area a park. I found myself hurrying, wanting not only to put The Shingles behind me but to put behind me all those who lived there, and who seemed inimical to me.

When the gatehouse with its steeply tilted roof emerged from fog, I could see warm lamplight glowing at the window, and for a moment I was tempted to stop and talk to Nan Kemble. She was a degree removed from those who lived in the house, and I had liked her at our first meeting. Perhaps she was even my aunt. But I really didn't want to talk to anyone at the moment. I only wanted to be alone so I could try to think.

The old iron gates stood open between crumbling stone posts, and I slipped through into Ethan Lane, myself a ghost in the enveloping mist. This part of the lane was a wilderness, with no houses, and a tangle of scrubby growth that I could glimpse on either side of me. For the moment my solitude was assured and I was grateful for this seclusion.

Yet as I walked on to where high hedges began——hedges

grown so wild that untamed privet became impenetrable with intertwined branches thick as my arm—I began to experience a sense of detachment, of eerie isolation in this dream world where rank vegetation ruled. It was as though I walked through one of Judith's strange landscapes, and I would hardly have been surprised to see a doll's face peering at me from within thick privet, or to have a unicorn come prancing along the lane. The smell of the sea had become heavy with wet earth, and there was an odor of decay all about me.

In my light jacket, I began to feel chilled, yet I didn't want to turn back. Now there were houses beyond the hedges, but they seemed to belong to another world, and only when I came to a driveway did I have a glimpse of habitation through the mist. The road had widened and I realized that I had left Ethan Lane for one of those town lanes that were less private, though still rimmed with high hedges on either hand. No sidewalks offered me a footing here, but neither were there cars, and I walked without fear down the middle of the road.

My sense of direction was already lost, but I didn't care. It was enough to be moving away from the Rhodes and everything connected with them. Yet my thoughts were still tied to what little I had learned.

If my mother, Alice, were alive, would I feel differently toward her than I did toward the others? I wondered. In her picture frame she had seemed so far removed from me that I'd had no feeling that she was my mother. Perhaps when I knew more about her, emotion would come. Of them all in that house, only Judith and John had won me to some extent, and she had only aroused my interest. But in those last moments in her studio even she had turned slyly against me for her own purpose and asked Evan to send me away. As though I would have opposed her!

I knew what was happening. I was slipping in spite of myself into the trap of trying to establish kinship with those at the house, and this was the last thing I must do. As a reporter I ought to stand removed from them all emotionally, so that I might retain objectivity. Yet in that I was not succeeding. What was worse, all my reactions were negative and that in itself seemed a disturbing and destructive thing. Best to finish my task with Judith—if she would permit me—and get away, even if I left my golden pendant behind. This was not a family I wanted for my own. Perhaps I could close that opening door, after all.

The sound of a car coming in my direction was deadened by the fog, and I was not clearly aware of its approach until it was very close to me and I saw its fog lights shining through the mist. It was coming faster than it should have with so little visibility, and I realized that the driver would not see me in time to swerve. I sprang aside with nothing to spare, so that fenders scraped by with hardly an inch of space. My escape was narrow and it shocked me out of my dream world into reality and awareness. The prickly intertwined branches of the hedge were against my back and I took long deep breaths to steady myself.

Ahead, the car braked, and I could hear it turning, coming back. The driver must have been frightened too and had turned around to make sure I was not hurt. I stepped out where the fog lights touched me, expecting him to stop and speak to me so that I could reassure him, tell him that it had been my fault for being out in the middle of the road.

Instead, the two orange eyes of the lights were coming straight at me with a sudden spurt of speed as the driver stepped on the gas. This time I didn't leap aside quite in time. A fender grazed my thigh, and I was thrown clear, crashing into the wall of the hedge, where I lay propped for a moment, feeling stunned and bruised.

I had not been able to see the driver crouched over the wheel, but in the light I had been sharply aware of the circular emblem that stood up on the hood. The car was a Mercedes.

Down the lane it was backing, turning, squealing in haste, and behind me was only the solidity of that wild, impregnable hedge. There was no doubting now the intent of the driver. I ran along beside the privet, stumbling because my leg hurt, trying desperately to find a way through, where there was none. Privet, untended, could grow thick as a jungle, and it was all of fifteen feet high, with no driveways to break its barrier and offer me a way of escape.

The car was coming back, coming more slowly this time, more deliberately—with a fatal deliberation. What was happening was mad, insane, impossible, but there was no time to wonder why a stranger in a passing car should suddenly attempt mayhem with me as the victim. If I were found dead or dreadfully injured in this lane, the authorities could only put it down to a hit-and-run driver and my assailant would never be caught. But where could I turn—how could I escape?

Then I heard the sound of another car coming down the lane from the opposite direction, saw another set of lights bearing upon me. I sprang away from the hedge, waving my arms frantically to flag down this second car.

The driver braked in front of me, and I heard the Mercedes accelerate, swinging away to pass us and disappear up the lane into the fog. Trying to catch my breath, I leaned over the hood of the car that had rescued me, gasping with fright and relief.

A man got out and came around to me. "Courtney!" he cried, and I looked up into John Rhodes' reassuring face. "What made you jump out like that?" he cried. "My God, if I hadn't been alert I might have run you down."

He was safety, he was my rescue, and I pushed myself up from the hood and clung to him, unable to get my voice back immediately. He held me gently, quietly, waiting until I could talk. When I'd caught my breath a little, I let words tumble out indiscriminately.

"There was a car! That other car that drove away. It was a Mercedes."

"A Mercedes? What about it?"

"It was dark blue, I think. I couldn't see the driver, but he tried to run me down. He tried to kill me!"

John held me away from him and looked down into my face as the fog swirled around us, shutting us in. "You're cold, shivering. Come and get into my car and I'll take you back to the house. You need a drink and bed. You've had a shock."

I let him put me into the front seat, glad of his kindness, his gentleness, glad to have someone stronger than I was to take over. He found a blanket in the back seat and wrapped it about me, held me for a little with my head against his shoulder, not speaking, not questioning or reproaching, just letting me recover. He was a man who knew what a woman needed in a time of stress. Knew it better than I knew it myself—I who had never turned to any man for reassurance and simple kindness.

Slowly I began to relax, and my shivering quieted. Yet I wanted to lean against his shoulder. I wanted this—from my father? Was it true? Could it be? Had the feeling I so longed for come to me at last? John Rhodes holding his daughter in his arms? But even if that was true, he couldn't know I was his daughter, and his rescue, the very solace he offered, was kind but impersonal. I was only a stranger in need.

I raised my head and sat up. "I'm all right now. Thank you."

"I'll drive you home. You've had a nasty fright. But you must realize that it's very hard to see in a fog like this. Lights do little good. I was almost upon you myself before I saw you. It may have been the same with the other driver."

I couldn't accept this. "That hardly explains why he turned around twice and tried to run me down—*tried* to hit me. It was deliberate. If you hadn't come along when you did I might have been killed."

He was silent, and I had a feeling that he thought me hysterical, thought I was exaggerating.

"It's true!" I insisted a little desperately. "Someone tried to kill me just now. Someone relentless, determined."

John turned the ignition key and as we drove along the curving lanes I could sense his continued disbelief, though he did not try to argue with me. I could hardly blame him. What had happened was so completely unlikely and unwarranted that I hardly believed it myself—except that there was a throbbing in my thigh which told me I had been struck and thrown.

By the time we reached Ethan Lane, the mists had thinned a little and I could see blue sky. John stepped up our speed, retracing the way I had come such a little while before. We drove through the gateway and past Nan's shop without slowing and in moments we had climbed the driveway beside the house and come to a halt on the brick apron before the garage.

A sudden thought seized me, and the moment the car stopped I got out, limping a little, and went toward the open doors of the long, low building. John came with me. There were several cars inside—but I was interested in only one: a dark blue Mercedes.

"Look!" I said and put my hand on the hood. The car was warm. It had recently been driven. I turned with a question in my eyes and John's hand came onto the hood beside my own, testing the warmth.

"It's not possible," he said quietly. "Who would want to hurt you?"

"Whose car is this?" I demanded.

"It belongs to Judith. But we all use it from time to time. There's always a key out here. Judith seldom drives it any more."

"Someone drove it," I said. "Someone who tried to kill me."

He shook his head soberly. "Please, Courtney. I would never take you for a hysteric but you really are letting something purely accidental go to your head. I can assure you that no one in the family goes in for attempts at murder."

"Can you?" I said. "Can you really assure me of that?"

His blue eyes seemed dark in the dim light of the garage and they regarded me with a look of distaste that I hated to see. That moment back in the lane, when I'd been able to rest with my head against him, was still intensely a part of me, and I didn't want to see him move away.

"I'm sorry," I said. "I'm upset."

"Do you want to go to the police?" he asked quietly.

If I did that, if I singled out this particular Mercedes, there would be a great deal of unpleasantness and I would become automatically persona non grata in this house. And I wasn't ready for that. Indeed, a new and tremendous curiosity—perhaps dangerous curiosity—had begun to gather force in me. Who among the Rhodes disliked me so much —or feared me so much—that an attempt upon my life had been made? And why?

"Let it go," I said. "I don't suppose that dark blue Mercedes cars are all that remarkable in East Hampton."

He touched my elbow, turning me toward the house. "At least I'll find out who may have had this car out in the last half hour. You can be reassured on that score."

I went with him silently up the steep steps to the house and he let me in the front door.

"Would you like a drink—something to steady you a bit?" he asked when we were inside.

I shook my head and walked away from him toward the stairs.

He noted my limp. "If you've been hurt, Mrs. Asher has had training as a nurse—I'll send her up. Unless you'd like a doctor?"

"I don't think it's anything." I turned back to him, suddenly wanting to touch him again, wanting to recover that brief feeling I'd had toward him in the car. "Thank you for coming along when you did. Thank you for rescuing me."

He took the hand I held out to him and his look was kind, but also a little puzzled, and I knew that I had lost contact with him because he did not fully believe in my account of what had happened. Nor could he be aware of the emotion that moved me.

I walked upstairs slowly and met no one. Nor was anyone waiting for me in my room, for which I was grateful. I got out of dust-stained white slacks and went into the bathroom to examine the purpling bruise on my leg. It was sore and a little swollen to the touch, and it would be uncomfortable for a few days—but I was sure it was only a flesh bruise, with no real damage done.

When I'd wrung out a cold cloth to press against it, I lay down on the bed and waited for the throbbing to subside. There was, however, no quieting the thoughts that whirled through my mind.

Someone in this house wanted to injure me. It was hard to believe that the driver of a random Mercedes had tried again and again to strike me down. But I was positive. There *had* been intent. And behind intent, I tried to fit the identities of those who lived in this house into the driver's seat of that murderous car. No one seemed to belong. Not Judith. Not Herndon. And John had been driving a different car when the first one sped away. Once more a twinge of feeling surged up in me. I was glad he was out of it. It had not been Evan, of course. Little as I knew of him, I was sure about that. Not Nan, of course. Stacia? Perhaps. I could imagine her trying almost anything.

But if Stacia was the only likely candidate, what would be her motive? Knowledge of the golden unicorn might give her my identity, unlikely as that seemed. Though I still didn't see how I could threaten any of them in any way. Yet someone did feel threatened.

The wet cloth on my leg had grown warm, but the bruise wasn't hurting as much. I got up to dress and went to stand at the window, looking out upon sun-drenched sand and a calm blue sea. As swiftly as it had come, the mist had disappeared, and the beach invited me with its sense of peace. About me the house seemed to press in, to threaten, and there was still a tension in me that had to be released.

Moving didn't hurt too much, and again there was no one about when I went downstairs and let myself out the door at the end of the house. This time I didn't wander along the terrace, but crossed it to the wooden steps that led down over the dune—steps weathered by rain and sun and salt air so they creaked a little beneath my feet, though the boards were sturdy and in good repair. When I left them, I walked with my heels sliding in loose sand until I reached the water's edge, where dampness offered better footing. My leg hurt a little again, but I could bear with it.

Disturbed only by occasional footprints and dog tracks, the sand was clean, with a few clumps of brown seaweed here and there, where broken shells had clustered. It was lovely to see a beach empty of the debris careless bathers could leave behind. Sun sparkled on clear green water, and it was hard to imagine a hurricane blowing up in the Caribbean, or a blue car hurtling out of the mist with murderous intent.

At least I felt safe here, and my tightened nerves were relaxing from the tension. There were houses stretching for some distance along the high ridge of dunes, set well apart from each other, their windows peering down at me, tall chimneys rising high. In empty spaces between them a tangle of scrubby growth gave a touch of wilderness, with here and there an unexpected pond. True, most of the houses were closed for the season by this time, yet I had no sense of the beach as a place dangerously isolated. I could see anyone coming for miles, and I'd been far more alone on that lane rimmed with hedges, beyond which were occupied homes.

Raising my head to the breeze from the Atlantic, I followed damp sand, with white-fringed waves curling in to reach for my feet. Gulls swooped overhead and far out on the gently heaving sea a freighter went by, its smokestacks leaving a pattern behind, like the contrails of a plane.

I had passed three of the beach houses and I had seen no one, heard no one. The sense of being totally alone helped to assuage the reaction I still felt from ny shattering experience. However, all too often twinges of pain from my leg reminded me, and before long I turned back. A real tramp along the beach—which must run clear to Montauk Point—would not be comfortable today.

When I came even with Rhodes property again, I started up across loose sand, approaching the house. But before I reached the flight of wooden steps, something caught my attention—something I hadn't noticed before because on my way down my back had been toward it. At the foot of the dune, where a matting of beach grass grew wild, a gray and weathered object stood, partly buried in the sand. It was a ship's figurehead, and I recognized the distant look on its face as the same I had seen in a figurehead in one of Judith's paintings—a woman's face, with the hair blowing back in some long-forgotten sea gale, her eyes staring wide, her lips pressed into a strange and haunting smile. As though, sphinx-like, she knew far more than she would ever tell. What an appropriate place for such an artifact to end its days. Here where there were still sea winds to be faced and storms to be weathered. Had it come from one of Ethan Rhodes' ships? I wondered. For some strange reason it reminded me of Judith herself. She too faced into the gales, always bent on her own course, imperturbable and never looking back.

"The ship she came from was called the *Hesther*," a voice said behind me.

I turned to face Evan Faulkner, and felt unexpectedly at a loss. In my mind I had done him an injustice. I had treated him coldly, with unspoken censure because of Stacia's lie. Yet I could hardly apologize for what I had thought. Somehow I managed a question.

"From Ethan Rhodes' ship that I saw a picture of in the library?"

"Yes—one of the few Ethan built that wasn't a whaler. In her day she carried cargo and passengers around the Horn to San Francisco, and Ethan named her after his wife. The figurehead really belongs in a museum, but Judith wants it here."

"I've been thinking how much she knows and keeps to herself." I looked again at the splitting wood of that weathered face and wondered what those staring eyes might have seen in all that sailing of the seas.

"John told me what happened to you," Evan said.

I turned to him swiftly, looking up into dark eyes that once more wore scowl lines between the brows.

"John doesn't believe any harm was meant me," I told him.

"I think he believes all right. Perhaps he didn't want to alarm you."

"What do you think?" I countered.

"We've checked with everyone in the house and no one admits to taking out the car."

"But the hood was warm!" I cried. "It *had* been taken out. John felt it too."

"Yes. That's why I believe you may be right and that it was a deliberate attack. Otherwise someone would have acknowledged having driven the car."

"Didn't anyone see it go—or return?"

"Apparently not. We've asked that question too. But the garage is always open, except when we lock up at night, and keys are accessible."

My legs didn't want to hold me upright any longer, and my thigh had begun to throb. Abruptly I sat down on the sand and pulled my knees up under my chin. After a moment Evan lowered himself to my level.

"Are you all right, Courtney? John said you might have been hurt."

"Just shaken," I said. "I can't imagine why anyone would want to harm me."

"How important to you is this interview with Judith Rhodes?"

"It's very important. She fascinates me. I want very much to do the interview." I couldn't tell him my other reason for being here—that reason I was trying to shut away and forget about. "Besides, I'm planning a book and she would fit into it perfectly, since there isn't another woman artist I really want to write about. Haven't you the slightest clue about the car? Or even an opinion?"

He smiled gravely at my urgent asking and I knew his smile meant that of course he would not tell me, even if he had such an opinion. He was too closely connected to the Rhodes, and I was an outsider—a stranger.

"It might be better if you returned to New York as soon as you can leave," he said. "I don't like what seems to be happening here."

I felt my resistance hardening. I said, "That's what Nan Kemble told me the moment I arrived. She mentioned quicksand and said I wouldn't know it when I saw it."

"An apt way of putting it. In any case, I don't think an outsider who's so deeply involved with the press is welcome here at the moment. Whatever it is, it's all strictly interfamily, and none of us wants publicity. Herndon should never have allowed you to come."

I pressed on. "These letters are a part of it, aren't they? Did Judith tell you what this last one said?"

His stiffness toward me was increasing. "Whatever it said is no concern of yours. At least it won't be if you leave shortly. Before something else happens that you might regret."

"But this, this family history, spat—whatever it is— isn't what I want to write about," I protested. "I only want to write about Judith as an artist."

I could see that he didn't believe me and that his prejudice against me as a reporter hadn't wavered. In a way he was right. He stood up, and in a moment he would turn away.

I spoke quickly, impulsively, "Judith told me that it was she who struck Stacia. I—I'm sorry."

"Sorry for what?"

An unfamiliar warmth was rising in my cheeks. I'd never thought myself the blushing type.

"I—I suppose I'm trying to apologize for—for misjudging you. I know it doesn't matter, but—" My hesitating words faltered to a stop.

"You haven't misjudged me."

I wasn't sure what he meant—only that he was throwing my feeble apology back in my face as something he had no use for. I pushed myself up from the sand and started toward the steps, but at that moment Stacia came running down them, her hair bleached pale in the sunlight. She had changed to denim shorts and a light blue pullover, and her legs were brown and graceful as she moved.

"Wait!" she cried when Evan would have turned away. "Don't go!"

She came to where we stood and slipped a proprietary hand through her husband's arm, though when she spoke it was to me.

"I'm sorry about what's happened, Courtney. Are you all right?"

I looked into her guileless face that was as conventionally pretty as one of those dolls' heads her mother liked to paint, and as devoid of real sympathy.

"I'm all right," I told her. "I had a bad fright, but no real damage was done."

"You poor thing!" She put her other hand on my arm appealingly, and we stood linked by her touch, and as far apart as any three people could be.

Her false pity didn't appeal to me. "John came to my rescue. He arrived in time and the Mercedes drove away."

"But who on earth would want to hurt you?" she asked sweetly.

Evan removed her hand and she dropped it to her side, aware perhaps of a rebuff. But she did not retreat. I had been wrong about her lack of feeling. There was sudden angry passion in the look she turned upon her husband, and I could see the answer to it in Evan's eyes—but whether it meant disliking, or an angry sort of love, I didn't know.

All I knew was that I didn't want to remain in the company of those two a moment longer. Something in me shrank from this sight of them together and from my own awareness of some strong, unhappy bond between them. I was the stranger. The injured stranger, but totally outside their circle, nevertheless. Without another word, I went past them, trying not to limp, though my leg was hurting more than ever. They let me go, absorbed in each other, and I climbed the steps and went into the house. At least the dog was not being allowed to run free, since my first encounters with him, and he was not about to harass me.

When I reached my room I dropped again on the bed, glad to take all weight off my leg, and lay there once more feeling terribly alone. More than I'd ever felt alone in New York. I hadn't even a man who would look at me angrily in that love-hate way, I thought—and rejected the very words as they went through my mind. If I hadn't a man to care about—or even hate—it was my own fault, and self-pity wasn't going to be my style this year. I had no desire to lie here feeling frightened and doubtful and sorry for myself. Resolutely, I got up and went to the dressing table, where I had put my notebook and pen. Now was the time to set down all those impressions I had gained this morning about Judith, and which I must record while they were fresh.

My hand touched the tissue where the pendant had been hidden in the drawer, and I stiffened. Something hard lay within the folds and I snatched up the paper and unfolded it to reveal a gleaming golden shine. The unicorn pendant had been taken, and it had been returned—and I was none the wiser as to the why of either action. I only knew that the sense of danger which had begun to haunt me had deepened still more. Without any understanding of how this could possibly be, I had become a target for disaster.

Carefully I turned the pendant about in my fingers, examining each tiny hoof. On the bottom of one prancing foot was something I had always dismissed as a mere scratch. Now I saw that it was more than that. I had no magnifying glass to help me, but I could just make out the shape of a crudely scratched "R." There was no longer the slightest room for doubt.

This time I fastened the clasp at the front of my neck, letting the pendant hang concealed by my collar at the back. I would wear it always from now on. With this precious keepsake, I would take no more chances. It was my only proof of who I was. Of me.

If only there were someone to whom I could turn. Someone who would talk to me honestly about what was happening and why I had unwittingly been caught in that quicksand Nan had labeled. I could hardly turn to the remote and correct Herndon, with his businessman's brain and probable inability to understand his wife. Nor to John, for all his kindness, because he did not believe in my danger. Not of course to Evan, who didn't like me and was tied to Stacia, whom I didn't trust. Certainly not to Judith—that strange woman of secrets and mysterious motivation.

It was no time to confront them with the past. What could I gain when I wanted only to find a sense of myself?

But at least I could put a lot of this down in words on paper. I sat at the room's small desk with my pad before me, and managed to fill three pages of helter-skelter impressions—not just of Judith, about whom I'd intended to write—but of all of them. Even of Evan Faulkner, who wasn't really a Rhodes, but to whom my thoughts kept returning in half-resentful, half-curious fascination. It was difficult to fit any of the people at The Shingles into the sort of pigeonholes I'd always taken for granted, and Evan Faulkner fitted least of all. What had it been like for Stacia to be married to such a man, and what did that marriage mean to each of them now?

I remembered his curt words, "You didn't misjudge me"—ominous, somehow, and disturbing.

When words ceased to tumble out on paper, I put away my yellow pad, slipped into a light coat, and picked up my handbag. I knew where I was going and to whom I could talk. As I reached the foot of the stairs, Asher came into the hallway to give me a dark look as he let me out the door. He must know by now what had happened to me, and he obviously didn't approve of someone in this house who tried to get herself killed.

Outside, I hurried down to the garage, where my Volvo had been left in the parking area. I had no taste at the moment for walking alone down any green lane, and I backed the car around and followed the driveway to Nan's gatehouse shop. There I left it and went into The Ditty Box, accompanied by the tinkling peal of the brass bell.

7

Lamps burned pleasantly around the main room of the shop, and there was a delicious odor of savory cooking somewhere at the back. Nan was nowhere in view and in spite of the ringing of the bell no one appeared from upstairs. Davy Crockett regarded me in ghostly fashion from his corner, and all the collection of things which had once led stormy lives at sea stood about in unwonted calm, seemingly aware of my presence and watchful of me. This was sheer whimsy, yet I felt strangely observed in this crowded room.

On a nearby glass case a sheet of paper had been placed conspicuously and I picked it up to read the words written in Nan's strong, assertive hand.

> I've had to go to town—will be back shortly. Make yourself at home. That's minestrone cooking on the stove—you're welcome to stay to lunch, whoever you are.
>
> Nan Kemble

I smiled at this informal greeting to any customer who

might wander into her unlocked shop, and decided to await her return. My nose led me to the small living area that opened through an arched partition at the rear—a room that held a tiny kitchen, complete with stove, sink, and cupboards, plus a crock pot of soup cooking slowly with that marvelous smell of aromatic herbs and vegetables. At the other end of the partitioned area I found a comfortable, well-worn couch, and a large bookcase which contained a catholic assortment of mystery novels, old classics, and volumes of modern nonfiction. Opposite a comfortable armchair, its probable shabbiness hidden by bright slipcovers, stood a television set on which had been placed a bowl of bronze and yellow chrysanthemums and a photograph in a silver frame.

A woman's face looked out from the picure and I recognized it as an older version of the young woman whose portrait watched from the dining-room wall. Alice Rhodes. I picked up the framed glass and carried it to a window where I could see the face in full daylight.

There was no mischief in these grave eyes and the lips did not smile. It was an intelligent face, but not a particularly warm one, and once more I tried to summon from my inner self some emotion, some feeling of relationship. Nothing came. I felt only pity for one who had died so young that she had not been able to watch her child develop and grow. She had never had a chance to be a mother, as I had never had the opportunity to be her daughter.

From the shop beyond came another tinkle of the doorbell and I went to the archway in the partition to greet Nan—and perhaps invite myself to lunch. But the moment I saw the woman who had come into the shop and stood reading Nan's note, I stepped back, just out of sight. It was Judith Rhodes, and I didn't want to face her. Perhaps she would leave before she discovered I was here.

She had changed into yellow corduroy slacks and a handsome brown suede jacket with brass buttons. Her long silky hair had been released from its velvet ribbon and cascaded down her back in a fall of black satin. She was a stunningly beautiful woman, I thought again, and then found myself hedging my own appraisal. No—perhaps not technically beautiful, but somehow giving an effect of beauty, which can be in itself enough.

Her serenity appeared to have been fully restored, if it had ever been shaken by the arrival of that anonymous letter in her studio, and she moved about Nan's shop with assurance. I must let her know I was here, I thought, but then she did so curious a thing that I halted in the very act of stepping through the arch.

Having read Nan's note she went directly to a row of built-in cupboards and knelt to open a lower drawer. From it she quickly drew a large carton that she carried to a nearby table. Hurrying now, she began to scrabble through the contents as though she must accomplish something before Nan's return.

Apparently a set of notebooks interested her most, and she picked up one notebook after another and riffled through the pages. I took less care now to hide myself. If she turned her head and saw me watching, never mind. From where I stood I could see that the pages she searched contained lines of handwriting, but she paused to read little of the content. Each time, after a brief examination, she set the book aside, reaching into the box for another and treating it the same way, until she had a pile of them on the table beside her. Her full lower lip was caught between her teeth as she concentrated—the only sign I could catch of possible anxiety.

When the bell sounded again, she paused with a notebook in her hands and looked without alarm at the door. Nan walked into the shop with a brown grocery bag in her arms, and saw her immediately. There was a moment of silence and I could almost sense a crackling of antipathy while each waited for the other to speak. Nan seemed vital and alive beside Judith's quiet that might have seemed apathy if I hadn't glimpsed the avidity with which she'd searched that box only moments before.

It was Nan who gave in first to whatever challenge had been raised between them. She set the bag down on a counter, ran fingers through the iron-gray bangs of her straight bob, and walked briskly toward the other woman.

"Hello, Judith. Are you looking for something?"

The answer came without confusion or effort at concealment. "Yes—I want to see those old diaries Alice used to keep. I don't find them here."

Nan's gray eyes appraised without liking, but she answered calmly enough. "Possibly because she never kept a diary that I know of. Exactly what is it you're looking for?"

Again there was a brief, silent exchange between them, with Judith's green eyes holding, but not quite dominating, Nan. I stood unconcealed at the back of the shop, while neither woman noticed me, so intent was each upon the other.

"I'd like to find the last book she wrote in before she died," Judith said quietly.

Nan took off the denim jacket she wore over jeans and green shirt. "Because you think there might be an answer in it to these letters you've begun to receive?"

"Yes. There's an answer somewhere, and it may lie in your sister's diaries."

"Except that, as I've told you, Alice never kept a diary. She used to write those stories constantly as you know— often stories for children. That's what fills most of those books. I used to read them when we were young. But there never was a diary."

"I don't believe you," Judith said with quiet authority.

It was time for me to betray my presence before this turned into an open quarrel, and I coughed gently, apologetically, so that both women turned to stare at me.

"I've been waiting for you to return," I said to Nan.

She smiled her welcome stiffly. "I'll be with you in a moment, Courtney."

Judith ignored me, her attention held by the cardboard box she had been so busily emptying. If it disturbed her to find that I had been in the shop all along, she didn't show it.

"You were saying that you don't believe me." Nan was less calm than Judith, and I heard the hint of anger suppressed.

"Only because there must have been something of the sort," Judith said.

"There wasn't. I remember asking Alice once why she didn't keep a journal, since many writers do. But she said all her words had to go into her stories and she wasn't interested in setting down daily happenings."

Judith began piling papers and books back into the box and when it was full she slid it into place in the lower cupboard. At no time had she asked permission, or made the slightest apology for what she was doing. As I had already observed, Judith seemed to cut through to the heart of any encounter with the least possible subterfuge and with no concern for conventions.

"Thanks, Nan," she said, as graciously as though she hadn't been brazenly helping herself. Then she turned to look at me down the room, surprising me once more with her lovely, breath-taking smile.

"I'm glad you weren't hurt by that car, Courtney. And I'm sorry I had to put you in the wrong light with Evan this morning. Please come back and we'll talk when we can be alone. Stacia was no help to us today."

She waved a casual hand, which seemed to include both Nan and me, and walked unhurriedly to the door and out of the shop.

Nan watched her go, her own face far more expressive than Judith's—of astonishment and annoyance. "Would you believe," she said, "that I haven't seen Judith Rhodes for three months? And then she just walks in and out like that, as though we'd met yesterday."

"As you warned me, she's going to be hard to interview," I said. "That's why I came down to see you. And also because I needed to talk to someone who isn't a Rhodes."

"I know how you feel. Alice and I used to have attacks like that. Especially when Lawrence was alive. We never really belonged to the clan. Why don't you stay to lunch?"

I nodded toward the note she had left near the door. "I've already accepted your invitation," I said, smiling.

"Fine. I'll give Asher a ring and let him know you won't be having lunch at the house. Would you mind taking this bag back to the fridge while I phone?"

I carried the bag out to the kitchen area, already reassured and feeling a little less strange than I did in the atmosphere of The Shingles. When apples and oranges and a carton of eggs had been placed in the refrigerator, Nan rejoined me, observing my awkwardness as I moved about the kitchen.

"You're limping. What happened to you? What did Judith mean about your not being hurt by a car?"

"That's one of the things I wanted to talk to you about. Someone tried to run me down when I went for a walk in the fog this morning."

"Tried to?"

"Yes. It was deliberate. Whoever it was turned around and came back to try again after the first miss. Someone in a dark blue Mercedes. John Rhodes drove by in his car just in time and the Mercedes speeded off. If he hadn't rescued me——" Having blurted everything out with no preparation, I faltered to a stop.

Nan was staring at me open-mouthed. After a moment she said, "Sit down, Courtney," and pushed me toward the comfortable armchair. When I'd dropped into it, she lifted the cover of the crock pot, sniffed, and stirred the contents with a spoon. "We can eat any minute now. I hope you're hungry—I've made a lot. I never know who may drop in."

"It really happened," I told her. "I can show you the bruise on my leg."

"I believe you. I suppose you've discovered that there's a Mercedes at the house?"

"Yes. John and I went into the garage and found the hood warm. It was the same car that struck me. I'm sure of it."

With neat, economic moves, she opened a gate-legged table, spread it with a cloth the color of green celery, and began to set out soup bowls and a round of dark brown bread with pats of butter.

"Have you any notion of who might have been driving the car?" she asked.

"No. None at all. I couldn't see the person at the wheel. I can't think of any good motive that would cause someone to try to injure me."

She drew two chairs to the table, and motioned me to my place as she began to ladle steaming soup into bright yellow bowls. I found that I was hungrier than I'd been since my arrival, and the soup was thick with vegetables and delicious, the bread crusty and filling. Nan made no speculations about what had happened to me. She did not even remind me that she had advised my going back to New York, and I let the whole matter of the car go. I didn't think she was wholly convinced, and there were other things I wanted to know.

I began hesitantly. "Several people have mentioned Alice's and John's baby—the child who died in an accident. Can you tell me anything about that?"

Nan swallowed a mouthful of minestrone. "Why does it matter? It was all so long ago—an unhappy time. I don't like to talk about it."

"I can't work in the dark," I said. "Judith seems to be distraught and tied to things that happened in the past. It's the past that's made her the way she is now—perhaps made her an artist. But I don't even know the right questions to ask. Was the child born in East Hampton?"

"No. Alice ran away to Europe when she knew the baby was coming. Anabel was born in Switzerland."

This surprised me. "Ran away? Why? I should have thought old Lawrence Rhodes would have wanted his grandchild born here."

"He didn't know the baby was coming. That was the whole idea. Alice had quarreled with him over the new will he was drawing up, and she wouldn't stay around to have the baby taken into his hands when it was born. So she and John went abroad. They took me with them to help in any way I could."

I suppressed the eagerness that rose in me. "So you were there when—"

"Yes." She nodded dully. "Poor little Anabel—to live so short a time."

"Please tell me about it."

"Before we got to Switzerland old Lawrence sent for John to come home. Of course his father still didn't know about the baby, and John had to do as he wished. Everyone always did as he wished. I stayed on to help my sister as best I could."

"You and Alice must have been very close."

"Not always. We had our disagreements. But at least we

could stand together against the Rhodes clan when it was necessary. I think our best and happiest time together was at the end of that trip, in Grindelwald. I'll always remember that little valley, with the great mountains behind— the Jungfrau and the rest. I'm glad we were together peacefully before they both died. But why must you know all this?"

Switzerland! Had I been born in Switzerland in the shadow of the Jungfrau?

"All these things seem to be part of Judith's background," I said carefully. "How did the baby come to be left with Judith afterwards?"

"That part was horrible—horrible! We brought Anabel home and Lawrence was told of her birth. But we didn't go straight to The Shingles. I think Alice had thrown something of a scare into old Lawrence, and when she went home she wanted to be in a better bargaining position than when she'd left. She meant to use her baby to get what she and John deserved from the old man—some real standing in the family. You see, it had always been Herndon he trusted—never John—and that wasn't fair. Even as an outsider I could see that. So we went first to our mother's cottage out near Montauk. It's a comfortable house on the water. Mother wasn't well, but she welcomed us, and it seemed a safe harbor compared with The Shingles. It wasn't, of course."

Nan's voice had altered as she spoke, tightening as though she held back emotion.

"Were you there when Alice died? And when the baby" —I couldn't help my hesitation over the word—"when the baby died?"

Emotion surfaced and she answered explosively. "No! No, of course I wasn't there. Perhaps none of it would have happened if I'd stayed. But I'd had enough of all of them. I'd been with Alice for months, trying to make things easier for her. By that time, however, I couldn't approve of some of the things she was doing. So I went out to San Francisco for a while. Unfortunately, only Alice had my address, so when she was drowned I had no way of knowing it. It wasn't until Judith answered a letter I'd written my sister that I learned what had happened. That was the first I knew the baby had died too. So of course I came back—though there wasn't much to come home to. My mother was more seriously ill and for a while she needed me." Nan broke off for a moment and then went on, as though she squared her shoulders. "Alice had left me something in her will, and Herndon fixed it with old Lawrence so that I could have this gatehouse to start my shop. Then in a few months Lawrence was dead as well. Tyrants do eventually die!"

Once the dam had broken, her words had poured forth without restraint, yet somehow I had the feeling that, in spite of this torrent, she held something back. I didn't think she was telling me all she knew about Alice's death, and I put another question.

"It was Judith who found your sister on the beach that day?"

Nan pushed her soup bowl away and I knew that I had spoiled her lunch. "Yes—when it was too late. Alice was a very good swimmer—but nevertheless she drowned."

"How did Judith happen to be out at Montauk?"

"John told me about that afterwards. They were all there, except the old man. When Alice and I returned with the baby, Lawrence wasn't well, and he sent the other three to Montauk to deal with her—Judith and Herndon and John. Lawrence wanted his granddaughter home, and he also wanted them to watch each other. He never trusted anyone, and he always liked to set them against one another whenever he could. At the time Alice died, the baby was sick with a cold. So Judith stayed out there, while Herndon and John brought Alice's body home."

The whole account had made me feel a little ill. There seemed to have been so little loving care for a young baby in what had happened. A picture was emerging in my mind of the old man who had been my grandfather. It was scarcely a picture to match old longings and fantasies, since Lawrence Rhodes must indeed have been a tyrant, and an unloving one. To him, I—if I had really been that baby—had only seemed another pawn in his game of power. Even to Alice, my mother, I had been a counter to use in the play against Lawrence's tyranny.

When I spoke there was a tension of resentment in my

voice, but Nan was lost in her own thoughts, still tortured by old memories and regrets, and she didn't notice.

"What happened to the baby?" I asked.

She seemed to shake herself in a visible effort to return to the present, and she stared at me for a moment before she dipped into the past again.

"The baby's cold got worse, and Judith, who wasn't used to babies, panicked. She felt she had to get her quickly to a doctor. My mother's doctor was just across the cove from our cottage and Judith felt she could get Anabel to him more quickly by boat than the long way around by road. All the Rhodes used to take to boats as easily as to their cars, and she thought nothing of wrapping the baby well and taking her across that small stretch of water. The doctor said nothing much was wrong, gave Judith a prescription, and sent her home. On the way back a sudden squall blew up and the boat capsized. Eventually the Coast Guard rescued her, but the baby was lost." Nan's voice broke on the last words. "I'll never forgive Judith—never! First my sister—and then Anabel."

I could have told her that somehow it was all a lie. Anabel—if I was Anabel—had never been lost from a capsized boat.

"What happened after that?"

She swallowed hard and steadied her voice. "Old Lawrence was wild, of course. I don't know what he'd have done to Judith if she hadn't been able to tell him that she too was pregnant, and there would still be that Rhodes heir he wanted more than life itself. Herndon returned to Montauk to bring Judith home, and from that day to this she's never gone out in a boat again. She seldom even walks on the beach. She only paints it—endlessly. The beach and the sea. Obviously she's ridden by guilt. And sometimes—sometimes I'm glad. But you've asked enough questions, Courtney. I haven't talked about these things for years, and I hadn't meant to talk about them now. Though it is true that these tragedies have indeed molded Judith."

Nevertheless, there was still one more qustion I had to ask. "Did your sister really want her baby?"

"More than anything in the world," Nan said flatly. "After all, it would have given Alice the status she needed in the family. No more about any of this for now, Courtney. And I mean that. None of this can be useful if you write a piece about Judith."

"Not directly, of course," I said. "But at least I can see her more clearly now."

"You'd better not see too clearly." Nan rose from the table, picked up my bowl, and went to the stove.

"No more soup," I said. "It was delicious, but filling."

She brought cheese and fruit and English whole-meal biscuits to the table and we finished eating, though not without strain. The easiness between us had been lost, but while I regretted that, my quest for answers had been furthered to some extent.

When the meal was over, Nan showed me about the shop, speaking with affectionate pride of her treasures, though I suspected that her intent was to hold me off and stem any further questions.

She was particularly pleased with her recent find of a sea chest with a painting on the under side of the lid, and carving on the outside, and she introduced me to her collection of whale-oil lamps and ships' lanterns.

"Though you can't always tell for sure that a lantern came from a ship," she ran on. "There were so many varieties and they were used on land as well as at sea. But this small pair here were a ship's running lights. I'm sure of that."

At the scrimshaw case she took out a whale's tooth, handsomely carved, and handed it to me. It was a small tooth, about four inches long, cone-shaped, thick at the base and curved slightly backward to a point. Around it were etched tiny land scenes—of trees and houses and a church, all enclosed by geometric designs. Probably these were the scenes a sailor had yearned for when he was at sea.

"I'd like you to have it," Nan said. "Just as thanks for all the reading pleasure you've brought me. And as a souvenir of your visit here."

The gift was too easily given, and I felt uncomfortable. When she went on, I knew why.

"Courtney, I hope you won't mention any of the things we've talked about. Not up at the house. It's all a sensitive area still. It's better not to open it up. I never intended to say so much."

So she was coaxing me. "Isn't it already open?" I asked. "Isn't that why Judith was searching for your sister's diary?"

Nan shrugged. "Those anonymous letters have her worried. Perhaps she's afraid someone is trying to bring up all those things she's kept buried for years. But that doesn't mean you have to open it up too."

"If Judith has nothing to hide, why should she be concerned?"

"Who says she has nothing to hide?" Nan's voice had once more taken on a harsh note that disturbed me. Nan Kemble still blamed Judith for the death of her sister and the supposed death of Alice's baby.

"There's one thing you ought to know," I told her. "Stacia was lying when she indicated that Evan struck her. He didn't. It was Judith. She told me so herself."

Nan considered this gravely. "I see. Yes—it fits the pattern. I'm glad to know it wasn't Evan."

"Pattern?" I said.

But she turned away and began to examine a stoneware jug. Clearly she was through talking to me, and I moved toward the door with her gift of scrimshaw in my hand—as a bribe for my silence? I didn't like to have such a thought occur to me, but I couldn't help wondering.

At the door I paused, prompted to try one more question. "Do you know anyone named Olive?"

This time she was plainly startled. "Don't tell me *she* has surfaced after all these years?"

"Who is she?"

"Someone who was there at the time everything happened. What do you know about her?"

"Nothing," I said. "She phoned Evan this morning and he didn't seem too pleased."

There was a new wariness in the look Nan turned upon me. "Have you any idea where this woman is? Has she come back to town?"

"I don't know."

Nan was lost in her own thoughts, and I knew she would explain nothing further.

"I'd better go now," I told her. "Thank you for the scrimshaw and for a lovely lunch. I was glad to get away from the house for a while."

She came with me to the door, but she didn't ask me to visit her again. "When will you be leaving East Hampton?"

"I'm not sure. I really haven't accomplished much in my one talk with Judith. I'm going to try again this afternoon, since she seems more amiable toward me now."

"Good luck," Nan said dryly. "But don't stay around too long. Or take any more walks by yourself."

So perhaps she did believe me, after all.

I went back to my car and got into the driver's seat. Someone had been there ahead of me. On the passenger's side lay the head of a doll with long black hair, its eyes peacefully closed, a slight smirk on parted lips that barely showed a space of pearly china teeth. The sight was ghoulish, and as I picked it up reluctantly the eyelids clicked open to reveal emptiness behind. The hollows where eyes should have looked out seemed more horrid than staring blue glass.

Stacia again? What did this mean—this infantile tormenting? Because she wasn't an infant. I'd had glimpses that had shown me the woman—sometimes desperate, sometimes angry, but anything but immature, for all her affectation of childish ways.

Then I saw that something had slipped off the seat when I had picked up the head. An envelope lay on the floor, and I wondered if I too was to receive an anonymous letter. But when I picked it up and took out the single sheet of notepaper, I saw that it bore The Shingles imprint at the head, and a name was signed at the bottom of the few handwritten lines—Stacia's name. I read the words.

I thought you might like this one, Courtney. Judith had the wig especially made for it. She cut the hair from her own head because she was foolish enough to think I might have fun combing it in different styles—the way she used to comb hers. Imagine!

That was all, except for her name. Silky black hair clung insinuatingly to my fingers, as though it still carried living electricity. I set the thing down on the seat and started the car. It was going to be necessary to have a talk with Stacia Faulkner. A very private talk in which the air might be cleared and certain rules laid down, if I was to be able to stay on in the house even a few days longer. One of those rules being that I would not stand for this sort of torment any longer. If she had anything to say to me, she could say it straight out, with no necessity for these vicious tricks. They were vicious—I knew that now. Not the pranks of a girl who had never grown up, but an intent to drive me up the wall if it could be managed—and I wanted to know why. Among other things, I wanted to know if she had been the driver of the Mercedes that had struck me down.

8

Inside the house I wandered around downstairs, with the doll's head bulging a pocket of my slacks. The living room was empty, and only the portrait of the woman who could be my mother dominated the dining room. I stood before it again, wonderingly, looking up into that mischievous face that was so different from the graver one in Nan's photograph.

Whatever had happened on that beach in Montauk and in the cottage that belonged to the Kembles, it was all having its repercussions now, and from the beginning it had concerned *me*. Through the pendant on the chain about my neck, the same pendant Alice had worn in the portrait, I knew how dangerously I was tied to whatever was happening. Someone here knew who I was—wanted me dead. How could I doubt my identity any longer?

I wandered on through the lower part of the house, to find the library door open, and Evan at work again on his task of pulling order out of the accumulation of years. He did not look around as I came to stand in the door, and I didn't go in. When I saw Asher at the far end of the hall I went toward him. The old man had apparently been taking Tudor for a walk and when he saw me he shortened his grip on the dog's chain and waited for me to pass. I stayed my distance.

"Can you tell me which room is Mrs. Faulkner's?" I asked.

He gestured toward the upper floor. "Mr. and Mrs. Herndon have the room at the south end of the floor. Mrs. Faulkner's room is at the opposite end."

I thanked him and went upstairs. At the north end of the corridor the door stood closed, but I could hear a radio beyond, and I tapped on the panel. The sound was switched off and Stacia called to me to come in.

She was sitting near a window when I opened the door, one hand on a thin notebook in her lap, and she looked around at me with a smile too winning to be true. Her fair hair hung over her eyes and she brushed it back as she looked up.

"Hello, Courtney. Do come in. I'm glad of company. Have you heard the news on the radio? The weather report says that our hurricane has started in toward the mainland and may hit Florida."

With the door firmly closed behind me because I wanted this to be private, I stood looking about the big, cheerful room, taking stock and not in the least caring about hurricanes. Storms of an outdoor nature had no interest for me at the moment, but only the inner storms that filled this house.

The room was large, and a bit more fussy than I'd have expected. A flowered satin flounce decorated the top of the four-poster bed, with a satin quilt to match flung over what looked like a puffy feather mattress. Stacia, still wearing her shorts and pullover, lay in a flowered chaise longue, with a small armchair covered in strawberry gingham opposite. Narrow bookshelves had been set against the wall on either side of a white fireplace, and on the floor were fringed cotton rugs woven in multicolored stripes.

It was hardly a man's room, and though it was moderately untidy, with a few clothes strewn about, I saw nothing that might have belonged to Evan.

"Sit down, do." Stacia gestured toward the gingham

chair, but I made no move toward it. As in every room in this house, the side overlooking sand and ocean dominated, and I went to an open window, where the eternally restless sound of the ocean reached me.

"I see you've collected a bit of Nan's scrimshaw," Stacia said.

I held up the ivory tooth. "She was kind enough to give it to me."

"Oh, Nan can be very kind. What did she want for it?"

Her words brought me around from the window. "What do you mean? She made a friendly gesture—that was all."

"Sure, sure. I'm very fond of Nan, but she's good at bargaining. That's why her shop is such a success."

I'd heard enough, even though I'd sensed something of the sort myself, and I took the doll's head from my pocket.

"This is your property, I believe?"

She nodded brightly. "So you found it? I thought it might interest you. Eerie, isn't it—when you think that black hair came from Judith's own head?"

For a moment I said nothing, trying to hold back an impulse to hurl words at her in anger. When I could manage to speak quietly, I went on.

"What are you trying to do, Stacia? Do you really think I'm a child who can be frightened by pranks?"

"I don't know yet," she told me frankly. "Breaking points are different for everyone. The only way to find out is to test. Isn't that so?" She laughed, with a touch of hysteria in her voice.

"I wouldn't know. I don't think I've ever tried to break anyone."

"Then you've missed a lot of fun," she said lightly.

"Why should you want to break me—if that's what you are trying to do?"

Her eyelids dropped lazily, so that long blond lashes lay upon her cheeks. "I think we both know the answer to that."

I decided that I had better sit down after all. The gingham chair was comfortable and there was a matching footstool for my feet.

"You found the unicorn pendant, didn't you?" I said. "Why did you take it away?"

"I wanted to make sure it was the right one."

"Who else did you show it to?"

She smiled at me—a triangular, cat's smile. "Why did you come here, Courtney?"

"I had the mistaken idea that I wanted to learn about my forebears. I wanted to know what sort of family I belonged to."

"I suppose you're Alice's mysteriously lost baby, aren't you? I always did think there was something fishy about that story."

"I don't know," I said.

"Odd to think we may be cousins. Have you considered that?"

"I'm afraid I have."

"You don't sound pleased."

"Should I be?"

This was mere dueling and she raised her foil. "It must seem strange to come suddenly into a whole nest of relatives. Nan would be your aunt, and Herndon your uncle, John your father. Even Judith would be an aunt by marriage. What are you going to do about a family like this?"

I wanted to put an end to such fencing and I attacked in earnest. "Nothing. Nothing serious enough to cause you to run me down in a car."

She lay very still, her eyes closed and the tiny smile gone from her lips. She looked frozen in ice—a small and oddly appealing sleeping beauty. When she opened her eyes the illusion was dispelled and I saw venom in her look.

"What do you expect me to say to an outrageous accusation like that?"

"I expect you to lie," I told her calmly. "The way you did about Evan striking you."

With a swift movement, she sat up, dislodging the notebook from her knees, so that it fell to the floor. "Listen to me, and listen carefully. On my twenty-fifth birthday, which is only a few weeks off, my grandfather's will goes into effect. I will inherit most of his fortune—this house and all the family treasures, most of the money—everything that's been held for me. He was mad at the whole family when he drew up that will—so I profit. And I don't mean to keep The Shingles for one moment longer than I have to. I'm already making plans to sell it—sell everything in it that isn't personally owned by the others."

I recoiled from such extreme venom, finding myself sorry for Judith for the first time.

"Why can't you leave the house to your mother and father? Judith works best here, doesn't she?"

"What do I care about that? Let her work somewhere else! You sound like Evan."

"I suppose I don't understand deliberate injury. Why do you want to hurt her?"

She leaned over to pick up the notebook, and I noticed that it matched the ones Judith had been rummaging through out in Nan's shop. But her movement was only a means of giving her time to think about her answer.

"Why do I want to hurt her? Because she's always hurt everyone else. Alice, John, Herndon, Grandfather—maybe even you. Why shouldn't she have a taste of what it feels like?"

"Do you really think she hasn't suffered too? It's there in her eyes. She hasn't won that serenity she wears so easily."

With an abrupt gesture, Stacia held the notebook out to me. "Here—you can have this, if you like. A heritage from your mother. Alice used to write stories, you know, and Nan gave me this book of them to read. Maybe you'd like it. I really don't care much for fairy stories."

I took the book from her. "Did Alice ever have any of her work published?"

"I don't think so. Grandfather Lawrence thought what she wrote was nonsense, or so I've been told. He didn't want his daughter-in-law to have such pursuits. You'd have to ask Nan about that. Anyway, I was telling you what I mean to do when Grandfather's money comes to me. I hadn't finished, and I'm sure you must be interested. I'm going to have the most marvelous time in the world. I'm going to buy anything my heart desires. I'll have a yacht, if I like, and some beautiful foreign cars. Not anything so dreary as a Mercedes. I'll have clothes. I'll travel. People will pay attention to me. Important people. Do you understand what I'm telling you?"

"It certainly sounds like a squandering spree. What do you do when it's gone?"

"It won't be gone. There's too much for one person like me to spend. Of course there will be investments—all that sort of dull necessity. There are banks and lawyers to handle such matters."

"What does your husband think of these plans?"

"He'll try to stop me, of course. He'll oppose me and try to save something. But he won't succeed. In the end he'll do what I want him to do. He always does. We're tied together, Evan and I. Remember that, Miss Anabel Rhodes!"

"That isn't my name. I'm Courtney Marsh, and I expect to go on being Courtney Marsh."

She lay still for a moment staring at me. "You already have everything, don't you? You're famous, popular. I expect you make quite a bit of money—though it wouldn't be enough to suit me. Why should you come here? Why should you want what belongs to me?"

"I don't want it. I don't want any part of it."

"I don't believe you. You'll want to get your hands on some of that money—perhaps all of it, if you can!"

"How could I possibly? Your grandfather left a will, didn't he? He thought I was dead. I don't come into it at all. I don't want to come into it."

She thought about that for a moment, a frown creasing her brows. Then she gave me a bright, false smile. "I suppose that's true. I suppose I really needn't worry about you."

"All I want is to finish my talks with Judith. As soon as they're done, I mean to get away from this house and all of you in it as fast as I can. I no longer want to know what really happened when Alice died, or what Judith did. Not anything! I'm sick of all of you." I hadn't meant to speak like that, but I was glad I had.

"You sound terribly fervent. I could almost believe you. But there is something else you want here, isn't there?"

I stared at her blankly. "I don't know what you're talking about."

"What about John? What about your father?"

"I don't know that he is my father. I don't know anything."

"It's as likely he's your father as it is that Alice was your mother. Did you know that our saintly, beautiful Judith was in love with John at one time—her own husband's brother?"

Judith and John? I pushed the thought away from me. I had come here wondering if she were my mother, but I had quickly turned to the more acceptable possibility of Alice.

"I don't believe you," I said.

"Then ask her! She never bothers to lie. At least not unless it's a big, whopping, earth-shaking lie."

"I don't intend to ask. As I said before, I don't want to know. I have a job to do and then I'm going away."

"I wish John were *my* father," she said, oddly wistful.

"What about Herndon? What about him if there was such an affair?"

"I wonder if Dad was ever aware of it. I think they fooled him completely. To this day, I don't believe he knows what happened. And I wouldn't want him to be hurt. In some ways he's the best of the lot. So don't go talking to him, Courtney."

Her switch to partisanship was as disturbing as her vindictiveness, and it was hard to deal with such chameleonlike changes.

"I don't intend to talk to anyone," I said.

"You needn't feel sorry about their being turned out of this house. My father has enough in his own right, and Judith isn't all that demanding. At least not when it comes to money. Of course John has the fixed amount Grandfather Lawrence left him. So no one will starve. I'm the one who needs the money."

She closed her eyes dreamily, and I watched her with distaste.

"When I come into my inheritance, John and I are going to spend it together," she went on. "I'm going to make it all up to him—his having to lose my mother and all that unhappiness. Soon I'll be able to give him all the things he's never had—in return for being so good to me all these years. After Grandfather died, Herndon kept a tight hold on the purse strings with the whole family. Except for Judith. If she wanted the moon, Herndon would get it for her."

"Even a unicorn moon?" I asked.

Her grin was impish, childlike, but her eyes were a woman's. "That's an interesting notion."

I had heard all I wanted to hear. Perhaps more than I wanted to hear, and I stood up. "I'll be leaving soon, Stacia, and you'll never need to see me again. Whatever you do with your inheritance is no concern of mine. I just want you to stop the tricks you've been playing on me. And I want to make it clear that it isn't necessary to try to be rid of me by striking me down in a car."

She left the chaise longue and came to stand close to me. "You really believe it was I, don't you?"

"I think it was—yes."

Her sudden laughter chilled me and made me remember her mother's laughter when I was with her in the attic studio. But when I started for the door, Stacia stopped me with a quick hand on my arm.

"Wait, Cousin Courtney. Wait till I show you one more part of your heritage."

I didn't want to stay, but her fingers tightened upon my arm, compelling me across the room to the wall opposite the ocean. There tall windows overlooked the driveway and what had once been that great park area, now overgrown with underbrush. Between the windows hung a portrait—and I was caught at once by the intensity of the blue eyes that looked out at me.

"Our grandfather," Stacia said softly in my ear. "Old Yellowbeard—our own personal pirate. Grandfather Lawrence. That was his sailing outfit, when he wasn't in his law office."

The man in the picture wore a brass-buttoned jacket and a captain's cap, and the lower part of his face was covered by a thick yellow beard. His mouth, what could be seen of it, was grim-lipped, and he had the square chin of a man who liked to get his own way. Did this man's blood really run in my veins? Could I possibly be tied as closely as Stacia to this man whose cruel grip upon this family was becoming more and more evident to me?

"What do you think of him?" she asked, still at my side.

"He must have been a formidable character."

"I gather he was all of that. I wish I could have known him. He knew what he wanted of life—and so do I. He never liked dull people. Maybe he trusted my father most, but he liked Uncle John best. How does it feel to be related to a pirate, Courtney?"

There was no way in which I could get through to my blocked feelings, whatever they were—and perhaps it was better so. If this man with the strong, purposeful expression was my grandfather, I could feel nothing at all about him. There seemed to be only an empty sadness in me—where I had somehow expected recognition in coming here, and an eager response of blood to blood.

"How did he die?" I asked. "I've been told it was a heart attack and that Judith was there when it happened."

"Yes. She was always there, wasn't she? John thinks she may have said something disturbing to him that brought on the attack. When the others rushed in he was trying desperately to speak, but he died before he could manage the words. Of course Judith never admitted anything. According to her, he thought he saw the unicorn moon, and it frightened him so badly that he died. That may have been true, but I think there was more. She didn't lie that time—she just kept still."

I had heard enough. More than I wanted to hear, and I started again for the door. Stacia came with me to let me out.

"I hope everything is clear now between us," she said.

I had no answer to that. I didn't even know what she meant. I had come to have something out with her, but I wasn't at all sure I had succeeded.

"I hope *you're* convinced that there's nothing here I want," I said. "I'll be leaving soon."

"But you can always come back, can't you?" she said softly.

I shook my head. "Not by any choice of mine."

Behind me, I heard her close the door with a sharp click that seemed to express displeasure and distrust. I was beginning to realize that Stacia lived in a world she made up to suit herself, and she acted according to rules that didn't apply to the normal, real world. A fact that made dealing with her difficult and sometimes a little frightening.

I carried the composition book that she'd given me back to my room along with Nan's scrimshaw and put them away in a drawer. I would look at the book later, perhaps read some of the stories, try to find some means of reaching through to the woman who might be my mother. The scrimshaw still made me a little uneasy, and I didn't like to consider what Stacia had said about Nan's bargaining. I wanted to like Nan—I did like her—yet I wasn't altogether sure of her either.

In any case, it was time to return to the studio and take advantage of Judith's invitation to talk with her again.

Before I left the room, the view drew me once more, and I went to look out at sunlight shimmering on the water, and at a beach that stretched for miles on either side, with only gulls and sandpipers to enjoy its emptiness. No wonder towns that had become summer havens had sprung up along the ocean, with all that beach available. Below me, on the terrace, something moved and I saw that Evan Faulkner was walking the flagstones. I dropped the white curtain to stand concealed, but I continued to watch him.

When he reached the end of the terrace he turned and came back, walking slowly, as though he carried some heavy weight on his shoulders. Once he paused and stood staring up at the house, so that I could see his raised face, though he could not see me. I was startled by his worn, unhappy expression. Whenever I had seen him he had been a man on guard, giving nothing of himself away, holding off any observer. In this moment when he did not know he was being watched, the troubled, inner man was evident—the face of a man in pain. I mustn't watch him in this unguarded moment, I thought, and I stepped back from the window, myself troubled and wondering. What lay between him and Stacia? How much did he love her, and how much could she make him suffer? Obviously she had a talent for hurting others—a talent she liked to use.

It was none of my affair, of course. Only Judith in her role of accomplished artist was my business, and I left my room and went up the attic stairs to her studio, trying to put aside this new image of a man whose face had begun to haunt me more than I wanted it to.

I could hear voices as I reached the landing, and the door to the studio stood open. There were three people in the big room. Judith, the central figure, was seated in a carved teakwood chair in the prayer-rug area, and she wore again her patchwork gown with its long, graceful lines and great squares of red and blue, yellow and green. Like a queen, she sat erectly, her arms resting on the carved chair arms, her silky black hair flowing forward over her shoulders. Nearby, John lounged against one of the big room dividers that held her paintings, while Herndon paced the attic, far the most disturbed of the three.

They all stared at me as I reached the door, and when I hesitated, Herndon started toward me, making a visible effort to control whatever emotion was driving him to restless movement.

"I'm sorry, Courtney, but I'm afraid this isn't the time—"

I was already turning away when Judith broke in, her voice quiet and controlled. "Come in, Courtney. Come and sit here and listen to this fascinating discussion."

She gestured to a heap of cushions on the floor near her chair, and I went somewhat reluctantly to sit at her feet, like a neophyte looking up at her teacher. When I glanced toward John he smiled wryly, as though he knew very well that this arrangement of Judith's was deliberate.

"I've got to get back to the office," Herndon said curtly. "In any case, we're getting nowhere."

Judith held out her hand to him. "Stay a little longer. Perhaps Courtney will have an idea for us. Sometimes an outsider's eye—"

Herndon sighed, but he ceased his pacing and sat down on the sofa across from his wife. With the new knowledge Stacia had given me, I watched all three—wondering about that long-ago affair with John, yet not wholly willing to trust anything Stacia said.

"I don't think this is the place for an outsider's eye," Herndon went on, though his look toward me had turned apologetic.

"Why not?" Judith leaned to place her hand on my

shoulder. "We've been talking about Stacia, Courtney. Perhaps you know by this time that her grandfather's will is going to put this house into her possession in a very short time. She's been announcing that she plans to sell it, no matter how the rest of us feel. We've been trying to find some way to stop her."

I moved uncomfortably on my pile of cushions, resisting the touch of her hand. "This isn't anything I can possibly have an opinion about."

"You're right, naturally," Herndon said, "and I think we'd better break up this hopeless conference right now."

"It's not hopeless," Judith said, and she smiled down at me gravely, almost affectionately. "Before I will move away from this house, I'll walk into the ocean and never come back. The way Alice did that day out in Montauk."

Herndon blanched, and there was a moment of silence. I guessed that she had startled both men.

"What are you talking about?" Herndon asked. "Alice didn't commit suicide, and neither will you."

Judith smiled at him almost tenderly.

"Alice was unhappy, wasn't she? Didn't we all know that she was unhappy enough to run away and have her baby abroad? And as soon as she came back, she must have known that she was trapped again in a life she had come to hate. Because of Lawrence. Always because of your father."

I glanced toward John, expecting him to say something—in denial or agreement—but instead he stayed where he was, leaning against the partition, with that faintly wry smile curving his lips. As though he sensed what Judith was trying to do.

"This is late in the day to cry suicide," Herndon said harshly. "That suspicion was never raised at the time, and shouldn't have been. Alice was devoted to her baby. We all knew that. She would never have killed herself."

"Wouldn't she?" John asked.

The two words were spoken quietly, and for some reason I looked not at John but at Judith, and saw the pallor of her skin—a pallor that made her tan look yellowish. Her hands, a moment before lying loosely on the chair arms, had tightened over the carved heads of temple dogs that graced the chair.

"What are you talking about?" Herndon challenged.

John shook his head enigmatically and Judith said nothing.

Impatiently, Herndon threw up his hands. "You're indulging in riddles, both of you, and that hardly helps us now. Nor do I want to hear any more about your walking into the ocean, Judith. I'll see to it that you don't have to move from this house. Stacia will be stopped in this—I promise."

I had never heard this forceful note from Herndon before, and I knew he would go to some lengths to spare Judith so painful a move.

"In any case," he went on, "Courtney can't possibly help in what is a private family problem. I'm sorry we've tried to involve you, Courtney."

"She might have an idea or two at that," John went on in the same quiet tone, but when I looked at him I saw dark humor in his eyes. For some reason *he* was baiting Judith.

"It doesn't matter." Judith ignored his words. "When the time comes, *I* will stop Stacia. You both know very well that this is the place where I must live and work. I won't be uprooted."

"A determined, but not very practical approach," John said.

I'd had enough of sitting cramped on a pile of cushions and I stood up, speaking to him directly. "What do you mean—that *I* might have some ideas about stopping Stacia?"

"Why not? Think about it."

"This is all nonsense," Herndon told him. He smiled at me kindly, apologetically, kissed Judith on the cheek, and went out of the room.

When he'd gone I turned back to her. "I thought we might talk some more this afternoon, but perhaps this isn't the time. Would you like me to return later?"

She didn't look at me. "Yes—later, please. I need to talk to John now."

I started toward the door, but John came with me, waving a hand at Judith. "We'll discuss this later," he said, and followed me down the room.

When I looked back, I saw Judith staring after us, a look of surprise on her face—and not of pleased surprise. Whatever she had expected, it was not that John would go off with me.

"Get your coat," he told me as we went down the attic stairs. "I want to show you something. You might as well use this time to improve your background knowledge of the clan, hadn't you?"

There was nothing else I wanted to do, and John Rhodes interested me a great deal. He was the only one who could at times seem warm and friendly. If I was Alice's child, he was my father.

"I won't be a moment," I said, and ran down the hall to my room. The sudden movement hurt my bruised thigh, but I ignored the twinge. I was looking forward to going wherever John Rhodes meant to take me, and I wanted very much to become better acquainted with him.

9

John was waiting for me in the lower hallway when I came downstairs, and I was aware of an exuberance in him that sometimes contrasted with the lazing aspect he could often assume. It was easy to see how attractive he must have been in his youth—and was still, for that matter. When I reached him he held out his hand and took mine in a gesture that seemed boyish, yet natural, and we went outside together and down the long flight of steps hand-in-hand as he drew me along energetically.

His car was low and small and maroon, with a bullet nose that suggested speed. I had ridden in it when he'd rescued me, but I hadn't noticed it then. Still expelling energy, he opened the door and swept me into the front seat, went around to the driver's side, and in a moment we were off and following the winding road that led to the gates. His mastery of the swift-moving car was evident, as well as the fact that he enjoyed driving, and enjoyed driving fast.

When he reached the gatehouse, I saw Nan outside, watering plants near the house. John gave her a gay salute as we swept through and I looked back to see her staring after us, unsmiling.

"You must be thoroughly tired of The Shingles by this time," he said as we drove through the lanes in the direction of town.

"I don't know whether 'tired' is the word," I said. "I've felt disturbed by the house and the family, perhaps. Especially after yesterday."

"Where I'm taking you, we'll have a chance to talk," he told me. "Peacefully."

"That will be fine. I'd like to know what you meant about my stopping Stacia."

He didn't answer as we turned down Main Street and drove beneath elm trees to a place where he pulled up to the curb and parked.

"Here we are," he said and waved his hand.

Away from us across the road the grassy embankment dipped to the foot of a sloping hill where gravestones and monuments climbed to the crest. We had come to the Old South Burying Ground.

"It's a good place to be alone," John said, "and there's a certain sobering influence. Besides, I want to show you something."

Again he took my hand with natural, friendly ease and we crossed the road and climbed the slope of hill to the place where a stile led over a fence that enclosed the cemetery. For a time we wandered inside idly, silently, no longer hand-in-hand, but still comfortable together. I was glad to be with him, to know him a little away from the house. Just as a friend. I mustn't think about who he might be.

Now and then I bent to read dates and inscriptions, finding that some of the stones went back to the 1600s, while some had worn so badly that the markings had been long effaced. Old trees hung their limbs protectively above the graves, and there had been plantings of cedar and yew. Yew to prevail against the powers of evil. I had read that somewhere.

"Our town prize," John said as he led me toward a large tomb on which rested the stone effigy of an armored knight—a tomb which bore the name of the first Lion Gardiner of Gardiner's Island, and which had been placed here two centuries after his death. But we didn't linger, as John had another goal. The stone we came upon was of granite and handsomely engraved with the name of ETHAN RHODES.

I glanced at John in swift questioning and he smiled at me. "You've been seeing the worst side of the Rhodes, Courtney. But Ethan was the good side, and I wanted you to see that once he really existed."

As I studied the inscription with long-ago dates, the blockage in me seemed to melt a little and unexpected tears came into my eyes. I blinked rapidly, not wanting John to see, wishing that I could have found this place for the first time when I was alone. I'd had no sense of relationship to Grandfather Lawrence, who was closer to me in years, but I felt that something had come down to me from old Captain Ethan. To him I could belong. My great-great-grandfather.

"I thought you'd like to see it," John said quietly.

I couldn't meet his eyes, still blinking away the tears in my own, not sure of his meaning. "Are other Rhodes buried here?" I asked.

"Only Ethan's wife, Hesther. Hers is the grave beside her husband's."

Because of the sailing-ship named for her, because of that figurehead in the sand below The Shingles, I felt acquainted with her. And because of the unicorn.

"This old graveyard hasn't been used for a long time," John went on. "It's only historic now."

A little way from where Ethan and Hesther lay, a green aisle ran between the stones, and I found a place in the sun and sat carefully down upon the grass, favoring my bruise.

"Do you mind?" I asked John. "I'd like to stay here for a little while. Just stay here and be quiet."

He nodded, but his own barely suppressed drive took him wandering among the stones, and I was glad he had the perception to let me stay alone. Now I could give myself over to emotion—as though, strangely, I had at last come home.

There was no one about. What traffic there was moved past on either side of this graveyard island and seemed remote from its peace and quiet. At one end the hill sloped down to the town pond, still in sunlight, its waters shining. A gull's feather lay on the grass near me and I picked it up to brush it softly through my fingers. Sitting here in this quiet, lonely spot, I began to feel calmer and less disturbed than at any time since I had come to The Shingles, so that I was grateful to John for bringing me here. I could even think of him now, think of what he might mean to me.

I had no feeling at all about my mother, but was it possible that I had found a father? Did I dare to think that? No!—I must be careful, I must leap to no conclusions. Nothing at all was certain except the fact that my golden unicorn had come from the Rhodes.

His step was soundless on the soft cushion of grass and I didn't hear him come back until he stood beside me. Now I could look up without tears and meet his blue, sardonic gaze. If John was my father there would be no sentimentality about the kinship, and that fact I would have to accept.

"Do you mind if I join you?" he asked.

"Please." I nodded to the space of grass beside me.

He dropped down and sat cross-legged, relaxed now, and at ease, not looking at me, but staring off toward the treetops where a redbird was singing. Unobserved, I could study the fine carving of his profile, the thick sweep of silvering hair—but could I find a resemblance? Did I really want to?

"Tell me why you think I might help Judith to stop Stacia," I asked him again.

He turned his head for a quick look at me and again his smile was faintly mocking. "Have you any doubt as to who drove that car that struck you down yesterday?"

Perhaps I hadn't any doubt, really, and I had said as much to Stacia, but I had no real proof that it had been she at the wheel of the car.

"Has Stacia admitted it to you?" I asked.

"She would hardly do that. Nor have I made any accusation. I think I understand her well enough, and perhaps with more sympathy than either Judith or Herndon. After all, I've grown up under Rhodes' suppression too. Not that I condone or excuse what she did—if she did it. But I have tried to understand."

"How could something like that possibly be understood?" I demanded.

"She would have acted on impulse, in passion of anger. That's in her character, I think. By now, however, she must be a little afraid of you—afraid of what you might do if you chose to accuse her."

I could only shake my head. "I don't think she's in the least afraid of me, and I have accused her."

"Why do you think she tried to run you down?"

"How can I possibly guess? I can't even imagine why. She knows I'm going away soon and that none of you will ever see me again."

"I wonder if that is already out of your hands?" John said.

I looked at him in surprise. "What are you talking about?"

"Are you wearing the pendant?" he asked softly.

My hand flew to my throat to touch the clasp of the chain and I found a new uneasiness growing in me. Now I could guess why he had shown me Ethan's grave and watched for my reaction.

He held out his hand. "May I see it again?"

"Again?"

"Of course. Stacia brought it to me when she took it from your room. She wanted to know what it meant."

He was waiting, so I reached up to release the clasp and gave him the chain and unicorn.

Holding it by the chain, he watched the tiny golden creature swing from his fingers in the sunlight.

"This had been in the Rhodes family for a very long time, Courtney. May I ask how it came into your possession?"

There was no point in trying to hold back the truth. "It was around my neck when my adoptive parents received me."

"Did they know who your real parents were?"

"No. At least I don't think they knew for sure. They died in a train accident a few months ago, and when I was going through their papers I came on a clipping—a reproduction of Judith's painting of the unicorn moon. There were words written in pencil in the margin that asked whether this was the unicorn in my life."

He gave back the chain and pendant for me to replace about my neck. "So you came here to find out?"

"That was part of the reason. I *am* going to write about Judith—I want to very much. But I've always wanted to know my own heritage. I thought I might find the answer here."

"And have you?"

"How am I to know? Do *you* know? Do you think I am Alice's child?"

His blue eyes had a bright challenge in them as he studied me for a moment without answering. When he spoke he formed his words carefully, without emotion, though not answering me directly.

"It's quite possible that I am your father."

My breath was coming raggedly and I felt shaken and more than a little frightened. Always people had said to me, "What if you do find your parents and they reject you?" Was this the moment of possible acceptance—or painful rejection?

"Don't look like that," he said. "We're guessing, aren't we? But if I am suddenly to discover that I have a daughter at this late date, I can't imagine being gifted with one I'd rather have."

The words were serious enough in their purport, but his tone was light, and I had the feeling that John Rhodes would hardly sweep me into his arms as a long-lost daughter. Indeed, he might well be afraid of such emotion, and if any sort of relationship grew between us, it would more likely be on a plane of friendship. It was probably too late for me to come into his life as a daughter, and over this I felt a faint twinge of regret. A twinge that was at least kin to feeling, though I knew better than to show any hint of emotion that might embarrass the man beside me, and put him to flight. He wasn't asking for a daughter at this late date.

"Why did it happen?" I managed to ask. "If I was the baby who was supposed to be lost at sea, why did Judith take me to New York and give me for adoption? And why wasn't it found out—what she did?"

"Lawrence—my father—was still powerful when it all happened, and he managed to take hold, sick as he was. The story of the accident was accepted. Both happenings are still accepted hereabouts—simply as two unfortunate accidents, which occurred close together."

My sigh was involuntary. How was I ever to know what had really happened? I only knew that a warmth of sympathy stirred in me for John Rhodes.

"It must have been a dreadful time for you," I said. "Yes!"

The word came out with such vehemence that I looked at him quickly and saw in his face the dregs of an old anger, left over from that tragic time. Beneath his gay and sometimes debonair manner, resentment against his father still lingered in John Rhodes. The damage the old man had done reached down through the generations— even to me.

John wasn't looking at me now. "I was, I still am, the eldest son," he said, and though the words came more quietly, I sensed their depth of meaning. Others had said that it was always Herndon old Lawrence had placed first, and at the time of Alice's death and the supposed death of the child, it was likely that little consideration had been given to John's loss. Even Herndon, his brother, would have been more concerned with protecting Judith than with his brother's suffering. And I could believe in that suffering now, no matter what tales Stacia concocted about an affair between him and Judith.

"You're still angry with your father, aren't you?" I said gently.

He gave me a startled glance and then smiled. "I didn't realize I was giving my feelings away. Yes, it's still there, and for a moment you brought it all back."

"I'm sorry," I said. "But what happened at the time? Couldn't *you* get any of the answers?"

"My father was only interested in closing ranks and avoiding any hint of scandal that would hurt the precious family name. He didn't want any of us to dig behind the surface he meant to present to the world. He and I had our last quarrel at the time and I went away. All he wanted was to protect the family name and believe what would best serve that purpose. I didn't come back to The Shingles until after he died."

"Did you and Alice want a baby?"

His look seemed far away—as though he searched some distant horizon. "We wanted one a great deal—Alice as much as I. For that little time she was a happy mother. And I was just beginning to feel like a father."

Instead, he had lost both his wife and child, and later he had tried, perhaps, to fill in the emptiness with an affection for Stacia. Sympathy stirred in me, but nothing more. He was too distant, too far out of my reach.

"Stacia seems to have a great affection for you. It comes through each time I talk to her."

"I'm not sure I've been good for her. I'm too much of an iconoclast."

As long as he was still receptive, not rebuffing me, I had to know more. "What about the selling of the house? Do *you* want this to happen?"

"Stacia hasn't consulted me. But perhaps in a good many ways it might be for the best."

"What ways do you mean?"

He didn't hesitate. "It's become too much of a shrine— a temple for Judith's talent. As a painter, it might be a lot better for her to leave here and never come back. She needs to test herself out in the world and stop painting beaches. There are other landscapes that she's never seen."

"Why does she want to stay? Is she afraid of the world outside?"

"Of course. She can only quiet her fears when she has the protection of the house—or so she thinks."

"Fear of what?"

"Discovery, perhaps. Discovery of herself—to herself. I don't think she wants to face that."

"But she seems so poised, so calm and sure of everything."

"As long as she has the house for a shield. I don't know what will happen if Stacia carries out her plan. But it may be interesting to find out."

"What will happen to you?"

He turned his head to smile at me. "I can drift with the wind if I have to. I'll make a landing somewhere. I'm still a pretty good designer of boats, you know."

"I've heard about the *Anabel,*" I said. "Why was it given that name?"

"Alice chose it. It didn't matter to me."

"And then she named the baby Anabel. Why was she so attached to that particular name?"

He regarded me thoughtfully, and when he spoke I had the feeling that he held something back. "It was a name that had some meaning for her, I suppose. A family name. But can you stop being a reporter for a little while, Courtney? This has been quite a quizzing, hasn't it?"

"I'm sorry. You're the only person who has been willing to answer all my questions."

"No, not all your questions. Not yet. Shall we go back now? You've had your break from the house, and perhaps Judith will be willing to see you again by this time."

He stood up, but I stayed where I was on the grass. "You still haven't told me how you think I might stop Stacia."

"Perhaps I've changed my mind about that. Perhaps I don't really think you can—or will."

He held out his hand and I let him pull me to my feet.

"Just one more question," I said. "When you rescued me after that car struck me, did you know then who I was?"

He shook his head. "Stacia showed me the pendant just after that."

"Thank you for talking to me. And for being a—a friend."

His clasp was warm, but his look still mocked me a little—as though he were warning me not to come too close, not to ask for more than he would be ready to give.

An awkwardness had grown between us and neither of us had much to say as he drove me back to the house. Outside Nan's shop two cars were parked as we went through the gates, and she was apparently busy inside with customers.

"Was Alice close to Nan in the old days?" I asked as we started up the drive. "Were they affectionate sisters?"

"Not particularly. Nan was the perennial spinster—starved for affection. Sometimes, I think she tried to live Alice's life."

When we reached the house garage, Stacia stood on the front steps above, as though she waited for us.

"Where have you been?" she demanded of John as we climbed the steps.

He answered her quietly, undoubtedly long accustomed to her moods. "We went to pay a call on a possible ancestor of Courtney's—Ethan Rhodes."

She stared at him. "So you've told her?"

"Told her what, my dear?"

"That I showed you the unicorn, of course." She turned to me. "I hate that cemetery. I don't want to be reminded that someday I'll be one of them. Has John been telling you ancient history? What do you think of us—of being related to us?"

"I don't know what to think," I said. "Though I like what I've learned about Ethan."

Stacia came down a step or two to slip her hand into the crook of John's arm. It was the same possessive gesture she had made toward Evan—as though she warned me away from property that belonged to her. If he were really my father, Stacia would not welcome that fact. She would be jealous of all those close to her—John, Evan, perhaps even Judith and Herndon, and she wouldn't want to share them with me. But that didn't seem a strong enough reason to make her the driver of that Mercedes yesterday.

"I want to talk to you," she said to John. "Let's go for a walk on the beach."

"Of course," he agreed. "Thank you for your company, Courtney." The words were formally courteous, the manner hardly that of a father thanking a daughter.

I watched as they went down the steps and around the house, then I walked inside and climbed the stairs to my room. I seemed to have no clear reaction to anything that had happened. Rather, I suffered from a state of confusion and uncertainty. For all the questions I had managed to ask, nothing had been resolved, no fundamental, positive truth had emerged, and I was no nearer to discovery than before. That is, emotional discovery. Perhaps all that had happened was that a few more possibilities had surfaced. I had no idea whether Stacia's words about Judith and John having had an affair were true, or merely one of her flights of fancy, and that was one question I hardly dared to ask John.

Remembering Alice's composition book that Stacia had given me, I took it from its drawer and sat down in an armchair to look through it. I expected no startling discoveries, and I found none. The stories were all for children, handwritten in a flowing script, which had a distinct character of its own, and most of them were fantasy. She had written gracefully, with an ear for rhythm and the right word, and she had not forgotten to entertain. It was too bad if she had never been published.

At the beginning of the book they were directed toward children of eight or nine, but as I turned the pages, not reading carefully, but scanning to get an idea of what her writing was like, I found that the tales became younger, with simple words, and a simple idea. Indeed, she had drawn in tiny illustrations in pencil here and there that showed talent in themselves, and were directed toward a very young child.

The inference seemed clear. Alice had been looking toward the arrival of her baby and she had begun writing for younger children, perhaps thinking of the time when her own child would be old enough to hear her mother's stories read aloud.

For the first time, I felt a pang of hurt as I thought of Alice. Reading these words she had written, I could no longer see her entirely as a woman driven by greed. She had, indeed, been looking forward with anticipation and love to being a mother. Her words told me that, at least. If I was the child she had held in her arms, she had known me—and I her—for so very short a time. The thought was saddening but it brought me something I could feel at last with my own emotions, so that I knew I still had love to give, even though this woman had been gone so long. If I tried, if I waited, I would yet find her.

However, if this was the book that Judith had been seeking in Nan's shop, there seemed no apparent reason why she had wanted it. The stories were make-believe, rather than reality—stories of sprites and elves and kings and princesses, of extraordinarily handsome princes—all stories of enchantment that told me little about the writer. Judith had spoken of a diary, while Nan had assured her that her sister had never kept a diary, and this, certainly, was no journal of daily affairs. When I came to the end of her stories, there were no more blank pages—she had filled the book completely.

I was about to set it aside when I noticed something I hadn't immediately observed. Still, clinging to the spine of the book at the back were snips of paper, as though pages had been torn away. I could see now that there had been more pages in the book, but that someone had taken the trouble to tear out those final sheets. Stacia must have done her work before giving me the book—knowing there would be nothing informative in it. Unless someone else had torn out those pages—perhaps Alice herself?

I went to the window to look out at John and Stacia following wet sand at the water's edge. They walked close together, though not touching each other, and though they had wandered some distance east along the beach, their figures were clear in the sunlight. John's head bent toward her, since he was the taller, and now and then she looked up at him with an eager raising of her own head. What was she plotting now? I wondered.

It didn't matter. Except that I had no way in which to turn. More threads had raveled into view, but only to make me feel that it was all too tantalizing to be tossed aside when my work with Judith came to an end. There must be some way of learning more before I left this house.

When a tap came on my door, I went to open it and found Mrs. Asher standing there.

"If you please, ma'am, Mrs. Rhodes would like to see you in her studio. She said to come now, if you have the time, please."

"I have time, of course," I told her. "I'll go right upstairs."

She hesitated a moment, as though she wanted to say something more, but though I waited, indicating inquiry, she seemed to change her mind and scurried off down the hall, always a little furtive in her behavior, and entirely unlike her assured older husband.

I went upstairs to Judith's studio, and found the door closed. When I knocked, she came to open it, shutting it after me and shooting the bolt.

"There," she said, "now no one can disturb us by walking in. I'm glad you could come, Courtney. This is a good time to talk."

For just an instant an unreasonable uneasiness seized me. It was nonsense, of course, to feel in any way uncomfortable about being shut away up here at the top of the house alone with Judith Rhodes. This was what I had wanted, so I must take full advantage of the opportunity, and forget about the unknown driver of a car that had borne down upon me yesterday.

As I followed her across the attic, I realized that something had changed in her since our earlier meeting in the studio, changed since I had seen her in Nan's shop. Some new mood had quickened her to a greater liveliness than I had noted in her before. As she walked ahead of me toward the center of the attic, her long patchwork skirt moving gracefully with her movements, she seemed less a woman who wore serenity as a cloak of protection. She was completely poised, but more truly so, as though some occurrence I did not know about had given her a new confidence.

"Come," she said, "sit down," and we found places for ourselves in the small living oasis in the middle of the vast room. "Now then," she went on when we were comfortable, "ask me anything you wish about my work."

Such openness, so unexpected a welcome, took me aback. I had been ready to press, to push, to struggle, and it was as though a door I had thrown my weight against had suddenly opened, so that I stumbled, trying to catch my balance. Had John or Stacia told her about me? I wondered. But I really didn't think so. The change in her didn't seem to suggest that.

Fortunately, I had my notebook to fall back on, and before I had left New York, I'd jotted down questions to ask her.

"Why do you always have a preference for sea and

beach scenes?" I managed to ask, though I knew the answer was obvious.

She waved a graceful hand at dormer windows that had been built into the roof. "That's what is out there—sand and ocean. In this house we live with them and their variety is infinite. The view is never the same from one day to the next. The sky changes, the water changes, things come in from the sea."

"What sort of things?"

"Driftwood, fish, all the trash men throw into the water. Not always romantic things. Though we had a dolphin once. That was exciting, although the poor, beautiful creature died before we could return it to the sea. Men from Evan's lab out in Montauk came and took it away. But I painted it first."

She rose and went to a stack of canvases leaning against a wall. When she had sorted through them she brought one back and placed it across the arms of a chair so I could see it.

The great shining creature lay on the sand in its last moments of life, its one visible eye faintly glazed so that it no longer beheld with joy and clarity the marvelous sea world that had bred it. The tail was slightly raised, as though the dolphin made a last faint struggle toward the life it was leaving. It lay half in the water, and half on the beach, its mouth barely open. Above, a single gull with outspread wings dipped inquisitively, and sky and ocean had a greenish tinge. For once, that was no fantasy—no dolls' heads, no unicorns.

"You should have this one on display," I said. "It's beautiful and sad and altogether wonderful."

"It's too sad," she told me and picked it up to return to its place against the wall. "I wept when the dolphin died. Somehow it belonged to life, and it wasn't fair that careless injury—perhaps from a passing speedboat—had cast it up on the land to end its life."

A remembered sadness swept over her and I realized for the first time how expressive her face could be, and how, when she relaxed her guard a little, her every emotion was visible. Emotion I'd hardly believed existed. But an interview must sometimes progress by prodding, by a treading on sensitive areas, because otherwise the real person doesn't come through.

"Someone has mentioned that after Alice's death you seldom walked the beach any more."

She raised her head and her calm green gaze regarded me, as though she knew very well what I was doing.

"Yes, you're right. The dolphin wasn't my first meeting with death on a beach."

I was silent. Indirectly, that was what I had meant and I felt ashamed of my question.

"Right now you can ask me anything, and I won't mind," she said, smiling at my confusion. "But I might as well admit that Alice's death didn't seem as tragic to me as the dolphin's. There—have I shocked you?"

"I don't know anything about your relationship with Alice," I said.

"I disliked her intensely. In some ways she was like our father-in-law—Lawrence Rhodes—even though she wasn't related by blood. She never let go of anything she wanted and she liked nothing better than to bend other people to her will. There were times when she was downright unkind to Nan, who seldom hit back. That trip abroad couldn't have been all roses. No, I couldn't be sorry when Alice died, except in a general sort of way, as one must regret any death."

The thought of those charming, sensitive little stories I had dipped into came to my mind and did not seem to fit with the picture Judith was giving me of a ruthless and dominating woman. But of course at one time Judith was supposed to have been in love with John, and she might have been prejudiced against his wife.

"Perhaps you'd better stick to the dolphin in your article," Judith told me gently. "Alice has nothing to do with what you're going to write."

"Not even if what happened to her kept you from walking the beach?"

"It wasn't wholly that. There were many complexities. And of course it didn't stop me altogether. It was just that I didn't want to go in the ocean for a while, or walk its shores when there were people around. I took my walks by moonlight, or at dawn. Nan wouldn't know about that."

Nan had not been mentioned in this connection, but Judith had guessed without my speaking her name that she was my informant. Always she was a woman of sensibility, as I was beginning to realize, and not one to be easily fooled. Yet I was here in what was still her house, and I didn't think she knew as yet about my real identity, or my possible connection with the Rhodeses. I had a strong conviction that Stacia and John were keeping such information strictly to themselves.

"Don't you tire of painting the same subjects over and over?" I asked. "Don't you have any urge to go where there are fresh scenes that might appeal to you?"

"Natural things are safer. Sometimes dangerous in their own way, but more to be trusted than people. However, I was painting human figures in that boat picture I've been working on. Unless a boat is a derelict—and I've painted a lot of those—there has to be a man at the tiller."

I left my place and went to where the easel stood with her current canvas upon it. Even though the painting was unfinished, perhaps it would tell me more than my previous casual glance had revealed. But when I came close to it, I stopped with a gasp of astonishment and looked back at the woman who sat so serenely in her chair, a light smile touching her lips as she watched me. Then I looked more closely at the canvas to make sure what I'd seen was really true. With some brilliant blue pigment an angry hand had brushed across boat, vague human figures, and stormy sea again and again, so that the painting was covered by defacing slashes of blue.

"Why?" I said. "Who did this?"

She shook her head at me, laughing softly. "No—it's not what you think. Stacia hasn't been up here messing around. I just got upset with what I was doing and vented my own annoyance. It's all right—I've recovered. Do you know—that's a picture I've never finished painting. I've tried it again and again. I've wanted to paint it—perhaps as a vindication—an answer to what people have whispered about me. Perhaps as a sort of defense."

It was disturbing to have this evidence that the serenity that seemed her most assured characteristic could break apart in so destructive a manner. I had to seek the reason.

"Does this scene you try to paint represent the time when Alice's baby was—was lost at sea?" I asked carefully.

"Yes. But as I say, I've never been able to finish painting it."

"Why not?"

"Because it's a lie," she said quietly. "Because the baby wasn't lost at sea and I'll never try to put up that defense again. It's perfectly possible that she's still alive and grown to womanhood by this time."

Unable to say anything, I returned to sit opposite her, waiting for her to go on. But apparently she had nothing more to add.

"Why did you tell me this now?" I asked.

"Because you're a reporter, and because the time has nearly come to tell the true story."

It was difficult to keep my voice steady and unshaken. "What is the true story?"

She only shook her head, the light smile curving her lips. "It's not quite time yet. I'm not sure when it will be."

Was I wrong about her not knowing who I was? I wondered. Had Stacia come to her with the truth about me, after all? Yet I didn't think so. I couldn't believe that she had any idea of my true identity, and I wondered what would happen if I pulled the little unicorn out and showed it to her. The temptation to do that very thing was strong, but I resisted it. Other moods could strike this woman—I had glimpsed some of them—and I didn't trust this new, open attitude of coming out to tell me some long-concealed "truth" at this late date. When it came to motivation, I did not understand Judith Rhodes at all, so it was better to hold something back and not play all my cards into her hands.

Someone rapped at the attic door and Judith turned alertly. "There! That's Evan now," she said, and bent toward me. "He's come for you, Courtney. We're going to stop Stacia! Between you and me and Evan, we're going to make it certain that she never tries to sell this house!"

She left me completely astonished, and flew down the

long room to the door. When she had slid back the bolt, Evan came into the room, and looked at once to where I was sitting, his attitude questioning.

"I've told her everything!" Judith cried. "And she's going with you. I know she'll help in any way she can. Run along, Courtney. And don't worry at all—everything will be fine!"

10

Judith's voice commanded me, and there was a pressure of will behind it. As I rose in bewilderment and started slowly down the attic toward the two near the door, I could feel my resistance rising. I had no idea what she was up to, and I suspected that she might be fooling Evan as well as me—certainly the "everything" she was supposed to have told me had little to do with the actual facts.

Evan waited expectantly, his look still questioning. He too knew better than to accept everything Judith said at face value. She might be known for her open telling of the blunt truth, but she was also a mistress of indirection.

"In the first place," I said, "I haven't the faintest idea what Judith is talking about. She has told me nothing specific, so I'm completely at sea about what you expect of me. Or where we're going, to accomplish what."

Evan's sigh bespoke exasperation as he shook his head at Judith. "Is this a railroading job you've done on Courtney?"

Judith slipped an arm about me as casually as though we were on terms of old and intimate friendship. "Of course not. You *must* help us, Courtney. You must help us all save The Shingles. That's what I'm asking of you.

You can do it so easily, and think what a good story it will make. Much more dramatic than anything you could write about Judith Rhodes, the painter. Though of course it does concern me as an artist, since I could never work again if I had to leave here."

"We need to start," Evan said to me. "We have an appointment to make and the time is short. If you'll come along, you can decide later what you want to do. Judith's tactics are sometimes imaginative short cuts, but they can work. Will you come?"

I could see where Stacia might get some of her own tendency to fantasize, but I was too much the reporter to refuse this opportunity, even if the means had been a bit high-handed. I stepped back from Judith's touch and met the bright green look she gave me.

"We'll talk again," I promised her dryly, and followed Evan out the door.

In the garage area, I saw that a kennel had been placed for Tudor, so that he was now secured by a sturdy chain —undoubtedly a concession made for my benefit. The dog stood up when we appeared, but, recognizing Evan, he offered no outburst.

"It's not far," Evan said, when we'd settled into the front seat of his station wagon. "I'm glad you're willing to come."

"I'm thoroughly confused," I told him as he turned the car onto the driveway. "I don't understand what this is all about."

"I don't wonder. To put it simply, we don't want to see Stacia carry out her present plans. This is a possible way of stopping her. And Judith is right in saying that it might make very good material for you to write about. I wish that she had told you the whole story herself, but since she hasn't, I hope you'll go along and listen to whatever develops."

"But I need some sort of clue," I protested. "What are you up to?"

"You might call it blackmail," he said.

"Blackmail! You and Judith?"

"In a way, I suppose we'd like to blackmail a blackmailer."

"You mean those letters that have been coming to the house are a sort of blackmail? Do you know who is sending them and why?"

"Not necessarily the letters. It's another little tactic—though the letters may be part of it. We haven't all the answers yet."

"Does Herndon know about this? Know what you're planning?"

"Not yet. Judith hasn't been able to bring herself to tell him. That's why she's asked me to help her."

"I can understand that," I said wryly. "I would hate to confess to my husband that I'd been living a lie for all these years. Especially when I had a reputation for directness and honesty."

He gave me a look in which there was no approval. "I suppose you're too young to have learned generosity."

Both look and words made me bristle. "How can anyone be generous with nothing to base generosity on?"

"Perhaps it's a quality that must be present before all the facts are in."

After that there was silence for a time, and I felt chastened and uncertain, yet at the same time rebellious. He didn't know *all* the truth, and in spite of his fine words, Evan Faulkner had not been notably generous toward me. Nor had I any valid reason which I could so far understand to be generous toward any of the Rhodes, whether the facts were in or not. All I knew for certain was that almost anything I did or said seemed to irritate and provoke this man. And I wished it weren't so. Against all reason, I envied Judith her champion, and that in itself was a disturbing and unacceptable thought.

When he spoke again, it seemed that he had reconsidered and intended to give me a little more to go on.

"I don't know all the details about what Judith did with Alice's baby," he admitted. "Or why she did whatever it was. But until I do know, I'd like to give her the benefit of the doubt. There may have been some necessity to get the child away."

"Judith doesn't always play fair," I said. "I never know what turn she may take against me. How can I be generous where I don't trust?"

He made no comment. By this time we were following Montauk Highway, running east through little towns that bordered the ocean. In one such village we turned off onto a narrow country road that ran between potato fields.

"I'll give you a little quick background," Evan said. "The woman we're going to see has been out of the area for a long while. She has apparently come back in order to stir up trouble, and she's staying here with a friend from the old days when she used to live in East Hampton."

"Who is she?" I asked.

"Her name is Olive. Olive Asher. She is William Asher's first wife and she used to live with him at The Shingles until they had a falling out and were divorced."

All my interest and attention quickened. The name "Olive" had been tantalizing me and I felt suddenly eager for the encounter ahead. When Evan drew the car up before a small cottage with a rose trellis over the porch, I got out quickly.

The woman who answered his ring had a thoroughly dejected look about her, as well as an air of uneasiness that was almost palpable. She wore dark slacks and a gray shirt over a dumpy figure that bulged in the wrong places, and her gray hair had the fuzzy look of a too-tight permanent.

"I thought you were coming alone," she said without greeting.

"This is Miss Marsh, who is staying with the Rhodes just now. I asked her to come here with me."

Olive Asher gave me a suspicious look, but when Evan walked past her into the house and I followed, she pulled the door shut behind me and waved us into a small sitting room.

"I'm staying here with Mrs. Blake," she said, "and she's out for a little while. We have to finish before she returns because she doesn't know anything about my—uh—affairs."

"Then let's get to the point as quickly as possible," Evan said. Since our hostess was apparently not going to invite us to sit down, he stood beside the small fireplace, with an elbow on the mantel, while I remained near the door. "Mrs. Rhodes has asked me to tell you that you are to stop making phone calls to the house. I have already asked you not to, and I have told you that any calls that come in will be transferred to me, so that you won't be able to annoy her again."

"Annoy her?" The dumpy little woman stood in the middle of the floor with her arms folded and spite in her eyes. "Maybe she's got it coming to be annoyed!"

"If you feel that way, why have you waited all this time to come here and bother her?"

"I'm hard up now—see? For a long time she made it worth my while to keep still. But now she's stopped sending what she owes me, and I'm not going to stand for it."

"What do you plan to do?"

"Talk—that's what! Unless she catches up on what she owes me. We had an understanding—her and me, way back when it began. She didn't pay me all that much to keep still, you know. But I've never been greedy. It was all right to send something every few months. Only she's stopped altogether now, and that's not fair. I have to protect my own interests, don't I?"

Evan regarded her with distaste. "When you say you're going to talk, just what do you mean?"

Her elbows waggled defiantly. "Maybe I'll go to Mr. Herndon. Or maybe to Mr. John. They never knew—they never knew anything. And after all, it was Mr. John's baby. Could be I'll even go to the police."

"Admitting that you were an accessory?"

"Accessory to what?"

"Kidnaping, perhaps."

She refused to be cowed. "You're bluffing. She don't want all this coming out in the open. You can't tell me! The police would still be interested, what with all this money coming to Mrs. Judith's daughter—when it doesn't belong to her at all."

"Who do you think it belongs to?"

"Why to that baby of Mrs. Alice's and Mr. John's. The one I helped Mrs. Judith smuggle away to New York—so that it looked like it was lost by drowning that time in the storm. It's not so easy to hide a baby—she couldn't have managed without my help."

"So you really were an accessory?"

"I don't care what you call it. I'm not afraid of her—or of you either."

Evan looked at me. "I hope you're listening to all this, Miss Marsh."

I managed to nod. "I'm listening."

"Good," he said, "because I know you'll want to write the details into your story."

Until now, Olive Asher had ignored me, but at his words she swung around and stared at me balefully. "What are you talking about? What has she got to do with any of this?"

"She's a reporter, Olive, and she will be writing it all up in an article she's doing for a national magazine. So you see it won't be necessary to pay you for secrecy any more. It's all coming right out in print—probably with your name included. And if there's any further annoyance from you, we'll be the ones to tell our story to the police. They don't look kindly on blackmail."

Olive's knees must have been ready to give way, for she dropped into a chair and stared at Evan.

"I—don't understand. What are you talking about? Mrs. Judith never wanted any of this to be known."

"That's not true any longer, as you can see," Evan said. "She wants it all to be known. She wants to find out what has happened to that baby. She wants to find the woman she is now and bring her here. So you see there's nothing at all you can do to trouble her any longer."

"But then—then *her* daughter won't inherit. And the other one will. How can she want that?"

"It's exactly what she wants. The girl who should inherit Lawrence Rhodes' fortune is Alice's and John's daughter—Anabel Rhodes. We're going to find her and see that justice is done, even though it's pretty late in the day. Do you understand now, Olive?"

"But what about the police when they find out?"

"Someone has to bring charges, but I don't think John Rhodes will at this late date. Not against his sister-in-law."

"What about this girl, if you find her?"

"She'll probably be delighted to have a fortune fall into her lap. She's unlikely to cause any trouble."

Words were tumbling around in my mind, but I couldn't speak any of them.

Olive sat in the heap she'd fallen into, turning her head from side to side in bewilderment. "I don't understand— I don't understand at all."

"You will if you make one more move against Mrs. Rhodes. And there's another thing you can answer me. Have you been writing anonymous letters to the house?"

"Letters? Why would I write letters? I've been phoning ever since I got to town."

"I see." Evan turned back to me. "Would you like to ask Olive any questions, Miss Marsh? Perhaps you'll want to set down a few details about what happened more than twenty-five years ago."

My own legs were not too certain under me, but I managed to stay on them as I shook my head. "No, I haven't any questions." This wasn't true, but I couldn't ask them now—not with Evan listening.

We left her humped where she was and returned to Evan's car.

"Judith won't have any more trouble with her," he said as we got in.

"Does that mean it's only a bluff and that Judith isn't going through with this plan?"

"She has to go through with it in order to stop Stacia."

As he started the car I looked around carefully, noting the number of the house, noting the street sign when we pulled away. Because there was one thing I knew out of all my confusion—that I would come back to this place, that I would return alone to talk with Olive Asher. As we drove toward the highway, I found that my mouth was dry so that it was hard to form words.

"Why are you mixing into all this," I asked at last.

"I'd like to see the house kept in Herndon's hands. For Judith's sake."

"How can you want to help her when she's done this vicious thing?"

"How can you know the circumstances? How do you know it was vicious? What if it was for the child's own safety?"

"So that's what she told you? How can you believe anything she says under the circumstances? Stacia—" Now that my words had started, they were pouring out without control, but Evan broke in.

"I can't regard Stacia as a sympathetic authority on Judith. And you are hardly an authority at all," he said coldly.

"Because she has you all hypnotized—you and Herndon and even John!"

His sidelong look was more puzzled than angry. "Why are you so upset about this, Courtney? Why have you set yourself against Judith?"

I sank back in the front seat, trying to get myself in hand. "How do you know this imaginary heiress won't sell the house herself?" I managed to ask.

"In that case, it's likely that she'll sell it to Judith and Herndon—out of gratitude. Where Stacia only wants to injure."

"Anyway," I said dully, "you haven't found this woman yet."

I must have sounded odd, because he gave me another quick look. "No, that's truth. But just going to the authorities with the facts will cause any payment to Stacia to be postponed. That will give us time to find Anabel Rhodes. Even if she's using another name, it shouldn't be difficult once we put someone on the trail."

I could think of nothing more to say, and we were silent most of the way back to The Shingles. Not until we had turned into Ethan Lane did Evan speak again.

"It will be up to you, of course, Courtney, as to how much of this you want to publish. Judith says you must be given the choice, but mainly you were a threat to hold over Olive Asher's head. Even though Judith means to go to the authorities, it will be hard for her if you write it all up in print."

"I can see that she'll hope I won't publish what I've just learned," I said dryly.

"I think Judith has suffered enough." His tone was quiet and reproving. "She's carried a load of guilt all these years. Nevertheless, she's putting no restrictions upon you. You can do as you please. Judith says she doesn't care any more."

"I don't know if she could ever suffer enough for what she did," I said.

"That's a harsh judgment."

"I was thinking of the child. Taken from her parents, given to strangers—"

"Alice was dead, and the child was only two months old. I'm not condoning what Judith did, but I don't think she should go on paying for it forever."

"I don't think you know anything about it."

"At least I know when I've trodden on a sensitive nerve —even though I don't understand why you're taking offense."

I knew I must be careful, lest I blurt out more than I wanted him to know. There was still a choice left to me— the choice of flight.

"Why *did* she do it?" I asked. "Why would Judith do such a thing?"

"I'm not altogether sure, since this is a question she won't answer, except in hints. There's the obvious reason, of course—that she knew she was going to have Herndon's baby and she wanted her child to inherit. But I have a feeling there was more to it than that. Something more complex."

Evan was no different from other men. Judith could put her spell on all of them, make them believe what she wanted them to believe.

"What will Herndon say?"

"He'll be upset, but he'll back Judith in the end. He always has."

"Then why did she come to you for help instead of going to her husband?"

"I've told you that. It's not going to be an easy thing to tell Herndon. And I've been close to Stacia. I know her. Her reaction is likely to be violent, and I need to be prepared."

I moved away from the thought of Stacia's violence. "What about John's reaction—since it was his child she smuggled away?"

"That's a question I can't answer."

"Isn't the biggest unknown quantity the girl you haven't found? What if she doesn't want to be an heiress?"

"That's unlikely, don't you think? In any case, she won't have much to say about it, once the law takes over."

"Why should she inherit instead of Stacia?"

"That has to do with the wording of the will, I understand."

We had reached the house, and afternoon shadows were lengthening. I felt increasingly cold—cold and a little sick—and my leg was aching. When Evan stopped the car, I sat for a few minutes without moving. What if I should tell him the whole thing right now? But I shrank from so irrevocable a step. As long as he and Judith didn't know, I could play for time—find out what I must do.

He didn't open the car door at once, and I became aware that he was looking at me strangely, as he'd done once or twice this afternoon, and the harshness he so often showed me was gone.

"What's troubling you, Courtney?"

"I—I don't know. I don't even know who I am any more, or what I want. Though I'm sick of people who think they have to search for an identity, and I don't *want* to be one of those. By the time a woman is twenty-five she ought to know enough about herself to be sure of what she wants."

"Not necessarily." Evan's tone was not unkind. "Maturing can be a long process."

I looked at him—straight at him. Into dark eyes that so often concealed what he was thinking and turned a defensive shield toward the world. Had his years with Stacia given him that look?

"Was it a long process for you?" I asked.

There seemed a difference in him that was almost a gentling as his eyes met my own.

"Some people are forced to it when they're very young," he said.

I nodded. "I'm still trying. Sometimes when you're on a treadmill you don't even know it. Until you tumble off. Then you can get badly bruised."

"What do you think you want from life, Courtney Marsh?"

The simple words carried an unexpected tenderness of tone, as though he had come out of all that remoteness that was his usual state, and was reaching toward me in a human way. I found the change both comforting and a little frightening. Frightening because of my own inner response and a desire to reach out to him that might be dangerous. Along that path lay rapids.

"I don't know what I want any more," I told him. "It's just that everything I was doing in New York suddenly became meaningless. I'd always known that a lot of it was artificial, but somehow I never got a real look at what I was becoming until the night of that Winser talk show. Then I didn't like what I saw. Now I don't know what I can put in its place."

"You're on the road to finding out, I think." He touched my hand—a light, reassuring touch, and I was all too aware of him close beside me. What would happen if I turned my own hand and clung to his? I had never needed anyone to hold onto before, but I did now. Yet there was nothing that could be said between us and I was silent, neither turning my hand nor drawing it away.

"We'll talk again, Courtney," he said, and I heard the promise in his words. The time was not ripe for either of us. Whatever current had leapt so unexpectedly between us had come too soon, and I think in that moment we both drew back. We were still capable of caution. Something had happened—and we knew that too—but we both stepped back.

"Thanks for coming with me," he said quietly. "Judith will be grateful. Don't judge her too harshly, Courtney."

He left the car and came around to open my door, and as I got out Tudor growled. Evan spoke to him and he subsided, but I gave the kennel a wide berth as we moved toward the house. When Evan started up the steps, I left, almost in flight, and walked around to the front terrace. To go inside, to face any of them right now was the last thing I wanted. On the terrace I ran toward the steps and hurried down—hurried so that no one could stop me, or even speak to me.

It was a relief to find the long stretch of sand empty and marked by few footprints, a relief to have ocean and sky to myself. Ahead of me two or three sandpipers ran away down the beach and I saw that the sky had begun to gray with coming evening, and clouds hid the sunset. Soon it would be time to go in for dinner, and I knew I should go to my room and change. But all I wanted was to stop the churning that had begun inside me, stirring up the wrong sort of emotion, scattering my thoughts helplessly, plunging me into a confusion that I didn't know how to straighten out.

One bit at a time—I must take only one bit at a time, I told myself. I wasn't as cold, now that I could walk briskly, ignoring the twinges in my leg. At my feet the rhythmic movement of the waves curling in soothed and quieted me a little. It was possible to stare out at the far, murky horizon and cease to think at all, cease to strive inwardly, giving myself up to the vastness all around that told me I didn't really matter, that nothing was real or important, and I needn't do anything.

But I couldn't escape into that nirvana for long. Sooner or later I had to think. Less than ever was there any loophole for doubt. I was Alice's and John's daughter and Stacia's cousin, and both Stacia and John knew it and were keeping silent. With good reason, as I could see. I didn't want to be Anabel Rhodes and have a fortune that was being held in trust dumped upon my defenseless shoulders. Money wasn't what life was all about. That much I knew. I had the things I wanted—the things I'd *thought* I wanted, though I was no longer sure about any of them.

There was an even worse aspect to all this because Judith meant to use that child she had given away—a child-grown-into-woman—to further her own desire to stop Stacia from coming into Lawrence's money. I didn't want to be caught in the middle, to become Judith's pawn, even though Evan Faulkner might think she was right and Stacia wrong.

Before long, the search would begin, and it would be far easier to find me than it had been for me to find the Rhodes. The law would be involved now, and it would batter down doors, push through all restraints in order to carry out impersonally the letter of a will made long ago. Even though Stacia and John might not speak out, I would be found. The trail would lead easily to Courtney Marsh, and then all the Rhodes and those connected to them would be furious with me for my masquerade, my pretense in coming here. I could well imagine how Evan would look at me then—and it would not be with tenderness.

In the meantime, what about Stacia—who knew my identity and was keeping silent? What did Stacia mean to do?

Suddenly, and without the slightest doubt, I knew my danger. Stacia was my enemy. There was something unbridled in her character, something disturbingly unbalanced, and I could easily see her at the wheel of the Mercedes, trying to run me down. She too would know the truth about the legacy Lawrence Rhodes had left, and she would know that the money might come to me—something she would never permit, if she could help it.

I shivered, thinking of the times I had been alone with her, realizing the threat she meant to me. I must go away, go quickly back to New York, where I could be safe from all the Rhodes for a little while longer, until I could decide what I must do before they came for me. My role was that of a fleeing prisoner, whether I liked it or not. So I must leave soon. Tomorrow, if I could. But first I would go back to see Olive Asher before she left town. There was more I wanted to know concerning what had happened during that time out near Montauk, and since Olive had played an active role, she was the one who could answer my questions. Perhaps she could even tell me more about my mother. Out of all this, there was only the one comfort for me—that Alice had wanted her baby daughter, had loved her, named her, valued her—no matter what anyone might say. I hadn't been an unloved discard, after all.

The one thought I put aside was that of Evan. What had happened—or nearly happened—between us just now in the car was something I could not, dared not, examine.

When I turned and walked back toward the house, I saw lights in the living room and dining room, and in some of the bedrooms upstairs. An unexpected regret ran through me at the thought of leaving The Shingles. Because my father was still in that house—a man who had been kind to me, perhaps unable to reach out to me, but with whom I might have found a closer relationship if given time. That was over now.

My steps slowed as I reached the foot of the wooden flight up to the terrace, and the thought of Evan was suddenly there, refusing to be denied. When I left here I would never see him again. Currents of attraction, however strong, die quickly when there is no further fuel to feed them. Evan belonged to Stacia. Even I, who was an outsider, had seen the bond between them. Old responsibilities could bind as strongly as love, and old passions of love and hate. Perhaps he would never be free of Stacia—and if ever he was, he would undoubtedly thank his good fortune to be free of all women and not seek some new entanglement. She had already damaged him.

My thoughts were depressed, futile, unlike me, and I felt impatient with myself and a little angry. Evan was nothing to me. That moment when I had wanted to turn my hand in his was ridiculous and didn't fit in with my conviction that attraction was never blind. You went into something with your eyes open, not with the helplessness of a schoolgirl.

From its place on the sand, the weathered figurehead stared at me with sightless eyes, its woman's breasts lifted to meet the raging elements of sea and storm. For a moment I stood still, returning that strange look that had seen so much. Hesther. Had she seen death at sea?

I thought again of answers to Alice's death, answers which were coming close to me. Had my mother been forewarned? Had anyone been watching when Alice died? Alice, who had been a good swimmer, yet had drowned mysteriously and been tumbled onto the sand by rolling Atlantic waves. My mother. What else did Judith have on her conscience besides what she had done with Alice's baby? Alice had been John's wife, and at one time, if what Stacia said was true, Judith had been in love with John.

I thought again of Judith's strange inference that giving the baby away might have spared it in some way. But who would have harmed a child? Judith could be the first choice for such a role. John was the child's father and could only have gained by having the baby live. Herndon? But of course not Herndon. And there was no point in considering Nan at all.

In any case, all this was long ago, and such speculation had little bearing on my life today. Better to stop the fruitless seeking for answers. *Unless.* Unless Olive Asher knew more about that time than she had originally revealed.

My walk on the beach had not calmed me. I touched the figurehead lightly on one cheek and turned to climb the steps. Feeling as though I'd been tossed by the same buffeting storms that had bruised Hesther, I went into the house. Anyone else in the world—almost anyone else— would be happy over the prospect of inheriting a fortune. But all I wanted was escape, and the opportunity to stay alive.

In the hallway, I met Asher hurrying to meet me.

"You're wanted on the phone, Miss Marsh," he told me, and something in his look alerted me—something both uneasy and suspicious. The library was empty and I went into it to take the call. The voice that answered my "hello" had a faint whine to it, and I understood Asher's look. He had recognized the woman who was calling me.

"Yes, Olive," I said, "this is Courtney Marsh."

"I need to talk to you." The whine became urgent. "If you're going to write all that stuff for your magazine, then you ought to know more about what happened."

"I'd already thought of that," I told her. "When can I see you?"

"You'd better make it soon. I can't stay around here. Can you come tonight?"

"I'll come after dinner," I said. "Around eight o'clock?"

"That'll be okay," she agreed, and rang off.

I stood for a moment longer with my hand on the telephone before I became aware that Asher had remained in the doorway, waiting.

"If you please, Miss Marsh," he said. "I know who that was. She's called here several times lately and she's up to no good. If I may say so, miss, I wouldn't go to see her as she wants."

I tried to smile at him reassuringly. "I understand, Asher. But I have to see her. There's nothing else I can do."

"Then take somebody from the house with you, miss. That woman isn't a good person. *I* know."

"I do understand," I repeated. "And perhaps I will take someone with me. Thank you for warning me."

He went off down the hall shaking his head, and I hurried upstairs to change for dinner, already a little late. It might be wise to heed his warning and find someone to go with me. Not anyone from the house—perhaps Nan Kemble, since I could trust her more than any of the others. She was tied into this through her sister and she should be willing to go with me. The thought of Nan was reassuring. I needn't tell her everything yet, and I didn't think she would ask. But at least with her along, I wouldn't have to face Olive alone. If necessary, she could wait out in the car for me so as not to throw Olive off whatever it was she wanted to talk about.

Dinner that night was a strange meal. For once, Judith came downstairs, and so did Stacia, the mark on her cheek turning a bit yellow. I could see that John watched Stacia unhappily, but for the moment he had lost any control he might have had over her, and she seemed bent on tormenting Judith all through the meal. Herndon tried to stop her once or twice, but she paid no attention, and I could sense a smoldering in him beneath his quiet exterior. I thought again of the possible complexities in Herndon Rhodes. Evan seemed preoccupied and gave his attention to the meal, ignoring us all, including Stacia.

Judith was as serene as ever, as though Stacia were no more than a naughty child. Her own purpose was already set and nothing could deflect her. The others attempted conversation to minimize Stacia's efforts, and eventually the unhappy meal was over. All that came out of it for me was a further determination to get away. I had no place here, yet I didn't want to tell anyone I was leaving until the last moment, lest some effort be made to interfere with my escape. "Escape" had become a truer word than I liked to think.

As quickly as I could after dinner, I went up to my room and put on my coat. Then I walked to the far end of the hall, where a flight of back stairs would take me down to a rear door, enabling me to slip out of the house without being seen. Or so I hoped.

As I walked through a darkness outdoors that lacked moon or stars, my way guided only by lights from the house, music came floating out from the living-room windows. Stacia was at the piano again, playing one of her disturbingly dissonant compositions—music that could cling to the memory with an unwelcome haunting. I would be glad to escape that sound too, as well as all the rest, and yet there was a strange loneliness in me at the thought of such escape. A loneliness I couldn't accept, and which did not bear too close an examining at the moment.

The garage area was quiet and empty, with a single light burning over the central door. Tudor stood up restlessly as I appeared, but this time he neither barked nor strained at his chain, but simply watched as I went toward my car and got in.

In Nan's shop lights were burning downstairs as I pulled up beside the door. For once, however, the shop was locked, and though I pounded the brass knocker no one answered. It was my bad luck to find Nan out, but that wasn't going to stop me. In spite of Asher's warning, I would not turn back. This was my one chance to see Olive Asher again, and I didn't mean to pass it up.

Even at night I was able to find my way, having noted the turnoff from the highway earlier, and because a helpful light had been left burning on the porch when I drew up before the house I had already visited. However, it was not Olive who opened the door, but a tall, rather gaunt woman, perhaps in her seventies, whom I took to be Olive's friend Mrs. Blake.

She stood in the doorway, not inviting me in. "Olive's gone," she told me curtly. "She's been called away. She said to tell you she was sorry, but she couldn't see you after all."

I had the sense of a sand castle crumbling in upon itself—as though someone had put out a deliberate finger, so that a structure I had built and counted upon had collapsed and left me with nothing.

Helplessly, I stood staring at the woman in the doorway, not knowing which way to turn.

11

Mrs. Blake's words had been a sharp disappointment, even though I wasn't sure why I had set any value on this meeting with Olive Asher.

"Is she coming back?" I asked after a surprised pause. "Do you know why she's gone away?"

The woman shook her head. "She had a telephone call a little while ago that made her very excited. She packed up right away and then a car came to take her to the station to catch the train. You didn't miss her by much."

I tried to make my tone casual. "Do you happen to know who was in the car?"

"It was none of my business, was it?" Mrs. Blake regarded me in disapproval.

"When does the train for New York leave?" I asked.

But she either wouldn't tell me, or didn't know, and it took a few minutes to pry out of her the information that it was a train that left from East Hampton.

I ran to my car and drove back to the highway, pushing the Volvo whenever there was a clear stretch of pavement. I didn't know why I was driven by this sense of urgency, but only that a chance was slipping away from me that might never come again. I had to make this last effort to retrieve what otherwise might be lost for good.

The train was braking into the station when I pulled up to park my car. I got out and ran toward the platform. Olive Asher, suitcase in hand, mounted the steps of a car ahead. Though I glanced around hurriedly, there was no one on the platform whom I recognized. If whoever had brought her here still lingered, he was keeping out of sight. Since there was no time to buy a ticket, I ran up the steps after her and followed her into a smoking car. A few people had come between us, but I recognized her gray head at the window side of a seat ahead. Quietly I sat down beside her and she didn't even glance my way, her attention on a packet of cigarettes she was fumbling from her handbag. I waited until the train had pulled out of the station on its journey to New York, and then spoke to her in a low voice.

"Hello, Olive. I'm glad I was able to catch you."

Her astonishment was evident as she dropped her cigarettes. I bent to pick up the pack and when I handed it to her she gave me a look of sheer misery. My presence had upset her more than a little.

"I really did want to talk to you," I said, "and I thought you wanted to talk to me."

When she had struck a faltering match and drawn in a long breath, she managed to find her voice.

"That's not necessary any longer, miss. Something unexpected's come up and everything's changed."

"Can you tell me what it is?"

She shook her head vigorously. "No—I don't want to talk about it. I don't want to talk to you."

"Because you've been told to keep still, told not to talk to me? Threatened, perhaps?"

She shrugged and stared out the window.

"I expect whoever it was made up for Judith's lapse in payments—isn't that so?"

This time I'd reached her. "Look, miss—you're a reporter and I don't have to talk to you."

"But earlier—"

"Earlier I didn't know this was going to happen."

I could see the possibilities. She had probably thought

she could get something out of me for whatever details she felt she had to sell. But someone else had cut in and outbid me—generously enough to send her quickly out of town.

"Did Mr. Faulkner drive you to the train?" I asked.

"Mr. Faulkner? No." She relaxed a little. "No, it was William who came for me. It seemed odd seeing him after all these years. He looks like an old man, for sure. What's his new wife like, miss? I suppose she's working at the house in my old place?"

"She's the housekeeper, yes." I answered absently, thinking about Asher as the mysterious messenger and wondering which one of them had been alarmed enough to send him.

"You're not going clear in to New York, are you, miss?" she asked.

The conductor had come around for tickets and I inquired about a stop two towns west on the line and paid my fare. When I looked at her again, I saw that she had cheered up a little. At least she knew now that she wouldn't have my company much longer—and I knew that if I was to get anything out of her, it would have to be fast.

"Of course," I began, "I'm willing to pay a little something for answers to my questions. . . ."

But she was already shaking her head. "I'm not going to talk. I'm not going to tell you anything."

"What difference can it make?" I pressed her. "This will be just a little extra for you, and no harm done. No one will ever know."

She was silent, and I tried to think of a possible question to start her talking.

"I suppose you went out to that cottage in Montauk at the time when Mrs. Rhodes—Mrs. Alice Rhodes—returned from her trip abroad?"

Apparently this seemed safe enough, and she nodded. "Yes, I used to help Mrs. Alice a lot in the old days, and she knew I was good with babies. So she sent for me before she got back in the country. In fact, I met her and Miss Nan in New York and went up to the cottage with them. Miss Nan was going on to San Francisco and Mrs. Alice didn't want to stay there alone with the baby to care for."

"You must have been a great help to her. But she didn't have to be alone for long, did she? I understand that Mr. Lawrence Rhodes sent both his sons and Mrs. Judith up there to take hold of the situation."

"That's right. He wanted Mrs. Alice and the baby home right away."

"Wasn't the baby sick?"

"Just a little cold—nothing more. Such a sweet little thing she was, and the image of Mrs. Alice."

"It must have been terrible for you when Alice was drowned, and not even her sister was there."

"Miss Nan? Oh, she was still around. She'd moved out of the cottage, but she hadn't gone away yet. I saw her myself the day it happened. They sent me downtown for something, and I saw her in the drugstore. She didn't know about her sister then, but before I could get over to her she went off, and I couldn't catch her. I didn't know she was flying out to San Francisco that very day. Nobody knew where to reach her for a while, and I always blamed myself for not getting hold of her that morning. She and her sister had a bang-up fight earlier, and I'll bet she felt bad about it later."

"A fight? What about?"

"I couldn't hear the words—just the way they yelled at each other. Miss Nan followed her right down to the beach where Mrs. Alice went swimming. But after a while when I looked out the window—because Mrs. Alice wanted me to keep an eye out for her—Miss Nan was gone and Mrs. Alice was swimming out there alone."

"If she was such a good swimmer, why did she want to have you keep an eye out, as you say?"

The woman beside me threw a quick, frightened glance in my direction and then stared out the window, drawing heavily on her cigarette. "I don't want to talk any more. It's all too upsetting. It was the worst time I ever lived through, miss."

"What did you see, Olive?" I asked softly. "What did you really see out there on the beach that morning?"

She answered almost frantically. "Nothing—nothing! I was in a back room looking after the baby. I didn't see a thing."

"But you know something, don't you? Something you've kept to yourself all these years?"

"Go away," she said. "Stop bothering me. I don't know anything!"

"But you knew about the baby. You helped Mrs. Judith when she wanted to pretend the baby had died. You've admitted that much."

"Sure. That's what she's been sending me little presents for. Because she was grateful to me for helping her."

"Only now she doesn't care any more if you talk about that. So what is it someone is paying you to keep still about?"

She gave me a quick, malicious look. "This is your station coming up, miss. And you might as well get off. Even if you stay aboard clear to New York, I won't say one word more. And that's that!"

This time I knew she meant it. There was nothing else to do, so I got off the train, found a taxi, and had myself driven back to my own car in East Hampton. All the way there I puzzled. Asher must have told someone that I was going to see Olive, so that person had phoned her, promised her an impressive enough sum of money, and then sent Asher to deliver it and get her aboard the train for New York. It could have been any of them, and I was no further ahead than if Olive had never come into the picture at all.

Though there was one thing that didn't fit. Although Olive claimed that Nan had still been in Montauk the day her sister had died, Nan herself had talked to me about that time as though she had been gone before the Rhodes had come out to take charge of Alice and the baby.

Discouragement had engulfed me by the time I'd paid off the taxi and was driving back to The Shingles through the lanes of East Hampton. It didn't matter, really, that I had learned nothing from Olive. All that mattered was that I must leave for home tomorrow and make it my business never to see any of the Rhodes family again. Let them hunt for me, if they must, but I would fight against accepting my grandfather's legacy. He didn't seem like a grandfather to me. It had all been far more disappointing to find out who I was than I had ever dreamed possible. Only now that it had happened, I couldn't erase what I knew about these people. Names and identities had entered my life that I would never be rid of. Not all of them my family. I had the depressing feeling that I would not quickly forget Evan Faulkner's face, or the way he walked and moved his dark head. I would remember the torment in his eyes that was beyond help from anyone. And I would carry for a long time the memory of his hand touching mine lightly. Stacia's husband. The last person to whom I wanted to be attracted in any way.

Lights still burned downstairs in Nan's shop when I went through the stone gateway, but this time I didn't stop. My headlights took the curving driveway ahead and I drove slowly. Never again would I follow this course toward the house in my car. Tomorrow I would drive away from it for the last time, and I would never return. Nothing could ever make me return. If the house came into my hands and I couldn't refuse it—I had no idea what the legal entanglements might be—I would give it to Judith and Herndon. It belonged to them.

Ahead, the high beam of my lights brought trees and undergrowth briefly to life as the car swung around a turn, then lighted the driveway straight ahead. Two people were walking there in the dark with only a flashlight to guide them, and I braked hurriedly. Nan Kemble and Herndon Rhodes stood full in the path of illumination. He drew her quickly to one side and I leaned out the window to greet them, though I didn't stop.

I heard Nan's voice call after me, and then I was approaching the house and I drove slowly across the bricks to the lighted apron, parked my car at the side where it would be out of the way, and sat for a moment staring up at the house above me. The thought had come to me again that everything I did was for the last time. In so short a while I had lived an eternity. This place and the people who lived here had become a part of my blood, of my experience, and a tie had been forged, whether I liked or trusted any of them or not. The new, strange sadness that seemed to pervade my thoughts grew from a feeling of what-might-have-been. If Alice hadn't died, and I had grown up with John as my father, if Judith hadn't taken steps to be rid of the baby . . . if, if, if!

But there was no point in sitting here brooding. I turned off the ignition and opened the door beside me. Across the brick paving the dog moved, stirred, growled. It was dark now, except for the light over the garage, and I had forgotten about Tudor. I was thankful indeed that he was chained near his kennel.

I must walk opposite him on the way to the steps, but at least I could give him a wide berth. I had taken only a few steps, however, before he began to bark furiously, straining at his chain, leaping against it, shattering my nerves. He had been willing to let me leave, but was unwilling to have me return. For just a moment I thought of running back to my car to get safely inside where I could shout for someone to come and quiet the dog. But that was foolish. He was chained and couldn't get at me, for all his leaping and striving.

Quietly, without hurry, I moved into the open. His barking grew more furious and suddenly I knew that its position had changed. The sound was between me and the walkway to the steps. The dog had moved—he was no longer chained.

I stood very still, and Tudor stopped where he was, still barking. I knew that if I took another step toward the safety of the house, he would be upon me. Slowly, carefully, I turned about to walk back to the car. I dared not hurry, dared not run, dared not scream, for fear of infuriating the dog. But now my car, only a few yards away, seemed miles out of reach. I took one step, then another. I'd begun to think I might make it, when I heard the click of his feet on brick, coming fast, and knew there was nothing I could do to save myself.

I did scream then, just as his weight struck me full in the back so that I was thrown to my knees and he was upon me, worrying my body like a rag. I felt his breath, the wetness of his tongue—and then pain in my arm. I tried to fight him off with my other hand, but he was a thousand times stronger than I, and in a moment I might have fainted from the hurt and left my face and throat unguarded, but in the distance I heard shouting and footsteps and I fought against the fog of unconsciousness as I couldn't fight the dog.

In a moment someone had pulled Tudor off me, someone else was struggling to restrain him, and I was picked up in Evan's arms and carried up the long steps and into the house. There was a sofa in an alcove in the back hall, and he laid me upon it gently. Behind him, orders were being given—that was Judith's voice calling for Helen Asher, and then Judith bending over me, examining my arm where blood came through the sleeve of my light coat. In the background I could hear John's angry voice.

"That chain was snapped! I just had a look at it and one of the links was damaged."

"You'll be all right now, Courtney," Evan said, smoothing the hair back from my forehead. His sympathy and the touch of his hand almost made me forget the pain that throbbed in my arm. I was dimly aware of faces looking down at me—they were all there, even Stacia and Nan and Herndon.

Judith said, "It's probably not bad. I think the coat sleeve protected her. Good, Helen—let me help you get her out of the coat."

Drawing my arm through the sleeve was painful, but my blouse had short sleeves and they didn't bother with that. I remembered my unicorn and was glad it hung at the back of my neck. Evan held me while they worked and I found comfort in leaning against him and letting everything go. I didn't want to think, I didn't want to understand—I just wanted to be, to stay there, protected.

"I'll let you take care of her, Helen, while I phone the doctor," Judith said. "Tudor's a healthy dog, but they'll want to treat the wound and give her tetanus shots, or whatever." She must have caught my look because she bent toward me again. "Courtney, I wouldn't have had this happen for anything. I thought Tudor was safe out there."

Beyond her Stacia said, "He's a guard dog. You can't blame him. That's what he's there for."

"Who put the chain on him?" John asked, still sounding angry. "Who last had a look at it?"

"It's an old one, sir," Asher said from the background. "It's been around in the garage for a while. Mr. Herndon fastened it on the dog."

"And it was in perfectly good shape when I put it on him," Herndon said. "I examined every link to make sure. Nan and I heard the dog barking, Courtney, but we were down the drive a way and couldn't get here quickly."

At his shoulder Nan regarded me anxiously, and I made a feeble effort to smile at them all. "I'll be all right. You came in time. Evan came in time."

He moved aside so that Mrs. Asher could work on my arm, and they all withdrew a little to talk among themselves, leaving me to whimper more privately. Helen Asher was doing what she knew how to do best, as a former nurse, and she worked with a competency that I'd never seen in her before, though at the same time I knew she was upset for her hands were trembling.

Judith came back just as Helen finished. "Dr. Grant will see you at his house. Will you take her in, please, Herndon?"

"I'll go along," Nan said.

I didn't want anyone but Evan, but he had risen to stand back and I saw dark anger in his eyes. I wouldn't think about that, or about what had made him angry, made John angry. I didn't want to think, but only to endure. At least I could walk now, and Herndon and Nan helped me down the steps and out to Herndon's car. Nan insisted that I lie down in the back seat with my head in her lap, while Herndon drove. She didn't try to soothe or reassure me, but she steadied me so that the movement of the car wouldn't jar my arm, and when we went into the doctor's office at the front of his house, she came with me.

Something about Nan tugged at my memory. Something that woman—Olive Asher—had said, but I didn't want to think about that either. At least she was kind and careful with me, and I couldn't believe that she meant me any harm.

The wound was not serious, the doctor said—punctures, rather than tears. I would have a sore arm for a few days, and I'd better not drive. When I'd been properly disinfected, bandaged, and given a booster shot, Nan walked me back to the car, where Herndon waited. Now I was able to sit up in the front seat, while Nan remained in back.

For the first time since they'd come to my help, I really looked at Herndon and saw the pallor of his face. But I didn't want to know why he looked so pale, or why Evan had seemed so angry, and John had gone shouting around. In my mind I had slammed a door upon something I wasn't yet ready to face—Tudor and the broken link in his chain. It distracted me now to talk a little, until the pain capsules the nurse had given me began to work. I turned in the front seat to look back at Nan.

"I tried to catch you this evening," I said, "but you must have been out."

"I'm sorry I missed you," Nan said. "Was there something you wanted?"

"I'd hoped you might come with me when I went to see Olive Asher."

There was a brief silence in the car and then Nan spoke to Herndon. "Did the others know she was back in town?"

"Of course," Herndon said. "We all knew. Asher recognized her voice on the phone, and when he learned that Courtney was going to look her up, he warned us. But by that time it was too late to stop her. Why did you go to see her, Courtney?"

"Evan took me there this afternoon, but I thought there was more she might talk about alone. So after dinner I drove to where she was staying."

There was a moment's silence in the car and Herndon turned his head briefly to glance at me.

"Did you think she might be of help in writing about Judith?" he asked.

"I didn't know, but I wanted to find out."

"And what did you learn?"

"Nothing. Someone else got to her first and bribed her to get out of town. She had left for the train by the time I got there."

Nan's gasp was soft, half suppressed, and it seemed to me that the man beside me relaxed a little. But I had to go on.

"I caught her train before it pulled out of East Hampton,

and I rode with her for a few stations. But she told me very little." I meant to say nothing about my knowledge of the baby.

"When I came back from San Francisco," Nan said softly, "no one would talk very much about Alice's death."

Herndon's silence seemed repressive.

"Never mind." Nan sighed. "It's all over and done with years ago. I don't want to know any more than I've heard already. In this case it's better to be an ostrich. I recommend the example to you, Courtney. It's safer and more comfortable." Her voice sounded hard, as though the years had toughened her.

"I don't need the example," I assured her. "I'll probably go back to New York tomorrow. That is, if I can drive."

"You won't want to drive with your right arm in that condition," Herndon said.

For just a crack, I opened the door I had slammed in my own mind. "I think I had better go. Twice now someone has tried to kill me. I don't want to stay around with *my* head in the sand."

In the back seat Nan was very still, offering no argument, but offering no contradiction either. Herndon took a curve too sharply and the tires squealed.

After a long silence, Nan spoke. "Why would anyone want to hurt you, Courtney?"

But I couldn't tell them why unless I told them who I was and I wanted to keep that a secret from those in the house who still didn't know. If it *was* a secret.

"In this case," I said, "reasons aren't necessary. The fact of two attacks is enough for me."

Herndon had begun to look so ill that I put my hand on his arm. "Don't worry. I still want to write about Judith, but I won't put any of this into my story. Perhaps I have enough material to make up a piece by this time."

"Thank you," he said, but I heard the tightness in his voice.

When we reached the gatehouse, he stopped the car and opened the door for Nan.

"Thanks for coming to tell me about Olive," she said to him. "I'll phone tomorrow, Courtney, to know how you are. Come see me if you can, before you go back to New York."

We waited until Nan had used her key to go inside, and then drove up the high dune that led to the house. As we reached the parking area, I threw a quick look around, but Tudor's kennel was gone and the dog must have been fastened up somewhere else. When we got out of the car, Herndon stopped me for a moment at the foot of the steps.

"You needn't be worried," he said. "Nothing more of this kind will happen. I give you my promise."

I heard him, but I didn't trust him. I didn't trust anyone at all except Evan. Old Lawrence Rhodes had left his deadly stamp upon this family—he had conditioned them through the years to stand together, to protect one another, to protect the family name. They were still doing just that, and even now there would be a subtle banding together against me. Related or not, I would always remain the outsider, to be regarded askance because of the weapon of publicity I held in my hands. John might be angry, Herndon might be perturbed, and Judith indignant, but not one of them would accuse Stacia or expose what she had done. The door was fully open now. I knew who had broken the link in that chain, and I knew why.

"Thank you," I told Herndon, but I didn't meet his eyes as I turned away and went up the steps to the door, where Asher was waiting to let us in.

John and Judith came together from the living room to meet us, but Evan wasn't around, and Stacia did not appear. Herndon assured them quickly that my arm would be fine, and that all I needed now was to get to bed and have a good night's sleep. There was an instant in which the three exchanged a look, and now my senses were wide awake enough so that I caught the exchange. They might be sorry I had been hurt, but they were still bound together to protect their own, just as I had thought.

When I started toward the stairs, Judith came with me and put an arm about my shoulders. "I'll see you up to your room," she said.

I looked past her, straight at John, who might be my father. But though he knew this, he was no good to me now. He turned from what must have been an entreaty in my eyes, accepting no responsibility, in spite of his earlier anger—perhaps unable to accept such responsibility. I felt a little sorry for him, but I couldn't reach him, and I knew it.

When he spoke it was to Herndon. "Evan's outside seeing to the dog. The kennel's been set away from the house, and Evan will take care that he's tied up safely."

"There aren't any words to say how sorry we are," Judith told me.

She probably meant it at this moment, I thought, and started up the stairs. Olive had said that as a baby I had looked like Alice. I was glad that Judith was not my mother. There had been times when she had fascinated me, times when I'd even thought I might give her a certain affection—but she was Stacia's mother. All three of them were bound together by a love for Stacia, no matter how furious she might make them at times. All I hoped for now was that I needn't see my cousin again before I left the house tomorrow.

Judith came upstairs with me, and I noted in surprise that a cot had been set outside my door, and inside the room Helen Asher was turning down my bed.

"We aren't going to leave you alone tonight, Courtney," Judith said. "Helen will sleep right beside your door. You may be in pain, or you may want something during the night, and she will be here to look after you."

I thanked her soberly, refused an offer of help to get into my nightgown, and waited until both women were gone from my room. No one was really worried about what I might want in the night. Helen was intended solely as a guard to keep the one they feared away from me.

My cousin Stacia.

What a lovely family I had inherited, I thought as I began to undress gingerly. I could feel homesick now for my *real* parents who had adopted and loved me all my life. How foolish I had been to come on this quest—to seek a goal that could only turn out in a disappointing fashion. Only Evan had come out of this experience as something that might have been. And I dared not remember Evan.

The thought of Alice was all I could cling to as I got into bed and eased myself down in a position that would disturb my bandaged arm the least. My leg, which had been hurt by the car, was nothing by comparison. I could forget it. I wished that I could have known Alice. Wished that Olive Asher had told me more about her. Before I left this house I must read further in those stories for children that she had written. Perhaps they could bring me a little closer to her. And perhaps Nan could tell me more before I left. I already had a feeling that driving home tomorrow would be beyond me.

The capsules I'd been given helped me to drop into a deep and undisturbed sleep, in which I didn't seem to dream. But at some time in the middle of the night I came wide awake, and all the horror of that moment I had lived through when Tudor had hurled himself upon me came back in vivid detail, and I almost cried out in fresh terror. My arm had begun to throb and I knew that was what had awakened me. I looked at my watch and found that enough hours had passed so that I could take something more for the pain, and I slipped out of bed and went into the bathroom. The water I drank refreshed me and I went once more to my favorite post at a window and flung back the draperies.

Moonlight fell brightly upon beach and ocean and the emptiness stretched for miles, somehow reassuring to see. It was only humans whom I feared at the moment. Nature could more often be trusted. Then, down on the sand, a shadow moved and I tensed at the window. My wristwatch had told me it was after midnight, but someone else who could not sleep was standing down there at the water's edge, looking out across the ocean. The figure was too far away for me to tell who it was, or whether it was a man or woman, or what nighttime torment had driven one of the house's occupants to seek solace at the edge of the sea.

For a moment longer, with the sound of waves filling my room, I stood staring up at the nearly full moon, but no shadows marred its surface. I reached for the pendant I still wore about my neck, hanging now in the V of my nightgown. The tiny unicorn felt warm in my fingers and the touch of it was somehow reassuring. If it was possible to bring me good luck, it had done that, hadn't it? Since I was still alive.

Before I returned to bed, I crossed to my door, which had no lock, and put my hand on the knob. I would open it just enough to make sure that my guardian still slept on the cot in the hall outside. Gently I turned the knob, and through the narrow crack I could make out the sleeping form on the cot, lighted by a dim hall sconce nearby. Helen Asher snored gently, and I was not altogether reassured. But she was all the guardian I had.

However, as I started to close the door, it suddenly resisted my touch and a slim hand came through the crack to pull the knob from my fingers, opening it the full way.

At arm's length from me, Stacia blocked the door's closing. Her short, fair hair was tousled and she wore pajamas and a pink silk robe. All this I saw at a glance, but it was the brightness of her eyes that held me, and the smile on her lips that was only the mockery of a smile.

I was once more afraid.

12

I stared at Stacia, unable to close the door against her hand.

"Aren't you going to invite me in?" she asked.

My throat seemed to close and I couldn't even call out to Helen. I was more afraid of Stacia than I'd been of car or dog—if that was possible—because this was a glimpse of wickedness undisguised. If there was such a thing as human evil, then Stacia exemplified it, and in this midnight moment, in this quiet house, the sense of that evil was paramount.

"How silly of Mother to put Helen outside your door," she said lightly. "We all know she sleeps like the dead. Come on, Courtney—don't stand there staring—I want to talk to you."

The illusion of evil faded a little in the face of her commonplace words, but I didn't want to be reassured by the commonplace. It was safer to believe the extreme and stay on guard.

With difficulty I managed to speak commonplace words myself. "What can we possibly talk about?"

"I should think there might be quite a lot for us to discuss, cousin dear."

This time I managed to challenge her. "For instance, that you tried to run me down in your mother's Mercedes? That you smashed a link of Tudor's chain, when you knew I was out of the house and would be coming back to the garage after dark? Are these the things you want to discuss?"

"Oh, come on, Courtney! What a vivid imagination you have. All I want to know is why you went streaking off to see Olive Asher tonight. I want to know what really happened."

My first wave of frightened reaction was subsiding a little in spite of my effort to stay on guard. Evil wasn't an entity in itself. There were only twisted and mistaken human beings, and Stacia was one of those—damaged long ago, perhaps because what *she* demanded of life was all that would ever count with her—but not driven by anything supernatural like evil.

I pushed past her out of the door and bent over Helen Asher. "Wake up!" I said, and shook her by the shoulders.

She started under my hand and blinked in dismay to find us looking down at her. Struggling out from deep waves of sleep, she spoke to Stacia.

"Mrs. Judith said no one was to bother Miss Marsh tonight. You shouldn't be up here, Mrs. Faulkner."

"Go back to sleep, Helen," Stacia said calmly. "I'm not going to hurt your patient."

Now that Helen was awake, I wasn't afraid any more.

"Just stay awake," I told her.

She nodded at me doubtfully as I waved Stacia into the bedroom and followed, leaving the door open a crack, and turning on all the lights. Stacia flung herself into a chair and curled her legs beneath her, while I managed with one hand to plump up pillows on my bed so I could sit up against them, pulling the covers over my legs.

"All right," I said, my voice low so that Helen couldn't hear. "What do you want?"

"I've told you. What did Olive Asher have to say?"

"Nothing. Someone had already reached her and bought her off, so she would leave town at once and not talk to me."

"But you got to her on the train, didn't you? I found

out about that. So she must have had something to say."

"About what?"

I'd expected Stacia to ask about the baby, about Olive's part in helping Judith with her plan, but she was following another road and her next words surprised me.

"What did she tell you about my mother finding Aunt Alice dead on the beach?"

"She told me nothing. We didn't talk about that."

Stacia shrugged. "I suppose you won't tell me."

I reminded myself that I was dealing with an imbalance here, an irrationality that must go clear back to her childhood and all those venomously destroyed dolls. I tried to speak calmly.

"What was she supposed to tell me? And what difference does it make now?"

"Those who are strong are the ones who are armed," she said sententiously, and I wondered who she was quoting.

"Armed for what?"

"Do you know who said that?" she asked. "Your mother did. It was in one of those dear little fairy tales Aunt Alice used to write."

"Why did you tear the pages from the back of that last composition book?"

She shrugged, her smile mocking me. "Those pages were just a little too revealing. I couldn't have them fall into her darling daughter's hands."

"What have you done with what you tore out?"

Her eyes danced. "Nothing drastic. They're in a safe place where no one will think to look. I haven't destroyed them. Not yet."

"Did something in her words make you curious about her death?"

"I've been curious about it for a long time. Because I *like* to be strong. I *want* to be armed."

"Against whom?"

"Ah, if you knew that, you'd know where to look for the enemy, wouldn't you? And then *you* would be armed. And we can't have that."

"Listen to me," I said. "Please pay attention. As soon as my arm permits me to drive, I'm going back to New

York. You needn't say anything about this." I touched the golden unicorn where it hung in the V of my gown. "Neither you nor your Uncle John—"

"Your father," she put in gently, derisively.

"No one needs to worry about who I am. I can't think of anything I want less to be than a long-lost heiress. I'll make a bargain with you. If you will let Judith and Herndon keep this house so they can go on living here, I'll never step into your lives again."

"But there's Olive now—and whatever she knows."

"As I've told you, someone has bought her off. Someone has frightened her badly and sent her away. I don't think you'll have any trouble with her."

She smiled at me, as sweetly as ever. "Unfortunate, isn't it? Poor old thing."

"Will you make the bargain?" I asked.

"I'll have to think about it."

I hunched up my knees and hugged them with my good arm. "What does Lawrence Rhodes' will say that makes you think I might be the heir? Didn't he leave everything to you?"

Stacia seemed to consider this—or perhaps she was only considering how much she wanted to tell me.

"I don't suppose there's any secret about it now. Grandfather was very cunning. He didn't want to leave everything to either of his sons, because he was angry with both of them at the time. But he *was* counting on a grandchild. The *first* grandchild. When he drew up his will he named no names. He didn't know when he did it that Alice was having a baby out of his reach over in Switzerland. And I guess Mother didn't know she was pregnant when he was changing his will around. So all he set down was that the first grandchild was to be his heir when she or he reached the age of twenty-five. When he did know about Alice's baby, I gather he was pleased, but he didn't change the wording. It referred to any child who happened to get born first in the family and reached the age of twenty-five. So then, of course, when dear little Anabel disappeared, the will still covered me—because *I* was then the firstborn to live, and I will inherit when I'm twenty-five. I mean to stay first, Courtney. That's what I came here to tell you—that I'm going to stay *first*."

"You're welcome to the place," I said. "But if you're going to turn Judith out of this house, then perhaps I'd better hang on for a while. With a bodyguard around, of course."

She jumped up like the nervous little cat she was, and prowled the room in her usual way. I hugged my knees and waited. At length she stopped opposite my bed, regarding me with wide blue eyes.

"How can I trust you? How can I possibly believe you mean what you say?"

Before I could answer, a woman's scream reached us through my open window—a sound shrill with terror. I was out of bed in a flash, but Stacia was ahead of me and we leaned in the window frame together. There had been only one scream, and then a flutter of small cries.

In bright moonlight we could make out figures below, the length of the terrace away—one of them lying prone on the stones. Stacia turned away from the window and ran toward the door. I caught up my robe, pulling it on as I went after her, noting as I ran past Helen Asher's cot that she was no longer there, wondering how long I had been alone with Stacia.

She was well ahead of me when I ran through the living room and out the door to the terrace. Asher was already there, wrapped in a woolly bathrobe, with a flashlight in his hand, while his wife knelt beside the limp figure, silent on the stones. Fright rose in me, and I found myself praying that it wasn't Evan.

Stacia had already dropped beside Mrs. Asher, pushing her aside, flinging herself upon the prone figure. "Uncle John!" she cried, while unreasoning relief went through me. "Uncle John, are you hurt? What's happened to you?"

Helen Asher was no longer the picture of a nurse in authority. "There's too much happening!" she cried and burst into tears.

Her husband spoke to her in stern displeasure. "Tell us! You've examined him, haven't you?"

Before Helen could find her voice, Judith materialized

beside us, wearing a long dark gown, her black hair hanging loose down her back. "What is it?" she demanded. "I heard someone scream. What's happened to John?"

Helen managed to collect herself and stop weeping long enough to falter an answer. "There's a—a lump on the back of his head, Mrs. Judith. Somebody's struck him down from behind."

I moved to where I could see the side of John's white, cold face, as he lay face down, and something stirred in me unexpectedly. This was my father—and now perhaps I would never get to know him. Perhaps it was already too late. I remembered guiltily that I had even preferred his being hurt to Evan's.

Down the terrace, wooden steps creaked and Evan Faulkner came from the direction of the beach. He was dressed in slacks and a pullover, as though he'd been up for a long time. Judith told him quickly what had happened, far more in control of the situation than either her daughter or the Ashers.

"He's not dead," she said. "But someone struck him down from behind with a heavy instrument."

"Where is Herndon?" Evan asked, and we all looked around, as though we had once more forgotten Herndon's existence.

Judith said, "I don't know. When I left my bed just now, I saw that his was empty. But he often stays up late at night, or gets up when he can't sleep to wander around the house. Sometimes he goes for a walk outside."

"We'll have to call the police," Evan said.

Judith stepped close to him and put a hand on his arm. "No police. Not yet. Let's see how badly he's hurt, and whether he knows who struck him. Who reached him first?"

"I did, madam," Asher said. "I don't know how long he was lying there. I went upstairs at once for my wife. But she is very nervous tonight, and when she saw him on the stones she screamed." He shook his head in disapproval. "After that, everyone came."

As if the voices speaking above him finally penetrated his consciousness, John moaned softly and put a hand to his head.

"Let's take him inside," Evan said.

Supported between them, he and Asher managed to get John on his feet and into the living room, where they helped him to lie down on a couch. Stacia remained close by his side, murmuring softly and now and then casting a deadly look around at the rest of us, as though we must be to blame. When John insisted upon sitting up, she knelt beside him to hold his hand, and he reached out somewhat shakily to touch her hair. As he would never touch mine, I thought, unexpectedly sad for something I'd never had.

Evan bent to examine the lump at the back of John's head and then turned to Judith. "The skin is barely broken. There's only a little blood, but a blow like that could have killed him."

"I have looked around for the weapon, sir," Asher put in, "but I've found nothing as yet."

"Did you see who struck you, John?" Judith asked.

He started to shake his head and then groaned. "God, what a head! No, I didn't see a thing. I came out on the terrace around twelve o'clock because I couldn't sleep, and I was sitting there in that folding chair smoking, when something hit me. I don't remember anything else."

"Nobody's sleeping tonight," Stacia said mournfully. "But I know why you were struck, Uncle John."

We all stared at her. Even John managed to focus upon Stacia.

"What are you talking about?" Evan demanded.

She gave him a spiteful look. "You're just like the rest of them! You're another Rhodes and you'll hush it all up. Someone tried to kill him because he knows about that time when Alice died. Doesn't he, Judith? He knows why Alice died by drowning that time out in Montauk!"

Even under such circumstances, Judith managed to look unruffled—a tall figure in her dark robe. She regarded her daughter for a quiet moment before she spoke.

"Yes, Stacia. I believe he does know. Perhaps it would be wiser if he would tell what he knows and be rid of the secret."

John moaned again, concerned only with the racking pain inside his own skull.

"Someone ought to find Herndon," Judith said. "He's got to be told about this, so we can decide what to do."

Evan went to a phone on the hall table and dialed a number. We could hear it ring several times before the receiver was lifted.

"Hello, Nan," he said. "I'm sorry to wake you, but I believe you saw Herndon earlier this evening. Something's happened up here and we can't find him. Did he give you any hint as to where he might be going?"

Apparently she answered negatively, and then began to ask questions, so that Evan had to explain, and we could all hear the sound of her voice raised in dismay at the other end of the line. When he hung up, Evan came back to the living-room door.

"I'll have to look around outside," he said and went out to the terrace.

Judith busied herself getting aspirin for John, finding a blanket to throw over him, sending Helen for a pillow and warm water to bathe the wound.

Stacia remained where she was, kneeling on the floor, in the way and of no help, but clinging to John's hand as though that were all that mattered to her at the moment. As though by clinging to him she could help his hurt, ward off his danger. He lay with his eyes closed, his face as white as the collar of his pajamas that showed above his dark red robe.

I had dropped into a chair in a far corner of the room, where I could rest and try to ignore the pain in my arm. I felt a little sick and even more shaken than I'd been earlier. I was right about evil, after all. It *was* abroad in this house—not merely in the person of Stacia, but somewhere else as well. Hidden, invisible, yet always there. I didn't belong with these people and I must get away.

Before Evan came back from his search, Herndon walked into the room, like Evan, fully dressed, even to his usual bright vest, and Judith went to him, not quite so calm, I thought, as she pretended.

"Herndon, we've needed you!" She told him what had happened and he listened gravely.

The news seemed to strike him like a blow and he walked over to bend above his brother. I had never seen any affection displayed between the two, but now when the older brother opened his eyes, Herndon spoke to him gently.

"You must have some notion about what happened, John," he said. "We need to know who did this."

John looked up at Herndon. "If I knew, would I say?" he asked, and Herndon stepped back from the couch and returned to Judith.

"Shall we call the police?"

"No! Certainly not." Judith was more positive than before. "He needs a doctor, not the police. You know what a scandal there would be if we called them in. It's not something any of us wants."

No, of course they wouldn't want it—because it was one of them behind what had happened, and old Lawrence Rhodes had trained them to close ranks and protect the family. And whoever had done this knew there would be just that sort of protection.

Herndon bowed his head gravely at Judith's words. "Perhaps the best thing that can happen to us now is to leave this house. Close it up and let Stacia do what she wants with it when she comes into her inheritance."

"Not my beautiful house!" Judith cried softly. "Never, never!"

Evan came back from his search and saw Herndon in the room, but neither he nor the others asked where Herndon had been, or why he had gone walking outdoors at such an hour. After all, Evan had gone out too. Restless men walked abroad at night, I thought. Both were married, both had wives beneath this roof, yet they walked abroad lonely by moonlight.

"I think you should all go to bed," Herndon told us. "Perhaps John will be more comfortable if we leave him down here. I'll start up the fire, and stay downstairs with him tonight. Come, Stacia, it's time to go to bed." His tone was kind, loving, and I knew these were the words he had spoken when she was a child. But she only looked up at him in angry rebellion—as she might also have done as a child.

Once more John opened his eyes. "Play for me, Stacia. Not one of those stormy tunes. Something gentle. Perhaps it will help me fall asleep. There's time enough to see a doctor tomorrow. I want to rest now."

Stacia jumped to her feet and for a moment I thought she was going to refuse, in no mood for gentle music. Then she walked to the piano and sat down to run her fingers over the keys in a rippling melodic sound. The last thing I wanted tonight was to hear Stacia's playing, and I left my chair and went quickly through the door to the stairs, with no one paying any attention to my departure.

Asher stood uncertainly in the hallway, and Helen had disappeared. On an impulse, I paused beside him.

"When Mrs. Judith sent you to take Olive to the train, did she know I wanted to talk to her?"

He looked clearly startled. "But it was Mr. Herndon who sent me, miss, and he didn't want you to talk to her."

"Thank you," I said. "Good night, Asher."

It had been only a small trap, and he had walked into it innocently. I started thoughtfully up the stairs. Somehow I had not expected Herndon Rhodes to be behind what had happened. Yet I supposed that Judith could have commanded him easily.

As I reached the landing, Evan came up behind me. "You're the one who should be in bed, Courtney," he told me. "I'll see you up to your room. You're looking rocky—and with good reason."

I gave up then. I stopped trying to be strong and invulnerable as he came with me up the stairs, and let myself lean on his arm.

"I'll have to stay another day," I said. "I won't be able to drive home tomorrow."

"I'll drive you to New York when you want to go," he said, "but do you have anyone to stay with you there?"

I shook my head. "There's no one now." A few months ago I could have summoned Gwen and she would have come to me at once.

"I don't think you should be alone in an apartment trying to take care of yourself," Evan said. "Not for a few days, at least. I know you want to get away from this house for a while—so why not come with me for a sail tomorrow?"

"With this?" I touched my bandaged arm.

"You won't have to do a thing. I'll fix a solid place for you to sit, and I know an empty beach we can sail to, where you can lie on the sand in the sun, and not be afraid. You have been afraid, haven't you?"

"Of course. I seem to have become a target."

His look hardened. "That will stop. You're not to be left alone again. I shall tell Judith that. So will you come with me tomorrow?"

He was once more as he'd been when we were together in his car, and when we reached my door I smiled my gratitude. A determination was growing in me. I needed to be alone with Evan and away from the house, where I could talk to him. I couldn't manage all this alone any more. He was the one person I could trust and I was going to tell him everything.

"There's nothing I'd like better," I said. "Thank you for thinking of it."

He put a hand gently against my cheek, cupping it for just an instant. It was the lightest of caresses—but it *was* a caress, and I didn't move away. Then, as quickly, he stepped back and waited until I'd entered my room.

"I'll send Mrs. Asher upstairs," he told me. "Though I think everything will be quiet for the rest of the night. You can sleep now."

When he'd gone, I turned out all the lamps but one, and got into bed. In what was left of the night, I wanted no more darkness. Moonlight through a window was not enough. Only after I had slipped beneath the bright quilt and found the right position to ease my arm, did I let myself relax and begin to feel, to think.

I put my hand against the cheek Evan had touched, foolishly tender as a young girl in my remembering. Would there be more tomorrow? What would happen when we were alone? What did I want to happen? What did this growing feeling I had toward Evan mean, and how far did I want it to go? Was I heading straight for a greater hurt than any I had ever known—and perhaps a greater danger? What still lay between Evan and Stacia I didn't fully understand, but I didn't think it was love—and I wasn't even sure that he meant to leave her. All I knew was that this feeling toward Evan was something stronger and more serious than any I had ever known toward a man. If I was to have him, I wanted him for keeps—and he was not available.

This was the way to stay awake for the remainder of the night, and I tried to empty my mind and forget about Evan. But into the emptiness I forced upon myself came a new thought to fill the vacuum. Only now did I remember something. Without giving it a single thought, I had gone downstairs in my robe, with the golden unicorn in plain evidence at my throat—for all of them to see.

If anyone had noticed particularly, I couldn't tell. Most of the focus had been upon John, not me—though the pendant had been clearly evident for anyone who chose to look. Whether it could make any difference or not now, there was no telling. Perhaps it would make a difference to Stacia, if others knew.

From downstairs came the whisper of soft music. Nothing stormy, as John had requested, but a lullaby from a favorite opera. *Hansel and Gretel,* of all things. Gentle, but a little eerie, lulling lost children to false security.

Nevertheless, the music soothed me as well, even though I knew it was Stacia playing, and I dozed off and slept into the morning.

When I awakened, the sun was long up and the scent of frizzling bacon drifted through the house. I thought first, not of my arm and the dog's attack, not of John lying white and still on the terrace, but of the fact that I was going sailing with Evan Faulkner this morning.

My arm seemed to have quieted somewhat during the night, so I knew there was no infection, though it was sore, and I was able to bathe and dress without too much difficulty. The bruise on my leg was only that—a bruise, and could be ignored. I put on slacks, with a red sweater. Once more I wore my pendant hanging at the back of my neck, though I didn't know whether this concealment came too late by now.

What would happen when the others knew? I wondered. Would Judith welcome me as the means of stopping Stacia? Evan had said she meant to institute a search for the lost child—but perhaps that was only a bluff to stop Stacia from selling the house.

And how would Herndon feel? I knew he loved his daughter, but he loved Judith more. Or was there much I still didn't understand in these complex relationships?

Helen Asher's cot was empty when I went into the hall, and I had no idea whether or not she had spent the remainder of the night outside my door. It didn't matter now. No one was in the dining room when I went downstairs, and the bacon scent came from the kitchen, where Asher and his wife were having breakfast. I went out to greet them and Asher rose quickly, his look guarded.

"Do you wish to have breakfast now, Miss Marsh?"

He looked old this morning, and there were smudges under his eyes—evidence of the night's disturbances.

I told him that coffee, toast, and orange juice would be fine, and asked about John.

While assuring me that Mr. John was up and about and apparently none the worse for what had happened, his tone seemed to promise dire calamity for all.

"Have you seen Mr. Faulkner this morning?" I asked.

The lugubrious look deepened. "Yes, miss. He is working in the library. And he has already asked Mrs. Judith about taking out the *Anabel.*"

So this was the source of his disapproval. William Asher, who had served the Rhodes for much of his life, did not like the idea of Evan taking me out for a sail. There was no way in which I could reassure him. I could hardly say to him that nothing lay ahead for Evan and me, and that I knew very well that Evan still belonged to Stacia, while I, who belonged to no one, wanted desperately to have one day out of all my life to remember. Just one enchanted day, when I could be with Evan.

Back in the dining room, I sat alone at the table, waiting until Asher brought my breakfast. I was hungry when it came, and while I ate hot buttered toast, heaped with East Hampton's specialty, beach plum jam, Judith came into the room and sat down at the table near me. If she had seen my golden unicorn last night, she gave no sign, but greeted me pleasantly, calmly.

"How is your arm, Courtney? Would you like me to drive you to the doctor's before you go sailing with Evan?"

"It's feeling better, thank you," I said. "Perhaps I'll

wait and see him tomorrow when he'll need to change the bandage."

She played idly with a silver salt shaker, her fingers not quite so relaxed as her bearing. "It's a long time since I've been out in the *Anabel*," she went on. "Old Lawrence taught me to sail, and years ago John used to take me out in her sometimes. Herndon never cared much for sailing. I suppose he's the only Rhodes who doesn't. But then, he was always a little jealous of John."

"Jealous of John?" I was surprised that she would admit to this.

"Of John's talent, let's say."

"But Herndon has everything. He's—"

"Let's not talk about the past, Courtney. Of course it's Herndon who counts today. Not John. But John did build the *Anabel*. She's a marvelous boat and I'm glad you're going sailing in her. Though of course Stacia will be furious."

I didn't want to talk about that.

"Asher tells me John is feeling better this morning," I said.

"Nothing ever keeps John down. He won't see a doctor, and he's up and around as though nothing happened, apparently without even a headache."

"What does he say about what happened last night?"

She regarded me brightly. "Perhaps we were all mistaken. I'm afraid Helen led us into jumping to a wrong conclusion. This morning John says he must have fallen and struck his head on the flagstones. He said he'd been drinking too much all evening."

Which meant she wasn't going to tell me anything. The ranks were still firmly closed.

"Do you believe that's what happened?" I asked.

She pushed back from the table and rose. "I suppose he must know what occurred. Helen gets hysterical at times, and she could easily have led us off down the wrong road."

"I expect it's safer to believe that," I said. "Even though he was lying face down. Just as it's safer to believe that it was an accident when a car tried to run me down, and another accident when Tudor broke his chain."

She gave me her slight, lovely smile. "All accidents—of course, my dear. What else could they possibly be?"

"It wasn't an accident that someone took the trouble to get Olive Asher out of town just when I was going to have a talk with her."

"You meddle too much," Judith said gently, and walked out of the room, leaving me to wonder whether I had been cautioned or threatened.

It would be good to get away from this house, if only for today. And it would be wonderful to talk to someone who might help me, give me unprejudiced advice. I still meant to tell Evan all about Anabel Rhodes, who had somehow turned into Courtney Marsh and come back to East Hampton under the foolish conviction that she could be made whole by finding her family.

But there was more than that—and I had better face it, accept it. Just the thought of being with Evan, of talking to him, made me feel hopeful that the day would turn out all right for me.

I finished my breakfast and went to look for Evan so that I could make this beautiful day begin.

13

The drive across the South Fork in Evan's car was pleasant, and when we reached Sag Harbor we parked and walked along the streets so he could show me the lovely old houses that had once been captains' homes, and the architectural curiosity that was the Whalers' Church, which had once boasted a spyglass-shaped spire—blown down in the '38 hurricane and never replaced.

Evan knew the history of the town, and he was anything but morose this morning, relishing the stories he had to tell. It was as though he too had been freed of the heavy haunting the house in East Hampton induced, so that we could be together with less strain than before.

Now more than ever, I knew this was going to be a beautiful day. A hurricane might still be creeping up the coastline of the continent, but I put all dire thoughts away from me. Nothing was going to trouble me now—not while I was with Evan.

He told me about the days when Ethan Rhodes had been a dominant figure in this town, and I was content to look and listen and even allow a sense of family to grow in me. Toward those who had lived before Lawrence Rhodes, I could feel a greater kinship. Eventually we walked down to the harbor, and Evan pointed out the sloop, *Anabel,* anchored out in the water.

"She's been well cared for," he told me. "John has seen to that, since she's his one perfect creation."

Evan helped me carefully into the *Anabel*'s dinghy. I was determined not to let any wince of pain from my arm show and I was beginning to feel so soothed and happy that I hardly noticed the twinges. As we approached the sloop, I could recognize the harmony of line, the grace of proportion as she rode the blue waters of the harbor, pristine in gleaming white, her single mast awaiting the sails that would give her life.

Watching her as we approached, I felt an unexpected lump in my throat. It meant something to me that my father had been able to create beauty such as this. If only I could find the closeness to him that I had longed for before I even knew that he was alive. Perhaps that still lay ahead of me. I could believe almost anything this morning.

When we were aboard, Evan helped me into the cockpit, where I was able to sit comfortably and rest my arm. I had tied my hair back from my face with a red scarf to match my sweater, and I felt free—ready to run with the wind like the boat itself.

We used the engine to get out into the bay, and then Evan tied the tiller so he could set the sails. With the noisy vibrations of the motor stopped, and water slapping against the *Anabel,* I felt lulled and enchantingly relaxed. Evan let the sails take over, and we glided swiftly across the water, with a glorious feeling of flying. There were gentle waves, a little foam spinning back from the prow, and I watched the man who handled this lovely winged thing so skillfully. He had shed his prickliness, his suspicion of me because I was something artificial that had come out of New York, and he seemed more relaxed and natural than I had ever seen him. He too had needed this escape.

We talked very little as we ran west away from Smith Cove and around a peninsula that thrust out into the water.

Islands and land, inlets and houses along the shore seemed remote and unreal. There was only the sun and the sea and our winged *Anabel*.

Eventually we came about and headed into the wind before dropping anchor off an empty beach.

"There were visitors here during the summer," he said, "but there'll be no one around now."

Again we got into the dinghy we'd towed behind us and rowed into shallow water, where Evan jumped out barefoot and pulled the small boat farther onto the beach, where it could rest safely on the sand. I took off my shoes, rolled up my slacks, and then jumped down into Evan's arms. He steadied me, released me at once—though I didn't want that—and walked beside me along clean, damp sand that felt firm and cool beneath my feet.

Judith had ordered a lunch packed for us and Evan made a small cache of our possessions, with jackets we didn't need in the warm sun, and the lunch box we would return to later, piled upon the sand. For a while we walked along the beach together, not talking at first, but somehow hand-in-hand—as if that were the only proper way to walk a beach.

It was all so beautiful, so utterly peaceful. Ahead of us were bluffs, a sagging snow fence to keep sand from drifting, a few stunted pine trees, while beside us grew patches of beach grass and bright yellow goldenrod. Farther inland rose thick, tangled growth, and I could hear birds singing. Winter was a long way off, and above us gulls soared and dipped, though their shrill cries seemed far away in the blue heights overhead, unable to shatter the peace of this lonely beach.

Yet it wasn't possible for me to relax and let all this peace and beauty be. I knew I must talk to Evan. I must let myself go and tell him everything. How to start without just blurting what I wanted to say, was the problem. Perhaps there would be a way if I got Evan to talk a little first, and I began tentatively.

"What was your life like—growing up around here?" I asked him as we walked along. "It must have been a wonderful place for a boy."

"It was. I could be outdoors all the time—summer and

winter. My father was what they called a naturalist in those days. He knew all about ecology before we used the word so commonly."

"And your mother?"

"She was a social science teacher in our local high school. She's retired now and lives with a sister out in Colorado. I try to get out there once or twice a year to see her. My father died when I was ten, but he taught me a great deal before that time."

"You were lucky," I said.

Something in my tone caught his attention. He led the way up the beach to dry sand and we dropped down on it together. The mood for talking was upon him too—everything was right, all was favorable for what I had to tell.

"What does that mean?" he asked. "That I was lucky? What about you?"

It was very easy now. "I was adopted when I was about two months old and taken to live in a small town in Connecticut. I meant that you were lucky to have your own real parents. But I couldn't have had a better mother and father, and I loved them as much as anyone could love their natural parents."

He caught the past tense. "What happened?"

"They died last June. In a train crash in Italy."

"I'm sorry." His hand reached for mine. "I can still remember what it was like when my father died, without warning, of a heart attack. It must make a great difference for you."

"I think I've been floundering ever since."

"That's not exactly the impression you give."

"I'm good at bluffing," I said. It was time to tell him, time to open up the whole subject while we were talking about me—yet I still wasn't ready. Something fearful in me held back. I didn't really know whether I could trust him to understand. Instead, I asked a question I hadn't meant to ask—at least not yet. "Have you always known Stacia?"

The peaceful spell was gone, and I had banished it. I could tell by the chilling in his eyes, but though I was sorry, I had known this quietness between us couldn't last forever. There were rapids ahead, and I flinched from facing them, even though I knew I must. Gentle waves rolled onto our beach, and I listened to the sound they made, waiting.

Evan picked up a bit of broken shell and tossed it in one hand. "As you must have noticed, there's no marriage left between Stacia and me. When I've finished this effort to preserve the Rhodes' collection, and when I've done what I can to save the house for Judith and Herndon, I'll go out to Montauk to live, near the lab."

His telling me meant something in spite of the chill in his eyes and his voice, and I tried to take heart.

"Does Stacia know?"

"She knows, but she hasn't accepted it yet. She never lets go of anything she thinks belongs to her."

"Has she always been like that—I mean, the way she seems to be now?"

"Judith says she has."

"All those dolls," I murmured.

"Yes—and worse. Things I learned much later. And yet—"

His voice gentled, and I knew he was looking back to the Stacia he must have known in the beginning, when she still cared enough to give herself to attracting him. How beautiful and desirable she must have been. Ever since I'd come to the house, I had seen the occasional flashes that sparked between them and I wondered if a man like Evan ever got over a woman like Stacia, even if their marriage ended.

"We won't talk about her," he said, suddenly curt. "It's over and done with. I just wanted you to know."

"Thank you," I said, and my own voice was so low I could hardly hear the words. In spite of the roughening in his tone, I knew what he had done, and I had to acknowledge this tentative reaching out between us in a thread so fragile that a wrong word might easily snap it. This was a man who was strong and independent and who had been bitterly hurt—a man reluctant to give his trust again.

"I've tried to talk to Judith and Herndon," he went on. "Judith accepts what's irrevocable. She's even encouraged me to break away. Herndon turns back from reality. He's the most successful escape artist I've ever known."

I was startled. "Escape artist?"

"He's not willing to face anything that seems destructive and damaging to established ways. He wants all his surfaces to be neat and orderly—to relate to neat formulas. When they don't, he closes his eyes and turns in another direction."

I knew so much less about any of these people than Evan did. And yet—?

"I wonder," I said.

Evan tossed the bit of shell toward the water. "What do you mean?"

"Of course I can't know him as you do, but I've sensed a greater complexity than that. Sometimes it seems to me that Herndon is capable of very deep suffering. I don't think Judith has given him as much as he has given her."

"That's true enough. But when it comes to a talent like Judith's, perhaps it's right for her to take whatever she can to nurture it."

I didn't believe this to the extent that he seemed to mean it. Not any longer. "Doesn't Judith fail in every connection except where her work is concerned?"

He thought about that for a moment, staring out at the water of the bay, and when he spoke the harsh note was back in his voice. "Perhaps that's true of anyone who has demanding work. Human relationships have to take second place."

"Do you really believe that?" I asked.

For just an instant unconcealed pain looked out of his eyes. "I've taught myself to believe it."

"That doesn't make it true. Though I used to think that too. Ambition was the law I lived by, the thing that drove me. I couldn't understand compromise. But I wasn't happy. I was always searching for something more."

"Searching for what, Courtney?"

"I thought it was for my family—my natural parents. I wanted an answer to the mystery most adopted children have to face. Do you know what it's like—not ever knowing, looking into faces you pass on the street and wondering if this one, or perhaps that one, is related to you?"

"I suppose I've never thought about it," he said gently.

I went on, trying to make him understand. "There's a

depth of yearning in all of us. A questioning that colors all our lives. Most people never do think of what it might be like to find themselves cut out of a piece of cloth that is separate from the bolt. We haven't any *past*. The things most children grow up with—stories about Grandpa Bob and Aunt Judy and all the rest are no part of the fabric. The relatives we hear about aren't really ours. We didn't come from *them*."

"Yes," he said. "Yes, I'm beginning to see."

"It's all taken for granted with those who have families. But not with me. Not with all the others like me. From the time we're children we ache to know. We think the answers will give us everything."

"I imagine answers can sometimes be pretty disappointing."

"Of course. But we never believe that—we never face it. And by the time we find out we may be left adrift again and unable to go back to what we had before. That's what's happened to me. Only now I can't ever again make a job all important."

"You have found out then?"

I turned to meet his eyes. "Yes, I've found out. That's why I came to East Hampton."

Realization dawned in him slowly. "The Rhodes? Do you mean—are you the baby Judith gave away with Olive Asher's help?"

I answered him starkly. "Yes, I am. I can't find any reason to doubt it. Evan, how long have you known that the baby didn't die?"

He swallowed hard, and I knew he found it difficult to speak.

"I didn't know until yesterday when Judith sent us out to talk to Olive. I'd believed, along with everyone else, that the story of the baby's drowning was true. But Judith didn't tell me that *you*—"

"I'm not sure she knows. About me, that is."

He went on as though I hadn't spoken. "—that you are Anabel. And Stacia is your cousin. Which makes John and Alice—" He seemed too stunned to go on, and his words halted, fell into silence.

"Yes to all of that," I said. "I've wanted to tell you,

wanted to consult you. But somehow there was never the right time or opportunity."

The air around us seemed to stir, as if somewhere out on the clear waters of the bay a storm was brewing, sweeping inland, sending a cold breath ahead.

"I see," he said, and now the chill was in his voice. "So you are the heiress whom Judith wants to bring back and use to defeat Stacia?"

"That's not what I want to be!" I cried. "I don't want any of that!"

"What proof do you have?" he asked coldly.

I drew the little unicorn from about my neck and showed it to him. I told him of the leads I'd found, and of the way everything seemed to add up, though of course the final proof was in a lawyer's files back in New York— the names of those who had adopted Anabel Rhodes, and given her for adoption. Only a court could order such facts released.

"I'm afraid it's all true," I said. "I've found a family I don't want, and who certainly won't want me."

"So you came to The Shingles and spied on us all to see if we would suit you."

The lash of his words made me angry. "What else could I do? How could I know ahead of time if any of my leads were true, or if I would be wanted by this family, once I found it? Or—and that's true too—if I would want them."

"Most people don't have such a choice. We have to take what we're given."

"Please," I said. "Please try to understand."

"I am trying. I suppose deception, the taking of an advantage with people who are hospitable and innocent of hidden motives, has always been something I've detested." He stood up beside me abruptly. "Let's eat that lunch we've brought and start for home."

We no longer held hands as we followed damp sand back to where we'd left our things, and I could feel tears of anger and frustration starting, though I blinked them back indignantly. He was a totally impossible and intolerant man. He lacked generosity and human kindness, and he was utterly harsh and cruel.

"I'll tell you something else," he said, as though he'd

read my mind. "I'm one of those people you spoke of who gives everything to his work and doesn't have time for anything else. I'm the sort of man who never should have married in the first place. Some of Stacia's problems go straight back to me. Some of the blame is mine."

When we reached our things, he picked up a lunch box out of the stack and held it out to me. "Do you want to unpack it?"

I opened the box with fingers that shook a little, spread the cloth that had been enclosed, set out food and the thermos of coffee.

"Who else knows about this?" he asked, picking up a chicken sandwich.

"Stacia and John know. Stacia found the unicorn in my room and took it to John the first day I was here. Whether anyone else knows, I haven't been able to tell. There's been no change in the way Judith and Herndon behave toward me."

"How does John feel over finding a daughter at this late date?"

"I don't know that either," I said dully. "He hasn't exactly opened his arms."

Evan was silent as he ate, but if the obvious motive that lay behind my "accidents" and their possible connection with Stacia occurred to him, he didn't put it into words.

"Stacia doesn't believe me either," I said, when the silence grew long. "She doesn't believe I mean it when I say I only want to go back to New York and never see any of the Rhodes again."

"In any case, it doesn't matter what she believes, does it?"

"I don't know what you mean."

"Once Judith institutes her search for the lost Anabel, the trail will lead to you—if that's who you are. And you can't sidestep an inheritance. So you're probably quite safe."

I could hardly swallow for the anger that rose in me. "I would hate to be like you! I'd hate never to trust or believe in anyone! I'd hate not to know honesty when I see it!"

"Honesty? You?" His laughter seemed to crack around the edges. "I was right in my first estimation of you when I watched that Winser television show. You've lived up to everything I thought about you then."

That was when I disgraced myself. I started to cry. But at least I tried not to let him see. I jumped up and began busily to collect the things we would take home with us, folded the trash into a paper bag, packed away the uneaten food, whether he had finished or not. And all the while tears wet my cheeks and I had to rub them away surreptitiously so as not to be reduced to complete humiliation.

Of course he saw anyway, and ignored—for which at least I was grateful. Yet strangely, even in my anger, I understood something of why he reacted as he did. Stacia was his major experience with a woman. He had been married to her since she was in her late teens and she had left her mark on him, so that he would never easily trust a woman again. Earlier, when we had walked along the sand, I had sensed a beginning of something between us, a softening in him toward me. I had already been drawn to Evan Faulkner, and there had even been times when he had seemed to turn briefly to me, and as we walked, something stronger had begun to make itself felt. Then I had destroyed it completely by telling him the truth he had to know.

What had begun as a lovely morning was long over and there was no comradeship between us when we returned to the sloop that my mother had named the *Anabel*. As we beat upwind across the bay, sailing home, I found that all words had been finished between Evan and me. Anger and resentment had put a stop to communication, and there was nothing left to say. My tears, at least, were spent, but something fresh, a newborn part of me, had been lost, wrenched away almost violently.

No—not wrenched away. If only it could be! This deep new pain was something I would have to live with from now on. Here beside him in the *Anabel* I knew what loving would be like when I'd have to love alone. At every turn I would think of him. Almost anything at all would remind me of my loss, and my self-sufficient life in an empty apartment would never again satisfy me. Work might become an anesthetic, numbing me as time passed. The moment I could handle a wheel I would leave, because here the reality of Evan's presence and the knowledge of how he despised me would be too much to bear. Now all I wanted was that anesthetic.

The afternoon was graying by the time we reached Evan's car and drove across the South Fork to East Hampton, each remote from the other, aware of a barrier that could not be crossed. Here again were the little green lanes of my recent fear, and we followed them through the gates of The Shingles and past Nan's shop. Only bare courtesies had been exchanged between us, and I didn't care what happened from now on. There was nothing I could say to him, nothing he could say to me. But he did give me one warning before I got out of the car.

"Be careful—if you can," he told me. "If I'd known earlier what I do now, I'd have urged you to go back to New York today. You must leave tomorrow at the latest. I can drive you in your own car, and return by train."

"That won't be necessary," I said, wanting only to be away from him. "I'll leave the minute I can drive."

Before he could say anything more, I got out of the car and ran up the steps alone. Even if he would never admit it aloud, he must at least be thinking seriously of Stacia as the one who wanted my injury, even my death. So let him think about it!

When I reached the door of my room, I hesitated, once more uneasy because I never knew when I might find Stacia waiting for me, or some evidence of a visit from her. But the room was as I'd left it and I busied myself with whatever came to hand, trying to ignore the double hurt that tormented me. The physical soreness of my arm was the lesser of the two. The loss of something I had never had seemed a far greater pain.

I wondered now what Evan would do with the information I had given him. Would he confront Stacia? Would he go to Judith and Herndon with the truth about me? It didn't matter. Nothing mattered except to stay alive until I could get away from East Hampton and begin once more to pick up the pieces of my life. I supposed I would care about that life again eventually. The cliché that time cured anything was undoubtedly true. But there was so little joy in waiting for a cure.

As a distraction, I took Alice's composition book from the drawer where I had left it and sat down near a window. As I opened it to the flyleaf, the name "Alice Kemble Rhodes" confronted me in her strong, legible handwriting. My mother's writing. I touched the page where her hand had rested, seeking. If only I could get through to her. There must be a way.

Each story had been dated at the time it was written and some of them belonged to the months just before I was born. I closed my eyes and tried to invite emotion, tried to let feeling come so that I could find the kinship I had so long wanted. But Alice Rhodes remained a misty figure, not nearly so real to me as Judith. Feeling could never be forced. It must be spontaneous, like the occasional flashes of emotion I had felt toward John.

This time I began to read the stories more carefully, not skipping in haste as I had done before. The same strong handwriting continued through most of the book, revealing the woman who had written these lines as a person of character and determination, as well as sensitivity. These were not a beginner's fumbling words, but skillfully written stories that should amuse children of any generation. It was another count against Lawrence that he had discouraged such writing in his son's wife.

Had some of these been written for me? Had she dreamed as she wrote of the time when she would hold a small child on her knees and read aloud? The thought brought a hint of tears, and if only I had time, I might find her yet.

As I'd noted before, the later stories grew younger and were graced with tiny drawings that might have pleased a child. But the eighth story in the book—the one that came just before pages had been torn out—was different from the others. It was older again, and I sensed at once that the writer had been trying to say something through the indirection of fiction. There was a change in the handwriting too, as it became less certain, less even on the page. It no longer marched with authority, but wavered now and then, as though the writer's hand might be shaking. Sometimes it hesitated, so that when the pen went on, a small space was skipped.

As I read down the first page of this final story, a name leapt to meet my eye. This tale was about the Princess Anabel, granddaughter of the Great King. A princess who would one day come into a magnificent heritage, providing she found the answer to three questions that her grandfather had put to her. Young Anabel lacked the answers, it seemed, but her mother, the Princess Royal, was very wise and she could tell her daughter all she must do to please the King.

I knew there must be allegory here, knew that Alice had been playing with bits of truth mixed into her fairy tale make-believe. Anabel was a name that had carried significance for her. I must still find out more about it and why she had an attachment to it. However, before I could discover what had been intended in the ending, the story stopped abruptly—with the rest of the pages torn out. So Stacia had thought them important enough to make sure I would never read them.

At least I had come upon the name "Anabel" again, and perhaps the person who might best tell me more about that name was Alice's sister.

I wanted to take no walks alone, but I could surely drive as far as the gatehouse in my car. In fact, it would be a way of testing my ability to drive. I returned the notebook to its drawer, beside the bit of scrimshaw Nan had given me, and left my room. Outside the door, I could hear voices from the direction of Stacia's room at the end of the hall—Stacia's voice in particular, raised in shrill anger. The second voice was subdued and I couldn't tell whether she quarreled with a man or a woman. Nor did I intend to listen. More and more, everything about my cousin Stacia disturbed and revolted me, and I hurried to escape the sound of her anger.

No one was about when I reached the garage area, and Tudor no longer had to be contended with. I found very quickly how many motions a driver needs to make with his right arm, but I gritted my teeth and drove to the gatehouse. By this time the sun had disappeared behind banks of gray cloud. The shop stood in the shadow of a great copper beech that made the dark, slanting shingles of the roof look like a witch's cap.

But Nan was not a witch and there was nothing here to make me afraid. Lights shown at the windows, but a note had been taped to the door and I read the words. Nan had gone to the library and would soon be back. The time on the note was 3:50, and it was only 4:10 now, so she was probably still at the library. I might be able to catch her and I would prefer that to waiting in so lonely a spot for her return.

My arm hurt quite a lot by this time, but I was determined—a trait that came from Alice, perhaps?—and it was only a short drive. I found my way to Main Street and located the library, housed in a charming low building of red brick and stucco that dated back to early in the century.

Nan was not inside and I was told that she had a favorite spot behind the building, where she sometimes went when she wanted to "escape."

Wondering why Nan Kemble, who seemed so well balanced and contented a person, had any reason to escape, I went outdoors, hunting for her. Around one end of the building I found a stretch of well-kept green, and a small sign dedicating these grounds as a memorial. Crossing the wide lawn, I found my way along a path that led between plantings and ended in a smaller green with a pool in its center where a stone child stood on a pedestal.

Trees and shrubbery enclosed the spot in shadowed seclusion, and Nan was there on a stone bench, with a book open on her knees. She wore brown slacks and a brown jacket to shield her against the graying day, and when I came upon her she was not reading, but watching a robin hopping in the grass not far away. She didn't see me until I stepped into that small, enchanted place that belonged to the stone child.

"Do you mind if I join you?" I asked as she looked up.

For an instant I had the impression that she did mind, that she resented my intrusion upon her thoughts, but then she gave me the warm, natural smile that banished any momentary doubts about my interruption.

"Come in and share," she said. "All libraries ought to have sheltered nooks like this. Were you looking for me?"

"Yes. I read the note on the door of your shop, and thought I might be in time to catch you here."

"I ran away," she admitted frankly. "I like my work, and I'm happy to keep busy—but sometimes I just close it up and run."

"I suppose we all do that," I said. "Or should. I closed up shop and ran when I left New York. I didn't mean to go back. But now I shall, as soon as I can."

"Your interviews with Judith have given you enough material?"

"I hope so. In any event, I've had enough of being run down by cars and bitten by dogs."

She nodded, quickly sympathetic. "It's dreadful that these things have occurred. But two accidents are enough, I think, and nothing more is likely to happen."

"Do you really think they were accidents?" I asked, aware that her hands, lying relaxed on her book, had tensed. But she offered no argument to refute my words, and when she spoke, her question brought me back to the present.

"Why did you come looking for me?"

"Stacia gave me a composition book of your sister's in which she'd been writing stories for children. I was curious about her use of the name 'Anabel,' among other things. Your sister seems to have used it for a boat and a baby, and for a princess in a story. Do you know why?"

"It was a family name on our mother's side. I expect she was throwing it out a bit defiantly in the face of all those omnipresent Rhodes names."

I realized that I had never given much thought to the Kemble side of my family, and had concentrated all too single-mindedly on the Rhodes.

"Are your father and mother living?" I asked.

"Father died when we were in our teens."

"And your mother?"

Nan's shoulders tensed and she regarded me without liking. "I prefer not to talk about my mother. Why should you ask me these questions anyway?"

So there were strains on her side of the family too, but her rebuff was unexpected and I apologized contritely.

"I'm sorry. It's just that something Olive Asher said has confused me, and I'm still trying to understand the pattern of what must have happened at that cottage in Montauk."

"Why? What does it matter at this late date? What did Olive tell you that opened all this up?"

"She said you'd quarreled with your sister before you left for San Francisco."

This time I'd startled her and she stared at me with unexpected anger in her eyes.

"That," she said evenly, "is none of your business."

"Everything that concerns Judith is my business."

"But this doesn't concern Judith." She seemed more agitated than I'd ever seen her. "Not at all! Our disagreements were between Alice and myself." She released the tension in her hands with a sudden gesture of rejection. "Oh, I told them, I warned them, that they should never bring a reporter here!"

"Because there's so much to hide?" I asked.

She looked away from me without answering, and I knew we had come to an impasse. But I liked Nan, and I didn't want her to be angry with me, so I tried a change of subject.

"I suppose you've heard about John's injury last night?"

She nodded and went off on a tangent, the hint of an angry response gone—or suppressed. "We're all worried about John. He used to have an aim in life, a purpose. But when he gave up his work with boats, he didn't find himself again. Now I'm told he's drinking too much. Stacia wants to take him abroad for a long trip when she comes into her money, but I'm not sure it will do any good. It was his drinking last night that caused his fall."

She sounded so assured that I wondered who her informant had been. "Do you really believe that?" I challenged again.

Her effort to reject tension was obvious. On the open pages of the book, her hands moved, the fingers flexing, relaxing deliberately, restrained now from any frantic movement.

"What do you mean, Courtney? What are you getting at?"

"I mean that I don't believe that any of these things were accidents," I told her. "Not what happened to me, not what happened to John. And I don't think you do either."

She was a woman of considerable vitality—which was one of the first things I had noticed about her, and she rose from her bench to face me with a movement that flung aside any pretense of calm.

"I'm sorry you think that," she said. "It's not true! I don't know why things have been so stirred up since you came here, Courtney, but you seem to have made a difficult situation a great deal worse."

That was unfortunately true. And something else was true. She really didn't know why my presence had wrought such havoc. Obviously, no one had told her who I was, and I certainly wasn't going to. I managed not to flinch or step back in spite of the anger that burned in her eyes.

"At least there have been no more anonymous letters," I said. "But the accidents go back a long way, don't they? As far back as your sister Alice's time?"

The change in her was sudden and shocking. The skin about her lips tightened and paled, though high spots of color still burned in her cheeks. This time I did step back because the look in her eyes alarmed me. She was not being warm and friendly now.

"What are you talking about?" she demanded. "What is it you think you know?"

"I don't know anything. Not really. But I do have some sensitivity when it comes to the touchiness of the people I've been talking to."

"Whose touchiness? Who has been talking to you?"

"Olive, for one."

"Olive!" She spoke the name explosively. "She's never been trustworthy. What did she tell you? What did she say?"

"Only that you were still in East Hampton on the morning when your sister died."

Her hand dropped from my arm and her knees must have betrayed her, for she returned to the stone bench and sat down. She looked completely stunned, as though something she might have shut out of her consciousness for years had suddenly returned to devastate her. In fact, she looked so dreadful that I bent toward her.

"Are you all right, Nan?"

She raised her head, but her look was blind, as though she hardly recognized me.

"I've been hiding," she said. "For all these years I've been hiding from myself because I couldn't bear to face what happened. I couldn't live with Alice's death or with anything else about that time. Now I've got to face it. I've got to bring it all out in the open, no matter how much I'm hurt."

Her eyes seemed to focus, so that she saw me leaning above her, and she must have recognized the listening look I wore. Without warning, she jumped up and ran away from me, out of the small enclosure, disappearing around the end of the library.

I let her go. There was nothing more she would tell me now, but I was as convinced as though it had been spelled out that Alice's death had been no accidental drowning—though what part Nan might have played in what had happened, I had no idea. Nor had I any clue as to what Olive knew—or thought she knew.

The one thing I could now realize fully was that my mother's death was not something lost in the past—a sad but nearly forgotten episode. The truth had been glossed over at the time, thanks to old Lawrence Rhodes, but now all the questions that had been suppressed were thrusting into the open, making new demands upon those still concerned. And someone was being spurred into what might be defensive action. Someone was frightened. This time it was not only the past that mattered, but the present.

Stacia, who hadn't yet been born at the time when Alice had died, couldn't have had anything to do with what happened then. There were only three who had been involved—Judith, John, and Herndon. And, of course, Nan. Yet surely there could be no damaging evidence left against any of them—except possibly in Olive's hands. And Olive appeared to have been successfully disposed of for the moment.

Yet those pages from my mother's composition book still remained, and I wondered if there was any possibility of getting Stacia to show them to me. At least this was something I might work on.

14

When I drove through the gates to The Shingles, I noted Nan's car was not parked outside her shop, but I saw it as I drove up to the garage at the house. Apparently she had lost no time in coming here—to confront which one of them?

The afternoon had darkened still more, though the garage lights had not yet been turned on, and the area was shadowy. Just as I was about to get out of the car, I caught movement near shrubbery that grew beside the steps, and Stacia stepped into the open, walking toward me. I drew back and ran the car window partway up. Walking beside her, his leash in Stacia's hand, was Tudor, massive in his Great Dane's dignity—and totally alarming to me.

"Don't worry," Stacia said, smiling as she approached my car. "He's always obedient. See—he isn't even growling at you."

I put out a finger and locked the catch on the door. "Just take him away," I said.

"Are you all that fearful? When I'm right here holding onto him?"

I asked the old question of her again. "Was it you who

smashed the link in his chain so he could break loose?"

She smiled at me sweetly, her blue eyes wide. "What if it was?"

"And it *was* you who drove the Mercedes and tried to run me down?"

"Not really," she said. "Oh, I was driving the car all right, but I wouldn't have hit you. I'd have braked in time. Honestly, Courtney, I only wanted to frighten you away."

She actually believed what she was saying, I thought. But I could remember too well the viciousness of both attacks to be convinced of her version.

"You can get out, if you want," she went on. "I won't let Tudor go near you."

"Thanks. I'll stay right here."

"Did you enjoy your day of sailing with Evan?"

I heard the note of spite in her voice, but I managed to answer quietly. "It was a lovely day for a sail, and the *Anabel* is a beautiful boat."

"Isn't she though? I've sailed her myself a good many times. Ever since I was a child." She took a step closer to the car. "But she'll be mine soon, and I don't want you to go sailing in her again. You'd better remember that Evan is already mine."

She was coming into the open now, admitting to her own dangerous tricks and ready to threaten me further.

"When I leave here, I don't expect to see any of you ever again."

"That's good! I hope it's true. But I didn't come down here for chitchat. Judith asked me to give you a message. She'd like you to come to her studio as soon as you can. You really have been neglecting the job you came here for, haven't you, Courtney?"

She waited for no answer, but turned Tudor around and walked down the drive, with the dog moving proudly at her side.

When I could be sure it was safe, I got out and ran up the steps to the house. I was beginning to feel weary from the long day, and my arm hurt, so that I'd have preferred to go to my room and rest, but Judith's summons had to be respected.

As I went upstairs I heard voices from the living room. Nan's—and who else's?

Judith was at her easel when I reached the attic, once more wearing a rust-colored smock and twill pants.

I paused in the doorway. "Stacia said you wanted me."

Her smile of greeting seemed melancholy as she beckoned me in. "Yes, I thought we might continue—if you still have any questions you'd like to ask me. I understand that you'll be leaving us soon."

"I still can't drive any distance," I said. "But perhaps I'll feel better tomorrow. And I would like to talk with you a bit more."

She motioned to a chair she had placed near her easel. "Do you mind if I go on working while we talk?"

"I'd like that," I told her, and sat down, only to find that the chair had been placed so I couldn't see the canvas on her easel. I shifted to a better vantage point in order to watch her at work and the sight of her new painting chilled me.

In the center of the canvas floated a large head with staring blue eyes and the mouth fixed in a smile as set as concrete, as set as the dimple in one obviously china cheek. The face was Stacia's, yet it was not Stacia because Judith was painting the face of a doll. A Stacia-doll. The effect was eerie and more than a little disturbing.

"What do you think?" she asked, glancing around at me.

"I—don't know. It's not finished yet, is it? What are you planning for the background?"

"More heads! A hundred more dolls' heads—watching her! The way all of us watch her now—because she's about to affect all our lives. Unless you can stop her, Courtney."

"I?"

"Are you wearing your little golden unicorn, Courtney? Are you wearing it now?"

So she knew, and I could only wonder how long.

"Did you see it last night when I came downstairs?"

"Of course. Alice used to wear it often, and I put it around your neck with my own hands—when you were Anabel Rhodes. The moment I saw it, I was sure. But I had to check with John first. He told me Stacia had brought it to him when you came. You've played quite a deception on us, haven't you, Courtney? All this pretense of wanting to write about me——"

"That part is real," I broke in. "I do want to write about you. That hasn't changed." My breathing had quickened and I felt cold there in the warm studio.

She watched me, her green eyes bright, for all her quiet manner. "And by now you must be aware that you are the first grandchild of Lawrence's will."

"Why did you do it?" I asked her. "Why did you give Alice's baby away?"

"It isn't necessary to go into all that old story. Let it be forgotten." She bent toward her canvas, putting a touch more crimson on one cheek of the Stacia-doll.

I wouldn't be dismissed like that. "Forgotten! How can you say that? Don't you realize how much I need to know? I have to know everything! That's why I came here—to find my family, to learn why I was given away."

"It didn't seem a mistake at the time," Judith said, her real attention on the canvas. "It seemed the only thing to do."

"So your own unborn baby could be Lawrence's heir?"

She turned toward me without resentment, paintbrush in hand. "There were other reasons, but I suppose that was the main one. And perhaps it was better for you to get away from this misbegotten family. Have you thought about that? Have you any glimmering of how Lawrence would have taken over your life? John could never have stood against him. But giving you away wasn't good for us in the long run, apparently. Not when you consider Stacia as she is now." Bright green eyes regarded me calmly, and her tone was as commonplace as though she spoke of the weather. "Stacia poisons everything she touches. She destroys. But you are going to stop her, aren't you, Courtney?"

"I'm not going to do anything!" I said sharply. "All I want is to go away and never see any of you again."

"Not even your dear father?"

I hesitated, hating the mockery in her words. "If I could meet him away from this house, with no demands made on either of us, I'd like to get better acquainted with him. But that isn't going to be possible."

"Do you know"—she spoke lightly, turning back to her canvas—"you might even have been my daughter instead of Alice's. That is, if I had married John, if I had left Herndon."

Another head was taking shape beneath her quick brush —a small one floating beyond the large central face.

A sick revulsion shook me. I didn't want any of them. All my search had come to nothing, and I wished I had never made it, leaving me with the undisturbed memory of Gwen and Leon, whom I loved, and who had loved me.

"Do you think I haven't suffered over the years?" she went on quietly. "Suffered for all those things I couldn't tell anyone. Only Olive Asher knew, because I had to have her help."

"And she's been blackmailing you all this time?"

"I never thought of it that way. I gave her small sums out of gratitude, and she was satisfied—until I stopped. It was small payment to make for peace and the right to do my work."

"Mind if I come in?" asked a voice from the doorway, and John Rhodes walked into the room.

"Come in, of course," Judith said. "Perhaps you'd like to sit beside your daughter and watch me while I paint?"

John raised an eyebrow. "So it's all out in the open now?"

I nodded. "I forgot I was wearing the unicorn when I came downstairs last night when you were hurt. How are you feeling?"

"Never better. But I may have been mistaken about falling." He looked straight at Judith. "It seems that something they call a weapon has turned up in the shrubbery along the terrace. It's a long wrench from the garage. Evan seems to be sure that it's what struck me down. Though which one of my affectionate family used it, there's no telling."

Judith had turned back to her easel, working as concentratedly with her brush as though she'd been alone. John walked around me and stood where he could see the canvas with its central face that caricatured Stacia.

"That's an ugly thing to do," he said. "Don't finish it, Judith."

"Why not? I have an ugly child!" Without warning, her serenity cracked like splitting silk and she whirled to fling her paintbrush across the studio. Then she ran to the little oasis of furniture set upon prayer rugs, and threw herself on the couch, her head on her arms, sobbing convulsively.

To see Judith take such leave of her control was shocking. It was as if the inferno she had lived with all these years had exploded into the open and she was being destroyed by emotion in the upheaval. Yet I couldn't believe that the mere act of giving me away after my mother died could have troubled her to this extent.

John watched her impassively, and when I made a move to go to her, he put his hand on my arm. "Let her cry. She's been bottling everything up for too many years. Let it all spill out."

He was not entirely without compassion, I thought, and he understood her very well. I wondered what life would have been like for them if he had left Alice, and she Herndon, and they had found each other.

I stayed where I was, aware of the touch of his hand on my arm, filled with a new longing to turn to him for comfort. But he had none to give. There was no one I could turn to—no one at all.

His fingers moved on my arm, so that his touch was almost a caress, and he was suddenly smiling at me, ignoring the tempest of weeping down the studio.

"I'm glad you're not the hysterical type, Courtney. We've enough of frantic females in this house today. Stacia—because you went sailing with Evan—whom she lost long ago. Nan full of self-accusation, with some wild bee in her bonnet. And now Judith. Poor old Herndon will have his hands full, but I expect I'd better go downstairs and fetch him. How is your arm, Courtney?"

"When I think about it, it hurts," I said. "But I'll live. I have to live long enough to get away."

"Get away where?"

"Back to New York. I can't take on what Judith wants. I don't want it. I don't want it at all."

"Nevertheless, it's inevitable. The way to stay hidden was not to come here in the first place, my dear."

"Whose side are you on?" I demanded. "What is it that *you* want?"

"I don't think I've ever found that out for sure," he said almost wistfully. "And as for whose side I'm on—always my own, young Courtney. You'll have to accept that. I'm not likely to change now."

I stood close to him for a moment longer, with his hand on my arm, while I looked up into the sadness in his eyes —the sadness of loss and old disappointment. *My father,* I thought. Without warning, startling myself as greatly as I startled him, I kissed his cheek—quickly, lightly—and then ran away from him toward the attic door, ran away from the sound of Judith's sobbing.

Nan was going out the front door as I came down the stairs, leaving Herndon alone in the living room. He stood at one of the long windows, staring out at sand and sea, but his look was blind and stricken, as though he couldn't see them.

I went to him quickly. "John thinks you'd better go up to Judith. She's upset and crying."

He gave me a brief, startled look as he came back from a great distance, and then went past me up the stairs. I didn't follow him back to the attic. He could manage Judith better than anyone else, and while there was more to be settled between Judith and me before I left this house, it would have to wait until she recovered.

I started up to my room and in the upstairs hall I met Stacia coming from her own room at the far end. She was carrying a cardboard carton and as she neared me she smiled sweetly.

"See what I have, Courtney?"

Reluctantly, because I wanted no exchange with her, I looked into the box and saw all the little heads staring up at me, rattling against each other as she shook the box.

"What are you doing with those?" I asked.

Her smile mocked me. "My mother isn't going to need these any more—not when she moves away from this house. So I mean to give them a proper burial. Perhaps a burial at sea."

I didn't care about the dolls. "Then you're going on with your plan for the house?"

"Of course! You didn't think I'd pay any attention to your so-called bargaining, did you? I don't think you're going to inherit, after all, cousin Courtney. So I must help my mother pack."

She laughed lightly and started past me toward the stairs.

"Have you seen what she's painting now?" I called after her.

She threw me a quick, vindictive look. "Yes! And she's not going to paint any more dolls. I'll see to that."

More than a little distressed, I went into my room and lay down on the bed, wanting only to close my eyes and shut everything away. In a little while it would be time for dinner and I needed to change into a dress. But for now I would go limp and let everything float away from me.

Of course it didn't work out that way. My thoughts were a tumult of confusion, as though on a stormy sea, with now and then a bit of flotsam floating to the surface. One bit was the wrench that had been used to strike John down on the terrace. Why? Why John? I could almost accept Stacia's feckless words about meaning to frighten but not injure me. Only now something far more vicious and dangerous was going on. Because of Alice's death? Because what had happened to my mother so long ago was finally surfacing into the present and frightening the one who had been responsible? What could John know that he had kept silent about all these years? Had he been protecting someone?

I thrust it all away from me and tried to think of Evan. But that memory brought me only pain, and after a little while the hurt in my arm seemed to surmount everything else, and I got up to take the capsules I was permitted. I wouldn't go down to dinner, after all. I couldn't face any of them at the dinner table. There was a house phone in the hallway and I went to it and listened for Asher to answer.

"I'm not feeling well," I told him. "I'll just skip dinner. Please make my apologies to the family."

Then I went back to my room, put on my nightgown, and got into bed, leaving my lights burning and my door closed. It had begun to rain and I wondered if this was the edge of the hurricane that had been moving slowly up the coast. I hadn't heard a radio all day, and I didn't know what was happening. The outside world had ceased to matter.

That was what happened in illness, I supposed—a self-interest predominated, shutting out all else. And everyone in this house was ill—including me—with a sickness of emotion that grew from the festering left by old tragedy. More than old tragedy. All that had happened seemed to have its source in one terrible old man—Lawrence Rhodes.

Rain beat against my windows, and was somehow a soothing sound. At least no one would be out walking on the beach or terrace tonight. Though Stacia might be getting soaked at her "sea burial." For some reason I thought of that sad figurehead from the *Hesther* out there on the sand, its weathered face lifted to the rain, as though it kept guard over the Rhodes, as though it summoned down punishment from the sky upon its own head, and took away the sting of lightning. It was indeed a sphinx—having seen all, known all.

I let myself drowse.

Later, when the dinner hour was over, someone tapped at my door, and I called out that I didn't need anything and just wanted to rest. But Judith opened the door and walked in. Tonight she wore a long gown of royal blue, with gold beads at the throat, and all traces of her tempestuous weeping seemed to have been washed away by the very tears she had shed. There was none of the swollen distortion that marred most faces after a bout of crying, and she came to the side of my bed and looked down at me with her usual calm repose.

"Asher told us you wouldn't be down for dinner. Are you all right, Courtney?"

Apparently we were to ignore what had happened upstairs.

"I'm just tired. I didn't think I could face the dinner table."

"I don't blame you, what with all of us at swords' points. But you *will* save us now, Courtney. We'll talk again when you're feeling better."

I propped myself on one elbow. "Yes, we'll talk. There's a great deal I want to know—and only you can tell me. I must know, Judith."

"I can tell you about the pendant," she said, as though she were making a generous concession. "Alice wanted it to be yours. She had put it around your neck soon after you were born. It was she who put it there, not I. And I felt almost superstitious about taking it off. I couldn't bear to, and I didn't see how it could identify you to your new parents."

"As though any of this matters now," I said. "It's all over, and I'm going away. Rhodes' problems aren't mine. You can't pull me back into your lives at this late date."

Her smile had an assured but faintly enigmatic quality. "We'll see, Courtney. Perhaps it won't be necessary, once Stacia realizes what's best for us all."

"That makes me the target again, doesn't it? She's already admitted to the other things—the car and the dog."

"Those aren't important. She wouldn't really have injured you."

"I think they're important. They're important to me. And I'm not a bit sure she didn't intend serious injury."

"No! Something much worse is happening. Courtney, I saw Alice walking on the beach last night. She loved to wear white, and she was down there in a long white robe. I saw her as clearly as I can see you now."

Here was new hysteria, and I couldn't cope with it. I turned my face away from her and said nothing.

She spoke almost sadly. "You don't believe me, do you?"

"Next you'll be seeing the unicorn moon."

"Not I. I'm not a Rhodes. But perhaps you, Courtney. You'd better watch the sky from now on. But I'll leave you alone for the present. This isn't the moment for all that heart-baring you want. I'll go downstairs and send up a tray. What would you like to eat?"

"Anything," I said. "Whatever there is."

But instead of going away, she came to stand beside

my bed and for an instant her hand touched my shoulder lightly. "Sometimes since I saw the unicorn about your neck, I've almost wished you were my daughter. Stacia has always seemed a stranger to me."

Remembering what she had said once before—"the eldritch child of a witch"—I looked up into her sad, beautiful face with its enigmatic green eyes. "Perhaps that's why she's a stranger—because you never loved her enough. Parents need to love a child—to keep it safe." This was something I could say from my heart.

"Yes. Perhaps you're right. Were you loved, Courtney? Were the parents you went to good to you?"

"They were wonderful. They loved me very much and I loved them."

"Then why did you come here?"

"They're dead, and I was foolish enough to think blood was important. I wanted to know who I was. Now I'm sorry to know. Perhaps if I could have stayed with Alice in the beginning it would have been different."

There was a flash of something in her eyes—perhaps an old resentment surfacing for an instant. "No! There was always something cold about Alice—something cold and grasping. She'd never have loved you properly, even though she bore you. I knew I was doing you a favor to get you away from the Rhodes."

So she must have consoled herself and quieted her conscience over the years for what she had done.

"If you take Alice away from me," I said, "you leave me with nothing. There's not even an illusion I can cling to."

"You don't really know us yet," she said calmly. "When—when everything is settled, you must come back for a happier visit. This will be your home, you know."

I stared up at her helplessly. Judith Rhodes lived in a world of illusion, and Herndon had always kept that world safe for her—like a cocoon around her. Perhaps that was why, in the end, she had never left him. He was the one who would never fail her, never condemn her, no matter what she did. The question came into my mind without warning.

"Why did you slap Stacia?"

The words were sudden enough to take her aback, and she stepped away from my bed, as though I had reached out toward her with some rough gesture. But her composure was quickly recovered.

"My daughter threatened me," she said quietly. "She threatened me in a way I couldn't accept. I don't often forget myself like that, and I was sorry afterwards. I went to John about it and he quieted her down. Unfortunately, she pays little attention to her father."

I let the matter of the slap go.

"I suppose I am thankful to you, in a way, for taking me to New York. It would have been dreadful to grow up here at The Shingles."

For a moment longer she stood looking down at me, neither smiling nor frowning. Then she went out of the room, moving softly down the hall, with my door left open behind her.

I felt too weary to get up to close it, and some twenty minutes later Mrs. Asher brought me a tray and arranged it on a table in my room.

"Can I help you out of bed, miss?" she asked.

"Thank you, but I'm not ill, Helen. Just tired. I'll be fine now."

She edged toward the door a few steps and then halted, so that I knew she had something to say.

"What is it?" I asked gently.

Her face worked for a moment, and then she managed the words. "You saw *her* yesterday, didn't you, miss?"

I didn't need to ask whom she meant. "Mr. Faulkner took me to see Olive Asher."

"Is—is she coming back to live in these parts, do you know, miss?"

I could reassure her about that, at least. "No—she was only here on a short visit. I don't think she'll be back at all."

"William said she'd try to stir up trouble about the old days. I think it worried him—her being here. And—and it scares me."

"There's nothing to worry about. She's gone."

She looked more relieved than the circumstances seemed to warrant, and I asked a question.

"Did your husband tell you what it was that made him feel concerned about Olive?"

She shook her head vehemently. "Oh no. He doesn't like to talk about that time. It makes him sad. He worked for Mr. Lawrence Rhodes when he was young, you know. And what with two of them dying so close together—those were painful days. And then the baby— But that Olive— she must have been a strange one. Sort of creepy, I think."

Before I could respond, Helen scuttled off abruptly, perhaps feeling that she had already said too much.

When she had gone, I got up and found that I had enough appetite to eat the soup and cold chicken and salad that had been sent up to me. Then I set the tray out in the hall for someone to pick up, and went determinedly about my packing. Tomorrow I had to leave—somehow. My arm had stopped hurting for the moment, and when I got back in bed I went to sleep quickly, the continuing rain at my window whispering a lullaby that was more soothing than Stacia's on the piano. Just before I fell asleep I heard her playing again. Something brilliant and a little staccato that I did not recognize. Another of her own compositions, perhaps? I didn't want to waste myself like that. I wanted to do something that mattered with my life. Even if I had to do it alone. Marrying wasn't everything. These days women were perfectly capable of living happily alone.

I touched the unicorn at my throat. In spite of everything, it was comforting to know that it had been my mother's hands that had placed it about my neck.

When I fell asleep, my pillow was damp beneath my cheek.

Awakening to a gray morning, I got stiffly out of bed to look from a window. It was no longer raining, but fog had come in from the ocean and drifted in wisps that obscured the beach below the dunes.

It was quickly obvious that I would not be able to put my arm to the strain of driving, but this, nevertheless, was the day when I must go back to New York. If no one else could drive me in—and I didn't think I would care to ask that of any of them—I would return by train and come back for my car later.

That settled, I should have felt cheerful and purposeful. Instead, I dragged through the chores of bathing and dressing, and went gloomily down to breakfast. They were all there at the table except Stacia, who was apparently sleeping late. Only Judith smiled at me with a forced cheeriness and I mumbled a "good morning" in response. Evan gave me one quick glance, seemed to dismiss my existence, and did not look my way again. I fought back the stab of pain. John and Herndon were engaged in some interfamily argument, and paid me little attention. I was glad enough not to be noticed until I'd had my coffee.

When Asher had brought it and I'd finished my first cup, I dredged up the energy to make my announcement.

"I'm going home today," I said a little too abruptly, so that the words sounded defiant.

They all looked at me, and Judith said, "But your arm, Courtney. You can't possibly drive."

"I don't mean to. I'll take a train for New York as soon as I can. I don't need my car in the city. If you don't mind, I'll leave it here until I can come back for it."

They all regarded me in a silence that was oddly tense, and I had no idea what any one of them was thinking. Evan was only a stranger.

Herndon spoke first, his voice quiet, the words unhurried. "Apparently I have been the last to be told who you are, Courtney. I wish you had come to me with the truth at once, so that you could have been given a happier welcome."

"I've had quite enough welcome in this house," I told him stiffly. "All I want is to go home."

"But now that we do know"—he went on, as though I hadn't spoken—"there are legal matters of some urgency to take care of, and a final identification to be made. I think you must really stay for a few days more, Courtney."

"You don't seem to understand." I said. "I don't want Stacia's heritage. I'm not Anabel Rhodes. I'm Courtney Marsh and I have my own life back in New York. If you think I'm going to cooperate with you in any way, you're mistaken."

"I don't think you have much choice," John put in quietly. "Stay and see it through, Courtney. It will be harder if you run away."

"I didn't run away in the first place!" I told them all, once more defiant. "I was *given* away. I was stolen—if you want to know what I think of it. I was taken away deliberately—away from my father and my family. Though that's something I'm glad of now. Today I can have a choice—and—and—" My voice broke, and I gave my attention to swallowing orange juice.

Judith made a soft moaning sound and Herndon leaned to comfort her. No one else said anything, and I couldn't bear to look at John.

When I could speak again, I tried more quietly. "I did have a talk with Stacia, and I promised her that if she would not sell this house I would go away and you'd never need to hear anything of me again. I tried to bargain with her. But I don't think she believed me."

"She wouldn't," Evan said, speaking for the first time.

"In any case," Herndon went on, "matters—legal matters—can't be worked out like that. You *are* here now, Courtney. You exist. There are no promises you can make that will affect the circumstances. You must accept the fact that all this is now out of your hands. Of course I should have been told. I should have been told at once so that wheels could have been set in motion."

I faced them angrily. "I didn't come here for that! I only came because I wanted to find out about my family. What if I refuse to save your precious house? What if I sell it out from under you, just the way Stacia wants to do?"

"But you won't," John said. "It's not in you to do that, is it, Courtney? Thank God you're not one of us. You're still capable of generosity."

"I don't think you know what I'm capable of!" I could hear the frustration in my voice, and knew I was flailing at the stone wall the Rhodes had raised against me.

Only Evan was not a Rhodes and I turned to him in pleading. No matter how much he disliked me, no matter how disgusted with me he had been, he was the only one who could help me now.

He was stirring cream in his coffee cup, but he must have sensed my silent entreaty, and he spoke without looking at me.

"I'll drive you back to New York, Courtney. But not until this afternoon. I have to go out to the lab this morning for something that's just come up."

"I won't be here when you get back," I said. "Not even if I have to take a taxi to New York!"

"Then you'll have to go with me to Montauk," he said, suddenly fixing me with a look down the table, his eyes dark with his own determination. "You can come out to the lab with me, and that will keep you out of trouble for the morning. This afternoon I'll drive you back to the city."

I was caught. I wanted to protest hotly that I couldn't be managed like that. I wanted to get away from Evan Faulkner, more than any of the others, because being with him meant pain. Yet I *wanted* to be with him. Some treacherous part of me wanted to acquiesce meekly, no matter how unpleasant the day with him might be. And while I was being pulled by my own ambivalence, Judith spoke up as cheerfully as though there had been no show of emotion around the table, as always unaware of others' feelings.

"I know what! We'll all go with you, Evan. I haven't been out to the Point on a picnic since I was a girl. It will be lovely!"

We stared at her in astonishment. This was Judith Rhodes, the recluse, speaking. Judith, who seldom left the shelter of The Shingles under any circumstances. What was up now? I wondered. Why was Judith suddenly determined that Evan and I shouldn't go out to Montauk alone? I didn't think she cared in the least about her daughter's marriage, but something must have moved her strongly to make her step out of the protective cocoon of the house.

Herndon seemed aware of none of this, perhaps as obtuse—or indifferent—to the rest of us as his wife. He actually looked pleased over the suggestion. "A very good idea. Since it's Saturday, I can go with you. Perhaps you can do some sketching out at Montauk, Judith."

"I'm tired of sketching, tired of painting. I just want a change!" Judith cried.

Herndon reached out to touch her hand. "Then you shall have it."

She looked around the table again. "Did anyone else see Alice walking the beach the other night?"

There was a startled silence before Evan spoke quietly. "What did you see that made you think of Alice?"

"A woman in a flowing white dress. Like the one Alice used to wear."

"That was only Stacia," Evan said. "She found an old box of Alice's clothes in the storage room. I saw her flitting around in that dress."

"To torment me," Judith said. She pressed her hands over her face. "Yes—we'll go to Montauk. I've got to get away."

I watched her warily, never sure of her direction, and more than ever doubtful of her motivation. John was watching her too, sardonically amused, and waiting to see which way the tide would carry us. He would go along with it, I knew, whatever happened. Right now Judith was the tide, and it was settled—we were going to Montauk.

"Are we taking Stacia along?" I asked.

"No," said Herndon firmly. "Let her sleep this morning."

"Let's hurry," Judith said nervously. "Let's get away before she comes down."

There was no telling whether Evan was pleased or not by this intrusion on his plans, but he offered no objection, and as soon as she had finished her breakfast, Judith went out to the kitchen to supervise the hurried preparation of a lunch to take along. I hoped that Stacia would remain asleep. Perhaps more than anything else, we all needed a respite from my cousin. It did occur to me to wonder if we might invite Nan, but no one seemed to think of it, and another person would crowd the car, so I said nothing.

Thus the die was cast, the plan was made, the steps begun that would lead to an ending we never expected. In the time while I was dressing in warmer slacks and a sweater, and binding my hair back with a green flowing scarf that left its ends trailing down my back—while I was doing all these ordinary and prosaic things—something new and determined came to life in me. I too began to make a plan.

From the first there had been an air of suppressing the truth about what had happened on the beach near that cottage in Montauk. The house was still there in the family—at least it must belong to Nan now. So perhaps I could get Evan to take me there while we were at the Point. What I could possibly find in an empty house on an empty stretch of beach, I had no idea. Nothing would be left to tell me anything of my mother's death—yet there was in me a new urgency to see both the beach and the house.

Now not only Judith had a secret motivation as we went downstairs to get into Evan's station wagon. There was purpose driving me as well, and I knew I would have to get Evan away from the others and convince him of what I wanted to do. I would find out nothing if they all accompanied us, but if I went with Evan alone, who knew what I might discover?

As we drove away from The Shingles I wondered idly what Stacia would do when she awakened and found us gone.

15

Fall in New York is often the best of all seasons, and September had been living up to the pattern until yesterday's rain and this morning's fog. There were still hurricane warnings, but the storm was far south off the Carolinas and no real coastal damage had been done. There was hope that the disturbance would lose itself at sea before it got this far north.

As we set off on what would be hardly more than a half-hour's drive to the Point, we found that the fog had lifted somewhat, and while mist clung to the water and rested in hollows, there was no driving difficulty.

No one talked now, and the atmosphere inside the car was hardly the gay one of a family household setting off on a picnic. John made an effort now and then, but no one helped him, and I didn't care about pretenses. I only wanted to follow through on my own purpose for this trip —even though I didn't really know what drove me. Once I got to the Kemble cottage, I would somehow know what to do. Afterwards, I would leave for New York as soon as possible.

Because he had put me there, I found myself in the front seat beside Evan, with the other three in back. Evan's attitude seemed to be that he was doing this simply to keep me out of further trouble, and he didn't have to be cheerful and conversational about any of it.

I was all too aware of him beside me, and sometimes I stole a guarded sidewise look, memorizing details against the time of drought when this moment would be gone and he wouldn't be beside me ever again. The present was only the flick of an eyelid before it became the past, and there would be nothing of substance to cling to after today. So at least I must try to be aware of these last hours when I could hold him in my sight.

The miles slipped away and we drove through the wild section of dunes that was Hither Hills State Park, and then "onto Montauk," as I had learned the old-timers always said. You went "onto" Montauk and "off" Montauk, and if you were a real native, you even put the accent on the last syllable and called it "M'n-tauk."

Before long we were in the streets of the town and I was reminded of some frontier settlement. There was an end-of-the-world look about this far tip of Long Island that reached out into the Atlantic. The country around was still a little wild, and the town had the appearance of being set down in the midst of a sandy wilderness of scrub growth. Yet, thrust up to a startling height in the middle of low buildings, was a tall office structure that seemed to have no relationship to anything else around. The only thing to match it in size was a huge château on a central bluff, which John said was called Montauk Manor. These two oversized buildings that matched nothing else were part of an attempted boom that was supposed to turn Montauk into the Miami Beach of the North back before the crash of 1929. The Montauk boom had crashed along with everything else, but the impressive structures remained.

We were going first to the lab, and Evan turned down a side road, where we checked in with the guard at the gates of the New York Ocean Science Laboratory. The area was located on Fort Pond Bay, and had its own pier, a seaplane hangar, helicopter pad, and numerous long, low buildings set out rather bleakly on the sandy earth like a government installation, which it had once been.

(241)

In the back of the car there was an uneasy quiet, and when Evan and I got out, the others followed silently. I had the strange feeling that each one of us knew that this period of calm was only a lull before the coming storm, and all I wanted was to escape before any of it broke over my head.

Only Evan seemed to change and throw off the atmosphere of The Shingles, now that we were on his own familiar ground. Obviously, his work was more than an anesthetic to him, and all this had been his life for a long time, compensating perhaps for the failure of his marriage.

As we walked toward a smaller building that stood apart from the rest, Judith hung back.

"I don't like the smell of fish," she said, and the other two stayed behind with her.

When I looked back I saw Judith and Herndon standing together, Herndon's head bent toward her, as though they talked together earnestly. John had moved a little apart, his expression faintly bitter, as though he sensed exclusion. What, I wondered, did he really think about that blow that had been dealt him last night?

I shrugged off an uneasiness about all three of them, and followed Evan into a long room that did indeed smell strongly of fish. With an absorbed interest that I'd never seen before, except when it came to the Rhodes' whaling collection, he began introducing me to his lobster friends in their various glass tanks.

"This little girl is special," he pointed out, designating one lobster in a tank alone. "She's a blue lobster, but you can see that she's molted. Her shell is completely gone and we've given her a hollow pipe to crawl into for protection when she feels like it. In the ocean this would be a dangerous time, since a lobster without its armor can easily be attacked and eaten."

I found myself responding with an interest I didn't need to simulate. For the first time I was seeing past his habitual guard to a man whose working life I knew nothing about. Even though this would no longer matter to me, I wanted to know all I could learn about Evan. I wanted to understand something of this part of him that I had never known existed. There was even a painful satisfaction for me in discovering him as a man who belonged to a wider life—a life which must have a more far-reaching effect upon the world outside than I had ever realized.

In the next tank were two lobsters with their gray shells intact and yellow bands fastened around their claws to keep them from trying to eat each other.

"It would be valuable to find a way to farm lobsters on a large scale," Evan said. "A good food shouldn't be an expensive luxury for the few. That's one of the things we're working on now, but lobsters grow slowly and they're cannibals, so it's not easy."

He was on his own ground, at home and thoroughly involved, so that I became vicariously involved too, and my vision and understanding of him began to expand. My loss would be all the more bitter when I went away, but my hunger to know all I could learn about Evan Faulkner was very great.

Outdoors he showed me where a pilot program was being conducted to assess the industrial potential of growing Irish moss, which was used in pharmaceuticals, cosmetics, and foods, and I found myself listening to his voice as well as his words—because after today I might never hear it again.

We crossed a wide road and entered another building where there was a huge model of the area showing how tides and currents could be studied and used. The scope of the laboratory was vast—biological and physical sciences of the sea, aqua culture programs, studies of shoreline erosion—the list was endless, the promise enormous. And Evan was playing an active, creative, imaginative role in much that was going on. He had devised some of the experiments and was developing others. The Rhodes and The Shingles seemed far away and I could almost forget the threat they meant to me.

After a while he took me into a big auditorium, where scientists in oceanography came from everywhere to lecture, listen to lectures, and pool their research. Men and women gathered here who cared about the future of the human race, and I felt an unexpected and glowing pride as I realized how much of a part Evan was taking in matters that concerned far more than this plot of ground, and could reach out across America and touch the world. I felt newly humble, and even grateful that this man might have loved me—if everything had been different.

Inside the building that housed the auditorium, we walked along an empty corridor, with the place to ourselves since it was Saturday, and as I became aware that Evan was watching me, I looked up to meet his eyes.

"Are you all right, Courtney?" he asked. "You're still pale. Does your arm hurt you?"

"I'd forgotten it. I'm all right. You made me forget. All this—it's so big—it matters. I'm glad to know a little more, Evan. More that I can remember."

I hadn't meant to say that about remembering. I didn't want him to understand how I felt. He was still watching me, and he seemed less unforgiving now.

"I made some pretty strong accusations when we last talked, Courtney," he went on. "I've been regretting them. I've had too much experience in distrusting and judging harshly, and I'm not sure I'll ever get over being that way. But that's no excuse for the things I said."

I didn't want apologies from him, and I moved on down the corridor. "It doesn't matter. I understand."

"I wonder if you do." He came beside me at once. "Perhaps we can talk again before you leave. I'd like you to understand—about Stacia, for one thing."

Stacia was someone I didn't want to understand, and I took abrupt refuge in the proposal I'd been waiting to make.

"Evan, that house—the one that used to be owned by Nan Kemble's mother—it's still in the family, isn't it? And isn't it located somewhere around here?"

He halted our progress down the corridor, regarding me intently. "Yes—that's right."

"I'd like to go there," I said hurriedly. "I'd like to see the cottage and the beach. Will you take me, Evan?"

"Why? Why do you want to visit that place? Isn't this a morbid notion?"

"You mean because it's where my mother died? But it's the only spot left where I might try to get close to her. At The Shingles I can never seem to reach her. Here—" I broke off because I was dealing with matters that concerned emotion—and Evan was a man of science. "It's just that after today," I went on feebly, "I have to forget everything connected with the Rhodes and the Kembles. This is my last chance."

He still hesitated and I sensed something I didn't understand. "It's occupied, you know," he said. "We mustn't disturb the people who live there. And I don't think Judith will want you to go. Don't be surprised if the others oppose your doing this. Perhaps you'd better not say anything ahead of time. We'll try after lunch."

He had agreed and that was all that mattered. I was willing to go along with anything he suggested, even though I didn't understand why anyone should oppose so simple a request. When he'd left me to go into an office on the errand that had brought him here, I sat on a bench in the corridor to wait. On the wall before me had been mounted the skeleton of a dolphin, with every bone set meticulously in place. I found myself studying it, trying to sense something of the strange existence this sea creature once had known—an existence hardly more strange to me than Evan's life.

When he returned and found me regarding the dolphin with a certain bafflement, he told me that it had been washed up on a beach near here dead, and the ocean had pounded those bones into a broken heap. One of the men at the lab had collected them and painstakingly wired them together, each in its proper place. The only bit missing was a single tooth, and a dentist in town had contrived a substitute.

I listened, feeling somehow subdued, thinking of Alice, whose body had also been rolled onto a beach. Morbid? Perhaps, but I was eager now for lunch to be over so that Evan could take me where I wanted to go.

When we walked back toward the car I saw that Judith was resting in the back seat, while Herndon and John paced the road nearby, their heads bent in earnest conversation. What were they plotting? I wondered suspiciously. Did any of it concern me? But of course it couldn't any more, since I'd be gone from their lives very soon.

"Let's go out to the lighthouse at the Point and have our lunch," Judith suggested as we reached the car.

No one objected, and Evan took the way east out of town—a fine road, almost empty of traffic at this season. The land rolled on either hand in low hills to the dunes, overgrown with pines and grasses. We passed summer homes occasionally, but no real communities as the road thrust east to the ocean.

The red sandstone lighthouse at Montauk Point is one of the most photographed and painted scenes on Long Island, and it has stood for nearly two hundred years, rising some sixty-eight feet into the sky from the rocks at its foot. Shipwrecks have been numerous down the years, and the foghorn still marks land and danger for the seafarer.

We left the car and walked toward the tower, rising before us in grace and strength. Fortunately, the earlier fog had lifted, or we could not have approached because of the shattering noise of the horn. Once the lighthouse could have been climbed, but the Coast Guard no longer permits this.

In frothing water where the ocean broke over rocks, a surf caster had just given up his try for striped bass, and was climbing to higher ground where he had left his car. The rocky beach lay deserted below us, but the sea was dotted with small fishing boats, and would be into October, as long as striped bass and blue fish were to be had. Farther out, Block Island was visible. All these things Evan pointed out to me as we moved about, and his mood continued friendly, though impersonal.

When we'd found a place to sit not far from the base of the tower, Judith began to unpack our lunch, with Herndon helping her. This was hardly a gay outing, and I wondered once more why Judith had put this plan together so impulsively, insisting upon carrying it out, and why she seemed watchful of Evan and me. The two of us sat on a grassy patch, apart from the others, and though Judith glanced doubtfully our way now and then, no one said anything.

Once I met John's eyes upon me, faintly mocking, yet without condemnation, and I knew that he understood me best. He knew very well that marriage between Stacia and

Evan was over and what remained to be dissolved was only a matter of time. Strange to think that under different circumstances I might have been able to confide in him, even to turn to him in my puzzling. Certainly he must have seen what was in my eyes when I looked at Evan. It didn't matter. I wasn't trying to fool anyone—not even Evan—and after today there would be no more looking at him.

We ate our lunch in a companionable silence for the most part, but since this was my last opportunity I tried to put a few more thoughts into words—just for Evan's ear.

"I suppose nothing ever matches what we imagine and dream of ahead of time. Such stories I used to build up as a child! All about accidental meetings under strange circumstances, where I would find my real parents, even my grandparents, and we would know and love each other instantly."

Evan nodded, and though his eyes were on a distant fishing boat, I sensed his understanding.

"And now I've found that my mother is dead, and I'll never be close to my father. I think I'm an embarrassment to him and he will be relieved when I go away. Just by existing I ask something of him that he can't give, and Stacia is more his daughter than I could ever be. Blood doesn't keep people from being strangers."

"Nor does marriage, Courtney." Evan stirred beside me. "Will you listen if I try to tell you something?"

I found myself stiffening, fearful of hurt, yet I didn't want to stop him. "I'll listen."

"I did love her, you know. I wanted a marriage that would last, and I didn't realize that she would never change, never grow. Perhaps it was my fault that I was able to have so little effect on her. In any case, it was all over long ago. I'd like you to understand that."

I was silent, wanting to believe, yet afraid to hope. I had seen the flashes of powerful emotion between those two.

"There's still feeling between us," he went on, perhaps understanding my silence. "Rage, I'm sure, something close to hatred at times—nothing I'm proud of, or that's pretty to see. Whatever it is; it's not love. I'd thought I could never love any woman again because of my experience with Stacia."

There was still nothing for me to say, and I dared not speak.

"Do you know what I see when I look at you, Courtney?"

I shook my head, not meeting his eyes.

"It's been an evolving process," he said, and in a sidelong glance I saw his wry smile. "You made it very hard, you know, with all that artificial veneer you'd built about yourself so skillfully. But it's been cracking away like a shell since I first saw you. Perhaps a little more every day. Now, you're almost out in the open, for the first time, I think, to yourself as well as to others."

"I've wanted the shell to crack," I said. "But it's been rather frightening."

"I expect it has. Meeting oneself can be alarming. But now I see a young woman with an appealing vulnerability, with a mind of her own, with a talent she cares about doing something with. A woman with a longing to love and to be loved that she tries to hide from the world. A woman who would, I think, be loyal and truthful, and generous, if ever she loved. A woman I have become very fond of. That's why I was so angry yesterday—when I stupidly believed for a little while that I was wrong. I'm not sure I'm ready to love again, Courtney, or even that you are ready to begin loving, but if we were alone and in a different place, I know I'd want you in my arms. Would you come, Courtney?"

I looked at him then, through tears that I couldn't hold back. "I'd come," I said.

He held out his hand and I put my own in his. His clasp was warm and I could return it—as though it were a kiss, an embrace. A beginning had been made between a man who was still fearful of loving, and a woman who had never learned how to love.

"If we're to stop at that cottage on the way back, we'd better leave now," he said, releasing me. "It's on the north shore of Montauk, off the main road near the water."

I packed up our lunch things and got to my feet. Evan

stood up beside me, but now, with the physical contact broken, there was a certain hesitance between us, as there must be between two, so recently strangers, who have begun to let down all guards.

"Courtney," he said, "when you get back to New York —what then?"

"I resigned from my job, but I think they'll take me on again."

"Why did you resign?"

"I didn't want that sort of life any more. I was going to work on a book. I meant to free-lance and live away from any city. But it's no use. I have to work at a job. I have to go back."

"Why must you?"

"So I can forget," I said a little desperately. "So I won't have time to think and I can forget about what has happened to me with the Rhodes, here in East Hampton."

Judith called to us just then, and I knew by his face that I hadn't convinced him. But now there was no more time left to explain. Perhaps while we drove into New York later . . .

We picked up our things, and when we returned to the car, Judith gave us a brief, curious glance.

"I'd still like to know why we came," John said to Judith.

She regarded him calmly. "It was better for us all to get away from the house for a while. Safer."

"For whom?" John said.

"For us, of course. With us away, there's nothing more Stacia can do."

"I wonder," John said. "I wonder if it's Stacia we must worry about."

He turned and started toward the car, a lonely figure— a man who would always walk alone. His very loneliness touched me, and I wanted to go to him, to make him the gift of some gesture that would acknowledge our relationship, yet I couldn't move. I couldn't yet make such a gesture spontaneously to my father, and unless it came from my heart, it mustn't be made.

Evan drove fast on the way back, not slowing until we

came to a side road and turned north to follow it. Judith stirred in the back seat.

"Where are you going, Evan?" Her voice was suddenly sharp.

He answered her casually. "Courtney wants to visit the Kemble cottage."

"No!" The cry was explosive as Judith's composure evaporated. "No, I won't allow her to go there! Turn back, Evan."

Evan kept on his way, deaf to her words.

I looked around at Judith. "Why don't you want me to see this place?"

"It—it's not healthy to go there. It's a place with terrible memories. I don't want to go there myself, and I should think you, of all people, would want to avoid it, Courtney."

"It's where my mother died, isn't it? So why shouldn't I see the cottage and the beach?"

"You won't need to go in, Judith," Evan said. "You can sit in the car while I take Courtney around."

"I think we should go back," Herndon put in quietly. "If Judith doesn't want this—"

John made a derisive sound. "She's not that fragile. And what does it matter at this late date!"

Judith turned to him with an urgency that seemed all the more disturbing because it was uncharacteristic.

"But there's the possibility—" she began.

"Don't," John said. "Let what will happen, happen. It doesn't matter now. And sooner or later Courtney will have to know."

Judith sank back in her seat and it was alarming to see that she could appear so unreasonably terrified of the place where we were going. What had she been hiding all these years? What had really happened there?

Before long Evan turned off onto a narrow, sandy road, running toward the water. Here there was an occasional house, and we drew up before one of these—an old-fashioned Victorian structure that was not what I would have called a "cottage," though it was nowhere as large as The Shingles. It boasted a wide veranda across the front and down one side, with a great deal of gingerbread carving on the supports and at the edge of the sloping roof. As

Evan and I left the car, I saw a mailbox out in front that bore the name "Kemble," and the sight startled me. Surely there were no Kembles living here now!

When I stopped at sight of the box, Evan held out his hand. "Come along," he said. "This may be a test for you. You wanted to see this place, so you'd better face whatever it holds for you. I don't know myself what may happen, but it may be better this way."

Behind us in the car there was utter silence and I didn't look back. We went up the steps together, but I stopped Evan before he rang the bell.

"Wait—let me look around a little, in case whoever lives here sends us away."

I walked toward the sharp angle of the veranda to the side stretch that overlooked the water, and came to a halt. A woman sat with her back to us—a woman in a wheelchair. She must not have heard our footsteps on the bare boards, because she did not turn her head. I could see by her profile that she was old—perhaps near eighty, with hair gone completely white, and cut short for convenience, though neatly brushed. Her features had been honed by the years so that nose and forehead and chin were bony and clearly etched, their lines unsoftened by the flesh of youth. She sat wrapped in a voluminous gray shawl, staring out at the water.

Evan stood back, letting me do as I chose, now that I was here. I stepped around to be within the line of pale blue eyes, and spoke to her gently.

"Hello," I said. "I'm Courtney Marsh, and I've been visiting the Rhodes in East Hampton. I believe my mother, Alice Kemble, lived in this house at one time and I wanted to see it before I go back to New York."

Her gaze remained fixed on some distant horizon and she made no response. Was she blind, deaf? I glanced back at Evan, questioning.

"I'd better ring the bell," he said.

But I had to know, and while he went to the door, I bent to the old woman in the chair, putting my hand lightly on her arm. "Can you see me? Can you hear me?"

Her look did not quicken and she gave no sign that she could feel my touch or hear my words. A sense of something like fright was creeping through me. Not because of her disability, whatever it might be, but because I'd begun to sense some dark aura, something that I knew was going to shock me deeply when I understood it.

In response to Evan's ring, a plump woman in a nurse's uniform opened the door, to regard him in surprise.

"I'm Evan Faulkner," he introduced himself. "And this is Courtney Marsh. We're from The Shingles. We were in the area and thought we'd like to stop in and see how Mrs. Kemble is doing."

"Of course," the woman said. "I'm Miss Dickson, her nurse." She came out to us and spoke softly to the old woman. "Now then, Anabel, do you think maybe you could give the young lady a nice smile."

I put my hand on the veranda rail to steady myself. Anabel! Anabel Kemble—for whom I had been named, my grandmother.

"It's one of her bad days," Miss Dickson said. "If I'd known you were coming I'd have tried to get her ready. But usually only her daughter, Miss Nan Kemble, comes to see her." The nurse turned the wheelchair so that the old woman was forced to face me, though she did not seem aware of us in any way.

I dropped on my knees and took her thin hands in mine, pressing them gently. "I would have come sooner if I'd realized you were here. You are my grandmother Anabel. Can you understand that? I'm your daughter Alice's daughter. I'm your grandchild."

Something in my words seemed to penetrate the distance in which she lived because she began to turn her head slightly from side to side, thought it trembled as she turned it.

"No," she said, and the word was so faint I could hardly hear it. "Baby—baby."

I pressed her hands. "Not any longer. I'm grown up now, Grandmother."

Weakly she tried to draw her hands from mine, rejecting me, but I didn't let them go. Miss Dickson looked thoroughly startled when I looked up at her.

"How long has she been like this?" I asked.

"I don't know exactly. For close to twenty-five years,

I suppose. I haven't been with her all that time—just the last three years. She's very good, you know. Sometimes she seems to listen to me. And she eats quite nicely. Not very much—but she does eat."

I could feel the tears on my cheeks. All the emotion that would not come before was rushing through me now. Anabel! For the first time I understood about the name, but it was too late because she could not see or recognize me. Alice had named a boat for her mother, named her baby for her. Used the name in a story. She and this feeble woman in the wheelchair had once been close.

Down the veranda there were sounds, and I saw that Judith had not been able to remain in the car. She and the two men were coming up the steps and across worn boards to where I knelt before the wheelchair. Looking up into the old lady's face, I saw exactly what happened. Something stirred faintly in her eyes, and thin, wrinkled lips moved as if to whisper. Her fingers moved like a fluttering bird in mine and I pressed them reassuringly.

"It's all right," I said. "Nothing will hurt you. Nothing will ever hurt you again." It was strange that I should sense it so clearly—sense how deeply she had been hurt.

But it was not my face she could see, or my hands she could feel. All her attention was focused on the three who stood in a frozen tableau down the porch. Again fragile lips moved and this time there was a whisper of sound and I bent to catch it.

"No! Wicked, wicked!" she whispered and then sighed as though the effort to speak was too much for her. She closed her eyes and leaned back against the cushions in her chair.

Miss Dickson came to her at once. "She's not used to visitors, Miss Marsh. I think you'd better go now." She bent above her charge. "There, there, dear. Everything is all right. No one is going to disturb you."

Judith turned and fled down the steps and Herndon went after her. John stayed a moment longer, regarding the old woman with a certain sad interest, before he too followed the others.

I had no further desire to walk the beach where my mother had died, or to enter the house that had known her presence. Evan saw my face and came to take my arm.

"I'm sorry," he said to the nurse, and then led me down the steps and back to the car.

Judith stood beside it, waiting for me, and she was angry now—angry with me. "You see what you've done? That poor thing deserves to be left alone. We never come to see her because the sight of us only seems to upset her. She is worse now—worse than ever. If you must know, Courtney, one reason I decided we must come along on this trip, if Evan brought you, was because I didn't want you to come to this house and see such an unhappy sight. It was better for you not to know. I think I must blame you, Evan."

Her indignation left him unruffled. "Maybe it's become necessary for Courtney to know anything that remains to be known about her family. Perhaps she even needs to be shocked a little, and jarred back into real life."

He opened the car door abruptly and I got into the front seat, feeling thoroughly shaken, and with tears still wet on my cheeks. The others sat in back again, with Judith murmuring, and Herndon trying to calm her, while John remained quiet.

When we were on our way, I spoke to Evan. "What did you mean about my being jarred back to reality?"

He looked straight ahead as he drove. "I mean that you're right in thinking that there's nothing for you here, Courtney. You knew the parents who brought you up— remember *them*. They're the real ones who cared about you. Not this family you've tumbled into with all its strains and self-guilt. You'll go back to New York now and forget us all. That's where reality lies."

"Yes," I said. "Yes, that's what I must do."

The drive back to East Hampton seemed quicker than the trip out, in spite of the accompanying silence. I felt a little sick, and frightened as well. "Wicked," she had said. But she had stared at all three of them, and which one she meant I couldn't tell—or even if she meant all three. It didn't matter. There was nothing I could do about anything now.

There were cars parked in front of Nan's shop when we went through the gates—Saturday would be her best day.

Though I wished I could talk to her once more, I suspected that it was better not to, better to leave without telling her of our relationship, or letting her know I had seen Anabel Kemble, who was her mother and Alice's. There was no point in opening up something which could not be continued, and which could mean nothing at this late date.

My bags were packed and waiting for me up in my room. There was nothing more I needed to do. We all got out of the car rather stiffly, as though we'd been on a far longer journey than to Montauk, and Herndon took Judith into the house at once. I had a feeling that she would not come out of it again for a long time. John climbed the steps with me as I ran ahead of Evan.

"I'm sorry, Courtney. If I'd known what was going to happen, I might have warned you. But we never thought it would be necessary for you to know about her. Her life is over, and it could only hurt you to see her. Nan gives her the best of care and sees her often, but there's nothing the rest of us can do. Herndon has always provided for her."

I held out my hand. "I'll say good-bye now. I wish—I wish I could have met you sooner."

The old mockery was in his eyes, and I wondered if he mocked himself most of all. He pressed my hand lightly and then let it go.

"I almost wish that too, Courtney," he said. "Almost. Probably it was too late a long time ago. Good-bye, Courtney."

This time I didn't try to kiss his cheek, and he made no move toward me. A wide, aching gulf yawned between us, but at last I could feel the ache.

Evan had a few things to do before he would be ready for the trip to New York, he told me, and asked if I could kill a half hour before we left. I assured him that I could easily, and let them all go past me into the house. I wanted to be under that roof for as little time left me as possible, and I walked instead around to the terrace above the beach and descended wooden steps to the sand for the last time. Mists were gathering once more over the water, and fog made strange patterns of familiar objects. The figurehead from the *Hesther* wore a wispy veil, through which her weatherbeaten face stared out at me. So veiled, she looked like some ghostly being, and I fled from her down to the water's edge.

The beach lay smooth and clean and undisturbed, except for foaming waves that lapped at my feet. Clusters of shells had been cast up here and there, and far ahead I could see a clump of seaweed flung upon the sand. There was no wind to drive the mists away and I walked with my hands thrust into my jacket pockets in the afternoon chill.

What lay about me hardly claimed my attention, because Anabel Kemble's face was so clearly etched in my memory, with its sharpened bone structure and honed planes. I was glad she had Nan to care for her. Regardless of how much they might spend, I would have hated to see her in the sole care of the Rhodes.

I passed two of the beach houses that glowered upon me over their dunes before I noticed that footprints had materialized suddenly in my path—indentations in damp sand, some of them already filling with water. They moved ahead of me along the beach, evidence that someone must have walked along dry sand above, leaving no trace, until descending to the brown sand at the water's edge, where marks would remain until washed out by the tide. I could see no one ahead of me, and there were no returning prints, but something small had been tossed upon the beach a few steps farther along and I walked toward it and looked down.

A bisque doll's head lay wigless on the sand, its eyes closed, as though it slept gently to the murmur of the waves.

So Stacia had come here for her "sea burial," I thought, and walked on, wondering if these were her footprints. If I saw her ahead, I would turn and go back at once. But mist concealed the distance and the stretch ahead was empty until I came upon the next little face on the sand, and then two more heads, and a few feet later a fifth.

Though the air was still, I felt a cold twinge of something close to horror.

From my first sight of one of these heads painted on a canvas by Judith Rhodes, I had been uneasy about them.

A sense of the eerie that I couldn't shake off had possessed me. There had always seemed something monstrous about Stacia's destruction of the dolls—almost as though she had destroyed something living, and this feeling of horror grew in me as I came upon head after head lying along the beach. Once I stopped to pick one up and found it wet and encrusted with salt and sand, as though it had lain in deeper water before being rolled onto the beach.

Had she tried to throw them into the ocean, and had the sea rejected them and tossed them back on the sand? How long had they been here? It had been yesterday that I had seen her with the box. And whose footsteps were these that seemed to follow the line of heads? They must be recent because tides would have washed them out since yesterday.

I dropped upon one knee and stared closely at a footprint. It had not been made by a bare foot, but by someone wearing shoes. Either by a man's shoes, or the flat-heeled sport shoes that might be worn by a woman—perhaps even by sandals. Long and rather narrow—a small foot for a man, perhaps a little large for a woman? I wasn't sure. As I knelt there a curling froth of white lace swept higher up the beach wetting my slacks and my own shoes.

The tide was coming in. I looked back at the marks on the sand and found them only a little smaller than these prints. In a little while mine and those of whoever had passed this way would be gone. Some of the heads would roll out to sea again, perhaps to roll back later.

I must hurry. Something lay ahead that I must know about. I must find out how many dolls' heads had been strewn along the beach.

The big patch of light brown seaweed was close now and I ran on to see if more heads had been caught in its wet meshes. Fog, which had grown thin, seemed to close in suddenly around me, so that when I looked back, startled, I could no longer see The Shingles. In fact, I couldn't see the nearest beach house. The beach was safe enough when it was visible to all—but not with fog shutting out the world. And not with Stacia perhaps ahead of me walking the sand, and lost to my sight in mist. Nevertheless, I went on.

She *was* there ahead of me, but no longer walking. I paused beside the clump of seaweed and looked down, feeling my stomach churn. It was not seaweed, but the old tan raincoat Stacia sometimes wore, and she was still wearing it. She lay face down, her blond fluff of hair wet and filled with shiny grains—encrusted as the dolls' heads were. All of her was wet and strewn with sand and very still. Her bare legs and feet protruded below the wet hem of the coat.

I bent and touched her—and *knew*. She was cold and unbreathing, and she had not died in the last few hours. The footprints did not match her small, bare feet, and they must have been made earlier this afternoon. They stopped at this point, moved about a little, then mounted the damp edge of sand and vanished into dry. Someone knew. Someone else had stood here looking down upon her, and had raised no outcry.

Desperately I cast around for help, or for danger—if it existed—but if it was there it hid in the fog. That was when I saw the carton of dolls' heads nearby on drier sand, with only a few of the heads left in it.

Frantically, I began to run—back along the beach, avoiding the footprints, avoiding the heads, lest I step on one and be thrown. I was gasping for breath when I climbed the dune below Hesther and met that wise, calm gaze that was long accustomed to storm and death at sea.

Only then did I catch my breath enough to scream for someone to come.

16

Evan reached me first as I climbed to the terrace, and Herndon and John came out of the house after him. The Ashers looked from windows at the far end, and then William Asher rushed outside, with Helen behind him. There was no Judith. I was vaguely aware of all this while Evan shook me out of hysteria and into coherent speech. The moment he understood me he ran down to the beach and disappeared in fog, with John and Herndon after him.

Asher seemed even more shaken than his younger wife, who stood trembling with a hand clasped over her mouth.

Somehow, I began to pull myself together. Evan's shaking had whipped me back to my senses and I remembered something.

"The footprints!" I shouted after them. "You mustn't destroy the footprints!" I ran to the top of the steps, but the men were already gone from sight in the mist along the water's edge, and I knew my warning was too late. The three would run along the firm sand, and whatever those prints might mean was already being lost.

"I—I'll call the doctor, Miss Marsh," Asher said, managing to rouse himself from his own state of shock.

"Yes—and call the police," I told him.

He gave me a gray look and went into the house, still visibly shaken. His wife looked after him anxiously.

"He's been sick since early this afternoon," she said. "He ought to be in bed."

I had no time to sympathize over William Asher. "Make a big pot of coffee," I directed. "Make it right away."

She made an effort to collect herself and we started toward the house together. Now I could hear the dog. I didn't know where they had put his kennel, but Tudor was howling mournfully in the distance—almost like a human crying.

"They're supposed to howl *before* a death," I said as we walked into the living room, and Helen threw me a quick, frightened look.

"I'm all right," I said. "I won't go to pieces again. It's just that I can't focus—I can't believe."

She hurried toward the kitchen and I stood for a moment before the fire that had been built against the damp mists of late afternoon. Flames crackled as cheerily as though death did not exist, but Stacia would never run along the beach again, never warm her hands at this fire or any other, never laugh mockingly ever again. Drowned? Drowned like Alice? But she hadn't been swimming in that cold water, and she hadn't been wearing a bathing suit.

Where was Judith? Someone must tell her. Or did she already know? My screaming must have reached every cranny of the house—even into the attic.

It was necessary to hold onto the railing as I climbed the stairs because I found that my knees were not to be trusted. My mind was leaping from thought to thought, and my stomach still had a tendency to quiver, but my shaky knees were the worst because they hampered movement. Nevertheless, I climbed the attic stairs to Judith's studio and knocked on the door.

There was no answer and I walked in, to find it empty. Her painting things had been put away, her brushes cleaned, and the canvas of the Stacia-doll had been removed from the easel.

I returned to the second floor and went to the room at the far end that belonged to Judith and Herndon. But the door stood open and when I looked inside there was no one there.

Somehow I seemed to be moving without my mind's volition, as though some instinct governed my choice of action. There seemed no need to wait until the men came back from the beach. I knew what I had seen. I had never liked Stacia, but I would not have wished this for her—however many problems her death might solve. That was a thought to put away from me at once. I didn't want to consider who might be served by her death, and I simply followed urgent instinct out to my car and got into it.

With an oddly distant concern, I considered that this was the day I should have had the dressing on my arm changed. It was also the day when Evan was to drive me to New York. Neither matter seemed important now. I started the car and backed around to head down the driveway. Twinges in my arm didn't matter.

There was no hurry and I didn't rush the Volvo toward the gates, but drove slowly because something in me had already decided where I was going and what I would find. When I reached Nan's shop, I parked the car out of the way and sat for a moment behind the wheel, trying to think what I must say, what I must do. But my mind had turned blank. I would have to act and find out afterwards what I intended.

The bell jingled as I went into The Ditty Box. Saturday's customers were gone for the moment, and there was no one in the front of the shop. As I walked toward the archway at the rear, I saw them sitting together in the little back room. Judith and Nan were drinking tea cozily together and they both looked up as I approached.

Nan's expression was strange—questioning and almost tentative, so that I wondered what Judith had been telling her. Judith, I thought, looked fleetingly guilty—though for only a moment—so probably she had been talking about me.

"Hello," Nan said. "Will you have some tea with us, Courtney? This is the first chance I've had to sit down all day, and hot tea seems just right."

"Thanks." I stood beside the table looking down at Judith's feet. "I'd like a cup of tea."

They weren't small feet, because she was a tall woman, and they were long and narrow and she wore thonged sandals with her twill pants. I had never seen her in high, block heels.

"Were you on the beach before we left this morning?" I asked her.

"I haven't been on the beach for several days," she said. "Why?"

All the shield of calm assurance that she could wear so successfully was back in place as she returned my look, but I had no way to tell what lay behind it. Earlier, at the Kemble cottage, I had seen her guard break down, but she looked completely calm and unruffled now.

As I sat at the round table, Nan brought a fresh cup and poured tea through a strainer. I took a deep draught of the hot liquid. No sugar, no cream, no lemon—just dark, hot, strengthening brew.

"Stacia is dead," I told them. I hadn't meant to break it like that, but I no longer seemed able to think a moment ahead of my own actions. It had to be said, and I had said it.

Judith was Stacia's mother, and at times she almost acted like a mother, in spite of all the strains between them. Nan had been fond of my cousin. I'd had no intention of being so brutal and direct, but perhaps in a way it was better because I'd cut straight through the very preliminaries that might have alarmed them both, even as they were uttered.

Judith didn't seem to react at all immediately, but set her cup down in its saucer and stared at me. Nan gulped a swallow of tea and choked.

"I went for a walk on the beach," I said, "and I found her. I followed a trail of dolls' heads on the sand and came to what I thought was a heap of seaweed. But it was Stacia. I think she's been dead for a long time."

I looked down at Nan's feet under the table and saw that she too wore sandals, open-toed.

Nan put both hands to her face and sat without moving. Judith seemed frozen, without expression—frighteningly like one of those immobile dolls that she painted. I reached out to her and touched her arm.

"I'm sorry. I should have let Herndon tell you. I—I can't think. It's not real. There were those dolls' heads on the sand, and a trail of footprints leading to where she lay, and—"

With an effort, Nan reached out to touch me. "Don't," she said. "Let's go up to the house. We'll want to know more, and there may be something we can do. Are you able to go up there, Judith? Or would you rather I brought Herndon down here?"

As though puppet strings had been pulled, Judith rose quite steadily, staring at us with that blank, frozen look.

"Oh, God!" Nan said. "I don't know what to do. It's going to hit her any minute."

"Asher has called the doctor," I told them. "And probably the police too."

The word appeared to jolt Judith and she looked at me as though she could see me for the first time. "The police?" she said.

"It has to be that way," Nan assured her. "Until they know how she died, the police are in it. Are you sure, Courtney, sure that—"

"I'm very sure," I said. "Can I drive you back to the house, Judith?"

"You'd better do that," Nan said. "She walked down when she came. I'll close up the shop and follow in my car."

Quite steadily, not wavering at all, Judith walked beside me to the door. If she saw the arm I offered her, she ignored it as we went outside. Nan closed the door with a slam that set the bell jingling and took Judith's arm on the other side, guiding her to my car.

In the front seat Judith sat looking out through the windshield while I put the key in the ignition.

"I don't have to leave The Shingles now," she said. "It will belong to us." She turned her head to look at me. "It *will* belong to us, won't it, Courtney?"

Her words and dull emotionless tone shocked me. "I'm sure I don't want it!" I cried. "I don't want anything!"

My course as I drove back was a little erratic. I didn't seem able to make the turns very well and my hands felt slippery on the wheel. In the mirror I could see Nan following behind.

When I drove up to the garage, Herndon was above us on the steps, and he came running down. He pulled open the door on Judith's side and helped her out. It was clear that he expected her to collapse in his arms, clinging to him in tears, but she did nothing of the kind.

"When she was little I loved her," she said quietly. "But I haven't been able to love her for a long time. She went beyond anyone's loving."

Herndon looked ill, and I thought he at least was grieving for his daughter, but his words shocked me still more. "She won't ever hurt you again," he said.

So this was to be Stacia's epitaph—that no one loved her, no one cared. But there was still John. And once Evan had cared.

Evan was on the phone when we went into the house, and John was nowhere about. Refusing Herndon's help, refusing to lie down on the living-room couch, Judith sat in a chair by the fire, poker-erect, her expression set, her eyes dry. I think she was hardly aware of Herndon's hovering. Nan and I stayed near the door, waiting for Evan to tell us what to do, or how we could help.

"Where is John?" I asked, as Evan's phone call went on.

Herndon stopped his futile ministering to his wife and looked at me down the room. "He stayed on the beach with her."

"Why didn't you bring her up to the house?" Judith asked.

"Evan said this was a matter for the police and we shouldn't move her. I agree, of course. He's talking to them on the phone now."

As he spoke, Evan came back to the room, his look grim, with all emotion suppressed. "They'll be here soon."

"How did she—how did she die?" Nan spoke from behind me and I looked around to see that she was crying. I had forgotten Nan, forgotten that she had befriended Stacia.

It was Evan who answered—Herndon looked as though he needed ministering to himself. "We don't know for sure. Drowning, probably. But ordinarily in a drowning it doesn't happen in shallow water and the body doesn't surface until later—if ever."

"It's like Alice!" Nan cried. "It's like Alice all over again!"

Judith spoke evenly, as though this were an ordinary conversation. "How do you know, Nan? You weren't there when Alice died. Were you?"

Nan turned and walked out of the room, perhaps to hide her own emotion.

"There were footsteps on the damp sand at the water's edge," I said, speaking to Evan.

He nodded. "Of course. You walked along that stretch both ways, didn't you? I saw your prints."

"There was a third set. I took care not to step on them."

"A third set? Then they're gone now. With the three of us tramping back and forth, they'd be wiped out. What did they look like?"

"Shoes. Long, not very wide. Or sandals. A small man. Or perhaps a woman. They seemed to start by themselves —as though someone came down from drier sand above. And they stopped near—near Stacia. Someone must have moved around there, and then the prints ended. Whoever it was must have gone up the beach because the prints didn't return the same way. With the tide coming in they wouldn't be there long anyway."

"I'd better have a look," Evan said. "When the police come, bring them down, Herndon."

He went out through the terrace door and I waited for a moment, troubled by Judith's cool calm, wondering what I might say to her. I couldn't believe that she was as unmoved as she seemed. However, she remained unaware of me, unaware of anything about her, and I went to look for Nan. First in the hall, and then in the library, but she was nowhere in sight. In the library I sat down at the long table where Evan's work still stood piled, and tried to think, to understand—to believe.

Out of my confusion and inability to accept what had happened, only one question emerged. A question almost irrelevant now. What had Stacia done with those pages she had torn from Alice's composition book? Perhaps looking for those pages would give me some purpose. Perhaps I could find them before the house filled with police and we were all being questioned and watched. Perhaps they might even hold the answer to her death.

No one noticed as I went upstairs and down the long hall to Stacia's room at the far end. The door was closed, but there was no need to knock this time. I opened it softly, stepped inside, and stood frozen, gasping in astonishment.

Across the room Nan appeared to be searching a handbag of Stacia's, while tears rolled openly down her cheeks. But it was the state of the room itself that arrested me and caused my startled gasp. Someone had been here. Someone had torn the room apart in a desperate search. Clothes had been strewn about, the contents of the closet emptied, and Stacia's possessions spilled from drawers onto the floor. The scene was one of utter chaos.

Nan made a disclaiming gesture in my direction. "Courtney, I didn't do this. Believe me, I didn't. I—I couldn't bear to stay around Herndon and Judith any longer. Someone ought to mourn Stacia, so I came here. I thought if I could just find some small thing of hers that no one would mind my taking—" She tossed the handbag aside and covered her face with her hands.

Perhaps she was sincere, but I didn't know her well enough to be sure, and a chilled part of my mind judged and did not believe her words. Whether she had searched the room or not, I didn't know. It would hardly seem that she'd had time. But she was here for a purpose—as I was here for a purpose.

"What were you looking for?" I asked. "I don't think you came to pick up a souvenir."

Her look was intent on my face and she must have read disbelief in my expression, as well as my words. "All right —you might as well know. Perhaps it concerns you. I wanted to find that composition book in which my sister wrote her last stories. Stacia hinted to me that it had told her something."

"I have the book," I said. "But Stacia tore out the final pages. Besides, wasn't that book in your hands for years? Didn't you read what was in it?"

"I used to read Alice's stories when we were young. But after she died, I couldn't bear to. When her things were packed up, John gave me the books, and I put them away. It was only lately that I took out the last one and gave it to Stacia. I thought she ought to read some of her aunt's stories and get acquainted with her. I'm afraid it was a mistake."

"Why a mistake?"

"That's when those anonymous letters started coming. Stacia was sending them. She admitted as much to me. She wanted to torment her mother. She always wanted to torment her because Judith put her painting first and Herndon put Judith first."

All that no longer mattered now. Stacia's jealousies and torment were over.

"I wanted those pages too," I said. "I thought they might contain something I needed to know. Because Alice Rhodes was my mother. You know that now, don't you, Nan? Judith must have told you."

For an instant her look warmed, but she didn't move.

"Yes, Judith told me. Just a little while ago. I—I'm horribly sorry, Courtney. I'd gone away. I didn't even know that Alice was dead, and when I returned they told me you were dead too. But now Judith has told me the truth."

"I'll never forgive her," I said. "I suppose it was better for me to be raised by the family I went to. I haven't any love for any of the Rhodes. Not even John—because he won't let anyone love him. But at the same time a woman who does what Judith did can never be forgiven."

"I know," Nan said. "I can't forgive her either. But she has suffered too. She showed more emotion just now, while she was telling me about your meeting with my mother this afternoon—your grandmother—than she's been showing over Stacia's death. I think she's paid a penalty over and over."

I could only repeat my own words stonily. "I'll never forgive her. I'll never forgive any of those concerned who permitted this to happen."

I turned away from Nan pointedly and moved about the room. One thing at least had not been disturbed. The portrait of Lawrence Rhodes still hung in its place on the wall. "Old Yellowbeard" Stacia had called him. His eyes looked out from beneath rough brows, and they seemed to scorn me as a poor thing, an unworthy descendant of his line.

"I didn't ask to be a Rhodes," I told him and turned my back on the portrait.

Nan looked a little sick, still concerned with the unforgiving words I'd spoken.

"We all believed you dead," she went on. "Judith fooled us all."

"I don't want to talk about it. I only wanted to read Alice's words. I think you're right that they told Stacia something. Perhaps they told her something that led to her death down there on the beach."

"Yes," Nan said. "I'm afraid of that too. And I think Judith is frightened underneath this pose of not caring. She's behaving unnaturally, even for her."

The sound of the doorbell reached us, followed by a chatter of voices downstairs. We both stood listening to the tramping through the house as the voices moved out to the terrace.

"Perhaps we'd better not be found here, with the room in this condition," Nan said. "I didn't do this and I don't want to be blamed. I think whoever did, found the pages."

Instead of leaving, however, we went to the window and looked down toward the beach. The fog had thinned and was drifting out across the water, so that what was nearest could be clearly seen. We could even look along the shore to where John stood beside that figure sprawled on the sand. Closer to the house, Evan was examining footprints, while under our window Herndon led two policemen and a man with a doctor's bag down the wooden steps.

When we'd watched for a few moments, Nan touched my arm gently. "Come along, Courtney—we'd better not know about this room. Neither of us."

"You don't profit by her death, do you?" I asked bluntly.

Tears welled in her eyes. "Oh, Courtney, Courtney, don't turn into a hating person. Don't let the Rhodes do this to you!"

"The Rhodes and the Kembles," I said, and walked out of the room.

I *had* turned into someone hating and hateful. Perhaps I hated myself most of all. There had been no need for me to be cruel to Nan, who was my mother's sister. Perhaps she was the one real link of family I might cling to. If I lifted a finger in her direction, she would come to me—I had seen that in her eyes. But this was something I couldn't do. All of them had been involved. All were to blame—even those who had been fooled and should not have been. Besides, Nan had been less than truthful on more than one occasion herself.

Down the hall in my room, I stood at the window again and watched the men down on the beach. They were all gathered around Stacia, some kneeling, some standing.

Perhaps I should feel relief over her death. She would never attack me again, yet there was no release in thinking of this. I couldn't be anything but shocked and saddened by her dying. In any case, it wasn't Stacia who should have been most feared. There was still another—someone who managed to remain hidden. The one who had caused her death, and who might be watching fearfully, even now, ready to strike out if there was danger of exposure for what had been done.

Someone passed the door of my room and I went to look out. Helen Asher was carrying a tea tray to the cluster of rooms across the hall on the land side of the house—rooms that had once been the generous servants' quarters in the days when the Rhodes had employed a great deal of help.

As I followed her, she glanced over her shoulder. "William's very sick. I thought this might help settle him a little."

Something I'd not thought of until now occurred to me, and when she turned the knob, I stepped to the doorway behind her. Asher lay on the bed, still clothed, with a blanket thrown over him, his face a bit green and worry showing in his eyes.

"I brought you some tea, William," his wife said and set the tray beside the bed.

He had seen me at the door and he paid no attention to Helen. "I'm sorry, Miss Marsh," he said. "Please tell them I'll be all right. I know they need me now. I'm just under the weather after what happened today."

"May I come in?" I asked, and Helen nodded reluctantly.

Asher's shoes lay on the floor beside the bed and I

picked one up and turned it over. Grains of sand clung to the narrow sole.

"You were down on the beach today, weren't you?" I said. "Down there earlier? Did you find her, Asher? Were those your prints I saw on the sand?"

A long shudder went through him. He closed his eyes and turned his face away from me.

"Please, Miss—" Helen began, but I pushed past her to lean over the man on the bed.

"I don't think you had anything to do with it," I said. "The footprints I saw on the sand must have been made long after she was dead, or they'd have been washed away. Maybe it's better if you tell me what happened."

He gave in—perhaps caved in would be closer to the term—and spoke without turning his head. "Miss Stacia didn't come down for breakfast and Helen said she wasn't in her room this morning when she went to make it up. So when lunchtime came I went along the beach to see if I could find her anywhere. She often liked a morning run. First I saw all those dolls' heads, and then—I found her." His agitation grew and Helen bent over him anxiously.

"Why didn't you tell anyone?" I asked.

"I was—frightened. I thought they might think that I—I mean, after all, she was dead and there wasn't anything I could do. I just—wanted somebody else to find her."

As Nan had wanted someone else to find the condition of Stacia's room. Thus delaying the inevitable. Was that what it was all about—postponing the moment when the things that had happened were officially "discovered"? Why?

"No one will blame you," I told him. "But I think Mr. Faulkner had better know about this. Will you talk to him if I send him up here later?"

"I'll talk to him," he said, and expelled a long sigh of something like relief.

"Drink your tea now," his wife insisted and held the cup toward him.

As I went softly from the room, he was propped against his pillows sipping tea.

It was a long while, however, before I could send Evan up to Asher's room. The police kept him all too busy, and I didn't want to present Asher's role to them unless Evan thought it necessary. Evan was taking charge, rather than Herndon, the capable businessman, whose only concern now seemed to be for his wife.

It was evening, after dinner, before Evan could be told, and he went upstairs at once to Asher's room. I waited in my own room for him to come out, and when he did he spoke to me briefly.

"There's no real point in involving the old man," he said. "She was dead long before he found her, and he seems to be afraid of something."

"Everyone's afraid of something," I said. "Or of *someone*. I think I am too."

Evan gave me a dark look and went away. That lovely moment out at Montauk seemed never to have been.

In the days that followed I continued to ponder that fearful "someone." Perhaps if it wasn't active fear, it was a desire to protect the Rhodes name again, as old Lawrence himself had taught William Asher to protect it. He was one of the family too.

In any case, nothing specific came out in the next few days. Stacia's funeral was a sad affair, with few people from outside the house attending, though she had lived in East Hampton all her life. She had never been one for close friendships, and except for a few former school friends, those who came did so mainly out of respect for Evan and Herndon.

The police were ubiquitous, of course, during those days. It was found that Stacia had indeed died by drowning, but no one could explain how it could have happened. The odd set of footprints I'd seen had been obliterated when the three men had first run down the beach, mingling their own and mine in a mass of trodden sand. It didn't even matter that the rising tide soon washed away all traces of our passing. Asher was questioned, but only in a general way. No one guessed that he had found her first, and the fact really did not matter.

Stacia's room, with its strewn possessions, was shortly

discovered, but no one admitted knowing anything about that either, nor did anyone suggest what the searcher might have been looking for.

And there were a few new developments.

One thing shortly emerged when the police talked to me. They had to be told my identity, and since I was instructed not to leave East Hampton, I had to remain at The Shingles while everything spilled out into the papers. Of course there were phone calls from New York—from my friends, and from the office. Jim Healy called me and wanted to talk, when I had no heart for talking. And he relayed the request that I write up the whole affair for the magazine. I reminded him that I was no longer employed and couldn't be commandeered to write anything. My idea of returning to the office had evaporated along the way.

A small matter that hardly attracted my attention at the time was the radio news that the hurricane that had been creeping up the coast had blown out to sea, to be dissipated in the Atlantic. Long Island breathed more easily for the moment, but the season was not over, though I didn't know then of the new "disturbance" that was stirring down in the Caribbean.

It can seem very strange when one looks in retrospect upon a pattern of disaster, to see that there was a time when two separate lines of activity had not yet converged, and when it would have been possible to escape that convergence.

Or would it have been? Was I not already fixed to my point in time when I must move inevitably toward what lay ahead? There is no way of knowing what might have happened if I had deliberately chosen another course. At the time, I wasn't thinking of hurricanes. I didn't dream of those lines that were so surely converging.

wind wasn't quite   as it had   or we would
not have been able   e into it as   did. Even then,

17

During those days that moved toward September's end, nothing at all surfaced to give us the answer to Stacia's death. If it had been murder—as the police suspected—there was no evidence to take to a grand jury. The investigation continued somewhat futilely and I was requested, courteously enough, to remain in East Hampton.

Besides, there was now a string of Rhodes' lawyers, trust lawyers, that I had to see, with Herndon supervising. I moved through all the discussions and arrangements in a dazed state, sometimes talking without being able to remember later what I had said. Papers were signed because I was told to sign them. Only now and then did my old self burst from its cocoon for a brief protest, but older, wiser heads always quieted me and explained methods by which I could do as I desired—if I must really be so foolish. But not right away. The movement of the law was ponderously slow. I did manage to sign over The Shingles to Herndon Rhodes, and he was quietly grateful to me for that, and insisted upon payment. Gradually I began to accept the fact that I was going to be a very rich woman. A rich woman who had nothing at all that she wanted.

More than once I reached for my old solace of writing, but when I tried to think about Judith Rhodes as an artist, all I knew of her as a woman got in the way and halted my borrowed typewriter, confused my thinking. I saw little of her during that time, and Herndon told me she was feeling ill and keeping to her room.

There was a difference in Herndon that was noticeable, mainly through his change in dress. The little touches of colorful flamboyance that had never seemed to match his personality were gone. No more plaid vests or startling ties livened his dress. He wore dark gray often, and the effect was so subdued that once, when Judith was with us, she remarked on it.

"Mourning is out of style," she said. "It's possible to grieve without turning to sackcloth. You look so drab, darling."

We had been sitting in the living room after dinner, and Herndon set down his glass of Drambuie, gave his wife a long, sober look, and walked out of the room.

"Oh, dear!" Judith said lightly. "I've offended him. He used to let me pick out his vests and ties, but lately he doesn't wear my choices any more."

Because he was being himself for a change? I wondered. Being his own man? I had never thought him naturally a bird of bright plumage. But it was a matter of small consequence and I didn't puzzle over it for long.

Both Herndon and John were about the house as usual at this time, with Herndon going off to his string of banks, John disappearing into his own pursuits. I held them off when they might have made any gesture of friendship toward me, since I could trust no one, and was only marking time until I could escape from this house for good. I didn't visit Nan again and she never came to The Shingles after that first tragic day. I was related to them all by blood, except for Judith and Evan, and I wanted nothing to do with any of them.

Evan I was trying not to think of at all, though I didn't group him with those who belonged to the house. I saw him only as a driven man in whom Stacia's death had brought about a terrible change. I caught him looking at me darkly in odd moments, but he spoke to me only when others were present—as though he were afraid I might bring up that past moment between us when he had spoken tentatively of love. He had returned to his work at the lab, and was gone for most of each day. I began to rise late because I dreaded early morning, so I never saw him at breakfast, and at the painful dinner meal there was little of light conversation.

One afternoon I talked by chance to John, and he spoke to me almost wistfully. The day was gray, with a feeling of imminent storm in the air, and I was sitting in the sand near Hesther, who by this time seemed my friend. I no longer walked the beach because it was a haunted place for me, but I had to get outside some of the time. John must have seen me from the house because he came out to drop down on the sand beside me. I had nothing to say to him, any more than I had to any of the others. It didn't matter that he was my father. I knew now that the chasm between us was not likely to be bridged. Yet this time, unexpectedly, he reached for my hand and held it lightly in his own.

"There's no need for you to look so driven, Courtney. This will all be over soon. They can't hold you here much longer. Then you can escape to any sort of life you choose to make for yourself. What do you think it will be?"

I could only shake my head. "I've always wanted to write. Not just for a magazine, but on my own. Books. Only now not even that interests me."

"It will," he said. "It will come back to you."

I turned my head and looked straight into his eyes. "Who killed her, John?"

His smile was sad. "If I knew, would I tell you? Isn't it better not to know? Not even to guess?"

"That's pretty cynical. Are you sanctioning murder? Are you going so far that—"

"Don't," he said quietly. "Perhaps I cared about her more than her mother and father ever did, but now we must think of the living."

"And protect whoever killed her?" I cried.

"Can *you* forgive her for the things she did to you?"

"Perhaps she never meant any serious harm. She told me that she expected me to escape each time—that she only wanted to frighten me. If she had wanted to kill me, there would have been more point to what she did. But there was no point in what happened to her either. You all knew that the house was coming to me and that I didn't want it. There was no *reason* for anyone to kill her."

He let that go. "I came down here to talk about you. It won't be long before they let you leave, and this may be our last chance."

Last chance for what? I wondered hopelessly. He still held my hand with that light touch that told me he was ready to release it at the slightest rejection from me. I wanted to return the slight pressure of his fingers, but there was no will in me. Not now, not yet, and I wondered if there ever would be. I could neither accept nor reject— my hand lay like an inanimate thing in his, and perhaps that in itself was rejection, for after a moment he drew his own away, and I felt an unexpected pang of hurt for him.

"What about you and Evan?" he asked. "Judith thought there was something promising there, and she knew Stacia no longer loved him."

This was a matter I couldn't talk about with anyone. It was something I hadn't been able to face even in the silence of my own mind. I only knew that Evan too was driven by demons and that he had no time for me now. What had barely begun was already over—destroyed by Stacia as surely as though she still lived.

John knew by my silence that I would offer no confidences and he spoke with that odd wistfulness.

"I hope you'll find happiness, Courtney. Don't follow any will-o'-the-wisps."

I had no answer for that and I stood up. "I'm going back to the house," I said, and left him there on the sand, giving him no opportunity to talk about whatever he had wanted to discuss with me. Was I running away because I was more afraid than ever of emotional involvement with anyone—even my father? Was that what was really wrong with me? I had thought for a little while with Evan that everything would change, but the only change seemed to be in a deepening of pain for me if I let myself feel. To love there must be need—the need of two people. Evan needed no one, and I was desperately afraid to need anyone. It was far safer to go on being numb and unable to feel.

From my window upstairs I looked out to see John still sitting there, staring out at the water, the weathered face of the figurehead watching him calmly from nearby. He looked unutterably sad and lost—and I knew that I had added to whatever pain he was feeling. Like Judith, John too wore a façade against the world. With him it was a shield of gaiety and gallantry, laced with cynicism to conceal the core of deep unhappiness. It was a façade I might have penetrated—but now there would be no more time.

That same day Herndon came home early from work and sought me out. "Come for a walk with me," he said.

I was weary of trust affairs, but I lacked the will to refuse. He took me, not to the beach, where neither of us wanted to walk, but along the empty driveway that lay between The Ditty Box and The Shingles. There had been another early frost, and the trees were turning in earnest now, flashing patches of red and yellow, with russet leaves drifting to the ground. It felt like rain, and there was a wind rising.

"I've wanted to talk with you, Courtney."

His tone was both kind and a little sad as we walked together, but my old resistance was rising and I didn't want any more of his manipulation.

"It seems to me we've done nothing but talk in the last week or two," I told him.

"I know. I *do* know that you hate all this, but you need to come out of your apathy, Courtney."

"Apathy?" I almost laughed. "How does hatred for something and apathy go together?"

"You hate what's happening, but you're drifting."

"Because I don't care," I said. "I've stopped caring about anything. Nothing seems to matter any more."

"Evan matters," he said.

I looked in surprise at the man who walked beside me, and saw to my distress how much older he had grown since Stacia's death. Perhaps I'd never given enough thought to Herndon, who had been more of a victim in all that had happened over the years than anyone else. I remembered that once Stacia had told me that he was the best of them all. And now he had spoken so strangely to me of Evan. Nevertheless, I resisted.

"He's not my affair," I said.

"He's very much your affair, and I'm fond of Evan. I don't want to see him hurt. Not again."

"Hurt—Evan? What are you talking about?"

"Let your heart tell you," Herndon said.

No right words would come to me. So often I seemed to have guessed wrong about Herndon, putting him down in my mind for the singleness of his devotion to Judith, not crediting him enough with sensitivity toward others.

"I don't think Evan needs anyone," I told him.

Quite gently Herndon took my hand and slipped it through the crook of his arm, patting it lightly. "Let's talk about you, Courtney. You are my niece, you know, though I can't very well ask you to think of that, since in your eyes I've had to stand for everything you disapprove. I must seem hard and distant to you, but that's not what I want to be. Perhaps there's still affection to give in this unhappy family."

I felt the sudden warmth of tears behind my eyes, unexpectedly touched by his words. How strange to have a gentle sense of affection come to me from this surprising source.

"Thank you," I said and let my fingers press lightly against his arm.

Perhaps there might have been more, but we both heard the car coming behind us and stepped aside on the road. To my surprise it was the Mercedes and Judith was at the wheel. I'd hardly seen her since Stacia's death, but she looked strong and purposeful now as she leaned toward us in the open window, braking the car.

"Will you come with me, Herndon?" she asked. "I've an errand to do, and I need you."

He asked no questions of this woman who almost never had errands away from the house, but gave me an apologetic look.

"I'm sorry, Courtney. We'll talk again." He went around the car and got into the seat beside Judith.

I stood back to let them pass and she gave me a brief, triumphant look that said everything. She must have seen us when we left the house together. Perhaps he had even tried to talk to her about me. In any case, Judith Rhodes would never for one moment allow a sharing of her husband's affection and interest. Not with Stacia, not with me. And whatever Judith wanted, Herndon gave—and always would.

With a faint pang of loss, I watched the Mercedes disappear down the curving drive in the direction of the gatehouse. Under other circumstances I might have found a more understanding relationship than I had ever expected between my father's brother and me. But Judith would always command him, and Judith was, in her own way, as greedy as Lawrence Rhodes had ever been.

I walked back to the house alone, sadness breaking through my apathy. But I was not yet through with these unexpected and intimate "talks." There was still another to come.

The next day was Saturday, though I had forgotten the day of the week until after lunch when I went idly down the hall to the library, to find Evan there, working on the last of his records. Before I could escape, he looked up and saw me.

"I'm sorry," I said. "I won't interrupt."

He rose from his chair. "Come in, Courtney. Come and sit down."

There was nothing kindly in his tone, and his words commanded me without sympathy. I sat obediently in the chair he pulled out for me and looked at my hands on the table, because I couldn't meet the dark anger in his eyes. Why should he be angry with me, and why should I sit here and listen? But I stayed on in silence while he talked.

"I've made up my mind about you several times over," he told me, "and each time you've turned out to be someone else. Now I don't know you at all. You've changed into a zombie."

I concentrated on a hangnail that seemed to be starting on one finger. He sat down beside me.

"You're letting this whole tangled Rhodes tragedy destroy you," he said.

Somehow I managed to speak. "I'm not the one who's been destroyed."

He ignored that. "What has happened to you? There are things you could accomplish here in the time that is left."

"What things? There's nothing here for me."

"You could reach out to those of your own blood—those who have been hurt. You could even reach out to John, if you wanted to. Perhaps John needs you more than you think."

"No one needs me," I said dully. "And I don't need anyone here."

"That has become obvious. What has changed you, Courtney? When you came here you were warm and alive and eager. What has taken all the life out of you?"

"It went out of me when I stood on the beach and looked down at Stacia," I said. "I didn't like her, and she tried to injure me and injure others too, but she didn't deserve what happened. And now I find I belong to a family that has been trained to such closeness, such self-protection, that murder is being hidden. Who is it? My father? My uncle? My aunt? They're all guilty because each of them is protecting the other—and I can't bear it."

All this poured out of me in a surprising flow, since I hadn't consciously thought about what I was saying. But there was still more that I couldn't pour out. Somewhere I seemed to have lost my chance with Evan through Stacia's death.

His tone gentled when he spoke again. "Yes—I feel that way too. I can't rest. I can't sleep nights until this thing is cleared up. I can't be my own man until then. I owe this to Stacia. She believed that someone had killed Alice and I think she was pursuing that trail in her own willful way. If she discovered the truth, perhaps that's what brought about her own death. She was fearless, always. She would face anyone. So now a double murderer must be exposed."

"Have you said this to the police?"

"I can't go to them with surmises, and there's no direction in which I can point a finger. The worst of it is that the Rhodes are all close to me and have been for years.

Closer, perhaps, than Stacia had become. Yet what happened the other time when Alice died is being repeated—the secrecy, the concealment. And that can't go on."

At least this was the way I felt too, though I could take no action about it.

"Do you think they all know who killed Stacia?"

"I can't tell. They've been trained all their lives—trained by old Lawrence himself—to close ranks and protect their own. Even Nan Kemble hasn't escaped his brush."

"Yes," I said. "I've seen that. I feel sick about being related to such a family."

He went on as though he mused aloud. "If there were anything—any small thing to go on . . ."

I remembered something and felt suddenly more alert. "Perhaps there is. That last day I heard Stacia in her room, quarreling with someone. I heard raised voices, but only hers came through. I couldn't even identify the other as a man or a woman, and I couldn't hear the words. I went away as quickly as I could. But I think she had made someone very angry."

"That's not good enough unless you can identify the other voice," Evan said.

"I can't." I felt listless again. "And I suppose I don't even care very much any more. I'm drifting, and I don't know how to get back to land."

He hardly seemed to hear me, and he wasn't looking at me now. It was Stacia's dead face that haunted him, as it haunted me. "I have to blame myself for a great deal. She was very young when I married her. Seventeen. Very gay and young and beautiful."

Since her death he could be more generous to her, and something in me hardened. "There were already the dolls."

"But I should have been old enough and wise enough to change her. I should have tried harder. I should have—"

"Do people ever change?" I asked flatly.

This time he looked at me. "Perhaps not. I would have needed to change too—and that was something I couldn't manage. Can't manage. Just as you can't manage to be anything else but what you are, Courtney. So go back to

(281)

New York as soon as you can, and take up your life again. Be a writer, be a success at what you're doing on the magazine. Don't let this money affect you."

"I don't have any money that I haven't earned," I told him. "I'm going to set up trusts, or funds, or whatever—where they're needed. I don't want any of it. Not Rhodes' money."

He was staring at me. "I guess I've been away from what's been going on. You must be frightening Herndon. Maybe it's all right if you don't change, Courtney—once you snap out of this apathy."

"No," I said, "it's not." It was as though I had begun to come to life a little, as though chips of ice were falling away. "I don't think I believe in my own question when I ask if people ever change. We have to change, don't we? We have to grow—or die. Stacia died—perhaps because she couldn't change. And I want to live, really. As soon as all this quiets down, I'll get back to my book. I'll close my apartment in New York, and go away to write it." Plans I didn't even know about were being made as I spoke, and an enormous relief was sweeping through me.

"Where will you go?"

"I don't know yet. Not East Hampton."

"Why don't you try Montauk? It's quiet out there—at the end of the world."

I couldn't look at him. There was never any telling how much or how little he meant. And I didn't want only a little. That was why I was afraid to feel—because I would want too much.

"I suppose some sort of investigation about you has been made," he said. "So that it's settled that you really are Anabel Rhodes?"

"Yes—there's no escape for me there. The lawyer's files in New York have been opened. Someone has even dug up my Swiss birth certificate and there are prints to identify me. I was born to Alice and John Rhodes. It's all down in black and white—the whole record that ties me to the Rhodes."

"But it doesn't really matter, does it?"

His words startled me. "What do you mean?"

"Blood doesn't matter all that much. Oh, there are

genes, of course—but you grew up in a different environment and Lawrence Rhodes has never laid a finger of his influence on you. You were lucky enough to escape this house before it could affect you in any way."

I sat quietly, considering. Had all that longing for my own blood family, for a mother and father and grandparents—had all that been purely emotional, now to be cast off? Was I to be free of all the dreaming at last? But when I closed my eyes, John's face was there—a man lost to himself long ago, and there was a new yearning in me to reach him, perhaps even to claim him as my father, to have him turn to me as his daughter. Could this feeling be the beginning of real affection? Not something to come in a blinding flash, but to grow between a father and daughter who had never known each other until now?

"Blood matters," I said. "It still matters."

The look he'd turned upon me had warmed. "Remember about Montauk," he said.

I nodded, not trusting myself to speak as I rose and started across the room. He came with me, and before I reached the door his hand was on my arm.

"You said you would come—when the time was right. Is this the time?"

That desperate something inside me was struggling to flee—out of fright, out of feared pain, warning me that not to feel was to be safe, not to feel was to avoid future wounding. And all the while a warming, trembling tide of emotion was rising in me, and would not be denied.

I went into his arms and for a moment he held me close, with his cheek against my hair. Then he tilted my chin with one finger and looked at me—as though he must know the very shape of my face, the color of my eyes, the trembling of my lips—and his very look was a caress. When he kissed me the old fears died. I knew who I was now, I knew what I wanted. I knew that running away from love would bring me nothing, even though staying meant the risk I had always been afraid to take. Now I had the courage and the will to meet life as I wanted to meet it.

When he raised his head it meant a denial of rising hunger in us both, but he held me at arm's length for a moment.

"That's only a beginning," he told me, and I heard the promise in his words.

"I know," I said. "I understand. There is still the matter of Stacia to be settled. And no one left but you to do it."

"Yes. An old debt to pay. Too late."

"Be careful then. I'll come to Montauk," I told him and went out of the room.

I was alive now, and awake to my very fingertips. Life lay ahead of me. I had a book to write, a fortune to get rid of, and a man to love. But first I must escape from this house. That was the first step along my new road, and it must be made at once.

It was already afternoon, but there was still time to push toward the thing I must do. I went to the telephone in the hall and dialed a number. One of the officers at the station answered and I told him what I wanted. He went away and conferred, and then I heard the police chief's voice in my ear.

"It's all right, Miss Marsh. You can leave anytime you want to. We're not going to hold any of you in East Hampton any longer."

I think I must have given a small whoop of relief when I hung up, because John came out of the living room to look at me questioningly.

"We're free!" I told him. "I can leave and I'm going back to New York as soon as I can get away."

His smile was not a happy one. "Good for you, Courtney. Though I'll miss you here. You're lucky to have something to return to."

"I haven't, really," I said. "I need to start all over and do the things I had in mind before I ever came to East Hampton. But at least I can go back and close my apartment, get rid of all my encumbrances."

"I envy you. Perhaps I'll take a fling down to the Bahamas for a while. It will be something to do."

I still wanted to reach out to him, but he was not inviting me now. Nevertheless, since my talk with Evan, I knew there was no need for our separation to be permanent.

"I'd like to see you again," I said. "This needn't be good-bye."

He hesitated, his look softening a little. "I don't know

if that would be wise, Courtney. I'd only disappoint you."

"How could you, if I'm not asking anything? John, the *Anabel* is such a beautiful boat. There ought to be more like her."

"That's what I mean." His tone was dry. "In the same breath that you tell me you ask nothing—you ask a very great deal. Run along, Courtney—and be happy."

He disappeared into the living room, and I had a feeling that our parting words had been spoken, that I wouldn't see him again, unless I made some special effort. And I might do that—sometime in the future. I couldn't ache with loss any more, because now there was Evan. Now there was hope.

When I'd climbed the stairs, instead of going into my room to pack, I followed the second flight up to the attic. Judith was at her easel when I reached the studio and she looked as though she had been working feverishly for some time. Though her long hair was pinned back, a few strands had come loose and hung across her cheeks—limp strands. Her yellow smock was smeared and her fingers stained, her eyes a little glazed when she looked at me.

"I came to say good-bye," I told her. "The police aren't restricting us any more."

She shook her head, like a swimmer coming out of water, and I repeated the words. This time she surfaced to the world away from her canvas, her look questioning.

"You sound glad, Courtney."

"I'm practically delirious. I want to get started on my own life."

With her palette hooked over her thumb and her paintbrush in hand, she took a few steps toward me, almost conciliatory.

"We've given you a bad time, haven't we? And I'm sorry. Herndon's been scolding me. Anyway, it's better if you never write that piece about me. I didn't want it in the first place."

"Oh, but I am going to write about you. I think I can now. And not just for an article in a magazine. I want to do a book. I want to collect the interviews I've written and add some new ones to make a book out of the whole. Yours will be my first new one."

She continued to look at me, her face calm in the old way, and expressionless. I didn't think she cared in the least whether I wrote about her or not, or whether I succeeded in doing a book. In a moment, after this small gesture toward me, she would return to her own imaginary world and it would be hard to draw her out again.

"I was talking to Evan a little while ago," I said, "about people changing. Have you been changed at all, Judith? I mean by all that has happened here?"

The attic was still, except for a spatter of rain against high dormer windows. The storm I had not thought about at all was beginning.

She nodded gravely. "Yes, I've changed. I can be quiet now. I can work."

"But that's the way you were before. That's not a change —it's a retreat."

"It's a marvelous, wonderful, blessed change!" she cried, and I heard a lilt in her voice—a lifting that I'd never heard before. The brightness of her smile startled me.

I must have looked shocked, because she shook her head in reproach. "Don't be so conventional, Courtney. Don't condemn me because I can't feel anything but relief to know that Stacia is gone and that she'll never trouble us again. She has damaged all our lives, including Evan's, and she would have damaged yours. But now I can work again. Perhaps I can feel free for the first time in years. Nothing more that is dreadful is going to happen. Everything will be all right now."

I turned my back and walked toward the door, feeling somehow sickened, and sorry to have this new glimpse of Judith Rhodes.

"Wait," she called after me. "You must understand why I took the action I did. If you'd grown up here, you might have been in danger. Don't you see that?"

"What action? What danger?"

She started to speak and then shrugged. "Perhaps it's better if you never know. But before you leave, you must look at what I'm painting. You'll need to write about the direction toward portraiture that I may be taking."

It would probably upset me further, I knew, to go back

and look at this new canvas, but I was drawn in spite of myself, and I moved to a spot not too close to her from which I could view the easel.

"You see?" she said. "Perhaps I have a talent for portraiture, after all. Perhaps I don't need to paint beaches any more."

The head on the canvas was indeed a portrait—and not this time the floating head of a doll. She had painted Stacia in a likeness immediately recognizable, yet with something added. In faintly-to-be-discerned structure behind the beauty of blue eyes and perfect features showed the underlying skull, the hollow sockets, the fleshless lips, in an eerie, shadowed counterpoint to the whole.

I must have gasped, for Judith, who had been lost in admiration for her own work, glanced at me and smiled benignly.

"It's been good therapy for me to paint that, Courtney. She was my child, but blood doesn't always tell, you know. I don't think I alone am to blame for what she became. I won't go on painting like this, of course, but it was something I needed to say about her—death beneath life. I'd like to paint you, Courtney. Won't you stay and pose for me?"

I fled down the room and out the door, clattered on the stairs in my haste to be away from the sight of her and the sight of that terrible portrait. This time I ran directly to my room and pulled out my bags from the closet, flung my clothes in a heap on the bed, and began feverishly to pack. I no longer wanted to know—anything. I wanted only to effect my escape from The Shingles and everything it stood for. It didn't matter if I had no chance to say good-bye to Herndon, or even Evan. Herndon I might write to, and Evan I would see again. We both knew that.

So with the rain slashing ever more loudly against my windows, and the sound of a muffled roar from the sea, I tossed my clothes helter-skelter into my suitcase. Driving to New York in a rainstorm would be unpleasant, but it would have to be done, and my arm was only a little tender now.

The suitcase was filled sooner than it should have been because of the haste of my packing. I removed the remaining contents of drawers and bathroom shelves, to dump everything on my bed. Then I unzipped my flight bag and began to thrust into it bottles and jars, toothbrush and cosmetic case, working with an almost frenzied haste. However, when I tried to shove my comb and brush into a side pocket of the case, they stuck because something was already there. Impatiently, I jerked out a wad of paper, dropped it into the wastebasket, and returned to my packing.

Then, as an afterthought, I considered that I might have thrown out some of my own notes, and I fished the wad out of the basket to flick through the pages. Handwriting across the sheets arrested my attention, and I felt a shock of recognition that was half dread, half triumph.

So this was where Stacia had hidden the pages torn from Alice's notebook—here in my own baggage, where no one else was likely to find them. My cousin Stacia had left me a legacy, after all. When I'd packed the last time, before the trip to Montauk, I had packed more neatly and hadn't touched the side pocket.

I forgot that the afternoon was getting on, and that I had a long drive in stormy weather into New York. When I'd flipped on the lamp beside the armchair, I dropped into it and began to smooth the rumpled pages out upon my knees. Now I would be given the answers. Now I would know.

For just an instant, the realization frightened me and I wondered if I wanted that much to know. Only moments before I had been sure that I wanted to know nothing, but only to get away. Yet now that I held these Pandora's pages in my hands, I knew I would have to read them.

Alice's last story had never been finished—that little allegory about the Princess Anabel. Instead, swiftly scrawled sentences changed into diary form—or at least the form of a statement. My mother had poured out her thoughts and fears and triumphs in this last writing.

They're all here now—John, Judith, Herndon. Lawrence has sent his troops to bring me home. But this time I have the power to bargain—now that I can give him the heir he craves. Now I can make him pay for what he wants and for all the earlier humiliation he has made us suffer.

I've told John there will be no divorce. He's read in my eyes what I feel toward him, and he knows I won't give in. He's a fool, of course. Judith has had her fling, and she has already gone back to Herndon. John hasn't faced that yet. He doesn't know what I know—that Judith is already carrying Herndon's child. For safety, mine has been born out of the country. Judith's a little afraid of me now, but she's too late—because I have my baby first. The first Rhodes heir. A darling, beautiful little girl named Anabel. Anabel, to spite them all. I want her to be a Kemble, not a Rhodes, and she will grow up having everything Lawrence wouldn't give John and me.

Other measures have been taken. I've told Herndon about John and Judith. He will forgive her, but I wanted to make sure he knew the truth. John, he will never forgive. And of course none of them will forgive me. They all hate me now. But I'm the strong one—I'm the one who will win. Money, power, and eventually a heritage of wealth for my Anabel.

As a further precaution, all this is being set down. If anything happens to me, perhaps Anabel will read it one day.

I paused in following the words, feeling as sick as when I had seen that painting of Judith's upstairs. Alice had been no better than the rest of them. Even Herndon could sacrifice integrity, loyalty, decency, when it came to protecting Judith.

There was still more and I forced myself to read on. She had scrawled dates in the margins of her entries, and this one was two days after the first.

I'm glad Olive Asher is here with me. She is the palace guard now, since she has never liked the Rhodes or approved of William's loyalty to old Lawrence, our resident tyrant. So she stays with me and tends the baby and watches.

In the morning, when it's warm enough, I like to go for a swim, and Olive stays at a window, or sometimes comes down to the beach with me, bringing Anabel. Today the baby has a cold so Olive will remain here to nurse her while I swim. But she will still look out a window from time to time and watch.

Here I turned to a new sheet and came upon a hole—a tiny oblong that had been deliberately cut in the paper. Before she had hidden these pages in my bag, Stacia must have taken the trouble to delete a name with scissors—the one name that mattered most. Alice's words went on after the blank.

—is down on the beach this morning. But I'm not afraid. I'm a better swimmer than any of them—and Olive will look out from her window. So I'll have my dip as usual. Let any of them threaten me, if they dare!

Good-bye, my little Anabel—I'll come back to you soon.

But she had not come back to me, and no one had noticed the pages in the back of her book of fairy tales until it had fallen into Stacia's hands. Strong swimmer or no, Alice had died in the water—and Judith had taken care to see that her own child would inherit the fortune Lawrence meant to leave to his firstborn grandchild. A precaution she had come later to regret.

Revulsion was like a gripped fist just under my ribs and I didn't know whether it would ever go away. All my life long I would remember this moment of revelation, and wish it had never come to me. Because now, staring at Alice's words traced across the paper in my hands, I knew the truth—just as Stacia had known and tried in some way to use that truth to satisfy her own cruel twist of mind. I knew who had been down on the beach that morning when Alice had gone swimming, and who had followed Stacia along the sand when she had carried that box of dolls' heads down to the water's edge.

It was time to act. I knew that I must go to Evan with my knowledge. But first, surely, I must be absolutely certain I was right. I needed time to think, to decide upon so terrible an action as I must now take. Yes—that was best. Flight first, for my own safety—though there was no particular danger for me unless my knowledge was discovered. I would leave, nevertheless, and go back to New York. I would get Evan to come to me there. How could I tell him the terrible truth here in this house?

If I was seeking excuses to wait, I didn't admit this to myself. The storm sounded louder now, howling and rattling windows, but I ignored it. The notebook pages were easily refolded and returned to the side pocket of the flight bag, where I'd found them. I zippered the case shut, managed with some difficulty to pack the rest of my belongings in the suitcase and force the lid down so I could lock it. When I'd pulled on my coat and tied on a rain bonnet, I made a last survey of the room, opening drawers, to make sure I'd left nothing behind.

Something rattled in one drawer as I pulled it open, and the doll's head Stacia had left there looked up at me, its eyes clicking open at the movement—a horrid reminder of sights that would always haunt me. In the next drawer lay the scrimshaw tooth Nan had given me, and I stood staring down at it, considering something that hadn't occurred to me until now. What if the name that belonged in that slot—? Hastily I took the scrimshaw from the drawer and put it on the bureau, put the doll's head beside it, wanting never to see either of them again. Now I had all the more reason to wait, because now I couldn't be *sure*. There was still another possibility.

I picked up my bags and went into the hall, to find Judith coming down the attic stairs.

"You're not leaving in this storm?" she cried.

I could hardly bear to look at her, and I merely said I was, and went quickly ahead. I could hear someone playing the piano in the living room when I came down, and as the music drifted up to me I recognized the lullaby I'd heard Stacia play when she'd sat at that piano. It was a ghostly, haunting sound, and a heartbreaking sound as well, pouring out notes of pain. Not a lullaby for a child's peaceful sleep, but music filled with hurt and longing.

When I reached the foot of the stairs, I went quietly to the living room and looked in. My father sat at the piano and his face was as sad as the music that followed his fingers. I couldn't bear the way he looked. Perhaps my emotion was partly a sense of abandonment toward him that I didn't want to feel. He had never invited me to be a daughter, so why should I feel that I ought to do something to help him? He had brought his own isolation upon himself, and I owed him nothing. I turned away to pick up my bags and carry them to the front door.

Judith had come down a few steps and stood on the stairs watching me. I think she must have known that she couldn't stop me from going out that door.

The storm battered the house with a force of wind that shook the walls, and I stood for another moment, bracing myself to face what waited for me outside. Then I reached and pulled open the door.

18

The roar and thrust of the storm hurled itself upon me. Tree branches thrashed as the wind howled through them, and rain came slashing in upon me in horizontal sheets, blinding and soaking me as I stood in the open doorway.

Behind me, Judith cried out, and at the same instant Herndon came running up the steps to push me back into the house and slam the door behind him, so that some of the tumult died away.

He saw my bags as he stood shaking rain from his slicker, wiping it from his face.

"Where do you think you're going, Courtney?" he demanded. "You can't possibly go out there now."

"I'm going back to New York," I told him. "And I *am* leaving now."

"Don't be absurd," he said. "There's a hurricane out there. The edge of it has already hit New York, and it's running east. I just heard a broadcast. You'd have to drive straight into it and you'd meet worse than this before you got there."

I made a last effort to escape and my voice rose shrilly. "But I must go! I want to leave now. If it gets too bad, I'll take shelter on the way. I—I don't want to stay in this house any longer."

"It's already bad. It was all I could do to get home." Herndon took the bags firmly from my hands and set them down near the wall. John had left the piano to come to the living-room door.

Herndon continued to talk to me with less patience than usual. "What's the matter with you, Courtney? Why this sudden urgency to leave? It would be insane to go out there now. We've closed the bank and sent everyone home. You can't go."

There was nothing to do but give in. Above me on the stairs, Judith spoke to her husband.

"While you're still wet, will you bring Tudor inside? He can't be left outdoors in this."

"I'll get him," Herndon said. "In the meantime, where is Asher? Hasn't anyone been listening to the broadcasts? We've got to shutter the house as quickly as possible— get ready for the storm."

They forgot me then. Herndon went outside, and Evan came out of the library to help. I left my bags in the hall, feeling useless in this emergency, while the others went to work knowing what to do. Back in my room, I tried to take stock of where I stood now. I was going to be all right, of course. No one knew what I had discovered, and there was no one to threaten me, now that Stacia was gone. Stacia, who had loved storms, would never see this one.

I sat in my room while the wind roared and clattered and shook the house. I waited in its emptiness, with only the sinister doll's head and a scrimshaw tooth for company—both reminders of possible danger. When the afternoon grew dark, I turned on lights. When the lights went out, I sat in darkness. I felt too thoroughly sickened by the things I had learned to be afraid of a mere lack of light. Even when the house trembled and shuddered under the impact of the wind, even when I heard shingles clattering on the roof, I didn't care. A storm—even a hurricane—was nothing compared with the tumult of horror and anxiety that churned inside me. Ethan Rhodes had built The Shingles to stand against storms, and it was not the assault on the house that frightened me.

When a lull came in the tumult outside, it was almost a shock. It was as though all the crashing and buffeting had become the normal thing, so that I had grown accustomed to it. Now what was this? Surely not the end of the storm, but perhaps the edge of the eye—that space of time at the center before we met the other side of the circle, and winds started hurtling in the opposite direction.

At the window I could peer out at a cloud-torn sky. Miraculously, there was a glimpse of moon—a moon still full, though slightly on the wane. It wavered before my eyes, vanished behind clouds, emerged again with a shadow across it. I stared, unbelieving, as the form of a unicorn took shape for an instant, then shredded into blown strips as the bright sphere vanished.

With my fingers on the pendant at my throat, I stepped back from the window. Not the Rhodes' unicorn moon! I had no wish to see that and be doomed. I was already frightened enough. Of course it had been only my haunted imagination that had created the illusion.

All track of time was lost to me, and I didn't know the hour until Helen Asher came upstairs to fetch me. She held a flashlight and murmured over my sitting there in the dark.

"There are candles in the bureau, miss," she said. "But you'd better come downstairs now. Cook's gone home long ago, but Asher and me have got together a cold meal. It's late, so come along now, miss." She was cajoling, as if to a child.

I didn't want to go. I didn't want to sit at the table, knowing what I did—knowing that perhaps two of those I sat with knew very well what the third had done. I was afraid too lest by some sign I didn't intend I should give away my knowledge. I didn't want to remember that I had ever seen that moon.

There was no help for me, however. Downstairs there were candles in the dining room, sending long shadows up the walls, smoking as gusts swept through the room—in spite of shuttered windows. The storm was in full voice again. I looked into no face but Evan's as I sat down at the table, and he regarded me sternly.

"Herndon says you were trying to leave in this storm, Courtney. What idiocy! Wait until it's over and I'll drive you in, now that the police don't need you here any longer."

I hoped it wouldn't be too late for me by the time the storm was over. But that was foolish, of course. No one knew. I must hold onto that belief. Stacia had hidden Alice's words well, though someone had searched her room for them. If I had found them, I would be expected to say something—wouldn't I? Isn't that what would be believed? My very silence was protecton.

Just as we finished the meal of cold meats, cheese, and fruit, a battery radio informed us reassuringly that most of the storm would pass well out to sea, and that the wind velocity was not as great as with some hurricanes of the past. The words seemed cold comfort in the face of the way we were once more being beaten by the elements.

Asher came in to report that the phones were out, and Evan rose from the table.

"If the phones are gone, so we can't reach her, I'm going down to the gatehouse to stay with Nan. She shouldn't be alone through all this, if she can't call for help."

I wanted to cry out to Evan not to leave, that I needed him too, but of course I couldn't. He was right to go to Nan. A feeling that what would be would be, was growing in me. It was as though all my life had been building toward this moment, toward this revelation that had come to me, and I knew now that I couldn't run away from it. Even to run as far as Nan's might put me in danger. I would have to stay and sit out the storm that had broken upon us from the skies, and then I would have to face the inner storm. My destiny lay under this roof. I was a Rhodes by blood, and a Kemble too, and there must be no more secrecy. As soon as Evan came back, I would tell him what I knew, show him Alice's pages. But until that moment I could only mark time.

When the others rose from the table, I rose with them. They had been talking among themselves, paying little attention to me, for which I was thankful. Even though they all knew my identity now as Alice's child and John's, I was still an outsider, and they could overlook my presence easily enough.

Accustomed by now to the continued roar and buffeting, I went into the hall and picked up my bags to carry them back to my room. I'd borrowed a flashlight from Asher, and I would light some candles and wait for the hurricane hours to pass. In the meantime, I would have my flight bag with its contents in my possession, where I could watch it.

Herndon and Judith went to their room, and I went to mine. When I looked down the dark hall, I could see them sitting before a fire, and quite cozy together, Judith talking animatedly. I wondered if she was telling her husband about that dreadful portrait of Stacia she had painted. I went into my room, found candles where Helen had said I would, and set them about in a cheerful number. Except that they cast an eerie glow that did not cheer me. More than once, I winced as wind slammed against the house, and set the shadows quivering. I tried hard to be still, so that the beating of my heart would slow its tumult.

There was no danger—none. Not yet. My heart didn't need to thump like this.

Once I got up to open the zipper bag and feel in the side pocket for Alice's pages to reassure myself. That was when everything crashed in upon me, and I knew that danger was *now*. The pages were gone, and now I knew which of my two suspicions was correct. Danger did not lie in the direction of the gatehouse—it was here, under this roof.

When I had been downstairs, I must have revealed my fright, my urgency to escape, so that one person had been alerted—and had looked into that available flight bag standing in the hallway. Now it was known that I knew— and there was no reason to trust me to be silent. Nor could I trust any of those three—not the one who was guilty, or the two who had kept silent all these years, and were keeping silent still.

One thing I knew—I must not stay here alone. With any one of them I might be in danger and without protection. No matter how fierce the storm, I must go out in it and try to reach Nan's shop, where Evan was staying with her. Only there could I find safety. If he had braved the storm, so must I.

With hands that had a tendency to shake, I managed to pull on my coat again and tie the plastic hood over my head. Then I opened the door cautiously and used my flashlight down the hall. Herndon's and Judith's door was closed, and the storm hid any possible sound of voices, or any noises I might make.

Nevertheless, I was quiet on the stairs, and thankful to find the lower hall empty. No music came from the living room now, though candlelight illumined the doorway, and a flicker of firelight made the shadows move. I turned off my flash and crept softly toward the outside door. The bad moment would come when I opened it and the storm rushed inside. That was when I must move fast, somehow getting down the steep flight of steps in the dark, and escaping to the driveway before anyone could stop me.

I had my hand on the doorknob when a soft radiance fell about me and I turned, startled, to see John standing in the living-room doorway holding up a hurricane lamp in one hand.

"Courtney!" he said in surprise. "You're not going to attempt the storm again, are you? I can't let you do that, you know."

I was caught and a sense of my own helplessness swept through me, weakening even my knees.

"I suppose it is hopeless to go out there," I said, and turned back to the stairs.

He came to me and took my arm gently. "I need your company tonight, Courtney. Perhaps this will be our last chance to talk. Come and sit with me before the fire."

In his face I could read the truth as he held the lantern high, and I knew that he knew what I had learned tonight. Hastily I cast a look down the hall toward where the Ashers had been sitting in the kitchen, and John shook his head.

"You don't want them for company tonight, my dear. And they'll never hear you if you call. No one will hear. Don't you think you'd better join me now for a little talk?"

My father, I thought. One out of the two from all creation who had given me life, and who might now threaten the life he had given. I had never wanted it to be my father.

His hand on my arm propelled me, and I found myself walking into that beautiful, comfortable room that held no comfort for me now. Long shutters had been closed against the storm, but gusts forced their way in, and not even the fire on the hearth could offer much warmth while that cold fury outdoors crashed on. Tudor lay upon the hearth rug, and when he saw me he stood up with a swift movement that gathered his feet beneath him and raised his great body instantly into a guard position. Involuntarily, I drew back.

John patted my arm. "You needn't fear Tudor tonight, Courtney. I'm here and he will obey orders."

He led me into the room and seated me in a chair near the fire, much too close to the dog.

"Sit," he told Tudor. "Stay," and the animal relaxed into a sitting posture, though still alert.

I could only stare at him helplessly. It sickened me now to think that I had felt moments of affection and longing toward this man.

He went to pour two glasses of wine and brought me one. "You may need this," he said.

I took the wine glass and glanced around the room. It seemed to be filled with movement as eddies of wind stirred the tall candles in their holders. The storm lantern added further light, but there were shadowy corners and unfamiliar black patches up the walls. It was a room that should have been quiet, peaceful, but the tumult outdoors offered no peace.

"It's really too bad that you had to find those pages from Alice's notebook," he went on conversationally. "I searched for them in Stacia's room, but you must already have had them. It *is* too bad. You and I could have got on very well, eventually. I could already see that you might do more for me in the long run than Stacia ever would. She was terribly greedy, you know—and possessive of what she regarded as hers. Of course I've read those pages too now, and I understand what Stacia believed she held over me. It was clever of her to cut out my name, but not quite clever enough."

Something new had come into his voice—a hinting of anger long suppressed. It frightened me, but I tried to talk to him calmly.

"You're right," I said. "She wasn't clever enough. The pattern of the way Alice wrote names was there. A longer cut could have meant either Judith or Herndon, but the short one could only mean John. Or Nan. For a little while I wondered about that."

"Nan!" He laughed unpleasantly. "May I ask what it was you had planned to do?"

I couldn't miss the past tense, or that quiver of rising anger in his voice. "What does it matter? I hadn't really decided. After all, I would be acting against my own father."

He smiled at me, falsely gentle. "If only I could have trusted you, Courtney. But I found I couldn't even trust Stacia. After all I'd done for her all her life . . ." Anger was in the open now—blazing in his eyes as he looked at me.

"I can understand about Alice," I said. "But not why you had to hurt Stacia. Weren't you two of a kind and on the same side?"

His smile stiffened, froze on his mouth. "Not exactly. Perhaps we both wanted money, and we'd always had it withheld from us. But Stacia was like her grandfather—my father. She was power-hungry. And after she had read those pages she came to the mistaken conclusion that she had power over all of us. And especially over me. That was where she made her mistake."

"What do you mean? She loved you, surely?"

"I think not. She could play that game while I was useful to her, but not a moment longer. When I refused to go along with what she wanted—which was to get rid of you —she was against me. Who else would have struck me down that night on the terrace, when she believed I meant her harm? Though I couldn't admit it to anyone afterwards. I had to deal with her myself. And I did." For the moment anger had died, and there was only cold, unbelievably treacherous fact in his statement.

I found that I was shivering. "What about Alice?"

He had no reluctance to tell me everything, still deadly

cold as he spoke. "Olive Asher saw me with Alice that day on the beach, and she told Judith what she had seen. Judith was still half in love with me then, Alice's words to the contrary, and even though she'd found it sensible to return to Herndon, she kept what she knew to herself and paid Olive off, sent her away. I was stupid enough to think she might turn to me after Alice's death, but she didn't."

He paused and anger was rising again—stronger now as old rage surfaced, old fury burst through, shattering the guise of sanity.

"Judith will have to pay for what she did," he went on. "Because I will inherit as the older son. I will have the money and the power, and I can pay them all off—make them grovel."

What he meant, of course, was that with me gone he would inherit, and my terror grew. I wanted to close my eyes, to shut out the terrible look in his face, somehow shut out the seething hatred in his voice. All these years this had been masked, hidden—while he waited. The new, dreadful voice went on.

"But she didn't turn to me. A few months after Alice was out of the way, it became apparent that Judith was going to have Herndon's baby. That was when she told my father the truth about what Olive had seen on the beach, and the shock killed him. She has never tried to tell anyone else, and she's been a little afraid of me ever since. But I would never hurt Judith—not physically. I'm very fond of her, really. It's just that she owes me a debt from long ago—and she'll have to pay it now. In full."

"She must have told Herndon," I broke in.

"No, strangely enough. Alice had seen to it that he learned about the affair between Judith and me, but he never let her know that he knew. He forgave her, but he couldn't be rid of me. My father's will stipulated that I was to live in this house as long as I wished, until the new heir inherited. But Herndon never knew that it was I down there on the beach that morning. That's one of the priceless jokes Judith managed to play on herself, without knowing it."

John laughed softly again, and I shivered at the sound. "Do you know," he went on, "what my loyal brother has believed all these years? He believes that Judith was behind Alice's death because Alice threatened her with exposure of our affair. He has given his life to protecting her. I don't know but what he might even have protected me, being a good Rhodes, and my brother."

"But Stacia loved you. She——" My words came out weakly and I broke off.

"Stacia always loved Stacia. She began to guess that from my viewpoint it might be much better for me if I made peace with you as your father. You would have been more generous toward me, since you're far more loving than Stacia. You haven't discovered it for yourself yet, but you are, you know. So we quarreled about a number of things that last day of her life. As I say, she had attacked me, and she threatened me further."

"I still think she had an affection for you. She was planning to take you away to Europe when she came into her money."

"But of course she couldn't do that, could she, once you had inherited?"

His words seemed so calm, so reasonable—and were so utterly twisted by the fury that drove him.

"Stacia was jealous and angry and bitter!" The furious words ran on. "And she became dangerous when she started sending those anonymous letters to stir everyone up again about Alice and Alice's baby. In the end she actually taunted me with exposure. So what could I do?"

So reasonable a question, rising out of total unreason. I had never known John Rhodes, and I didn't know him now. I only knew that my flesh crept when I thought of him as my father.

"What did you do?" I asked faintly.

"The same thing I did with Alice. There are pressure points that can make a person quickly unconscious—and I'm strong enough. The water took care of the rest. It was very simple."

So calm, so clear, so reasonable, except for that cracking of his voice on certain words.

The sickness in me was growing, I didn't know what he meant to do with me, but I knew it would be terrible. And the most terrible thing of all—the thing that kept beating at me in reminder—was the fact that John Rhodes was my father.

As though he had read my thoughts, he spoke to me with that dreadful, seemingly gentle note in his voice. "I've really liked you, Courtney, and I never wanted to hurt you. But if it will comfort you, you might as well know that you are not my daughter."

For a moment I could only stare at him blankly. "But then—then who—?"

"No! I'm not going into all that. It's too long a story, and it doesn't matter any more. There isn't time. Though I must tell you something else. Do you know what I saw tonight, Courtney? Earlier, when the storm died down at the center, I saw the moon—"

"I saw it too," I said with a sense of fatalism.

"Then you noted that odd configuration of clouds?"

"Yes—like a unicorn."

"Of course I don't believe in any of this, but you know what the legend says, don't you?"

I answered as though he had hypnotized me. "That when a Rhodes sees that moon it can mean either great good fortune, or utter disaster. But perhaps I'm not a Rhodes?"

His smile gave me no answer. "Tonight I think that moon will carry out both prophecies—one for you, and one for me. Perhaps it won't be very difficult for you to figure out which will be for which."

"What will it profit you?" I asked between stiff lips.

"Profit? I'll have your silence assured, of course. And then there is the inheritance—since I am the elder son the trust will come to me."

I was very cold, and fear seemed to pulse with every beat of my heart. "John," I managed, "you can't get away with another accident. And you can't do anything to me in this house."

He regarded me calmly. "I can get away with anything I choose. No one has ever known the man I am. I've hidden from all of them—behind the cheerful, unambitious play-boy! I've taken their beastly treatment—but now it's my turn. Though you're right about the house. Let's go outside."

Without turning my head, I tried to measure the distance

behind me to the door, to a place where I could make the Ashers hear me if I called out to them. It was hopeless to think of reaching Judith and Herndon upstairs.

He must have seen the movement of my eyes. "I'm faster than you are, and in this uproar no one will hear, however loudly you scream. Come outside with me, Courtney. Like Stacia, I've always enjoyed a good storm. I like to test myself against the elements."

I stayed where I was, my hands gripping the arms of my chair.

He picked up an oilcloth slicker from another chair and pulled it on, buttoning it high, and turning up the collar. When he bent to fasten a lower button, I sprang from the chair and hurled myself toward the door, forgetting the dog. But Tudor, though he snarled and showed his teeth, was still obedient to the command to "stay" that had been given him, and it was John who caught me and pulled me back with a jerk that wrenched my still tender arm. I cried out in pain, but he did not let me go. It was all in the open now—the rage gone out of hand.

"Don't try that again," he said. "You'll excite the dog."

Tudor was on his feet, watching me, alert for the slightest command.

John directed me in a voice turned low and deadly. "We'll go out through the terrace door. Come, Tudor— guard."

The dog was beside me at once, huge and menacing. Futilely I felt for the unicorn under the scarf at my throat, touching its golden surface.

John flung open the door to the terrace room, letting in a roar of wind, while the unprotected candle flames around the room dipped, smoking and trembling. John pushed me ahead of him into wild darkness and closed the door after the dog came through.

Earlier, someone had dragged all the terrace furniture in and stacked it in this semishelter, where it blocked our way. The night screamed with sound, and cold rain slashed our faces as John pushed me past tables and lawn chairs, with Tudor close on our heels.

On the terrace, the full buffeting struck us, but John made no surrender to these banshee forces. Perhaps the wind wasn't quite as strong as it had been, or we would not have been able to move into it as we did. Even then, the terrible thrust of it was greater than anything I had ever felt. My arm ached with pain, and I stumbled and might have fallen if John hadn't held me firm by the other arm.

Out here the night was pitch black and wet sand stung my face and gritted between my teeth. Wind tore and whipped my hair into a wet tangle. All around us there was a howling, as though demons had risen from the ocean and been let loose on the land.

Again I felt John's hand pushing me from behind, and I heard the whining of the dog, who liked this night no better than I, but who would do as he was told. I could see nothing now, but John knew his way instinctively, and he was thrusting me out from the terrace to stand on the rim of the high dune. The beach must have vanished as waves boomed across it and broke against the dune, sending spray into the air, eroding the embankment and carrying sand back into the sea. The treacherous undertow would be working tonight. My face felt like ice and my lips were stiff with sand and salt spray.

John's voice sounded close to my ear, so the wind couldn't snatch his words away. "We can't risk the steps in the dark. Dig in your heels as you go down the dune. Slide with the sand."

I shouted back at him. "No! I won't go down."

"Tudor!" John cried, and the dog pressed against me. He was so close that I could hear the growl in his throat and I knew that I might feel his teeth in another moment.

"You have a choice," John shouted in my ear. "The water or the dog. I don't mean to lay a hand on you. This time I don't need to."

There was a madness in him that I was powerless to oppose. If I went down the dune the waves would snatch me away, drag me out to sea in the undertow, where I would drown, as I was supposed to have drowned twenty-five years ago. And John would concoct some story that would leave him free of guilt. But if I stayed, Tudor would gladly obey any order of John's. I would be driven into the sea in either case.

As my heels dug into the sand, I felt it slide beneath me, taking me down a few feet. The water was close now, black and unseen, but painfully felt as it hurled itself upward, soaking me in icy wetness beneath my coat. I fell backward from the force of wind and water, sliding farther down the sand, so that water came over my ankles and up my legs. I had already lost my shoes and my feet were numb. My wounded arm had gone numb as well, but I managed to thrust myself to my feet, so that I was standing in the surge of water that rose up the dune. John had slid along beside me. "Go down, Courtney! Go all the way!"

Water would be better than the dog. Perhaps I could fight the water as I couldn't fight the dog. Perhaps I could struggle out of the sea and make my way up some dune farther along the beach. Darkness was the one thing in my favor. The moment I was away from John's touch, he couldn't see me.

I took another step into the sea and was promptly knocked down by a wave, submerged, with water in my mouth and the deadly suction drawing me out. I came up choking, pulled up by John.

"Go out farther," he shouted. "Let the water take you. It will be easy that way."

He let my arm go and I flung myself away from him, away from the dog. Another wave battered me down, but I came up choking farther along the beach, and John wasn't grasping me now. If I could manage the struggle against waves and wind until I came to a place where I could climb up the next dune, out of sight in the darkness, I might escape. I could hear him shouting behind me, coming nearer, and knew that he was in the water too, pursuing me—to make sure of what he wanted to happen.

My hands were stiffening in the bitter cold and my feet and legs were without feeling. I struggled in water up to my knees, trying to stay on feet I couldn't feel—a struggle that seemed to go on forever. John shouted again, but he must be floundering too. I rose and fell, choking, my lungs burning, my eyes afire, fighting against that fatal suction that tried to pull me out to sea. Only the fact that I was not in deeper water saved me.

Then without warning a blaze of light shone directly into my face, and I heard voices through the crash of wind and water. More lights flashed upon me. A hand grasped my tender arm so that I cried out again in pain—and was engulfed by darkness.

19

Before I opened my eyes, I heard the crackle and felt the warmth of a roaring fire. Well wrapped in blankets, my wet clothes gone and a warm nightdress on my body, I lay on something soft drawn close to the fire. There was no more sea, no wind, no icy water sucking me down. As my eyes began to focus, I saw that this was the hearth where Tudor had lain earlier in the evening, but he wasn't there now. And I was warm again, the water gone from my lungs—warm and safe. My hand felt for the pendant and it was still there at my throat. Whatever had happened, I hadn't lost it.

"She's coming to," a voice said.

My eyes blurred and then cleared as I looked up into Nan's face, and saw Evan beside her. Behind them I could see Judith, unmoving as a statue, her face white. Fear started up in me, and then I remembered that she was not the enemy.

"John," I said. "He's out there. And the dog. He tried to—"

Nan and Evan exchanged looks and again she bent over me. "Hush, Courtney. We know. The men have been searching, but I'm afraid we'll have to wait till morning. Tudor came in by himself."

"But how—how did you find me? How—"

This time Evan leaned toward me. "No more talk now. It can wait until you're stronger."

I tried to struggle up from my cocoon of blankets. "I'm all right! I'm fine! I—"

"You're going up to bed," he said, and picked me up, blankets and all. I stopped my struggle, feeling languorous and safe in his arms, willing to let everything go. Again I saw Judith's face, sad and lost as Evan carried me toward the stairs.

Nan came with me, and when I'd been tucked into my bed Evan stood beside me for a moment longer, looking down into my face. I saw in his the strain he must have been through hunting for me in that howling darkness.

When I tried to speak, my words sounded ragged, my voice hoarse. "It's over. I don't need to run away now. You won't let John—"

"Hush," Nan said again. "We think he's been lost in the water."

"You're not going to run away ever again," Evan said quietly.

"What a lovely thought to go to sleep on," I murmured and he leaned down to kiss me. Drowsily I murmured something sweet and foolish, and then he went away. I was vaguely aware of candlelight, of Nan sitting in a chair across the room, of the lessening storm sounds outside. And then I was asleep.

I never knew when the hurricane beat its way out to sea on its eastern course, leaving the island drenched and ravaged behind it. Though, as I learned later, it hadn't been one of the worst storms, and damage was not too great out here in the South Fork. I slept and if I dreamed, nothing stayed with me. Dawn pressed at the window when I next opened my eyes, to see Nan asleep in her chair. The moment I stirred, she awakened, and as she came over to me I felt new energy surge through my body, while my mind brimmed with unanswered questions.

"You should have gone to bed," I told her.

"I wanted to stay," she said. "How do you feel?"

"Wonderful! Free again. But I want to know everything. How did they come in time? How did they find me?"

She moved about the room, stretching her arms over her head, wriggling her shoulders back to life, and then drew a chair closer to my bed and sat down, regarding me soberly and rather remotely.

"Judith talked to Herndon last night. She told him the truth—as far as she knew it—about John. What Olive Asher had told her—that he was guilty of Alice's death. And probably of Stacia's. Herndon went through the storm to fetch Evan back to the house, and I returned with them. It was a good thing I had a man on each side of me to pull me along in that wind. Herndon didn't know you were in any danger then, but he wanted to confront John, and he didn't want to do it alone. Luckily Asher was uneasy. John thought he'd seen the unicorn moon, and he told Asher, so the old man stayed alert for anything that might happen. I think he may have been suspicious all along, but next to old Lawrence he loved John. Nevertheless, he couldn't let anything else happen."

There was a deep weariness in Nan's voice and she paused to rub her fingers across her eyes. I waited, not urging her.

"Asher was trying to listen in the hall, and he heard some of what John said to you. When he realized that John meant to take you outside, bringing the dog with him, he was frightened. He knew he couldn't stand against John alone, and it was sheer luck that brought the three of us back in time. Asher told us where John had taken you."

"He's not my father," I broke in. "Oh, Nan, I'm *glad* he's not my father!"

She was silent, watching me across the room.

Perhaps she was the one who could tell me, I thought. I still needed to know the answer. "Nan, if I was your sister's child, perhaps you know who my father was?"

"Yes," she said, "I know."

There was something strange in her voice—something controlled and cold, so that I felt no sympathy in her. If she was my mother's sister, she felt nothing toward me.

"You'd better tell me all of it," I said.

She seemed to brace herself and I saw her touch her lips with her tongue, as if they were dry. When she spoke it was in the same cold, remote way.

"You weren't Alice's baby either, Courtney. You were named after your real mother—Anabel. That was a little whimsy of Alice's because it was a name I never liked, even though it was our mother's too. I never used it, though it's my right name."

It seemed an eon before I could speak. I couldn't immediately grasp what she had told me. At the window the light grew brighter with the new day.

"Please tell me," I managed at last.

Hesitantly at first, she began to speak, and then with the words pouring out—as though they had been suppressed for so long that the pressure of release was too much to resist. Yet she still spoke without feeling, with nothing I could reach out to, even if I'd wanted to.

"There are no good excuses for what I did, and I can only tell you how it seemed to me then. I was young and I was pregnant and I had no husband. It was a situation made for Alice's machinations. The one thing she wanted more than anything else was an heir to satisfy old Lawrence and make certain of her own power in the family. She had given up hope of having a baby—even if John had given her one, it might not have been in time to provide that *firstborn* heir. So she promised me a home and a mother and father for my child—something I couldn't give. She promised that the baby would be raised as a Rhodes, with all the care and benefit that implied. And I didn't know the Rhodes then as well as I do now. Worst of all, she threatened to ruin your father if I didn't do as she wanted."

"Who was my father?"

Nan went on as though I hadn't spoken. "I went abroad with Alice and we fooled old Lawrence completely. My sister and I looked a lot alike in those days, and it was simple to switch passports when we went into Switzerland. So you were safely born to Alice and John Rhodes."

Nan paused, and for a moment the room was very still. Then she went on.

"After I saw you, I wasn't sure any more. When we came home to the cottage in Montauk, where our mother was staying, I began to fight against Alice's plan. As soon as Lawrence knew about the baby, he sent Herndon and Judith and John out to the cottage at once, to bring Alice and the baby home. When I told her I was going to tell the truth and keep the baby, no matter what, she brought up that big gun of hers and again told me just what she could do to your father if I didn't take myself off and do it quickly. On the other hand, if I behaved, I could come back to East Hampton later and be a loving aunt to my own child—so the little girl wouldn't have to grow up without knowing me. I could even watch over her and know what happened to her. Alice and I fought bitterly, but she was older and stronger-willed in those days, so she won and I went away. If only I'd stayed a little longer—"

Her voice broke, but she controlled her emotion quickly and stared at me, stony-eyed. Her look said, "I loved that baby—but I don't know *you*. I can't love *you*."

After a moment she continued.

"You know the rest. Olive saw John and Alice down on the beach and I think she told our mother. Mother went to pieces emotionally and mentally, and she's never been right since. I didn't learn of Alice's death until months later, and then I came straight home—to find that my little Anabel was also supposed to be dead."

"Judith told me she gave me away partly for my own safety. But why wouldn't I have been useful to John—presumably as his child."

"You could have been. But since he knew you weren't Alice's child or his, he was afraid of what might happen when I came back to town. Lawrence would never have forgiven our tricking him. In any case, when I returned to town, you were supposedly dead, and Herndon had gone back to Judith, as I always knew he would."

"Herndon?"

"Yes. While Judith had her brief fling with John, Herndon was left hurt and terribly wounded, and I'd always loved him. Perhaps I had something of comfort and affection to give him at that time that Judith never did. And for a little while he turned to me. He was the decent one of the lot, Courtney. He was the one Lawrence trusted, and if he hadn't been bewitched by Judith, life might have been different for him. Of course he never knew that Alice's baby was mine—and his."

I tried to shut out her words that carried emotion only for the past, with nothing left over for the present. I closed my eyes and turned my head away from her. Even in the last words she had written in her notebook, Alice had carried on the lie—that I was her child.

The cold, clear voice went on. "You owe me nothing but contempt, Courtney. Ever since Judith told me the truth about you yesterday and I knew what even she didn't know—that you were *my* daughter—I've been trying to find some way to ease this story in the telling. But there wasn't any easy way. I've never forgiven myself, and I won't blame you for the way you feel. I'll never ask—or want—anything of you. It's too late for all that."

When I heard her leave her chair and walk to the door, I turned my head. "Nan," I said, "wait."

Suddenly and clearly, watching her across the room, I could understand. I had already told her that I would never forgive those who had taken part in the deception. The control, the coldness, the remoteness of her manner—all these were a defense because she couldn't bear to be hurt any more, and she didn't dare expect anything from me except rejection for what she had done. I was out of bed in a moment, running across the floor in bare feet and nightgown.

"I've come all this way to find you!" I cried. "I've come through all the years of my life to find you, and you can't go away from me now!"

The tears she had held back brimmed her eyes, spilled down her cheeks, yet she was afraid to reach out to me. So I put my arms about her and held her close, with my own wet cheek against hers.

There were years of words to be bridged, understanding to be learned, both a mother and a father to become acquainted with—yet the human heart could span all this in an instant, and with my cheek against Nan's, I knew I had come to the end of my search. Though strangely, even as I held her, I thought of Gwen and Leon and how fortunate I had been. They would have been truly happy for me now. Perhaps I was luckier than most—to have had two sets of parents.

When we'd cried a little and laughed a little and could stop hugging each other, she managed to speak again.

"Herndon still doesn't know. I'm fond of him, Courtney, but there aren't going to be any more secrets. I can give him the gift of you now, when he needs it most. And Judith—well, Judith will have to accept the past. She has her painting, and I know he'll stand by her. I always knew that."

But there was someone else I had to tell before we told Herndon. I couldn't love Herndon as a father yet—and whether I ever would must wait on time and on how he felt about me as well. Yet something had begun between us when we'd walked together only a short time before.

Now, however, it was Evan I must talk to, and I wanted to see him quickly.

Outside, when I reached the terrace, the view was one of devastation. Part of the beach had been lifted to the terrace, it seemed, grasses and foliage were flattened, and everything outdoors bore scars of the storm. The wooden steps had been broken and partly washed away, but Evan was climbing the altered bank, and when he saw me he came quickly up to my side.

"How are you, Courtney?"

"I have to tell you something," I said. "Will you listen, please?"

He listened gravely, not touching me, and I knew he was glad about Nan. As I talked I looked down the sandy bank and saw that the old figurehead had been shifted by the storm, but had somehow not been swept out to sea. Hesther no longer stared off toward far horizons, but with her sand-beaten face turned inland, she seemed to be watching me with an air of wise understanding. *So another Rhodes has come home,* she seemed to be saying— *a Rhodes from Ethan's time, perhaps.* I touched the shining surface of my golden unicorn and knew the bond was there.

But now there had been enough of talking.

"Hold me," I said to Evan. "Just hold me and tell me a lot of foolish things I need to hear."

His tenderness was healing and I knew that all my searching was over. I had come home indeed—at last.

ABOUT THE AUTHOR

PHYLLIS A. WHITNEY's exciting succession of novels—including *Listen for the Whisperer, Snowfire, The Turquoise Mask,* and most recently *Spindrift*—has established her as one of the top-selling authors of romantic suspense. *Time* magazine has called her "the only American in her field with a major reputation."

Miss Whitney, who was born in Yokohama, Japan, has spent her life working in the field of books—as bookseller, librarian, reviewer, teacher of writing and bestselling novelist.

Fawcett Crest Books
by
PHYLLIS A. WHITNEY

THE GOLDEN UNICORN	2-3104-6	$1.95
SPINDRIFT	2-2746-4	$1.95
TURQUOISE MASK	X2835	$1.75
SNOWFIRE	Q2725	$1.50
LISTEN FOR THE WHISPERER	Q2761	$1.50
LOST ISLAND	2-3078-3	$1.75
THE WINTER PEOPLE	2-2933-5	$1.50
HUNTER'S GREEN	Q2603	$1.50
SILVERHILL	Q2810	$1.50
COLUMBELLA	X2919	$1.75
SEA JADE	Q2572	$1.50
BLACK AMBER	Q2604	$1.50
SEVEN TEARS FOR APOLLO	Q2508	$1.50
WINDOW ON THE SQUARE	Q2602	$1.50
THUNDER HEIGHTS	Q2737	$1.50
THE MOONFLOWER	Q2738	$1.50
SKYE CAMERON	Q2804	$1.50
THE TREMBLING HILLS	X2807	$1.75
THE QUICKSILVER POOL	2-2769-3	$1.75
BLUE FIRE	Q2809	$1.50
EVER AFTER	P2298	$1.25

FAWCETT CREST
BESTSELLERS

THE GOLDEN UNICORN *Phyllis Whitney*	2-3104-6	$1.95
THE PEACOCK SPRING *Rumer Godden*	2-3105-4	$1.75
MAKING ENDS MEET *Barbara Howar*	2-3084-8	$1.95
STRANGER AT WILDINGS *Madeleine Brent*	2-3085-6	$1.95
THE TIME OF THE DRAGON *Dorothy Eden*	2-3059-7	$1.95
THE LYNMARA LEGACY *Catherine Gaskin*	2-3060-0	$1.95
THE GOLDEN RENDEZVOUS *Alistair MacLean*	2-3055-4	$1.75
TESTAMENT *David Morrell*	2-3033-3	$1.95
TRADING UP *Joan Lea*	2-3014-7	$1.95
HARRY'S GAME *Gerald Seymour*	2-3019-8	$1.95
THE SWORD AND THE SHADOW *Sylvia Thorpe*	2-2945-9	$1.50
IN THE BEGINNING *Chaim Potok*	2-2980-7	$1.95
THE ASSASSINS *Joyce Carol Oates*	2-3000-7	$2.25
LORD OF THE FAR ISLAND *Victoria Holt*	2-2874-6	$1.95
REBEL HEIRESS *Jane Aiken Hodge*	2-2960-2	$1.75
CIRCUS *Alistair MacLean*	2-2875-4	$1.95
CSARDAS *Diane Pearson*	2-2885-1	$1.95
WINNING THROUGH INTIMIDATION *Robert J. Ringer*	2-2836-3	$1.95
THE MASSACRE AT FALL CREEK *Jessamyn West*	C2771	$1.95
EDEN *Julie Ellis*	X2772	$1.75
CENTENNIAL *James A. Michener*	V2639	$2.75
LADY *Thomas Tryon*	C2592	$1.95

Send to: FAWCETT PUBLICATIONS, INC.
    Mail Order Dept., P.O. Box 1014, Greenwich Conn. 06830

NAME _____

ADDRESS _____

CITY _____

STATE _____ ZIP _____

I enclose $_____, which includes total price of all books
ordered plus 50¢ for book postage and handling for the first
book and 25¢ for each additional. If my order is for five books or
more, I understand that Fawcett will pay all postage and handling.

Fawcett Crest Books
by
VICTORIA HOLT

BRIDE OF PENDORRIC	22870-3	$1.75
THE CURSE OF THE KINGS	Q2215	$1.50
THE HOUSE OF A THOUSAND LANTERNS	X2472	$1.75
THE KING OF THE CASTLE	X2823	$1.75
KIRKLAND REVELS	X2917	$1.75
THE LEGEND OF THE SEVENTH VIRGIN	X2833	$1.75
LORD OF THE FAR ISLAND	22874-6	$1.95
MENFREYA IN THE MORNING	2-3076-7	$1.75
MISTRESS OF MELLYN	Q2509	$1.50
ON THE NIGHT OF THE SEVENTH MOON	X2613	$1.75
THE QUEEN'S CONFESSION	X2700	$1.75
THE SECRET WOMAN	X2665	$1.75
THE SHADOW OF THE LYNX	X2727	$1.75
THE SHIVERING SANDS	22970-X	$1.75

Romance, Mystery and Suspense by

DOROTHY EDEN

AN AFTERNOON WALK	2-3072-4	$1.75
DARKWATER	2-3153-4	$1.75
THE HOUSE ON HAY HILL	X2839	$1.75
LADY OF MALLOW	Q2796	$1.50
THE MARRIAGE CHEST	2-2032-5	$1.50
MELBURY SQUARE	22973-4	$1.75
THE MILLIONAIRE'S DAUGHTER	Q2446	$1.50
NEVER CALL IT LOVING	2-3143-7	$1.95
RAVENSCROFT	22998-X	$1.50
THE SHADOW WIFE	2-2802-9	$1.50
SIEGE IN THE SUN	Q2736	$1.50
SLEEP IN THE WOODS	2-3075-9	$1.75
SPEAK TO ME OF LOVE	X2735	$1.75
THE TIME OF THE DRAGON	2-3059-7	$1.95
THE VINES OF YARRABEE	X2806	$1.75
WAITING FOR WILLA	P2622	$1.25
WINTERWOOD	Q2619	$1.50